# "Provoking baggage!" the Earl exclaimed.

"Nothing frightens you, does it? You are the most shameless hussy."

Elizabeth knew he'd begun to recover himself, at least enough to be embarrassed about all he'd just told her. No doubt it was the first confession of this sort he'd ever made. And a man as strong as Neil couldn't be comfortable baring his soul that way.

"Kiss me half as well next time round, and I may tell you how I got that way." She pinched his cheek. "Now, why don't you take a short nap while I go and make you breakfast?"

"Damn it, Bettsy, don't be so bloody kind! I'm trying to warn you I can be dangerous!"

"My God, you *are* blue-deviled this morning! Now, shut up and lie down or I'll kick you in the shins. You haven't seen a vicious rage until you've seen one of mine!"

Dear Reader,

Every year at this time, the editors at Harlequin Historicals have the unique opportunity of introducing our readers to four brand-new authors in our annual March Madness Promotion. These titles were chosen from among hundreds of manuscripts from unpublished authors, and we would like to take this time to thank all of the talented authors who made the effort to submit their projects to Harlequin Historicals for review.

This year's books include a second-place finisher in the 1995 Maggie Awards, *The Wicked Truth* by Lyn Stone. In this delightful story set in Victorian England, a woman with a ruined reputation and a straitlaced physician join forces to discover the real culprit in a murder they are both under suspicion for.

The other three titles are: *Emily's Captain* by Shari Anton, the story of a heroine whose father sends a dashing Union spy to get her safely out of Georgia against her wishes; *Heart of the Dragon* by Sharon Schulze, the medieval tale of a young woman searching for her identity with the help of a fierce warrior; and *The Phoenix of Love* by Susan Schonberg, a Regency novel about an unusual marriage of convenience between a reformed rake and a society ice princess who must overcome tortured pasts and present enemies before they are free to love.

Whatever your taste in reading, we hope you'll find a story written just for you between the covers of a Harlequin Historical.

Sincerely,

Tracy Farrell
Senior Editor

Please address questions and book requests to:
Harlequin Reader Service
U.S.: 3010 Walden Ave., P.O. Box 1325, Buffalo, NY 14269
Canadian: P.O. Box 609, Fort Erie, Ont. L2A 5X3

# The Wicked Truth

## Lyn Stone

# Harlequin Books

TORONTO • NEW YORK • LONDON
AMSTERDAM • PARIS • SYDNEY • HAMBURG
STOCKHOLM • ATHENS • TOKYO • MILAN
MADRID • WARSAW • BUDAPEST • AUCKLAND

ISBN 0-373-28958-8

THE WICKED TRUTH

Copyright © 1997 by Lynda Stone

This edition published by arrangement with Harlequin Books S.A.

® and TM are trademarks of the publisher. Trademarks indicated with ® are registered in the United States Patent and Trademark Office, the Canadian Trade Marks Office and in other countries.

Printed in U.S.A.

## LYN STONE

A painter of historical events, Lyn decided to write about them. A canvas, however detailed, limits characters to only one moment in time. "If a picture's worth a thousand words, the other ninety thousand have to show up somewhere!"

An avid reader, she admits, "At thirteen I fell in love with Bronte's Heathcliff and became Catherine. The next year I fell for Rhett and became Scarlett. Then I fell for the hero I'd known most of my life and finally became myself."

After living four years in Europe, Lyn and her husband, Allen, settled into a log house in North Alabama that is crammed to the rafters with antiques, artifacts and the stuff of future tales.

Love and thanks to Bonnie, Pat, Sabrah and Tammy,
my critique group for this book;
to my daughter Pam, my Edith Head who also designs
clothes with words;
to my son Eric, who teaches me to
listen with my heart;
to Dennis, Katie and Sarah, who raise love
to an art form;
and especially to Allen, the absolute master of
research, historical and hysterical.

# Chapter One

*London, November, 1858*

"You can't think to marry that wicked little tramp, Terry. She gulled you into proposing, didn't she? God, I can't believe how naive you are!" Neil Bronwyn knocked back his whiskey with an audible gulp and poured himself another. He felt like taking a stick to the boy. "Whatever possessed you to announce such a thing? And at White's, of all places? Everybody's laughing."

"You think I care? Just because you're eight years older, you think you can tell me—"

"Shut up and look around you, man," Neil said with a sweeping gesture of his glass that threatened the Aubusson carpet. Havington treasures dotted even the study of the town house—expensive cherry, Ming dynasty vases, silver-crested crystal decanters, a Rembrandt drawing, a solid gold paperweight with the family crest. A long-dead countess, immortalized by Vigée-Lebrun, glared at them from over a classic mantel designed by Wren. Probably turning in her grave, Neil thought. "Recall who you are, for God's sake—an earl now, with all the responsibilities that come with it. Your name and title are who you are, Terry."

"I will marry her," the boy said simply. There was no

belligerence now, no wrathful, rebellious tone. The angelic face with its guileless blue eyes looked calm and determined. The narrow shoulders were firmly set against Neil, who was easily twice his size. He admired the lad's resolve, if not his cause.

Until the rascal spoke. "I will have her, Neil."

"Then take her to bed if you must! But marriage? Hell, you're only twenty-one. You have no conception of what commitment is all about, and *she* wouldn't know the meaning of the word. I know you don't believe me, but she'll play you false before the ink dries on the license."

Neil mellowed a bit after his outburst, both from the whiskey and a sharp wave of sympathy for the lad's infatuation. He'd been where Terry was and survived it. The scar had healed. Almost. Watching his nephew struggle through a similar coil didn't bear thinking about.

"She's not that sort, Neil, regardless of what you think. I know you mean well," Terry said with a protracted sigh, "but I'll remind you that I *am* of age. The time has passed when you need to wipe my nose."

"If you'd keep it clean, I wouldn't have to," Neil scoffed. "I promised Jonathan on his deathbed that I would—"

"I know, I know. Watch after me." To Terry's credit, he didn't show half the resentment Neil knew he must be feeling. "Neil, he was a good father to me and to you as well, even if he was your older brother. You've always been more like a brother to me than an uncle. I do appreciate your concern, but..."

"But you're the earl and will do as you damn well please, eh?" Neil asked, knowing the answer. The boy had a head like marble.

"Just so. I am the earl," Terry said unequivocally.

"Then I bid you good night, *my lord,*" Neil said quietly. He set his glass down carefully on the mantel and strode to the door.

"Aw, Neil." Terry came after him and caught his arm. "Don't leave angry."

"Just leave, eh?" Neil offered a tired smile with the tired joke. He loved his nephew and hated to see the boy distressed. But damn it all, how could he stand idly by and do nothing while Terry wrecked his future? "Meet you at the races on Saturday?"

Terry nodded once and let go of his sleeve.

"I'll see myself out," Neil told him. "And, Terry...please think very carefully about all the repercussions of this, won't you?"

Lost in his thoughts, Neil strode down the brick walkway to his waiting carriage. Terry left him no alternative but to approach the woman. Hell, he couldn't even buy her off; she already had a bloody fortune. Perhaps if he appealed to her sympathy, Lady Marleigh would be willing to set her sights elsewhere. Not likely, though, if all he heard was true.

Old Marleigh's daughter had a reputation as black as the devil's hoof, smutted beyond repair by every wagging tongue in London. The *Gazette* published accounts of her antics almost weekly. She had to have worked damned hard to ruin herself so completely in the four months since her father's death. Totally wild, they said, as amoral as an alley cat. Worse than Caro Lamb, old Byron's paramour. And God knew that one had been a trollop of the first water. Decades later her adventures were still legend, just as Lady Marleigh's were becoming.

Neil peered out into the night as his carriage trundled along toward his bachelor digs near the hospital. The foggy night and his mission left him with a chill that his fox-lined cloak couldn't warm. Godamercy, he should be with the army now, where he could do some good. Horrible as it was, he'd at least felt useful. What the hell was he doing here, trying to sort out Terry's life when his own lay in pieces?

If only Jon had lived. Coming home on leave had been a mistake. Would it have been any easier if Neil had heard of his brother's death while in the Crimea? Would he still be alive if the fox hunt to entertain Neil had never taken place?

Jon's deathbed request had forced Neil to resign his commission so he could stay and look after Terry. Pitiful job he had made of that! The three months he had needed to study the latest medical developments—first in Florence, then in Boston—had been three too many away. He never should have left Terry at such a vulnerable point—orphaned, young, newly titled, inexperienced. And ripe for plucking by a jaded little tart who knew exactly what she was doing. Women like that were a scourge!

Jon had always been so careful about the Bronwyn name and the Havington title. How adamant he was, even as he drew his last few breaths, that Neil protect the boy and give him proper guidance until he gained maturity. With both his mother and father dead, Terry would have no one else, Jon had said.

Why couldn't Jon have survived and handled this himself? Neil cursed his brother's carelessness in taking a jump beyond his mount's ability. He despaired at the helplessness he felt watching his brother die. All those years spent becoming a physician and he could do nothing. Jon lay dead only half a year, and now his only son planned a marriage that would destroy him socially, politically and probably emotionally as well. No, by God, Neil vowed, he'd do his duty by Jon, and by Terry as well. He'd put a stop to this if it was the last thing he ever did.

Neil pulled out his watch; it was a bit past ten. He ran a gloved thumb over the timepiece, considering whether it might be too late. Then he raised his malacca cane and rapped on the top of the carriage. When it slowed and his driver peered down through the small opening, Neil ordered, "To St. James's, Oliver. Marleigh House." Might as well have done with this distasteful business now. Tonight.

Elizabeth Marleigh stuffed her traveling case to bursting and sat on top to pack it down for fastening. Footsteps in the hall-way gave her just enough time to drag it off the bed and see if she could lift it. "What?" She answered the knock.

"Sorry, milady, but there's a doctor downstairs in th'

foya wishin' to speak wi' you. Says it's frightful urgent,'' the tweenie said, sounding upset. "Mr. Thurston's abed and I didn't know where ta put—''

"Tell him I'll be down directly,'' Elizabeth interrupted. Who had called a doctor? Thurston complained so constantly she hardly paid attention anymore. She hadn't seen him up and about for several days, though. No doubt he'd been just as useless in his prime, when he'd been in her uncle's employ. She ought to have turned him off when her father died, but he had nowhere else to go. Butlers in their dotage were in short demand. Maybe the doctor would recommend retirement and she could let Thurston go with a pension. Well, with her away in Scotland, there would be very little for him to do but rest and recover, anyway.

She quickly buttoned the jacket of her traveling frock and pushed her untidy hair back off her brow. With her regular maid gone and Thurston indisposed, no one would question her plans or know where she had headed.

The doctor waited at the bottom of the stairs, his hat and cane gripped tightly in one leather-gloved hand while he tucked away his timepiece with the other. Ready to leave already, thought Elizabeth. Thurston must not be too seriously ill, then. "So, how is he faring, Doctor?" she asked, eager to have the interview over so she could be on her way.

"Truly besotted, I should think," the doctor answered with a quirk of one dark brow.

The small movement drew Elizabeth's notice to his face. Good Lord, he was handsome...and familiar. But no, she'd have remembered meeting this one, she was certain. She shook her head to clear it. He was just the physician and they were discussing Thurston. "Sotted, you say? He drinks?" She'd never known Thurston to indulge before. "Peculiar."

The doctor grunted impatiently, shifting his cane to his right hand. "Don't treat this lightly, my lady. I'm asking you, pleading if I must, to let him go gracefully. And as gently as you may."

"Let him go? Of course, I was just thinking I should have

done so months ago." She wondered where Thurston would
go. Perhaps her cousin, Colin, would offer him a cottage on
the estate for retirement, just for old times' sake. The old man
fairly worshipped the son of his old employer. "He'll be upset,
of course, but you're quite right. I'll make it as painless as
possible, I promise you."

He smiled then, and her knees almost gave way. *Devastating* was the word that came to mind. The man was devastating.
Dangerously so. Women patients, ill or not, must fall at his
feet with astounding regularity. He was well over six feet tall
and built like a brick wall. The somber black waistcoat, trousers and knee-high boots emphasized his build. A snowy shirt,
one with the new turndown collar and soft, unstarched cravat
gave him a sort of Bohemian air. He carried a wide-brimmed,
low-crowned hat, also black, fashionable but still a bit daring.
As was his scent, not the usual bay rum or witch hazel most
men wore, but spicy and unidentifiable, subtly teasing.

There was an easy grace about him, a comfortable acceptance of his form that communicated itself. Dark blue eyes,
almost black, glittered like gemstones in their lush, black-rimmed settings. Midnight hair, carelessly brushed back, tickled his collar. A deep wave of it fell over his forehead and
right temple, softening his strong features. His nose was long
and nobly formed, accented by sharply planed cheekbones.
Smooth skin, slightly tanned, spoke of outdoor exercise. Of
course a doctor would take care of himself. This man looked
as though he worked at it. And his mouth...

Elizabeth cleared her throat and held on to the newel post
for support. Men didn't affect her this way. They just didn't.
Or they never had before. She felt so stunned she hardly heard
his next words.

"I hadn't expected such understanding," he said. "You're
being a real brick about this, Lady Marleigh, and I want you
to know I do appreciate it."

"Thank you for saying so, but it's no great thing. I can
easily find someone else," she mumbled automatically. Then
she squinted at him. "Have we met before, Doctor?"

"No," he said amiably, still smiling. "I don't believe we have. Perhaps it's just the family resemblance—the eyes, I'm told. Most people remark on it. I'm always flattered, but Terrence—"

"Terry! You're Terry's uncle! I recall he mentioned you were a doctor just returned from serving with the army. What a coincidence you've come…"

Then the truth dawned—the awful truth about why he was here in her foyer. She shrank inside, a painful shrinking that made her feel queasy. Her face hardened and felt as though it would shatter. "You didn't come about Thurston, did you?" she asked in a near whisper. "This isn't about him at all."

His smile vanished. The beautifully molded lips drew into a thin line, white around their edges, before he spoke. "I'm sure I don't know a Thurston. If he's another of your conquests, I have no interest in him. All I want is for you to withdraw your affections—and your claws—from my nephew."

Elizabeth fought the rage rising inside her. She had almost forgotten for a moment—for a sweet, blessed moment, while talking to a man who didn't pounce before greeting—that she could expect no more than revulsion, leering or lust. She ached to slap his face, to scream at him and tear out his hair. How could she have believed for a second that he was any different? "And if I don't withdraw, Doctor? If I refuse?"

He drew himself up to full height, seeming to tower over her even though she stood on the second step up. "Then, my lady, you must believe that I'll do anything necessary to remove you from his life." He paused—for effect, she thought—before adding ominously, "Anything."

Oh God, he was the one! It was *him!* Fear gripped her like a vise and she couldn't move. Her eyes cut from one side of the deserted foyer to the other, searching for help. Why had she dismissed all the servants? Only a bedridden butler, a wine-soaked cook and a hen-witted between-stairs maid were all she had left in the house. None of them could do the least bit of good against this threat. Terror choked off her breath and she felt faint.

"Do you understand?" he asked in a gravelly tone that chilled her blood.

Elizabeth nodded.

"Then take care of it."

Without a further word of farewell, he turned on his heel and marched out the door. It banged shut with a whoosh of cold November air.

Elizabeth collapsed on the stairs and clutched the rail for a long moment until her heart stopped pounding in her ears. Then, with a haste that threatened her footing, she raced up to her room, grabbed her overstuffed valise and ran down the back stairs to the carriage house.

Humphrey stood waiting, and the coach was ready, just as she'd ordered earlier. "North," she gasped breathlessly as she shoved her case at him and scrambled inside. "And make haste."

The wheels bounced over the cobbles, vibrating the inside of the carriage as though coach springs hadn't been invented yet.

Elizabeth tried to calm herself by calculating the time it would take to reach Scotland. No one would expect her to go there. Hardly anyone knew about her father's old hunting box. It wasn't grand enough that he would have invited any of his cronies to it. He had purchased it in his youth and kept it strictly as a refuge for the times he wanted to spend alone. She would never have known about it herself had they not gone to Edinburgh earlier this year. A quick stop on the way home to insure the lodge was properly stocked was the only clue he'd ever given that it existed.

She would take the carriage to Edinburgh, dismiss Humphrey and ride alone to the lodge. It would be a perfect place to hide.

The doctor couldn't kill her if he couldn't find her. Oh, she understood full well why he wanted to, but it did seem a little extreme. Why had he waited until tonight to warn her? He must be a fool to think she needed three attempts on her life to scare her into heeding his demand.

She would never have married Terrence Bronwyn, anyway. Hadn't she told him as much time and again? He seemed to have some misguided notion of restoring her to society. Saving her from the wolves of the ton, as he had put it. Righting the wrongs. She'd reminded him it was a bit too late for that. Those wolves had already ripped her to shreds, and there wasn't a damned thing he could do about it.

Now that she knew who wanted her dead, all she could do was disappear for a few months until Terry—and this murderous uncle of his—forgot about her. Maybe she'd never come back. Life alone in a hunting box couldn't be nearly so bad or so lonely as life in her London town house.... By the time they left the cobblestoned streets for the open road, Elizabeth had drifted into a fitful sleep.

Neil almost turned back an hour into the journey. It was fairly obvious now that the woman wasn't on her way to meet Terry. When he'd seen her carriage careen past his at breakneck speed, a possible elopement had been his first thought. Where the devil was she going in such a lather? Curiosity prevented him from abandoning his surveillance. That, and the possibility that she might be meeting someone else. Now that would be helpful. As soon as Terry found out about her rendezvous with another man, surely he would wake up to the facts, see her true character—or rather, the lack of it.

A guilty thought worried its way up from the back of Neil's mind. She might be running from him after that intimidating little speech of his. Terrorizing women wasn't a thing to be proud of, and Elizabeth Marleigh had definitely been terrified.

"She deserved it!" he said aloud. "Fractious twit." Who did she think she was to play fast and loose with the earl of Havington? She'd admitted her willingness to give over that Thurston fellow, whomever he was. Hopefully, she'd be showing poor Terry the gate next. The lad would get over it, of course, but not if they became locked in a meaningless marriage.

Neil could see how Terry had become entranced, though. The girl was a goer—wicked as sin, but with the innocent air of a schoolroom miss. Who could resist that? If he didn't know all she'd been up to, Neil admitted to himself he might have… *No!*

He certainly had more sense than to involve himself with another like her, even temporarily.

Emma Throckmorton had been enough to make a man swear off women entirely. Well, almost entirely. Neil hadn't had the slightest urge to commit himself to more than a quick night's pleasure in the last six years. No, he had learned his lesson quite well, thank you. The moment he found himself looking cow eyed at a woman again he'd take a bloody scalpel to his wrists and be done with it. Less suffering that way.

This Marleigh woman might be one of the most beautiful he'd seen in some time, but beauty meant nothing. Her hair was odd—a lovely color, red-gold, but no longer than a finger's length all over her head. He had to admit the feathery curls set off those liquid brown eyes entirely too large for her face, that pert nose with its flaring little nostrils and the generous mouth enclosed by dimples. The whole of it came together like a well-written sonnet—marvelous to admire but imperative to leave alone.

Devil it all! Her face counted for little but good skin and a fortunate arrangement of features. And body parts, of course. Oh yes, luck favored Lady Marleigh in that respect as well. She possessed a slender bone structure that would age quite well. Dainty women were the worst kind, in his opinion, for a man to tangle with. Neil catered to the robust type himself, women who were sturdy enough to look after themselves, women who didn't rouse his protective instincts. He and his nephew would both do well to stay away from the likes of Elizabeth Marleigh.

His thoughts ran on along the same lines until he felt the carriage pull to a stop. Instantly alert, he stuck his head out the window and met little but dense fog. Only small, wavery blobs of light penetrated the gloom.

Oliver leaned over the side to speak. "Inn up ahead, sir. Think it's th' Dowdy Maid. Th'other rig pulled up just now so I stopped outa sight. Whatcha want ta do?" The driver shifted his close-fitting cap and scratched his head.

"Pull up beside the stables and wait. Maybe they stopped to eat."

"No, sir," Oliver said. "They'll be in fer the night. Stable lad's unhookin' the team and her man took her bag inside."

"Well, keep the team hitched. I'll be going back to town shortly." When they reached the stables, Neil alighted, left his puzzled driver and approached the inn.

Stepping just inside the doorway, he carefully kept to the shadows. Elizabeth Marleigh's back looked tense and ramrod straight as she argued with the innkeeper. "I must have a private room, sir," she said.

"Sorry, there ain't none available. Ye'll have to sleep in the common." The man eyed her with suspicion, probably because she was not attended by a chaperon or even so much as a maid. It just wasn't done, even in these enlightened times, Neil thought. At least not by respectable women.

"Oh, but you see, my husband is joining me later tonight. He'll be expecting his comfort when he comes to meet me." She turned on the charm. Very convincing charm, Neil admitted. Of course, the coin she pushed forward didn't hurt her effort any. He could imagine the batting eyelashes even though he couldn't see them.

The man pointed up the stairs and handed her a large key. "Number three."

With a nod, she hefted her leather valise and headed up the stairs.

So her *husband* was joining her, eh? Neil thought about Terry's insistence that he meant to marry the woman come hell or high water. Could Terry be meeting her here? If not, why hadn't she simply declared earlier that she had already terminated their relationship?

Lord, he'd stumbled on their elopement in progress!

This demanded drastic action. He had to do something before Terry arrived, something to stop this tragedy from taking place and ruining his nephew's future.

Neil slipped back out into the swirling fog, virtually feeling his way to the carriage.

"Oliver, when I go back inside, pull up in front and leave the door open for me. Hold that lantern over here."

The driver complied as Neil reached in for his medical bag. He extracted a small, brown, stoppered bottle and pocketed it, stowing the bag under the seat once more.

"I'll have a patient with me. When we come out, I want you to drive west to Bearsden, posthaste. No stops."

"All th' way to Middlesex? In this soup? But, sir—"

"I know the place is not staffed, but we'll need privacy. Absolute quiet." Neil shot the man a pointed look that dared him to question the business any further.

"Aye, as ye say, sir. Bearsden 'tis then. Posthaste." He saluted with a tug of his cap and a sly, gap-toothed grin.

Neil reentered the inn and looked around the taproom. The Marleigh driver hadn't come in, probably intending to sleep in the stables. Neil approached the burly keeper. "I'm to meet my wife—short woman, reddish hair, dark eyes. Which room?"

The man squinted and pursed his lips. "Maybe she's here, maybe she ain't."

Neil sighed, plopped two guineas on the bar and cocked his head. "She's been quite ill, the poor dear, in hospital until yesterday. Did she seem all right?"

"Can't say. Don't care. Third room on the right, top o' th' stair," the man said, hefting the coins in his hand.

The stairs creaked under Neil's weight, and he fingered the bottle in his pocket as he climbed. At the third door he stopped, saturated his handkerchief with the concoction, re-stoppered the bottle and knocked softly. He heard her answer, "Yes?"

"Hurry, darling, you must hurry! He's coming!" he whispered frantically, hoping she'd take him for his nephew.

It worked. The door opened a crack and Neil pushed his

way through. She opened her mouth to scream and he covered her face with the wadded linen. She fought him, struggled wildly for a few seconds and then collapsed against his chest. Quickly, he lifted her deadweight in his arms and laid her on the bed.

How light she was, like swan's down. So delicate. He turned her this way and that until he had her securely bundled in her cloak. Then, cursing, he awkwardly shut her overstuffed suitcase and carried them both downstairs.

"A relapse," he explained to the wide-eyed innkeeper. Managing the door latch with some difficulty, Neil exited the inn with his burden, dumped her into the waiting coach and climbed in behind her. He arranged his little charge in a comfortable position as Oliver barreled through the fog toward Middlesex.

The tiny witch would have a hell of a headache when she woke up, but nothing compared to the one she'd probably give him. What did one do with a shameless, greedy female secluded in a deserted old manor house to make her want to stay awhile?

Neil dismissed his scruples and smiled. The possibilities seemed deliciously endless.

# Chapter Two

*Bearsden Manor, Middlesex*

Sunlight streamed through the window and sliced across her face. Elizabeth forced one eye open and quickly clamped it shut against a shard of brightness. Her head ached abominably and her stomach churned like a kettle at full boil. She tried to roll off the bed to find a chamberpot, but froze when a huge hand settled on her shoulder.

"Stay where you are," a deep voice warned.

Elizabeth screamed.

Terrorized, she struggled with all the wildness of a cornered fox. This was it. He'd kill her *now!* But not, by God, without a fight! She struck out with her fists. Desperate to live, Elizabeth flailed against him until her body heaved violently.

He dodged to one side as her stomach emptied the little that was in it. Heedless of indignity or even death, she retched endlessly before collapsing back against the pillows.

Fear shifted to anger and frustration. She'd done all she possibly could and it wasn't enough. Her eyes wouldn't open. They joined the rest of her body in total and complete exhaustion. "Do it, then," she rasped. "Just do it."

"Look, I'm sorry about this, but it's your own fault." The voice was calmer now, only tinged with irritation.

Elizabeth braced herself for whatever came next—hands around her throat, a knife, a pistol ball? What did it matter? Her muscles felt disconnected and refused to react. Rage deserted her suddenly, left her empty, spent. She was just too tired to care anymore. Let him do his worst. Everyone else had.

If only her voice would work, she could curse him. One parting shot: *See you in hell, you bastard!* No, she wouldn't go there. She'd already paid for all her sins. Surely.

Thoughts scattered as she grasped for something pleasant to distract her from whatever pain might ensue. His words now were seductive, scary, threatening, luring her back from every comforting scene she tried to picture. Couldn't the wretch just be quiet and get on with it? Her muzzy mind couldn't grasp the content of what he said, but she sensed exasperation in his tone. Was the idiot trying to talk her to death?

His muttering ceased as he tugged her this way and that, rustling and yanking at the bedcovers. Then there was a peaceful stillness, broken only by the sound of pouring water. Her limbs lay weighted, lifeless. Her eyelids felt too heavy to open. The odor of sickness faded.

A cool cloth was swiped across her face and neck. Ah, that felt good, brought memories of Mother. Good memories to die with. "Mama," she whispered, hoping her mother would be waiting to welcome her. Her father, too.

"No, I'm not Mama. Here, drink this," the voice ordered, gruff and impatient. "I said *drink!*"

She drank. *Poison, then.* Of course. He *was* a doctor. She welcomed the creeping oblivion, weary of fighting a useless battle she couldn't begin to win or even understand. The weeks of sleeplessness and watchfulness had only delayed the inevitable. Death in a water glass. Ironic.

Her last thought contained relief and a little regret. She ought to have married old Purvis Hilfinger when she was sixteen. She'd be in Northumberland right now, raising babies and counting sheep. Ah, counting sheep...one, two, three...

\* \* \*

Neil started to cover her. He ought to undress her so she would be more comfortable, at least get her out of that pinching corset. God only knew how long she had worn the damned thing—all day before, probably, and certainly throughout the night. 'Twas a wonder she could breathe at all.

He placed his hand lightly on her chest. Breathing was too shallow and she looked pallid as a corpse. A bad reaction to the chloroform? Nonsense, the queen herself had used it. He'd employed it on hundreds of patients without any ill effects.

But none of them were women, his conscience reminded him. Maybe he'd used too much and for too long a time. What did he know of delicate constitutions such as Miss Marleigh's or even of female medicine in general? Nothing outside the medical texts and an occasional treatise on feminine complaints. There'd been cadavers in med school, of course, and as an intern he'd observed indigent patients. But Neil could count his actual female patients on the fingers of one hand. Hardy trulls every one—camp followers he'd treated for the grippe or diseases better left unnamed.

Military medicine was virtually all he knew. Battlefield surgery, dysentery, saddle sores, the odd appendectomy. What if, in his desperation to protect Terry, he'd done real injury to this fragile girl? Suppose she died right here in his bed?

Neil shook himself. Where the hell had he put his objectivity? Her functions had simply slowed because of the drug and her constrictive underpinnings. Stupid to react like some corkbrained first-termer who'd never attended a bedside before. *You've given her a stimulant, now take off the damned corset and see if she improves!*

Still he hesitated. She was no willing paramour who wanted him to see her naked, but a helpless woman he'd rendered unconscious. This was wrong, all of it. After taking the oath to preserve health and life, he'd purposely put someone at risk.

Hell, he always got too involved with his patients, but how could he help it? The responsibility for another's life was daunting, too much like playing God without a rule book or the proper power to pull it off. As with Jon.

If only he had thought this out first and found another way to prevent her meeting with Terry. Neil cursed himself for reverting to that inborn proclivity to act on impulse. He thought he'd had that conquered years ago.

"I'll make it up to you, you know. Anything you want." Anything but let you wed Terry, he added silently, reason returning.

*Nonsense*, he thought. *What unmitigated foolishness. She's just a hardheaded adventuress with a nose full of chloroform who needs a bit of care to bring her around.* So get on with it.

Bending over her, Neil released the row of tiny buttons on her bodice and stripped her as efficiently as he had all the battle victims he'd tended.

The breathing improved immediately, Neil noticed with relief. Her skin color looked better, too. *Peaches and cream, soft, silken...beautiful.* He forced his gaze away from her breasts, embarrassed at his lack of decorum, guilty at the way his body reacted to the sight of her. He cursed the impulse to touch her.

Stalking across the room, he snatched one of his old linen shirts out of the wardrobe. It smelled of cedar and starch, but not unpleasantly. She'd certainly prefer this to his rummaging through her valise for a night rail. The weathered case looked ready to explode at a touch. He didn't think he could deal with a scattered sea of her frilly furbelows.

When he'd dressed her and neatly tucked her in, he bundled her soiled clothing along with the sheets he'd removed and stowed them outside in the hall. Then he pulled the bedroom draperies shut and sat down to wait. Exhausted as she was, it might be awhile before the mild stimulant kicked in and she woke again.

What the devil would he do with her then? Several things hopped to mind. His lecherous thoughts had dissipated a bit, only to return now with hurricane force. Neil suspected that was going to happen with disturbing frequency as long as he kept her here, his guilt notwithstanding.

The delicate little piece looked like a tuckered-out child lying there. This feeling of tenderness toward Elizabeth Marleigh bothered him. It was undeserved on her part, and maddening on his. But she seemed so vulnerable. Her cap of red-gold curls framed such an angelic face, barely free of its baby roundness. This one was no infant, though, and most assuredly no angel. He'd do well to remember that and keep his sympathy—and his hands—to himself.

Why had she embarked on such a wanton life? he wondered. If she had controlled her baser nature, there would have been no impediment to her wedding his nephew—a beautiful, wealthy heiress for a fine, fledgling earl. The Marleigh name was one of England's oldest and most respected. That is, until she had destroyed it with those foolish escapades of hers.

Neil passed his thumb over the watch Jon had left him, rubbing it like a talisman, renewing his promise to keep Terry safe. He looked down at the case and the glint of gold mocked him, made him think of the Marleigh woman's gilded curls.

She had ruined herself, but, by God, she wouldn't ruin Terry! If hiding her here was the only way to prevent the marriage, so be it. Perhaps when the lad found her missing at their appointed rendezvous, he'd become disenchanted and give up thoughts of marriage. He might search for her, of course. Probably would, given Terry's tenacious nature. But he would never look here.

Bearsden had stood vacant since Neil's maternal grandparents died. He felt no sentimental attachment to the place and should have sold it long ago. Still, for some twisted reason, he'd kept it cared for, and even visited occasionally. He doubted Terry knew the property existed.

How would Lady Marleigh explain to her young lover an absence of a week or so from town? Yes, this ought to work. If Neil could just keep her here in the country awhile, word would get around that she had struck up with another paramour.

No one would take her seriously even if she told exactly what had happened. Who would believe it if she named him as her abductor? A respected physician stealing away with the likes of her? Neil could hardly believe it himself. Or countenance the fact that he'd really done it. Leaning his head to one side and clasping his hands across his middle, he allowed himself to doze....

Neil awakened with a start, almost falling out of the wing chair. The patter of hurried footsteps on the bare floor of the hallway brought him to his feet, running. He tore out of the room and down the hall, catching her at the top of the stairs. Clamping his arms around her, he forced her forward against the banister.

She landed a backward kick to his knee that almost sent them both plunging headfirst over the rail. Neil tumbled her to the floor facedown, clutching her this way and that, struggling to subdue clawing hands and kicking feet.

Lord, she was strong! It was like trying to stuff a wildcat into a sack. His fingers closed over hers, squeezing them into fists while he threw one leg over both of hers. She finally went limp, her back heaving against his chest. Neil relaxed his hold and started to speak. She leaned forward and bit the back of his hand.

"Ow! Damn you, stop! Stop it! I'll thrash—"

She bit harder. He clamped his own teeth over a mouthful of her curls and yanked her head back sharply. She let go of his hand with an ear-piercing screech. Neil rolled sideways and landed on top of her, their hands imprisoned beneath her and her face pressed to the hardwood floor. "Be still or I'll throttle you, you wildcat!"

All the life seemed to drain out of her once more and she stopped breathing. Silence reigned for a full minute. He frowned down at her. Was this another trick to throw him off guard? The one eye he could see didn't blink, but stared at the wall. Tears poured out in a steady stream, but she didn't sob. Didn't move. He could feel the rapid beat of her heart under their joined hands.

"Will you fight if I let you up?" he asked.

No answer.

"I won't hurt you."

She still said nothing, just stared at the baseboard, weeping silently.

"I *promise* I won't hurt you."

He gave up waiting for an answer and moved off of her. She sucked in a deep breath and shuddered, making no move to rise. The shirt he'd put on her had become wound around her waist, so her lower body was bare. Neil froze at the sight of her pert little buttocks. He fought the sudden stirring in his groin.

Fury at his unwanted arousal made him gruffer than he meant to be. He yanked at the tail of the shirt to cover her. "Get up!"

Slowly she pulled herself to her knees and stared at him, wide-eyed and tense. Her lower lip trembled and the tears continued to freshen and fall.

The sight undid him completely. He caught her to him and held her as he would a frightened child, smoothing her soft curls and pressing her face against his chest. "Don't cry. Please don't." Gently, he lifted her, carrying her back to the bed.

She made no attempt to get away, no move at all, as he settled onto the edge of the mattress beside her. Still, her eyes never left his, and he hadn't yet seen her blink.

"All I want to do is talk to you," he explained, keeping his voice soft and using his best doctor-patient tone. "That's it— lie back and take a deep breath. Another. It's all over now." He stroked her wet cheeks with the back of his fingers.

"Get it over with," she whispered. "I don't want to...dread it anymore."

"What?" he asked, still soothing her with his hands, patting, caressing. "What shall I do?"

"Kill me," she squeaked. Her chin lifted and her eyes narrowed in a brief show of bravado.

"Don't be absurd!" He grunted in disbelief, shaking his

head. "Surely you don't think...? I have no intention...I'm certainly not going to *kill* you. What gave you that idea?"

She wore the look of young men after their first battle—uncertain that they had survived it and already dreading the next one. "You said you'd do *anything!* And even before that I knew it was you who... The boat, the knife and the chocolate..." Her voice dwindled on a defeated sigh.

"What the devil are you talking about?" She must be in shock. God, he hadn't meant to frighten her this badly. She really believed he wanted her dead for some reason. Well, he remembered, he had implied...no, had actually threatened her.

This was really getting out of hand. No one, even someone like her, deserved to feel such fear.

"I don't want you to die," he said earnestly, hoping to ease her mind, convince her. Ought he to use her Christian name? Patients always responded better to the familiarity. "Do you understand me, Elizabeth? You are in no danger. I just don't want you to marry my nephew. That's the only reason I brought you here—simply to get you away from Terry. That's *all,* I swear."

She didn't believe him. He could see her disbelief and virtually smell her fear. The poor thing still expected a death blow at any moment.

"Look, you little dimwit, if I wanted you dead, you'd never have awakened. Don't you see? I could have done you in a hundred times over, dumped you somewhere and dusted my hands of it. You needn't be afraid, Elizabeth. I do *not* want you dead."

For a long minute she studied his face intently, biting her lips and breathing hard. She shifted uncomfortably and straightened her back. When she finally spoke, her words were soft. "Would you...leave me alone then? Please?"

He understood immediately. She had been abed all night and most of the morning without relieving herself. She looked somewhat calmer now, sane enough to trust to herself for a while.

Hopefully.

Neil glanced at the room's only window, which he knew from experience was impossible to coax open. Should she break it, there was a thirty-foot drop beneath. One who clung to life so tenaciously was hardly suicidal enough to jump.

"Certainly. We can talk downstairs. There are towels on the stand, water in the pitcher, and the necessary room's in there." Neil waved as he stood up. "Your bag's in the wardrobe. Why don't you dress and come down to the study when you feel up to it? The door will be open. If you need to rest awhile, it's all right. I won't disturb you."

She still didn't fully believe him. Neil dragged forth the practiced reassurance he doled out like laudanum to the wounded. "I promise you, you're safe, Elizabeth. My word as a gentleman." Ha! She'd surely credit that after his conduct up to this point.

"Will you let me go?" She sounded a bit stronger, he thought, but very doubtful.

"Of course I'll let you go," he answered patiently. *In about a week,* he purposely didn't add.

Slowly he descended the stairs, lost in his thoughts. "Lord, what have I done?" he asked himself, rolling his eyes heavenward. "This is sheer madness."

Here was a side of himself kept well buried since he was a child. It had emerged only once in the intervening years.

With Emma.

Recklessness and disregard for consequences had already ruined his life twice. How many lessons did one need?

First his mother had left him, unable to deal with the wild child his aged father had spoiled rotten. How well he recalled the last incident before his father died.

Neil had had the best of intentions. Listening for days to his mother bewail the fact that she needed a grand hunt scene painted for the dining room, he had sought to oblige. He knew exactly how, he'd thought, after weeks of watching a visiting artist capture his mother in oils. His own attempt on the wall above the buffet wasn't bad for a five-year-old. She didn't agree. After her screaming fit, Neil made hasty amends. Mother must be pleased.

"What takes paint away, Jed?" he had asked the footman.

"Bird shit," the disgruntled man replied, busy scrubbing the nasty stuff off the lord's glossy carriage.

Well, chickens were birds, Neil reasoned. He'd visited the henhouse and set to work on the unwanted picture that very afternoon. Now that he looked back, he wondered that Mother had stayed as long as she had.

Married at sixteen to a man three times her age, Norah Guest Bronwyn had probably whooped with delight when her husband expired six years later. Until she realized she was only a dowager countess, stranded in the country with her own little hellion and an eighteen-year-old stepson—the new earl—who loathed her.

Without a word of explanation, Norah had packed her things and Neil's, deposited him at a second-rate boarding school and hared off to God knew where. He hadn't seen her since. But later, as a man, he'd met dozens of women just like her.

As far as he knew they were *all* like her—flighty, shallow, feather-headed females set on taking all they could get at the least possible cost.

Even after he'd realized that, he still felt responsible for her desertion. If only he'd been well behaved. If he'd been quiet, agreeable and more circumspect, she might have taken him with her or stayed and at least tried to love him. She wasn't all she should have been as a mother, but he knew the fault was mostly his own. He should have been different.

With that thought dominant, he'd reformed his whole personality by the time he was twelve. He grew determined to find affection somewhere, somehow, and hold on to it. His older brother had doted on him after he changed, delighted with Neil's newfound maturity. Didn't that prove the theory?

Thank God Jon had been too preoccupied with estate business to notice Neil's relapse at the age of twenty.

He'd thought Emma different from his mother. Showed how green he was—green as a goddamned summer cabbage. The old impulsiveness had reared its ugly head, caused him to think he could behave irrationally, love without analyzing the thing to death and get away with it. Lo and behold, another gut punch.

Now here he was, dead center in another harebrained fiasco that reduced his former lapses to insignificance. Why hadn't he considered the repercussions first?

This incident would forestall Terry's marriage, all right, but at what cost? The poor girl was scared out of her wits. And Terry might believe every word she said when this was over even if no one else did. Why in God's name hadn't Neil stopped to think before he acted? Hindsight was hell. Would he never learn?

Neil lifted his second glass of brandy as she appeared in the door of the study, interrupting his tardy self-recriminations.

She wore an unbecoming, dark, broadcloth dress buttoned up to her chin, and carried her valise. Like a child dressed in nanny's clothes, he thought. Her shadow-smudged eyes dwarfed her other features. She faced him with that chin up, however. Tentative though it was, she had found her courage somewhere.

"I'd like to go *now*," she said in a small, insistent voice.

"No doubt," Neil answered with what he hoped was a re-assuring smile. "Sit down and have a bite to eat. Only biscuits and tea, but that should do you. How is your stomach? Still weak?"

She nodded and dropped the case to the floor with a thud. Carefully, she inched her way to the chair he indicated and sat on the edge of it, watching him warily.

"You really are quite safe, Elizabeth," he said as he handed her a cup. "I may call you that, may I not? I truly mean you no harm." How many times would he have to say it to get that look off her face? he wondered.

Her brow screwed into a charming little frown as she seemed to consider his words. "Very well. I've thought about it at length. I suppose you'd have done your worst by now if you really meant me to die." Her voice grew stronger with every word. "But why did you frighten me so before? I could have expired of heart failure! And why all this? Why did you abduct me?"

Neil had a ridiculous urge to praise her for her recovery. Her anger was righteous, but he couldn't let it sway him now.

"I told you that. Because you were eloping with Terry, and I'll not have his future destroyed. I had to stop you somehow."

"Eloping? Are you mad? Why would you think that?" Then she pressed her forehead with the heel of her hand. "Of course, the silly dolt told you he had proposed. What am I to do with him? He won't hear a no." The dark eyes hid under shadowed lids and she sighed. "He has a good heart, but he's such a fool sometimes."

"Well, I agree with you there," Neil said with a short, bitter laugh. "He's not the first young pup to sniff after a skirt and call it love."

Her head came up with a jerk. "Love? Is that what he told you? Well, I suppose he would say that." She smiled, and the sadness in her eyes surprised him. At least she didn't gloat.

"I overheard you tell the innkeeper that your *husband* was expected. I figured that it was Terry," he said, sipping his brandy thoughtfully.

"You assumed wrongly, Dr. Bronwyn. Making up that story was the only way I could avoid sharing the common room. I never had any intention of meeting your nephew at the inn or anywhere else. Terry's simply the only friend I have, and he thinks he can save my good name if he combines it with his. Sweet idiot."

"Naturally you would say that." He took another sip, peering at her over the rim of the snifter.

"You don't believe I refused his suit?" she asked, looking so troubled he almost believed her.

Neil regretted what he had to admit, but spoke nonetheless. "Let us say that I doubt you enough to insure that no wedding takes place. In order to guarantee it, I must ask you to accept my hospitality for a while—perhaps a week—until his, uh, ardor cools. I promise you'll be perfectly safe."

She nodded thoughtfully. "All right."

He couldn't hide his shock at her ready agreement. She displayed no slyness, no taunting and no further fear. Just "all right," as though they were cementing a minor business deal? What did she think to gain? Her capitulation was too easy.

"I think I understand why you thought it necessary to do what you did," she explained. "I can't say I'll ever forgive you, but what's done is done. Staying here for a while will suit my purposes as well." She nodded once. "Yes, I'll stay."

Then she smiled.

*Oh God, that smile.* So she would turn her charms on him now, would she? Now that she couldn't have Terry? Neil beat back the thrill that shot through his soul. Not bloody likely would he succumb to her! Not if he were careful.

"You really will be safe here, you know. In every way," he said. "Please understand, I have absolutely no designs on you."

"Well," she said with sad sarcasm and a roll of those lovely dark eyes, "won't that be a novelty?"

Impudent chit. He wanted to wring her neck. "No doubt it will. The trout all jumping at your boat, are they? Can't believe there's one won't bite your bait? Well, I'm no randy hatchling, young lady, and I've had more seasoned anglers than you toss hooks in my direction. Just believe me, *I* am off-limits!"

She laughed. The bloody tart laughed so hard she was spilling her tea. Hysterical henwit!

When she had calmed a bit, she pressed a hand to her chest, gasping for breath. There were tears on her cheeks again, but they weren't the product of fear. Well, maybe an after-product of some sort, he decided grudgingly. Relief now that she understood she was safe.

"I should have brought a net!" she said, and was off again, bending double in her chair, holding her sides with laughter.

"I fail to see the humor!" He drew indignant shoulders back, took a deep gulp of brandy and waited for her to subside.

It took awhile.

"I'm sorry," she said, wiping her eyes with her serviette. "It's just that you looked..." her lips compressed, holding back a further outburst "...like a carp."

Neil squeezed his eyes shut and relaxed his mouth, knowing she was probably right. He squelched the urge to laugh with her. How in hell was he going to deal with the little tramp when she was so damned appealing? It was as though she erased every resolution he'd ever made to maintain his decorum. Even when she mocked him, he found her so enchanting he wanted to kiss her.

There was a reckless thought. He must remember what she was. "I know all about you, *Lady* Marleigh," he said.

She sobered as though he had doused her with icy water. "So, you've heard it all, have you?"

"Oh, yes indeed. That orgy at Hammershill, the statue, the midnight swim, your...ménage à trois. Have I missed anything? Do fill me in." He begged to God she wouldn't. Neil hated the snideness in his voice, but it grated on his soul to think of her cheap theatrics. How could she be so flagrant? Why did he have to picture her dancing naked, cavorting with another...no, *two* other men? Christ, he wanted to shake her!

"I guess that covers it rather well," she said quietly, all traces of laughter gone, cut away by the knife of his sarcasm.

Neil heard the catch in her voice and hoped it meant she regretted those foolish actions. He hoped she cried from now until doomsday for all that could have been. For what he might have offered.... No! Not him. He'd never have offered her a damned thing! Nothing.

The front door knocker clacked loudly, echoing in the high-ceilinged foyer outside the study. "Stay here and eat your biscuits," he ordered curtly. "And drink that tea."

Who the hell would be calling on him here? The house had been closed for years, his presence a secret. Could be the caretaker he paid to make a monthly check, he supposed. Neil pulled the study door shut as he strode to the front entrance.

The man who stood waiting frowned in greeting. "Hullo, Doc. I recalled your mentioning the house here once, and hoped I might find you. I'd looked everywhere else."

Neil froze, subconsciously barring the way inside. *Scotland Yard?* Had someone reported his abducting the girl? Surely not this soon. No one had seen him but the innkeeper, and the man had no idea who he was. But what the hell was Mac-Linden doing here? They hadn't even seen each other since Neil returned to London.

"Lindy? What do you want?" Then, with effort, he recovered himself and forced a laugh. "I'm sorry, old man. You quite took me by surprise. Come in, come in." Neil stood aside to allow him entry. Guilt must have sapped his reason. It was absurd to think the authorities would send a *friend* to arrest him.

MacLinden curled the brim of the dapper bowler he was holding, turning the hat round and round. An uncharacteristically nervous gesture for Lindy, Neil thought.

As a rule, Trent MacLinden was the soul of composure. Even the blinding pain of his war wound hadn't affected him this way. His eyes, a dark, mossy green in the weak lamplight, didn't meet Neil's. Even the ruddy mustache, shiny from a recent waxing, worked impatiently as Lindy raked his upper lip with his teeth.

Judging by their previous ease in each other's company since serving together in the Crimea, it was a sure bet this was no social call. Something was definitely wrong.

"Didn't mean to be rude, old son," Neil apologized. "It's just that the sight of the estimable Inspector MacLinden strikes fear in the hearts of us mere civilians. Congratulations on your promotion, by the way. I only heard of it when I arrived in town this week. You're a real top peeler now! We should celebrate."

"Thank you. I'm here in an official capacity, Doc. Could

we perhaps sit down?'' Lindy headed for the closed door of the study.

"In here." Neil redirected him to the parlor across the hall. This had to be about some other business. There was no way Lindy could know about the woman. Not this soon.

He closed the door behind them with a prayer that Lady Marleigh had fallen asleep over her teacup. If she came bursting out of the study, hurling accusations, he'd just have to confess.

With a distracted sweep of his hands he yanked off the dust sheets covering two overstuffed chairs. Large as it was, the room smelled musty and airless. Neil felt trapped—by the age-grayed walls, by the impending disgrace, by his own reckless idiocy. What else could have brought Lindy here but the abduction?

Terry would hate him if the truth came out. And arrest was a real possibility.

Neil would receive a light sentence, probably—at least he hoped so. It was a first offense and he hadn't harmed the girl. Not really.

He was so preoccupied forming his defense, he almost missed Lindy's announcement.

"Terry's dead, Neil."

# Chapter Three

*Dead?* Terry couldn't be dead. He was alive and well at Havington House, planning to attend the races on Saturday.

As Lindy's words began to register, Neil staggered a little and caught the back of a chair. Disjointed scenes flashed rapidly, one after another: little towheaded Terry bouncing along on a pony, sharing biscuits with his hound, wielding his first razor, graduating from Harrow. Arguing about his right to wed.

"God, no," Neil whispered, fighting off the pain. It grabbed him like a vicious animal, shook him, sank its teeth to the bone.

"I'm sorry, Neil. So sorry to bring you this news."

"He *can't* be dead! I just saw him. You've made some mistake, Lindy. Surely!" Neil recognized his own reaction from the many he'd had to deal with as he'd delivered similar news to families of friends when he'd returned early from the war. And even from his own experience six months before, when he'd watched Jon breathe his last. Even then, with the evidence of death staring him in the face, there had been a moment when he'd refused to believe it. Denial, the mind's refuge.

If there was the remotest chance of an error, Lindy would have qualified his news. Terry *was* dead.

Neil sat down and dropped his head on one hand, pressing

his eyes with his fingers. Mustn't weep. He would do that later, when he was alone. If he let go now, he might never stop. Lindy would be embarrassed, as would he.

"How?" he made himself ask. *Painlessly,* he prayed.

MacLinden laid a hand on his shoulder and squeezed hard. "He was killed, Neil. Murdered."

Fresh pain. Neil's throat burned with a need to scream. Only a whisper emerged. "Ah, no!"

"Yes, and we know who did it. I want you to come back to town with me now. There'll be an inquest, funeral arrangements and all that. I'll help, of course. Goes without saying."

Neil focused on fury—anything to lessen the godawful anguish. Murder was inconceivable. Everyone loved Terry.

Neil felt an urgent need to kill someone. A very specific someone. "Who, Lindy? What bastard did this thing?"

MacLinden sighed. "It was a woman. The woman he planned to marry, evidently." He paused. "Lady Elizabeth Marleigh. Last evening, she shot him through the head."

"No!" Neil shouted the word, realized he had and lowered his voice. "No, that's impossible, she couldn't have done it!"

"Well, she did. We found one of her father's fancy dueling pistols beside the body. Her butler says the set has been in the family for years, a gift to the old earl. Even has the Marleigh crest on the grip. The woman's run for it, but we'll find her."

"You don't understand, Lindy. Elizabeth Marleigh couldn't have killed Terry. I was with him until ten o'clock last night and went directly to her. She's been with me ever since."

MacLinden narrowed his eyes and worried his mustache with a forefinger. "Never out of your sight, you say?"

"Not once. I...followed her to an inn, brought her directly here, and we've not left."

"Where is she now?"

Neil marched to the door as he answered, "In the study."

"Wait," MacLinden cautioned. "Wait a moment. Are you telling me *you* are involved with Lady Marleigh?"

Neil paused and thought about the answer. "Yes, in a way. I guess you might say that."

Trent MacLinden battled with his professionalism. He prided himself on his objectivity, and his superiors at the Yard depended on it. That, plus his ability to ferret out culprits from seemingly nonexistent clues, was precisely why he'd been recently promoted to inspector.

Doc was his friend, one of his best friends—the man who had saved his right arm after a Hussar's bullet smashed through it. Lindy couldn't allow the authorities or anyone else to suspect that Neil Bronwyn had had a hand in his own nephew's murder, not even by association.

In MacLinden's experience with lawbreakers, brief as it was, he knew that a strong motive combined with opportunity usually equaled guilt in the eyes of the law. Neil Bronwyn clearly possessed both. That was an indisputable fact Lindy couldn't hide. Lady Marleigh did as well. Everyone on the case had already established that fact and were searching everywhere for her. By giving her an ironclad alibi and declaring her innocence, Neil risked arrest himself, for complicity.

Allowing the lady's arrest now was out of the question, of course, or Neil might hang with her. Lindy certainly couldn't have that, not after all the man had done for him.

If not for Neil's assistance in applying to Scotland Yard, Lindy would be dishing up meat pies alongside his father in the family inn in Charing Cross. And if not for Neil's flagrant usurping of a senior medical officer's surgery in Balaclava, he'd be dishing them up one-handed.

God, he still shivered when he thought about it. That saw biting into his skin. His own screams. Neil's intervention.

Devil take the Yard! Lindy would do as he'd always done and go with his instincts. He wouldn't let anyone so much as hint that Neil had killed his nephew or countenanced anyone else doing so. It was Lindy's duty to ask the question, however. Just for form's sake.

"Doc, forgive me, but this is necessary. Have you conspired in any way with this woman to help her or hide her guilt?"

He watched Neil immediately switch from grief to outrage. "Good God, man, how can you ask such a thing?"

"It is my job. That's what they pay me for. Have I your word of honor you had nothing to do with the murder?"

Neil's shoulders straightened and his gaze was direct. "By all that's holy, Lindy, I do swear it. And I promise you Elizabeth Marleigh could not possibly have done this."

"Let's see what she has to say for herself, then. Perhaps she might know someone capable of the deed." He brushed past Neil and headed for the study, not breaking stride as he entered the other room.

"Lady Marleigh?" He greeted her perfunctorily as she turned from the window. "How do you do? I am Inspector MacLinden, Scotland Yard, L Division."

She looked pale and upset as her wide-eyed glance darted from him to Neil and back again. Putting people off balance was a technique that worked quite well. Helped him keep the upper hand, especially with the nobs. Pretty little nob she was, too, with those dark chocolate eyes and springy bronze curls. Younger than he'd have thought, from all that was said about her.

He cleared his throat and gave her a few seconds to wonder just why he was here. There was confusion in her eyes, and maybe a little relief? Interesting. He dropped the bombshell. "The earl of Havington is dead. Shot. With one of *your* pistols."

Her mouth opened, worked as though she was searching for words. The eyes widened so that he could see white all around the darkest brown irises he'd ever seen. Then the heavily lashed lids dropped like a curtain, and she toppled to the floor in a tangle of skirts.

"Hang it, Lindy, that was coldly done! Get my medical bag, upstairs, second room." Neil knelt by the woman as Mac-Linden went for the doctor's satchel.

When he returned with it, Neil offered her a few sniffs of a bottled substance—something awful, by the way her nose twitched—and brought her around.

She woke still muddled, but her memory returned almost visibly. The lost look rapidly transformed into the same

shocked expression of very real grief he'd seen earlier on
Neil's face.

The woman—by association with Neil—was innocent.
Lindy was relieved he didn't have to take her in now that he'd
seen her. A pity that his own decision to declare her guiltless
wouldn't extend to his chief. Nope, MacLinden knew he
wasn't going to be able to handle this one by the book. And
God help them all if he couldn't turn up a killer. So much for
professionalism.

MacLinden watched patiently as Neil did his doctor tricks.
There didn't seem to be quite enough intimacy in their words
or touches for there to be a real affair. Yet. The attraction was
there, though, at least on Neil's part.

Unusual, that. In the four years they'd been friends Lindy
had never seen Doc show any real interest in a woman beyond
an infrequent tumble. Tumbles quietly accomplished and never
bragged about...at least not by Neil. The women weren't quite
so noble, but then women did love to talk. The man was leg-
endary and didn't even know it. Hadn't a bloody clue.

If Neil didn't know about this girl, though, he ought to be
warned before he got in over his head. An ass for an arm was
a fair trade. Ought he to save Doc's ass for him? Lindy wondered.

No sooner had the girl's sobs ceased than MacLinden
launched his questions. He found that insensitivity was the key
to being a good investigator. "So, Lady Marleigh, do you
shoot?"

"No, I do not," she answered, visibly shoring up her composure. Her chin lifted and she took a deep breath.

"Were you in love with his lordship or not?"

On the last word, he glanced pointedly at Doc, who looked
ready to kill him on the spot. Obviously didn't care to have
his ass saved. Hmm. "I repeat, were you in love with young
Havington?"

She answered in a near whisper, "No, I was not."

"You were to marry him?"

"No, I was not." Her response was defensive.

"What was he to you then?"

She shuddered, expelled a long sigh and looked out the window, doubtless seeing little through her tears. "He was the only friend I had left." Then, almost inaudibly, she added, "The only one."

Doc stood it longer than MacLinden imagined he would. "See here, Lindy, you can do this later. You can see she's overwrought. I'll just take her to her room and give her something." He reached for his medical bag.

"Not if you mean to sedate her. We must get to London tonight, and all the questions must be asked before then if I am to help you both." It felt strange giving orders to a man he'd once thought was God in a uniform. Rather bracing, in fact.

"What do you mean, help us? I swear to you she had nothing to do with this. You don't mean to arrest her anyway?"

"No, not if I can help it, but we'll have to do some tricky dancing to avoid that until we find the real murderer. My position's too new to carry that much influence with my superiors, and they're absolutely convinced she's guilty. You'll both have to do exactly as I say."

They nodded in unison. Power was a heady thing, MacLinden thought with an inward grin. He'd really have to watch that it didn't puff him up. Doc and the woman had no choice but to trust him to get them out of this mess. At least it should prove a lot more interesting than simply hauling the girl in and going on with a new case. And Lindy would be able to discharge a portion of his debt to Neil Bronwyn, the man who had kept him whole when no one else would have. He rather looked forward to the whole thing.

Elizabeth tried to climb out of the numbness, but it persisted. Poor Terry. Gone in a flash of powder. She'd never see him again, never be touched again by his gentle optimism.

There was nothing to do now but sit by while the red-haired, freckled-faced Scot chewed on his pipe and decided her fate. Her father's gun had done the deed—one of the gift set of dueling pistols, she supposed. Those were the only weapons she knew of except for his hunting guns, which were in Colin's possession. One didn't have to be a genius to figure out that she was the prime suspect.

"Lady Marleigh, do you know anyone who might have wished Terrence Bronwyn dead?" This question was kinder, as though the inspector were trying to placate Dr. Bronwyn. She sensed the camaraderie between them. Ah, they were friends, then. Good friends, apparently, for MacLinden to overlook the evidence of her guilt on the doctor's word alone.

"No, everyone liked his lordship very well," she said. "Since we've known each other, I only saw him cross once. That was at the theater just last week. We always came late and left early to...avoid crowds." She looked from the inspector to the doctor and nodded when she saw they understood. Then she continued, "A man approached Terry's box during the second act and called him into the corridor. I tried not to listen, until Terry's voice became rather heated. That was so unlike him, you see.

"Terry said something to the effect, 'Not one more bloody damn farthing until I have it all. Do you hear me?' When he returned, I asked him about the matter. He laughed and said it was merely a small venture he was looking into that was proving more difficult than he had anticipated."

Inspector MacLinden listened intently, writing all the while. "This person he spoke with was unknown to you?"

"Yes, but then I know very few people in the city. I had only a glimpse of the man. He was rather tall and slender, with long side-whiskers. About fifty I should say, with a distinctive voice."

"You'd recognize him if you saw him again?"

"Very possibly. I'm certain I would know the voice. Rather deep and sonorous." She began to get excited. "You think this man might have killed Terry, Inspector?"

MacLinden sighed. "Anything's possible. He could very well be only a business acquaintance. Did his lordship speak of anyone else with whom he might have had recent dealings?"

She paused to think, toying with her rings. "No, we rarely spoke of his day-to-day affairs. We mostly talked of...my problems and his ideas for a solution to them."

"Do you think there might be any connection between your relationship and his death?" MacLinden asked. "He did propose marriage, according to his boasts at White's."

Elizabeth thought about it. Everyone would have hated the idea of Terry taking a wife like her. His uncle, Neil Bronwyn, certainly did. Such concern would hardly be a motive to kill the prospective bridegroom, though. More likely, someone would try to kill her.

In fact, someone *had!* She tensed as the possible connection dawned. Should she tell the inspector? Would he believe her or think she was simply trying to throw him off track?

"Something has occurred to you, my lady?" he asked.

"There have been three attempts on my life," she said calmly. It wouldn't do to shake and tremble as she'd been doing or the inspector might think her mad. Or even worse, guilty.

"How and when did these attempts take place?" MacLinden asked, his pen poised over his small notebook.

"The first, three months ago at our family estate in Kent," she said. "I took the rowboat across Penny Lake to visit my old nurse, who has a cottage there. It's a weekly trip, always on Tuesday, whenever I'm in the country." She paused. "Someone tampered with the boat. I nearly drowned."

"You swam out?" he asked, scribbling idly.

"I sank like a stone. Then I shed everything but my shift so I could swim to shore." *And be ogled by Colin's guests,* she thought, wincing. That part of the story was hardly a secret.

MacLinden nodded. "And the second attempt?" he prompted.

"That would be the knife, two weeks later. A bumping noise in my chamber woke me. I rose to light a lamp and a dark shape rushed at me. A long blade flashed in the moonlight coming in the window. I ran for my dressing room, which has a stout door that locks. There was a swishing sound when the intruder struck at me. I slammed the door and locked it.''

She brushed a hand over her face, hoping to wipe away the spine-prickling memory.

"And so you escaped. Are you certain it was a knife?"

She swallowed heavily, feeling sick. "It—it cut off my braid." With nerveless fingers, she gripped the nape of her neck.

"Good God!" The doctor brushed a hand over her cropped curls. She recoiled automatically, noting his look of horror.

Eager to have done with the questions, she rushed on. "The third time took place a week ago. My maid, Maggie, sent my breakfast up with one of the kitchen girls. I allowed Ruby— that's the girl's name—to drink the chocolate. She began to act very strange afterwards, reeling about and clawing the air. She screamed nonsense about snakes and demons as though she were mad."

"And then?" the inspector asked calmly.

"Colin rushed in with Thurston and Maggie. Before they could subdue Ruby, she ran to the balcony and dived off."

"She's dead?" MacLinden asked softly.

"Yes. Her—her neck was broken in the fall."

"A poison?" the inspector asked, looking at the doctor.

"Hallucinatory agent, more likely," the doctor said. His agitation was evident in the way he was crushing her fingers in his. "Have there been any further attempts?"

Elizabeth looked from one to the other. "None that I know." She cleared her throat and pulled her hands away from Dr. Bronwyn's. "Could I be excused for a few moments?" The effort of remaining calm had exhausted her.

"Yes, of course," the inspector said. "However, we ought to be off within the hour if you could manage."

She nodded. "May I ask where we're going?"

"To Havington House in London," MacLinden said. "I'm

afraid you'll have to reside there with our new Lord Havington until we straighten this out."

Elizabeth took her leave of the men. There seemed no point in resisting. At least the inspector had a plan.

MacLinden remained silent until the woman closed the door. Then he turned to Neil. "Acquiring the title and the lady is going to look very suspicious, Doc."

"Don't be a fool! I've no interest in either one and you know it. I only met the woman last night. I brought her here against her will to prevent an elopement, or so I thought. Terry was determined to marry her and it would have ruined him. You know what sort she is. You read the papers."

"I read them, yes. I wondered whether you had," MacLinden said thoughtfully, folding his notebook shut and stuffing it in his pocket. "Be that as it may, someone out there has snuffed out a peer of the realm—very probably the same person who tried to destroy Elizabeth Marleigh. Clearly, someone took the murder weapon from her town house specifically to implicate her," he continued. "The matching pistol is also missing. None of the servants seem to know how long the guns have been gone. Without doubt, this is all somehow connected."

"I agree. But who and why?" Neil asked.

MacLinden shifted in his chair, crossing his legs at the knee. "There's the fellow Terry had words with at the theater, possibly a blackmailer, from the conversation overheard. Could be the maid who sent Lady Marleigh the tainted chocolate. It may be the lady's cousin, Colin Marleigh, who inherited the earldom after her father died. Excellent motive there, eh?" He sighed and shrugged. "Then, of course, we mustn't rule out the less obvious, a disgruntled employee, or the odd maniac with a grudge against the nobility. Lots of possibilities at this point and damned few clues. Some of the puzzle pieces may have rolled under the table. That's very often the case."

"We have to solve this, Lindy, before he harms Elizabeth."

"Oh, we shall. Our success hinges on keeping the lady hidden, yet available to assist. She'll have to remain the focus of a search, as though we at the Yard believe she's guilty. Otherwise the killer will go to ground. I'll need her near for questions, and she's the only one who might recognize the man at the theater.''

Neil saw the plan's worth. ''So we'll hide her in the least-obvious place—at the scene of the crime?''

''Just so,'' MacLinden said, twisting his mustache.

''The servants probably know her. Given her, ah, relationship with Terry, I expect she's been there before.'' Neil's frown darkened. He looked as if he wanted to say more on the matter, but held his tongue.

MacLinden nodded. ''Have the staff leave the town house before she arrives. Then tough it out with her alone there if you can. She'll need the freedom to come and go with you, but no one must guess her identity. That means a foolproof disguise.'' MacLinden chewed somberly on his pipe stem, then brightened. ''Wouldn't she make an admirable *valet!*''

''Valet? Are you daft? She's too obviously female to get her up like a man! Besides, I've never *had* a valet.''

MacLinden smirked. ''Well then, my fine new earl, you won't be so critical of her services, now will you?''

# Chapter Four

It might work, Neil thought. It just might. She would sleep in his dressing room, of course. Or perhaps even his bed. She'd be expected to attend him at his bath, dress him, be in intimate contact most hours of the day. Well, at least she was no stranger to men. Any woman who could deal with a ménage à trois shouldn't quail at dealing with one man's requirements, whatever they were.

What of his work? Could she accompany him to hospital for rounds when he began his work there? No, that course was out of the question now, anyway. An earl wouldn't be expected to carry on with employment of any sort, even as a physician. London society would choke at the very thought.

He could content himself with research, he supposed, and the occasional emergency. *Research.* The idea rather appealed to him, the more he thought about it. God knew he'd done enough cutting, stitching and dosing of patients in the Crimea.

Truth told, he'd realized too late in the game that he hadn't the proper objectivity to practice surgery. A patient's pain was his pain. He suffered right along with each and every one. Every death he witnessed was a partial death for him. The grief had nearly done him in before he'd resigned his commission. He couldn't even pretend he looked forward to more of the same.

Since that time, he had traveled a bit, trying to catch up

with the advances in modern medicine before setting up a civilian practice and attending hospital duties. But research? That seemed the ideal solution. With the Havington fortune available, he could devote himself to it.

The very thought of Terry's death providing any kind of advantage troubled Neil. Perhaps he should look at it another way. Could he turn the horrible tragedy of Terry's death to some good purpose? He still felt guilty about using the Havington wealth he'd inherited, but if he must, what better way?

Besides incorporating his new career move with the murder investigation, Neil had to figure a way to deal with his private feelings toward the lady-cum-valet. She heated his blood like an aphrodisiac. And was probably just as dangerous.

In spite of that—or perhaps because of it, given his rash behavior so far—he would offer to make her his mistress. Out of necessity, they would be sharing quarters. His body would be clamoring for her constantly, even if his mind was repelled by what she had become. No doubt she'd agree to the arrangement. Hadn't she already serviced half the population, anyway?

All he had to worry about was getting rid of his anger over that very fact.

He admitted he was being too prudish by half when it came to Elizabeth Marleigh. A woman's past had never troubled him before when he'd decided to bed one. He'd had women of his own class before, accommodating widows and those of the fashionably impure. She was not a whit different than they were.

Who was he fooling? he wondered, even as he thought it. Elizabeth Marleigh was like no one else he'd ever met. At least, in the way she moved him.

He'd just have to accept that she was what she was, that she had a wayward streak wide as the Thames at high tide. And he'd have to protect her in spite of it. Someone had tried to kill her, and she was in grave danger of arrest for Terry's murder. In that, at least, he knew she was an innocent. He must keep her safe.

The fact that she roused this feeling in him, this caring beyond his natural compassion, scared him half to death. No way could he allow himself to become emotionally entangled with a woman of her caliber. He had to remember she was reckless, a flouter of convention and as shameless a trollop as he had ever had the misfortune to know. Hell, she didn't even deny it.

Why, then, did she appear so vulnerable and defenseless? So sad? How could she twist his heart with her tears even as she stirred his lust to a frenzy? It was downright disturbing....

MacLinden was gone when Neil ceased his mental meanderings. A soft rustle of fabric drew his attention to the doorway.

"I'm ready to go," Elizabeth said. Her eyes were red rimmed from crying and her lower lip a bit swollen from the way she worried it with her teeth.

Neil ached to close his arms around her and give her comfort. He also wanted to throttle her for making him want to. He picked up her valise where she had dropped it earlier. "We ought to get under way, then."

"I expect so," she agreed.

"How is your acting ability? You're to pose as my valet. MacLinden and I have decided it's best to keep you disguised, and that's the best role we could devise."

A wavering smile lifted the corners of her lips. "How devious. I fear you'll have to teach me the duties, my *lord*."

"I doubt there's much left for you to learn, my *lady*," he said, answering her sarcasm.

"Subservience does not come naturally to me, I warn you," she retorted. He noticed a spark of determination, perhaps even calculation, lurking in the depths of her eyes.

"If the rewards are substantial, surely you can learn to, ah, service my needs?" Was that pointed enough to stick in her craw? he wondered.

"Coercion does not become you, my lord." Anger made her voice harder than he'd ever heard it. If he didn't know better, he'd have thought she looked a bit wounded.

"I prefer persuasion, but whatever works." Lord, why was he being so nasty? Because she made him want her, made him abandon all his ethics and good sense. There seemed to be no limit to his foolishness where she was concerned. She'd hate him before they ever got this ruse under way. Maybe she did already. Judging by her expression, she was certainly off to a running start.

"Let us understand one thing, Lord Havington," she said with a sharp lift of her chin. "I wish to stay out of gaol for obvious reasons, but if it comes to a choice between a cell there and forced intimacy with you, I'll take my chances in prison."

Neil resented the heated rejection. She was supposed to thank him for this, damn her fractious hide. And from all reports, he was the *only* one she had rejected! "They still hang women, you know," he warned, hating himself more with every word, but unable for some reason to stop baiting her.

She rewarded him with a scornful frown. "Society has already hanged me, my lord. All that's left is for me to stop kicking. Before I do that, I plan to find out who killed my best friend. I've no time to spend on my back with my legs in the air while I'm about it. The valet idea is a stroke of genius and I applaud it, but I will not be your whore." Elizabeth took a deep breath. "And if you try to force me, I'll confess to murder and name you my partner in crime. Then we'll see how *you* like dangling from a noose!"

With that, she snatched her valise out of his hand, turned on her heel and marched out into the late afternoon.

Neil couldn't reconcile the jolt of admiration he felt with his former opinion of her. He desired her, pitied her when she wept and hated her when he thought of all her liaisons. Now he admired her? He shook his head, hoping the marbles would roll back into place.

She'd really set him back on his heels with that little speech of hers. Well, the battle lines were drawn now. He'd see just how long her lusty little nature would hold out when confined to his company exclusively.

He might not be the most desirable man around, but, by God, he'd be the only one available to her. And he'd make her beg.

They arrived in London very late. The inspector's endless questions and the bouncing of the carriage prevented any semblance of rest.

Elizabeth spent the remainder of the night with Inspector MacLinden at the doctor's bachelor rooms while the new earl roused Terry's servants and packed them off to his country house.

The divan proved wretchedly uncomfortable, but Elizabeth flatly refused to take the doctor's bed. She felt horribly out of sorts when MacLinden awakened her before dawn to take her to the Havington town house. Exhaustion and fear of discovery made her weak at the knees as they left the safety of Neil's rented rooms. However, luck held, and she and the inspector encountered no one about at the ungodly hour.

When MacLinden abandoned her to Neil Bronwyn's care, the wretch of a doctor had another unwelcome surprise to impart. The rakehell proposed they share a bedroom! Not bloody likely.

"You cannot insist on such a thing! The adjoining chamber will do just as well, and we'll both be much more comfortable." She watched him deposit her suitcase on a shelf in the back of the huge cherry wardrobe and busy himself stacking Terry's hatboxes in front of it. His words sounded muffled. "I promised Lindy you'd remain within my sight at all times. You'll sleep here, in the master chamber with me, and that's the end of it."

"But, my lord, you can't expect that! It's not—"

"Proper? Don't be ridiculous. And call me Neil, at least in private. The title only reminds me of how I came by it. Even you can't be so cruel as to throw it up every time you address me. It was bad enough having to take over Terry's bed."

"Well, you *are* the earl, whether you like it or not, and believe me, I can think of worse things to call you." She made a rude noise with her lips. "And this *is* highly improper, *Neil,*" she said, emphasizing his name with a sneer. "Surely you could grant me privacy to sleep."

"And have you sneaking out in the night to God knows what mischief? Your little escapades will have to cease, at least for the duration of the investigation. I won't have you arranging assignations, however secret. There's still that Thurston fellow you mentioned, who might very well be a prime suspect. I doubt you're so eager to get rid of him now that Terry's...gone."

Elizabeth thought seriously about kicking the derriere he presented as he bent to open the bottom drawer of the bureau. "Thurston is my butler. He's old as Hadrian's Wall and in terrible health. I thought you were at my home to see to him the night we met," she said.

Abruptly Neil straightened and faced her. She noticed a fleeting expression of what appeared to be surprised relief before he covered it with a scowl.

"Be that as it may, Elizabeth, you'll have to sleep in here. You've little need to preach propriety after all you've done. Even were we living openly together, copulating on the front lawn, no one could think worse of you than they do now."

"You're cruel," she said softly, and turned away so he wouldn't see her tears. "Mean," she added for emphasis.

Suddenly he reached for her arm and took it, a gentle gesture that she shrugged off as he spoke. "I apologize, Elizabeth. That was uncalled for and I have no earthly idea what made me say it."

"I don't care," she said, lifting her chin and rounding on him. "I've had enough of this! I'm sick of trying to explain. That's what you want, isn't it? Explanations for my lewd behavior, my shoddy little peccadilloes? Well, my fine lord, you'll get no vulgar details and no plea for understanding, do you hear? You'll get *nothing* from me. And if you continue to bait me so, I'll surrender and take my chances with the courts!"

He looked abashed. "Fool! That's suicide at this point and you know it."

"Yes, I've considered that," she said. "Seriously."

"Suicide?" he whispered, obviously appalled. Then he grabbed her, his arms locking around her like a vise. His lips felt hard against her ear. "Nothing's so bad as that, Elizabeth. Believe me, nothing! Promise me you'll never think it again," he demanded. "Promise me!"

Elizabeth let herself lean against him, hungry for a touch of human concern, however fleeting, no matter what stirred it. She burrowed her face into his linen shirtfront, ignoring the hard bump of a shirt stud against her cheek. Warmth enveloped her, comforting and yet disturbing, smelling subtly of exotic spice and the light starch of fresh linen. Strong hands on her back grasped urgently as though he searched for the source of her despair so he could tear it away.

Elizabeth fought the urge to slide her arms around him and promise him anything he wanted to hear. *No!* Trusting was what had gotten her into this mess. He might be a doctor and basically kind, but he was still a man for all that.

"Elizabeth..." The word emerged a soft entreaty, a longing sound caught somewhere between regret and desire.

Frantically, she pushed away, terrified that he meant to prey on her momentary weakness. "I didn't mean that I wanted to die, you dolt. I merely meant I thought of the repercussions of surrender. Don't pretend solicitude. False sympathy disgusts me. Don't touch me again."

With one hand reaching out in a conciliatory gesture, he watched her with a concentration that was unnerving. After several moments he shrugged his massive shoulders, dropped his hand to his side and looked away. "All right."

Tension grew in the silence that followed. Nothing broke it but the ceaseless rain pattering against the window. Finally, Neil moved, and she sighed, realizing she'd been holding her breath.

His eyes avoided hers and he began with a forced lightness, "Well then, we'd best see to your disguise. Terry's things should be a near fit since he is—was..." Neil swallowed hard. The false cheerfulness had disintegrated and he finished through clenched teeth. "He was small. Only a bit taller than you." The heavy silence returned, uncomfortable and laden with grief.

Elizabeth moved close enough to touch his arm, and he whirled to glare at her, daring her to complete the move. "If his...if the clothes don't fit, can you sew?"

"Of course I can sew," she said with a touch of indignation. He must think her totally lacking in women's skills. Well, socially acceptable skills, anyway.

She looked on as he plundered Terry's things, tossing unmentionables, a folded shirt and stockings from the bureau to the bed. His sangfroid apparently restored, he turned to the wardrobe and thumbed through the hanging suits. With a satisfied nod, he plucked out a somber gray wool and tossed it down beside the linens.

His face reddened and he bit his bottom lip, releasing it with a little sucking sound. "You ought to, well, use something to, ah, diminish your upper proportions, I suppose."

"Bind my breasts, you mean?" Elizabeth restated with a lift of her brows. She loved to watch him blush. That he could even do so took her completely by surprise. He was a doctor, for heaven's sake. She couldn't resist testing the extent of his capillary functions. "What of the, ah, lower proportions, my lord? Perhaps a nice sausage?" She laughed and shook her head. He was positively scarlet, even his neck.

"Deal with it as you see fit," he said with a strained gruffness. Then, under his breath he added, "You truly *are* shameless."

"Didn't want to disappoint you," she quipped, her good humor resurrected by his embarrassment. "Go find me some boots while I change."

As soon as Neil disappeared, she hurried out of her clothes. The male apparel held a certain fascination. How wonderful to leave off all the cumbersome petticoats and the blasted corset. She wrapped a length of smooth linen toweling around her chest and pinned it securely. Not much to worry about, she thought, for once blessing her lack of abundance there.

When she buttoned the trouser flap, though, she looked into the full-length mirror and frowned. No, this would never do. Her earlier joke to make the doctor blush turned serious.

Searching the bureau drawers, she selected a stocking, rolled it up and stuffed it down past her waistband. Definitely not, she decided. Casting around the room, she spied Neil's medical bag by the door. A moment's plunder turned up a roll of cotton bandages, which she shaped appropriately—she hoped—and replaced the rolled-up stocking. Now then! Much better. She wriggled her hips, turned sideways and back and grinned. Yes, that looked right.

Wetting her hair from the pitcher on the nightstand and plying the hairbrush from her reticule, Elizabeth smoothed her short curls straight forward toward her face. She thought the overall effect looked rather convincing.

"Ready!" Deepening her voice a good octave, she called out to Neil, who had not yet returned from the dressing room.

When he appeared in the doorway, he dropped the boots.

"Well?" She assumed a pose, one hand resting on a slender hip as she'd seen Terry do a hundred times. Cocking her head, she raised her chin and regarded him through narrowed eyes.

If his shocked expression was any indication, the disguise was successful beyond hope. Of course it was. All she had to do was think how Terry would act, copy his mannerisms, his expressions, his voice. Elizabeth nodded. Yes, this was definitely going to work.

Neil swallowed heavily and shook his head. No, this was definitely not going to work.

Oh, she'd somehow gotten her chest flat enough beneath the starched shirt. But his eyes traveled the length of her legs, encased as they were in the fitted gray wool of Terry's trousers. Shapely, feminine legs, topped by sweetly rounded hips that were all too evident below a belt-cinched waist.

And below the waist…? "What in God's name have you got in your breeches?"

"What a naughty question, milord! You'll never know. How's my hair?"

He jerked his eyes away from her lower body and noticed her head, topped by a soft, wavy cap of red-gold minus its tousled ringlets. The style reminded him of Terry's Brutus, a cut affected years earlier by Lord Byron, casually brushed forward to frame the face. A bit out-of-date, perhaps, but it neatly disguised her lack of side-whiskers.

"We should darken it," he muttered, wanting nothing more than to slide his fingers through the shiny stuff and feel the shape of her head against his palms. "Your color's too distinctive. I'll see to some dye stuff."

Grudgingly, he stepped forward and picked up the jacket he'd laid out. "Here, put this on. And these," he ordered, picking up the boots and handing them over.

He nodded when she had finished dressing. The loose coat hid the worst—or best—of her curves and the straight sides of the boots covered the shape of her calves. Her face still looked like an angel's, though. A very feminine angel's. He fumbled around in his pocket and withdrew his spectacles, the ones he wore for close work when his eyes were tired. "Here, try these."

She hooked the wire frames around her ears and assumed a frowning, purse-mouthed stare. Neil thought she looked charming, like a child playing dress-up and fooling no one but herself.

"I guess you'll do." He sighed. "Let's see you walk."

Elizabeth strutted around the room, hands swinging in a parody of Terry's loose-limbed gait, and then rested in a negligent, purely masculine pose. He had to admit her movements matched those of a young dandy. "Perhaps you missed your calling, Elizabeth. Quite the little actress, aren't you?"

She grinned, her face lighting at what she took for praise. "I may never go back to skirts!"

Neil cleared his throat to cover a chuckle. The scamp was clearly enjoying this despite the reasons for it. Why that should surprise him, he didn't know. Her adventurous nature was the talk of the town.

He let his gaze wander over her, looking for things to improve. What the devil did she have in her trousers? Whatever it was, it would have been vastly flattering on a man twice her size. "Maybe you ought to reduce your...endowments just a bit, Elizabeth."

Her eyebrows shot up. "Certainly not! And don't call me Elizabeth."

He laughed at her indignation and shook his head. "It's too large, my dear. *Much* too large. People will stare, believe me."

"Well, if they're staring at that, they won't be staring at my face, now will they?" Inordinately pleased with her reasoning, she pranced back and forth, practicing in the unfamiliar boots. "What will you call me?"

"Percival, I think. You look like a Percival," he teased.

"No, no, something manly. How about Drummond or Buford?" She opened the humidor on top of the dresser and stuck a cheroot in one corner of her mouth. She gripped it between her teeth so that it took an upward slant, exactly as Terry used to do.

Neil felt a sharp pang of loss at the sight, recalling the first time he'd caught Terry smoking. "Don't," he said before he could stop himself.

Her eyes flew to his, and he knew instantly that she understood. Jerking the cheroot out of her mouth, she tossed it back into the humidor without a word.

A moment passed before she broke the silence. "Well, all right, Percival it is then, if you insist. And Betts, short for Elizabeth. Papa used to call me Betts. Yes, Percival Betts!"

Smiling rakishly, she offered her hand for him to shake. "I am born."

MacLinden rapped on the bedroom door before he entered. "Security downstairs is fine. Your Oliver seems to know what he's about. Good man," he said, noting Elizabeth Marleigh's transformation. "And so you appear, my lady! I must say, though, you're too well turned out for a valet."

He walked around her, observing from all angles. His gaze locked on the front of her trousers and he raised a brow. "Perhaps we ought to pass you off as a patient—a medical curiosity, I should think."

Lady Marleigh looked indignant, Neil laughed out loud and MacLinden couldn't stifle a grin. "Why, such a virile specimen as yourself ought not to languish as a mere servant," he continued, teasing. "Why don't we set you up as the doctor's protégé?"

"Not a bad idea, Lindy," Neil mused. "A valet wouldn't accompany me everywhere, but an assistant certainly might."

The lady shook her head. "I know nothing about medicine!"

"Doc does have a point," MacLinden said, brushing off her protest with a wave of his hand. "The clothes really are a bit too fine for a hireling, anyway. All right then, we'll introduce you as the son of a family friend. You've studied medicine in Edinburgh and come to London to sharpen your skills in…?"

"Research," Neil supplied with a satisfied nod. "I'll be involved in research. That should keep us fairly well isolated for the most part, but give us leave to poke about as we will."

"What of your patients?" MacLinden asked.

"I have none as yet," Neil explained. "I've been abroad until recently, as you know. I was to take up my new position at St. Stephen's next week and look about for an office to let for my private practice, but I've had to make other plans."

"Now you're the earl and such wouldn't be appropriate, eh? Noblesse oblige and all that?"

"Just so," Neil agreed dryly. "I'll set up my own laboratory here in the conservatory, but I needn't be in a hurry to begin any actual work. The organization of it will be a perfect cover, since I would need an extra pair of hands about. Dr. Percival Betts should serve nicely, don't you think?"

"Percival?" MacLinden asked, pursing his lips in distaste.

"Dr. Percival Betts at your service, Inspector," Elizabeth said, offering her hand to shake as she had done earlier.

"She is born," Neil said with a wry twist of his lips and a quirked eyebrow.

"Better than fully *grown,* I daresay," MacLinden remarked with another pointed look at the lady's crotch. "Do something about that, will you, before Doc's cronies decide to write you up in the medical texts?"

# Chapter Five

Neil sighed and pinched the bridge of his nose. The whole ridiculous scenario was giving him a headache. "I have a horrible premonition that the first time you show yourself, everyone's going to point and say, 'Oh look! It's Lady Marleigh in breeches! How utterly daring of her, and let's call the peelers.' This is insane. Why don't we just hide you?"

"Because you *need* me to help find the killer! I promise you no one will know me," she said, apparently upset that he questioned the effectiveness of her disguise.

Lindy agreed. "She's right. We do need her to keep an eye out for this man Terry met at the theater. As for the disguise, I don't believe I would recognize her if I met her on the street, unknowing. Look at her objectively, Neil. Unless she comes face-to-face with someone who knows her quite well, I think she should be perfectly convincing."

Neil paced. He wished he didn't feel so disoriented. Seeing the woman got up like a man and playing the part so well unnerved him. "A big part of London's male population probably *does* know her quite well!" he said.

"No, they don't," she argued. "Father and I just came down from Edinburgh shortly before he died. We hadn't yet accepted any invitations in town when it happened. Then there was the hurried journey back to Kent for his burial. I was veiled at the funeral and spoke with almost no one. Cousin

Colin took care of everything. I stayed secluded until—" She broke off with a distant look and swallowed hard.

"Until?" Lindy prompted.

"The weekend at the Smythes' estate," she said, forcing the words out as though they hurt her throat. "Colin encouraged me to accompany him to Lady Smythe's for a quiet weekend. Said it would ease our grief. I didn't want to go. Father had been laid to rest only three weeks before."

"But you did go," Neil remarked with more accusatory force than he intended.

"Yes," she answered defiantly. "I went."

Lindy tapped the heel of his pipe thoughtfully and cleared his throat before speaking. "Well, there's Lady Smythe we must avoid, I suppose. And of course, the men. What about those with whom you..."

"*Consorted* is the *nice* word you're looking for, Lindy," Neil supplied. Then he turned on her. "What about the two men discovered in your room with you?" The thought of it made him want to shoot the men and to shake her for her stupidity.

"Their mission did not include writing odes to my eyebrows. I doubt they looked once above my neck!"

"They bloody well did a damned essay on the rest of you, though, didn't they?"

"Children, children!" Lindy soothed. "Let's keep to the matter at hand." He grasped Neil's arm, but the new earl jerked away angrily and stalked to the window, looking out.

Seemingly satisfied that the outburst was over, Lindy continued the questions. "Now then, *Betts,*" he said, indicating to both of them that he intended her to *be* Betts from now on, "you say you don't think Lords Frame and Tilburn would recognize you in disguise?"

Neil noted that she didn't even look surprised that Lindy knew the identity of the men. Everyone knew.

"They were thoroughly foxed that night," she said thoughtfully. "And I had never spoken with them before." She met Neil's eyes as he turned, and there was no shame in hers, just renewed anger. "They were only there for a moment," she added.

"Damned swift, then? Must have disappointed you no end."

"Shut up, Neil," Lindy barked. "Have done with your bickering or I'll do this in private!"

Neil stiffened with surprise. Lindy never used that tone with him. "Next you'll have me defending her *honor,* I suppose!"

"Watch your mouth, *my lord,* or I'll rearrange your teeth for you, and don't think I can't do it. This arm can bloody well pack a punch, thanks to you. Now sit down over there and mind your manners." The inspector jerked his head toward the bed.

Lindy was right. Neil sat. Why was he acting such a bastard about this? What right had he to judge Elizabeth just because he was enamored of her and mad as hell about it? He almost wished Lindy had made good the threat and planted him a facer. He admitted he deserved it.

Lindy kept at her, but at least his voice was kind. "The incident with the boat—how many saw you then?"

"Lots, I suppose. Maybe ten or twelve people, but I was bedraggled as a drowned cat and I still...had my hair." She fingered the short tresses just above her ear. When she saw Neil watching the gesture, she quickly pocketed her hand and lifted a defiant chin. "I don't recall speaking to any of the guests Colin invited down. Twice I was accosted in the hallways, but it was rather dark. After that, I mostly kept to my room."

*"Accosted?"* Neil certainly wanted to follow that up.

"Shut up!" the others said in unison, turning on him with eyebrows raised as though he'd said something out of turn. Neil held up his palms in a mute apology that he in no way meant.

"Have you attended any public events during your stay here or kept company with anyone else?" Lindy asked, as though Neil hadn't interrupted.

She lowered her head and answered softly, "No. You see,

we've never gone about much in society and have done no entertaining since my mother died. I was thirteen then. My friends, or the few I claim, are of rather modest means and live in our village.''

"A veritable recluse," Neil muttered sarcastically, clamping his mouth closed when Lindy shot him another warning look.

"Well then!" MacLinden summed up her revelations. "We have nothing much to worry over, do we? Keep well away from Colin Marleigh and Lady Smythe and there should be no problems. Needless to say, do keep a sharp eye out for anyone who looks familiar and avoid him or her at all cost.''

He turned back to Neil. "You and your 'assistant' should begin to frequent Terry's haunts, I think. Perhaps Boodle's and White's would be good places to begin. Men talk freely at the clubs, don't they, and who knows what you might glean? I have no entrée to either place so you two could assist me greatly in the investigation. You might do the theater a few times and see if you spot or overhear anyone who resembles the man who approached Terry. You can manage all that, eh, Betts?''

"My pleasure, Lindy," she said, her good humor apparently restored by MacLinden's show of faith. The challenging tilt of her head dared Neil to object.

He nodded at Lindy. "Wednesday night," he suggested. "Terry always went to White's for cards on Wednesdays.''

"Very well, then. But first we have to get through the funeral," Lindy said. "I'll be with you, of course, both out of respect and in the event that anything untoward should happen. If Betts is unmasked, you see, I can take her into custody immediately and whisk her away.''

The three of them looked at each other wordlessly. Neil knew Elizabeth felt every bit as apprehensive as he did about her appearing in public dressed as a man. How she could put up such a courageous front was beyond him. Lindy must be terribly worried about the effect on his new position at the Yard if the truth came out. And as for himself, he thought it would take an act of God to get through Terry's funeral under the best of circumstances. Dread didn't begin to describe his current state of mind.

Later that afternoon, Trent MacLinden handed his favorite bowler to the same aging excuse for a butler that he'd interviewed at Marleigh House only hours after Terry Bronwyn's murder. He carefully hid his surprise at finding the man now established at the country estate of Colin Marleigh.

He supposed it wasn't that unusual, though, come to think of it. As far as Thurston knew, Lady Marleigh had disappeared, and the vacant Marleigh town house hardly needed a butler. Where else would the old man be expected to go but to her cousin, the earl?

"Good afternoon, Mr. Thurston. I've come in hopes of a word with Lord Marleigh. Do you remember me?" Lindy asked.

"Of course, Inspector. His lordship's meeting with his steward at the moment. If you'll follow me?"

Lindy measured his steps to the butler's rather dragging gait. Light from the clerestory window above the front door threw reflections off Thurston's hairless pate. The man's sour odor and rumpled appearance must be anathema to his new employer, Lindy thought. He might look like an unmade bed, but he had a voice any actor would envy. The gnarled hands shook as the old man reached for the door handle and pushed it downward. The heavy portal swung open without a sound.

"Inspector MacLinden, Scotland Yard, milord," Thurston announced in his well-modulated baritone.

"Oh very well," Marleigh mumbled absently, his attention still on the papers he was folding away. "That will be all, Hinkley," he said to the man Lindy assumed was the steward. "While I'm away I'll expect reports at least every other day, as usual. You have my itinerary?"

"Of course, milord." The steward bowed himself out, and Lindy watched Thurston follow and quietly close the door behind them.

Lindy waited patiently while Colin Marleigh busied himself

locking away record books and the other paperwork he'd apparently been discussing with his man.

True to his training, Lindy used the time to observe the young lord, who appeared to be in his late twenties. Marleigh was short and rather stocky, tending toward portliness around his middle. Straight blond hair lay in thin, pomaded strands across an extremely high forehead. A virtually lipless mouth was compressed into a nearly perfect horizontal line.

His nose might be noble, Lindy thought, but the ears were doubly so. They protruded outward from his head like clamshells. Some effort went toward disguising them by employing bushy dundreary whiskers in front and longish, fluffed-out hair behind them.

Given the stick-straight hair on top, Lindy suspected the man's vanity had bowed to using curling tongs for the locks at the back. The thought prompted a laugh, but he neatly squelched it by clearing his throat. It solved two problems. He got his lordship's notice.

"Scotland Yard, you say? Then you're here about my cousin," Marleigh said, looking up at last through cold, green eyes.

"Lord Marleigh." Lindy gave a curt nod and what might be construed as a bow if one were generous. He didn't like the concept of obeisance to anyone, even royalty, though he recognized the need to play the game. It had proved a hard object lesson in his early army days. "Good of you to see me without an appointment."

Colin Marleigh managed to make his shrug look regal. It barely caused a ripple in his impeccably tailored Tweedside coat. "Could hardly refuse, could I? Lady Elizabeth's servants came to me with what happened immediately after you questioned them. I'm afraid there's nothing I can add to what they've told you."

"You could help immensely, milord, if you would give me a bit of insight as to the lady's character." Lindy saw no reason to beat about the bush. "Do you believe Lady Elizabeth capable of the shooting?"

Marleigh's sharp green gaze shifted down and raked the carefully arranged desktop. Lindy wondered why the question bothered the man. Surely it was expected. After a long exhalation of breath, the young lord finally looked up. "No, Inspector, I think not. You see..."

The words had drifted off into a protracted silence. When nothing else was forthcoming, Lindy prompted, "Yes, milord?"

"She's a shy little thing for the most part." Marleigh rested an elbow on the desk and leaned forward, massaging his forehead with long, white fingers. "Perhaps. Maybe in one of her spells. I confess I don't know for certain, but I hate to believe she would actually, well, shoot anyone." He glanced up, the look almost pleading in its intensity. "Do you think?"

MacLinden shook his head sorrowfully and sighed. "It certainly appears as though she did. She had best access to the weapon. She knew the victim quite well, and Lord Havington would have allowed her entry without suspicion."

Lindy paused as he watched the earl fidget with a jeweled letter knife. "However, we are wondering about the motive, you see. Have you any idea what might have prompted her? That is, *if* she is guilty."

"Madness," Marleigh said in an agonized whisper.

"I beg your pardon, milord? Madness?" Lindy blustered loudly, breaking the mood of quiet suspense he thought the earl was trying to engineer.

"Yes, by God, the woman is mad!" Words tumbled out now as Marleigh threw up his hands and shoved back his chair to rise. Agitated, he began to pace. "She's been nothing but confounding of late! Haring around in her underthings, making assignations with bounders she wouldn't have given the time of day four months ago, indulging in screaming fits that would raise the dead. You can't feature the embarrassment that woman has caused me since her father died!"

"Why, that's terrible, milord," Lindy declared, looking aghast at the news.

"Damned right it is!" Marleigh seemed to calm a little now

that he'd made his point. Then he sat down again, his face sorrowful. "If only I'd confined her when I first admitted it to myself, poor Havington would now be alive." He hung his head and let his hands drop by his sides, clenching his fingers as if in frustration. "I feel responsible."

"I see," Lindy said, smoothing his mustache. "What did you think about her contemplating marriage to Lord Havington?"

"Was she?" Marleigh looked properly shocked. "He certainly never approached me for her hand, and she never said a word. There were rumors, of course, but then there always are. I never pay attention to gossip."

"He announced it at White's earlier on the night he died."

"Fancy that," Marleigh said, shaking his head. "The match might have worked wonders, but I doubt it." He sighed. After a moment of uncomfortable silence, he brought the interview to a close. "Well, if you have no further questions, Inspector, I'll be off. My coach should be ready by now."

"Where might I reach you if I need to speak with you again, milord?" Lindy asked politely, stepping toward the door and pulling it open. Thurston, waiting just outside, handed him his hat.

"I shall be searching for my cousin, if you must know," Marleigh said. "The poor woman could be anywhere, terrified of what is to happen to her. Despite her unstable condition, Inspector, I really can't see Elizabeth committing murder, or think of any reason why she should even if she were capable."

The earl placed a restraining hand on Lindy's arm as they reached the front door. "If you happen to find her before I do, MacLinden, may I count on you to treat her gently?"

Lindy regarded the man, trying to perceive how sincere he was. Not very, he concluded with a nod. "You certainly may depend upon that, milord. I shall give her my every consideration."

The next day, Elizabeth fully assumed her role as Dr. Percival Betts. In their preoccupation with getting her dressed appropriately for the funeral, both she and Neil were able to avoid dwelling on the event itself. Arrival at Gormsloft Castle brought on the realization that their final, respective farewells to Terry were all too imminent.

Pitifully few mourners came to the lichen-covered chapel at Gormsloft. Neil had mentioned that the castle was the oldest and smallest of the Havington properties, dating back some three hundred years. The only servants about looked ancient enough to have been there since the castle was constructed.

Feeling extremely vulnerable and exposed, Elizabeth walked a few paces behind Neil as he approached Terry's coffin. She brushed the brim of her beaver stovepipe back and forth against her left leg, wishing it were proper to keep it on her head. Terry wouldn't have cared a jot for such a breach of respect. He'd have laughed himself silly at the sight of her.

The tight feeling in her throat increased. Oh, she wished he *could* see. She wished to God he were alive to see instead of lying in that satin-lined, mahogany box. From where she stood now, she could just see a slice of his forehead and the tip of his nose. Another step forward and his whole face would be visible. She drew in a steadying breath to brace herself and moved up to see him.

Oh God, his hair was combed too neatly. Too neat for Terry. A sound escaped the constriction in her throat and she swallowed hard, twice, to stifle a full-fledged sob.

The doctor turned slightly, his eyes heavy lidded and admonishing. *If I can do this, so can you,* they seemed to say. Grasping her hat in one fist, her cane in the other, she locked her knees against the urge to flee.

Holding her breath, Elizabeth kept her eyes on the earl as he approached the edge of the casket. He carefully tugged off his right glove, and his bare, long-fingered hand reached out hesitantly. He touched Terry's forehead, gently disturbing the carefully coiffed waves so that they rested in their usual disorder. His fingers trembled and then curled into his palm. Neil bowed his head. His slowly released sigh was the only sound inside the chapel.

Elizabeth forced herself to draw a breath and let it out. Through a sheen of tears, she focused on a spray of flowers beside the coffin, counting the petals of one particular bloom, seeking the Latin name in the recesses of memory—anything to block grief from her mind until she could master her emotions.

When she had herself in hand, she looked back to see that Neil had stepped aside slightly, still staring down at the remains of his nephew.

Knowing she must, she moved to the edge of the bier and gazed on the face she had last seen smiling. He looked waxen, his lips too finely drawn. Satin billowed so high around his head the ears were almost completely covered. *I won't think why that is! I won't!* she warned herself, as her breath caught in her throat.

"Touch him," Neil whispered—a dare, a plea, permission? "To say farewell."

Following his example, she tucked her hat and cane under one arm and removed one glove. Then she laid her fingertips on Terry's left cheek. The coldness of his skin stunned her and her heart lurched in her breast. Her throat worked desperately. This couldn't be all that was left! Not of her warm, exasperating Terry who was never still for a moment, always laughing, teasing, wriggling with enthusiasm. Her hand curled in a fist before her eyes, the knuckles white as Terry's skin. Neil's grasp on her elbow pulled her away and turned her, breaking the horrified spell.

Wordlessly, they returned to the family pew, sat down and replaced their gloves. The sound of the scuffling feet of other mourners covered his next words. He leaned toward her so that his lips were near her ear. "Weep later. Promise yourself you can, and dwell on that. Delay it."

She realized what he was doing. In the midst of his own grief, he was giving her advice on how to cover her own turmoil. He must know that, as a woman, she'd never been called upon to conceal her tears. Men always were.

"Count the flower petals," she returned in kind, nodding.

She patted his thigh gently, offering the little consolation she could. He shifted uncomfortably, and Elizabeth snatched her hand away, suddenly aware of the intimacy of her unthinking gesture.

"Whatever it takes," he mumbled, fiddling with his watch fob. He eased the watch out of its pocket and held it for a moment. Then he put it back impatiently, as though realizing it would not appear proper to glance at the time now. So he was anxious to have this over. His habit with the watch irritated her, especially now, even though she had felt much the same ever since they'd arrived.

For a moment there, she'd thought he was concerned about her. A warm feeling of comfort had begun to develop. Now she understood. If she were unmasked by one of the guests, he could be adjudged guilty along with her, as an accomplice. A coldness rivaling that of death drove out all warmth. She felt desolate, empty.

Others—she counted only fourteen, including servants—made their way to the coffin, and out of mourning, respect or curiosity, took their turns at view. She recognized no one among the mourners.

One by one they approached Neil and muttered their regrets and comforts. Due to her proximity to the earl, she was next to receive the handshakes and murmurs. Those in attendance obviously believed her to be a close friend of the family. She quirked a brow at the thought. And so she was.

When everyone was seated, the service began. She grasped every word and examined it for truth as applied to Terry. In turn, she had to hold back tears, laughter and outrage. When the vicar finally closed his mouth, her relief was so great she wanted to scream with it. The clear, pure tenor of the vicar's wife rose in an a cappella version of "Amazing Grace." Elizabeth soothed herself with the thought that Terry at least would have appreciated that. All the rest would have been a grand old joke—the vicar's syrupy eulogizing of a budding rake he barely knew, his ignorance of Terry's blatant irreverence in the face of a solemn occasion. God in heaven, she wanted to hear him laugh about it. She smiled for Terry.

Neil's dark look promptly erased it.

Elizabeth used the fear of discovery to distract herself from her grief. She dedicated her every gesture, each facial expression to his memory, calling up his actions and reactions like required recitations in the schoolroom.

Thankfully, the entombment would take place after the mourners had departed. Terry would lie beside his father and the mother he had never known in the stone vault behind the chapel, with all the former earls and their families.

Elizabeth left the chapel, head down, avoiding the others. Dismal fog hung about the churchyard like a pall, persisting long after it should have burned away. She craved sunshine, but perhaps this suited. Terry would never see the sun again.

Due to Gormsloft's proximity to London, none of those who had driven down for the ceremony would be staying the night. After less than an hour of desultory mingling outside the ancient stone chapel, the gentlemen returned to their coaches and departed for town, their noble duty done. On with life.

Neil excused himself to oversee the entombment, and MacLinden ushered Elizabeth inside the old keep to wait. They sat at the table in the drafty old hall while the caretaker's woman went to fetch tea.

The inspector drew out his ever present pipe and gripped it between his straight, white teeth. He drew on it once as though it were lighted, causing an irritating little sucking sound. "The service was rather nice, wasn't it?"

Elizabeth stared at him, incredulous. She recalled the pious, beak-nosed vicar and his nauseating nonsense about Terry's being the flower of England's youth. Terry would have choked. And all that trash about his death being God's will made her see red. Her thoughts spilled out. "God's will, indeed! I wanted to smack the fellow in the teeth with my cane!" She huffed and shivered. "Bloody fool. Why couldn't he just call down God's vengeance on the bastard that shot Terry and be done with it?"

"Now, now, steady on, Betts. Man's just doin' what he can to keep his living here. Not his fault he's no talent for the pulpit. You're just overset."

Lindy ran a finger around the rim of his bowler as he changed the subject. "Didn't happen to notice a familiar face or voice, did you?"

Elizabeth shook her head. "The man from the theater? No, I'm afraid not. Matter of fact, I didn't see a soul I know personally." She frowned at the thought. "Not many attended. Probably because of Terry's relationship with me."

"Quite possibly," he agreed. The good inspector certainly wasn't one to gloss things over, she thought.

They fell silent for a while. MacLinden sucked on his pipe. Elizabeth glared at him until he wrinkled his nose in apology and tucked it back in its special pocket.

Not long after tea, Neil returned and curtly announced he was ready to leave. MacLinden bade them a perfunctory farewell and took his own rig, intending to stop over in Charing Cross.

For Elizabeth and Neil, the three-hour ride back to the city was silent but for the creaking of the coach springs and the sound of hoofbeats. From under lowered lashes, she studied her companion from time to time. Encased in tense silence, he gripped his engraved gold watch in a bare, fisted hand as he stared out the window into the darkness. His thumb rubbed the watchcase in a hard, circular motion, as though the thing were a talisman to ward off pain.

They arrived at the town house well after nine. Elizabeth pulled her stifling cravat loose and sank down on the bed in the countess's chamber of the master suite. Neil had finally agreed to allow her to sleep here, but not before locking her hall door so that the only way out was through his room. He was alone in the adjoining room now and the silence was deafening.

Was he crying for Terry? His eyes had looked bloodshot throughout the day's ordeal, the irises so dark a blue they appeared black. She felt a new respect for men and their capacity to remain dry-eyed in situations such as this. Even though she'd wept copiously the night before, the funeral had nearly destroyed her composure all over again.

Because of the autopsy, Terry had not lain in state at the town house, but had been carried directly from the morgue to the mortician and then to the chapel at Gormsloft. Though she had braced herself for it, seeing his sweet face composed in death had come as a frightful shock. It had taken all her concentration to hold herself in check.

Divesting herself of her male attire, Elizabeth drew on one of Terry's dressing gowns. She hugged it about her as though she could draw some of the young earl's former warmth. Then she cried again for the friend who was gone forever.

Later, she woke to a clinking sound from next door. She slid out of bed and was lighting the lamp as the door opened. Neil appeared, balancing a tray on one hand.

"I suspect you ate little at tea. Are you hungry?" he asked. Elizabeth stepped away so that he could deposit his burden on the bedside table beside the lamp.

She wrinkled her nose at the smell of burnt toast. "You cooked?"

He shrugged his shoulders. His voice sounded constrained and hoarse. "Not very well, I'm afraid. There's ham, compliments of Lindy's mother, and I've done up some eggs. Bread's a mite singed at the edge, but there you are. Tea's good and hot." Not once had he looked up.

They stood close enough to touch. Elizabeth reached out. She couldn't seem to help herself. It was the first time in memory that anyone had given a thought to her comfort who hadn't been paid to do so. Even her father had ignored her for the most part after her mother died. Now Neil, despite his suffering, worried that she might be hungry.

"Thank you, Neil," she said softly, squeezing his arm.

He raised his eyes then, and she saw they were red rimmed and swollen. The look of pain on his face proved her undoing. With a muffled cry, she slid her arms around his waist and squeezed hard, wanting desperately to ease his suffering.

"Oh, Neil. I'm truly so sorry. I wish..." But there was nothing she could say. She knew there was no way to wipe away the hurt he was feeling. Her own was just as deep.

With her head against his chest, she could feel as much as hear his voice. The timbre sounded strained and raspy. "You loved him, too."

It was not a question, but she answered, "Oh, yes. How could I not? He was so good, so kind and caring. Dear to me."

She felt Neil's hand on her head, pressing her to him in a protective and reassuring way. "He was more than a nephew, you know. Like a younger brother. Or even a son," he said in a stronger voice. "He would want me to take care of you. I think he must have loved you very much."

"We met through an advertisement he placed for Roman coins. Papa and I both collected, you know. Terry visited us quite regularly on weekends long before Father died. We remained good friends, even after..."

"After all the others?" Neil's voice took on a hint of bitterness now. "Terry overlooked all that, didn't he?" He drew away from her and turned his back. "It doesn't matter now."

"It does matter," she said, trying to explain now that they had formed a bond of sorts. "Terry knew there was never—"

Neil interrupted her with a curt backward wave of one hand and a gritty warning. "Don't lie, Elizabeth. Not now. All I need to know is that you were his lover and he would want you protected. For his sake, I'll do that," he said, and stalked toward the open door. "Drink your tea before it cools."

The door closed quietly, but she knew he had ached to slam it. His anger was a sorry replacement for grief, but maybe that was what he needed. He had wept enough today.

Perhaps it was better if he continued to believe she and Terry had been intimate. That might keep him at a distance until this physical attraction between them dissipated, or at least until the investigation of Terry's murder was complete.

Trouble was, her feelings for Neil were fast progressing beyond the pull of his well-honed body. She was not blind to the fact that he felt something stronger than lust for her. Nothing could come of it, though. At least not anything honorable. He was now in the same position Terry had been: an earl in danger of ridicule by association with a social pariah.

Elizabeth cursed her reputation and, not for the first time, her stupidity in letting herself come to such a pass.

Neil immediately regretted his harsh words. She was suffering, too. Later, when his grief lessened, he'd apologize.

She had done well today at the funeral. Not many of Terry's peers were present, however, and of those few, only men came.

The boy's attachment to a woman of Lady Marleigh's character had alienated more people than Neil had thought. Even Terry's untimely death hadn't canceled that. Didn't the lad's goodness of heart matter? Couldn't they understand that he'd been ensnared by her beauty and was a victim of his own innocence? Victorian society grew more pompous and restrictive by the year.

Well, no matter now. Terry was beyond their censure, and the only thing left to do was find the son of a bitch responsible for the murder and see him hanged. It was the driving force behind Neil's existence at present—finding the murderer and proving the lady's innocence in the matter. Above that, keeping Elizabeth Marleigh's body and soul together in the event that her life was still in danger. Which it doubtless was.

Regardless of what she had allowed herself to become, Neil had no desire to see Elizabeth lying lifeless on a slab with a medical examiner prodding her death wounds. The very thought chilled him to the core. No, he must keep her safe. For Terry's sake. Surely that and his own devout respect for life were enough justification for going to all this trouble.

*Liar.* He cursed his own vulnerability where she was concerned. Never in his life had he panted after a woman. Even if Emma Throckmorton had turned his head and then tried to twist it off, he had kept his pride and composure to the very end of that farce. He suspected that if Elizabeth Marleigh ever spurned him as Emma had, that hard-won composure of his wouldn't stand a chance of survival. Not that he planned to give her the chance. No, best to keep her at arm's length at the very least.

A sudden picture crept into his mind and stuck: a tumble of dye-darkened waves sweeping a finely arched brow, narrow shoulders padded under a baggy tweed jacket, fake male parts as large as his own stuffed down trousers half the size of his.

He smiled in spite of himself. She was a treasure, that one. A badly tarnished treasure, to be sure, but tempting as hell. Plucky little Betts.

Even old Lindy was not immune, judging by the way he smiled at her. Neil recalled the rush of anger he'd felt when Lindy turned his rough-edged charm on her. Jealousy, of course. Only a fool wouldn't recognize it for what it was, and Neil was certainly no one's fool. Well, not on a regular basis, anyway.

Facing problems was not always easy, but the problem of his attraction and his possessive leanings toward Elizabeth Marleigh was best admitted up front. Then he could deal with it. If nothing else, the guilt he felt over desiring Terry's mistress ought to help Neil keep his hands to himself.

If only he could forget that impulsive hug of hers, such a healing thing, so warm and altogether right.

Neil slept restlessly that night and rose at dawn to a house empty of servants. Clad only in a loose shirt and breeches, he slipped out to the walled garden in back of the house to complete the exercises he usually did in the privacy of his room.

After filling his lungs with brisk morning air, he executed the controlled movements that stretched each muscle to its fullest extent. Now tensing, now releasing. Concentrating carefully, gathering speed and power, he performed each sweep of his limbs with practiced grace and force. The ritual provided a certain calmness of spirit, while the chilly air energized his body.

Increased blood flow and cooling sweat temporarily exorcised a few of the demons haunting him, thank God. The pain of Terry's loss remained a steady, constant ache, but Neil knew it would become bearable in time. He feared the problem of his growing desire for Elizabeth Marleigh might take a bit longer. He rolled his shoulders forward and then back, shaking the kinks from his arms. He was a fool to let a woman, especially this woman, tie him in knots again.

Absurdly eager to see her even as he cursed his idiocy, Neil went to the kitchen and made tea while waiting for her to wake.

It pleased him to find she was not a late sleeper. Without any fanfare, she joined him in the kitchen and dished up a simple breakfast while they discussed the day's schedule. Neither mentioned the funeral or what had happened afterward.

"Shall we ride later?" he asked, stacking his dishes and passing them to her across the table.

"Why don't you teach me to dance?"

"Dance? You mean you don't know how?"

She shook her head as she pumped water into the wash pan. "That dance you did in the garden this morning. I saw you from the window. It's very…powerful. Graceful."

"Oh that." He pursed his lips, wondering if it was worth an explanation. "I learned it from a classmate whose father was a sea captain. It's an oriental form of exercise that teaches discipline and defense."

"Fighting, you mean?" she asked idly, scrubbing a plate.

"Sometimes." Recalling how he had employed it once made him uneasy. "Forget about it. What say we get our chores done and take a turn around the park? You need fresh air."

The chores included Neil dictating endless lists of supplies for the laboratory. Elizabeth wrote in her fine, slanted hand, asking occasional questions about the use of a substance or instrument. The mundane activity soothed him after the frantic events of the past three days. It seemed to affect her the same way.

Later that morning, they rode together in the park, he on his sturdy roan and she on a mare Oliver had rented for her.

No one looked askance at the modestly dressed physician and his dandified assistant as they took their exercise.

Neil was still terrified she would be found out. It amazed him that she had brought off the disguise at the funeral. And today, trotting about Hyde Park, he saw not so much as a second glance at his companion when they passed other riders on the paths. There would be no mourning or blur of passing horseflesh to distract anyone at the clubs, however.

The whole plan was so outrageous, it might work after all. Who in his right mind would ever suspect that an earl's daughter would undertake such a daring role? People generally saw what they expected to see. Perhaps she would be safe enough if the two of them kept to dark corners and drew as little attention as possible. They were only to listen, anyway, and pick up what information they could from the gossip.

Neil uttered a small prayer in any event. "Please God she has the good sense not to overplay the part." Recalling that confident swagger of hers didn't ease his mind at all.

# Chapter Six

*Confident! She must remain confident.* Slouched uncomfortably in the corner of Neil's carriage, Elizabeth twisted the head of her cane and squirmed with apprehension. She raked her bottom lip with her teeth until it felt raw. Attending the funeral was one thing, given all the distractions of the service, but socializing with Terry's peers in the all-male setting of White's was quite another. What if she failed to maintain her pose as a man? She knew without doubt the discovery of her real identity would incriminate Neil as well as herself. Lindy couldn't save either of them if they were found out.

Neil was hiding her, after all, while Scotland Yard implemented a countrywide search. The papers were full of speculation about Terry's death and her own disappearance. She imagined the entire populace talked of little else. Now here she was, about to enter London's most famous male refuge as though she belonged.

Sucking in a deep breath and struggling for composure, Elizabeth forced her chin high as they exited the coach. From the stiff set of his shoulders, she sensed that Neil's apprehension matched her own.

"For God's sake, don't wander away from me," he warned. "And don't initiate any conversation, just follow my lead. Heads up, Betts, here comes our test."

She watched him paste on an amiable smile as two young

gentlemen approached them near the entrance. Elizabeth remembered them as two of the handshakers from the funeral.

The dark-haired one was short, quite stout and rather pudding faced. He reminded her of an overfed spaniel with his drooping brown eyes and eager nature.

The other one was the complete opposite—handsome in an effeminate sort of way and skinny as a reed, with stylish, wheat-colored curls arranged not unlike her own. He appeared to be a bit shy, hanging just behind and to the left of his friend. They both smiled engagingly and came to a halt in front of Neil.

"Turner, Biddenton." Neil greeted them with an outstretched hand and inclined his head toward her. "You've met my colleague, Dr. Betts, I believe?"

"Yes, hullo." Turner, the slender blonde, nodded to her but directed his words to Neil. "Dreadfully sorry about Terry, sir. Sorry as can be, all of us."

"Thank you," Neil said sincerely, but the underlying bitterness in his voice seemed to make them uncomfortable. "Good of you both to pay respects. So many did not."

"Indeed…well, dashed mean of 'em if you ask me! Prudes, the lot," Biddenton remarked with a scowl. "Who cares where Terry parked his boots at night, eh? He wasn't serious about th' marriage, you know. Couldn't have been, I don't think. They'll catch the bitch who did it, sir, make no mistake. And when they do…!" He exchanged a confirming nod with Turner.

Elizabeth felt her stomach clench, and turned slightly away.

"Let's not dwell on it tonight, eh, Biddie?" Neil said. "Could I buy you fellows a drink?"

She heard apprehension in his invitation. Well, they must start somewhere, and these two certainly seemed talkative enough.

The ruddy young Biddenton ran a chubby hand through his thin black hair, combing it forward with his fingers. "Could do with a spot of brandy, thanks. Just came from the tables. Ain't the same without Terry, y'know?"

"I know," Neil agreed. "Grab that space over there, Betts." He steered them to an empty table in a darkened corner.

Elizabeth used the time to study Terry's friends. She recalled their introduction at the service. Schoolmates of Terry's at Harrow. Biddenton was a viscount, Neil had said, and Turner the younger son of a baronet.

"So, Dr. Betts, this your first trip to London?" Turner was asking her as they settled in.

Elizabeth cleared her throat, hoping her voice didn't sound too unnatural. "No, no, been here once before when I was a lad. Ain't changed much. Mite different from Edinburgh, though. Bit wilder, I should think."

"No doubt there," Biddenton said, laughing. "Oughta let us show you around, what? Doc won't mind, will you, sir?"

Neil grinned, his white teeth almost glowing in the low light. "In a few weeks, perhaps. Betts and I have much to do setting up my lab. I'd not like him rolling in bottle-eyed every morning."

Biddie nodded enthusiastic thanks as the waiter delivered their drinks and a plate of cheese and small pasties. "Oh, we'd take care he don't overdo. Nice to know where the petticoats hang, don't you see. Right, Tun?" He popped a pasty into his mouth and chewed voraciously.

Elizabeth raised her glass and rocked it, swirling the amber liquid as she'd seen Terry do on occasion. "Daresay I can locate a ruffle or two on my own," she said with a wink, "should the need...*arise*."

Neil groaned and rolled his eyes in disgust.

"Ha, well said, Betts!" Biddie said, chuckling as he licked the crumbs off a finger and reached for another of the tiny pies. "Fellow's a bit of all right, eh, Tun?"

"Excuse me, Lord Havington." A second waiter hovered at Neil's elbow. "Lord Hobbs requests a private word with you. At your pleasure, of course. He waits in the reading room."

Neil shot Elizabeth a guarded look as he pushed back his

chair, reluctant to leave her alone with the men. She nodded once and lifted her glass. "Aw, go on, sir. Not as though I'm off to the stews just yet." She blinked sorrowfully at Biddie and pulled a frown. "He promised Da to keep me in a dry beaker on the shelf, y'see." They all laughed and shooed Neil away.

He paused, held her gaze for a moment in silent warning and then strode away, picking a path through the occupied tables.

"So, Betts—" Turner leaned forward on his elbows with a wicked gleam in his eye "—keeping you on too tight a leash, is he? Dashed stuffy, that one. Always was. Ought to've seen him raking Terry over for gettin' caught with a bit of muslin in his rooms our last year up. Ha! Like th'old fellow's never bounced the bed ropes himself!"

Suddenly Biddenton pushed away from the table and stood, clutching his throat. His eyes bugged out as he staggered back, making a strangling sound. Those at the surrounding tables merely glanced at him and then away.

"Aww, don't chuck it up, Biddie," Turner groaned.

With dawning horror, Elizabeth saw Biddenton's terrified eyes bulge as he gagged. Quickly, she leapt from her chair, stepped behind him and landed a two-fisted blow between his shoulder blades. Biddie fell forward against the back of a chair, its high, padded back catching him just under the ribs. A piece of meat popped out of his mouth onto the table, and he began coughing violently.

She shoved him around so that he plopped down, gasping, in her own vacated seat. "Calm down, Biddie. Arms high. Breathe deep. Slowly now." Elizabeth relaxed a little when she heard him wheeze in and out a few times.

He shuddered and drew in another ragged breath, clutching her supporting forearm in a bruising grip. His face was still beet red.

"Jesus!" Turner croaked, and laid a hand on Biddie's heaving shoulder. "Christ amighty, man, you were *choking!*" His words rang out over the sudden buzz of conversation.

Biddie nodded as his breath rattled. He shut his eyes and sucked in noisy draughts of air.

"Hey!" Turner shouted. "Betts saved your friggin' life, old man. Drinks! 'Nother round over here!"

Elizabeth watched Neil plow hurriedly through the commotion of patrons who were now leaving their tables to gather around. "What's happened?" he asked as he reached their table. He gripped her as though he meant to drag her out of the place by the scruff of her neck and fight everyone off with his other hand. His eyes flared a warning, raking the table until they found Biddenton. Fascinated, Elizabeth watched the metamorphosis from defensive male animal to civilized physician.

"Biddie got something stuck in his throat. Little Doc here unstuck it! Gad, he could've died! Choked to death with me thinking he was only tossing his supper!" Turner lowered his voice. "Thank God for your presence of mind, Betts."

"Are you all right, Biddie?" Neil asked. Elizabeth watched with interest as Neil ascertained the answer for himself, checking the man's respiration and grasping a chunky wrist for the pulse.

Biddie rested his head on his free hand. "Right as—as rain, sir." He looked shaken and was trembling visibly.

"Ho! This calls for a celebration," Turner shouted to the room at large. "Drinks, everybody. Drink to the little doctor!"

A loud *huzzah* rang out and she heard the clinking of glasses. "To Little Doc! Here, here!"

Elizabeth held up one hand in acknowledgment of the salute. Her nose wrinkled in a helpless expression when Neil shot her a look of exasperation. She could see she was in for a tongue-lashing, but what was done was done, and she refused to feel guilty about it. Biddie was alive, after all.

Forcing a cheerful grin, she accepted the fresh brandy Turner offered her and raised it to Neil. "To my mentor!" That gained her an even darker scowl and set glasses to clinking again. So much for sitting quietly in a dark corner with her mouth shut. Neil looked livid.

* * *

Twenty minutes later, Turner bundled Biddie into a hansom cab at Neil's insistence and promised to take him straight home.

Elizabeth curled in the corner of Neil's carriage, trying to escape his glare. She dreaded the ride to Havington House, knowing that what she'd done had drawn dangerous attention to herself. Neil made his fury clear with sharp looks and huffy sighs.

"Ought I to have let him die then?" she asked defensively before he could speak.

"No, of course not," Neil said with a curt, backward wave of one hand. "It's just that...damn it, Elizabeth, you were supposed to remain unobtrusive! Now every one of those young bucks will be clamoring to make your acquaintance." He snorted, staring out the window at the dark, wet night. "Quite the hero."

"Jealous?" she asked, knowing that would stir his anger to an even greater froth.

"That's a stupid thing to say! You did exactly right, all you should have done. All *I* would have done. I only wish it hadn't been necessary." He slumped back on the seat, leaning his head against the leather squabs.

"Nobody else was doing anything. They all just sat there like peas on a plate while Biddie lost his breath. I gave him a thump to get him going, is all. I thought about running my finger down his throat, but he might have bitten it off."

Neil's eyes softened in the carriage light with something strangely resembling admiration. "Never mind. In spite of the risk of discovery, it was a good night's work, Betts. Biddie's alive because of you."

She smiled, inordinately pleased. "That's twice you've called me 'Betts' in private. Does this mean you think of me as your man now?"

Head still tilted back against the seat, Neil regarded her through lowered lashes. "I could never think of you as any-one's *man*, Bettsy." When he spoke, his voice drifted over her like a warm, suggestive touch. "Not after having seen all that's beneath that superfine suit you're wearing."

"Highly improper of you to mention that, *Doctor*," she said, wary of the turn of conversation, shivering at the thought of his eyes on her body, awake or not.

"Propriety has no place between us, Bettsy. I'm amazed you understand the concept at all."

"Two degenerates in league, then, are we?" All the hurt his words caused her surged out in spite of the fact that she meant to speak lightly.

"How could you have done all those things, I wonder?" he asked in a thoughtful voice, his gaze drifting out the window. "I wish to hell I understood you better."

"You'll never understand me at all, Havington," Elizabeth said, closing her eyes and feeling as dejected as she ever had in her life.

She jumped when he moved across the carriage unexpectedly. Even more surprising, he took her in his arms, holding her as if someone might try to take her away. She melted against him, the tension of the night's excitement turning into another sort altogether. The cool silk of his waistcoat brushed her open lips, exciting nerves there, making her wish for the warm, more mobile contact of his mouth. Exotic spice and male heat enveloped her, touch and scent blending, gathering together with the enticing vibration of his voice.

"I don't care," he whispered against her ear, exposing all his anger and urgency and need. His hold on her tightened further. "Do you hear me, Bettsy? I just don't care anymore."

The kiss startled her as much as his words. Lips hard at first slowly softened as she murmured a welcome against them. His taste, that of good brandy and something vaguely unique, filled her with incredible longing. Elizabeth drew in a deep breath as his mouth moved to a spot just below her ear.

Her arms slid around him of their own volition, as naturally as her mouth found his again. This time his kiss was open-mouthed and desperate. Hungry. As hungry as she felt. She met his tongue with hers, eagerly matching everything he did, learning and inventing as she went. A disappointed moan escaped her when he finally dragged his mouth away.

His words almost escaped her foggy senses. "God, I want you!"

She tightened her arms around him, one elbow accidentally brushing against his arousal just as the carriage lurched to a stop.

"Damn it to hell!" He moved her aside with a rough push.

Elizabeth shook her head, dizzy with desire and confused at his abrupt abandonment. "What?" she muttered.

"We're home." He tugged his coat together and avoided her eyes. "Your hat and cane," he reminded her gruffly as he shoved open the door and climbed out.

She recovered immediately, his curtness dismissing her languor as effectively as a slap in the face. Snatching up her accoutrements, Elizabeth exited the carriage, stumbling in her haste, and followed him into the town house. *The wretch!* She hefted her cane, thinking it might not be such a useless trapping, after all. She itched to break it over his head.

Neil turned into his study, shooting her a frown over one shoulder, his blue-black gaze halting her in her tracks when she would have followed. "Go to bed, Elizabeth," he ordered with barely restrained fury. "And lock your door! We needn't make this any more complicated than it already is."

Elizabeth stood in the foyer for a moment after the study door slammed shut. What exactly did he think to prove? Surely he knew she'd have gone to his bed for the asking if he hadn't turned so fractious.

The truth disturbed her, but she tried never to lie to herself. She wanted him as much as he wanted her. Badly as she hated to admit it, refusing him tonight in the carriage had never even occurred to her. Thank God he'd come to his senses.

Then the reasons for his denial crystallized. He hated his lapse of self-control, for one thing. That probably more than anything had triggered his anger. And her reputation put him off to the extreme. He made that quite clear every chance he got.

Carefully, she laid her hat and cane on a side table and began to climb the stairs. Why should she care what he thought? He had kidnapped her, insulted her at every turn, and now this! He'd pushed her away as though desiring her were the worst thing in the world. Perhaps for him it was.

She knew why he treated her as he had and really couldn't blame him for it. Neil had stolen her away only to prevent a disastrous marriage with a nephew he loved. Given his limited knowledge of the situation, there was very little left for him to do. And the lashing insults? Well, he had good cause to believe she deserved them. Had she ever uttered one word to deny the accusations? Her pride kept her from begging him to believe her side of what had happened. Pleading the truth certainly hadn't helped with Colin or the Smythes.

Neil acted as though the slurs against her hurt *him* in some way. The fact that he didn't try to ravish her at the first opportunity proved he was different from most men. If Neil Bronwyn had a fault, it was that he cared too much about people.

Elizabeth undressed, pulled on a nightshirt and slipped into bed, wondering how he would react to her in the morning. Neil was right about an affair between them complicating matters, but she fervently hoped the incident in the carriage tonight wouldn't halt their growing friendship.

She would do almost anything to recapture that fleeting moment before he'd kissed her, when she thought she had seen warm admiration in the depths of his eyes.


Neil dashed the brandy snifter against the cold logs in the grate. *Why?* Why hadn't he taken her straight up to bed? God knew he wanted to. She *wanted* him to. Stupid, idiotic, stiff-necked pride would be the death of him!

No, he had a surfeit of pride, all right, but there was more to his reticence than that. He wasn't sure he could bear to discover that she was as proficient in bed as she was at kissing.

He could still taste her, feel the quicksilver of her tongue, the flame of her eagerness igniting him like dry tinder. Her scent lingered, a faint hint of lavender and Elizabeth stealing through Terry's cologne, which she'd dashed on earlier to disguise herself for the club. The throaty little sounds she'd made during their kisses echoed in Neil's head, tormenting him.

"Damn me for a fool!" he thundered, and stormed out the French doors onto the terrace. Even the cool night air did nothing to dispel his heat.

He stalked about for a while and then returned to the study, frustrated. Brandy straight from the decanter dulled his hunger just enough for him to risk going upstairs. Carefully avoiding so much as a glance at her door, Neil entered his adjoining room, undressed and went to bed. Eventually he slept.

Screams rattled the windows. Neil jerked himself awake, cursing the fog of brandy and exhaustion.

"Bettsy!" he shouted and tore across the room, pausing only to grab a poker from the fireplace. The door opened immediately when he pressed the lever. Thank God she hadn't locked it!

The room was empty of life except for the hysterical figure tangled in the bedsheets. Neil dropped his makeshift weapon and ran to her. She fought the covers like a tigress and switched her struggles to him when he tried to unbind her.

"Be still," he ordered, yanking the fabric aside. "It's me! It's Neil! Wake up, Bettsy!" He shook her gently.

She made an incoherent little noise, half sob, half laugh, and buried her nose in the crook of his neck. "Dreaming," she muttered. "Sorry."

"It's all right," he soothed, caressing the disheveled curls on the crown of her head. "Awake now?"

He felt her nod. "Want to talk about it?" he asked.

"No," she said, then added perversely, "he cut off my hair. He swung the knife and I felt the..." She pulled back slightly and turned huge, tear-filled eyes up to his. "He put it on the statue and they all thought that I... It wasn't *me!*"

Neil drew her to him again and lay down beside her, cradling her fiercely. "I know, I know. It's over and done. Don't think about it, love. Just don't think about it."

"But I *didn't!*"

"No, no, of course you didn't. It's all right. Lie still now. Take a deep breath." He cradled her head against his chest and ran his fingers through her tousled hair.

Neil recalled the story he'd heard at Varian's. One of the rowdy swells Colin had invited down from London swore he'd seen Elizabeth from a third-floor guest room at Hammershill. Dressed in a diaphanous night rail, she'd clambered into the fountain. There, she'd slung a long switch of hair—her own, apparently—over the head of Aphrodite's nude statue.

She had kicked about playfully in the water, showing a fine length of leg and then, laughing merrily, had run back toward the house, where he had lost sight of her in the shadows.

"Wickedly enchanting and mad as a hatter," the man had said of her, laughing as he recounted it. Marleigh's elusive, daring cousin had apparently kept to her rooms and taunted them with her absence, except for cavorting in the moonlit garden to tease those looking out the windows. Thinking of it made Neil's chest ache.

"A lusty jest and a blatant invitation to lewd advances." The *Gazette* and the gossips had had a field day.

What had made her do such a senseless thing? Neil wondered. Had her father's death caused a temporary madness? Perhaps she couldn't even recall the episode afterward and had invented the knife story to explain it away. Or had dreamed and believed it real.

Her account had sounded credible when she'd told him and Lindy about it at the country house. But how much of that was fantasy? No one in her right mind would take up her severed braid, brush out the plait and hang it over a statue's head immediately after she'd been threatened with death. And she certainly wouldn't dance in a fountain for the guests' entertainment. Someone else, then? Hardly.

No, some horrid thing had overset Bettsy, unbalanced her somehow in spite of her courage and strength. She would recover, had to, and he would help. He hugged her closer, kissing the top of her head and soothing her with his hands. She was so soft and giving, snuggling against him, seeking his warmth. The scent of her invaded his nostrils, all lavender and sweet Elizabeth.

Neil ceased to think rationally. All he wanted was to feel. Her breasts, bare but for the thin layer of batiste, pressed to his chest with gentle insistence. He imagined the hardening of their lovely peaks, certain he could feel them. Soft, slender legs met his, entwined their coolness with his heat.

His mouth sought hers. He'd distract her from the nightmare just for a moment, stop her trembling, and then he'd leave. Ah, she was so sweet, so soft. The kiss deepened as she relaxed and began to participate. How could he end it? He knew she didn't want him to stop. Not now. Not ever.

As naturally as breathing, he traced her spine with his fingers, causing her to arch against him. That sound again, that marvelous keening sound deep in her throat, echoed his own need so exactly.

She moved against him, a sinuous writhing that threatened what was left of his sanity. "God, Bettsy, I need you," he murmured as she found his lips again, parting her own. Insistent. Insatiable. Impossible to resist.

Nothing existed beyond the nectar of her mouth and the blazing fire between them. The sensation in his palm grew acute as he found her breast beneath the nightshirt. Impatiently, he released the treasure long enough to bare her completely.

No time to look. Later. Later, he would feast his eyes, he promised himself.

Greedily, she drew his hand to her again, and he squeezed her almost roughly, willing her to hurry, to catch up, to be as ready for him as he was for her. Unable to linger, he stroked down her ribs, her waist, over her hip and home. He swallowed a groan of pleasure when he felt the honeyed sweetness, the slippery, welcoming heat embrace his fingers.

Her sudden resistance reared violently. Neil groaned as she shoved against him with surprising strength.

"No!"

"No!"

Their words tumbled out simultaneously—her meaning quite clear and his an effort to stop her denial. Their eyes locked and their breath became suspended. He held on to her when she tried to put distance between them.

"Why not?" he whispered, hating himself for the pleading note in his voice. He'd never begged a woman in his life and, by God, he wasn't going to start with this one.

His body, already aching with suppressed desire, tensed even further as he pushed away from her. "Excuse me, my lady. I'd thought we were past playing games."

She reached out and touched his shoulder, drawing her hand back as though stung. "Neil, I can't do this. I'm sorry."

"Can't or won't?" He rolled off the bed, reached to retie his robe and realized that he was completely naked. Well, let her look, then. Straightening to his full height, he raised his eyes and put all the disgust he'd ever felt for womankind into one furious glance. "Good night, Lady Marleigh. Pleasant dreams."

Four angry strides took him to the connecting door, which he closed behind him with a deafening slam.

The sound echoed in his brain and reverberated through his body with a satisfying tremor. He looked down at his clenched fists and past them to his toes, digging into the Turkey-red carpet. His stubborn arousal raged, mocking his fury and refusing to subside. "Damned traitor!" he cursed.

It took Neil a full ten minutes of inward railing, plus another shot of brandy, to reach any semblance of calm. He set the glass down on the bedside table with a thunk and tried to reason out what had just happened.

A hell of a time for her to change her ways, he thought, scowling at her door. Perhaps she hadn't changed at all, but was playing some sort of twisted game. He slapped his palm hard against the bedpost, ignoring the sting. She had wanted him to make love to her. He *knew* she had. Even a sex-starved idiot couldn't have mistaken her initial response.

Why had she called a halt? It wasn't as though her virtue

was at risk. Ha! Surely she didn't think he'd grow besotted enough to offer marriage if she held out. Had she done the same to Terry?

It grew increasingly difficult to distinguish sound reasoning from jealous conjecture and thwarted desire. His body still hovered on the edge of lust. Impossible to think straight. Maybe he was making too much of a simple refusal. Maybe she just bloody well hadn't felt like doing it all of a sudden.

Neil forced his disappointment down and made another attempt to analyze the situation. They had become friends. Perhaps she didn't want to mix things up. He had even suggested that sex between them would do that. He had certainly been rather sharp with her earlier, when they had returned home.

*Aha! Revenge.* That was it! The little cat was getting back at him. She had been fully ready for him when the carriage stopped and he'd sent her packing off to bed. Actually slammed the door in her face.

He smiled grimly. Yes, revenge made perfect sense.

She didn't hate him, wasn't trying to trick him. All she wanted was to show him how he had insulted her. He could simply apologize in the morning and pick up where they had left off. Women weren't so hard to figure out, after all.

But they could damn sure dash the hell out of a good night's sleep.


Elizabeth punched her pillow for the hundredth time and finally gave up. No point lying awake and worrying about what had just happened, but she had little choice in the matter.

Neil would hate her now. That would simplify matters, but it wasn't any easier to take. She knew he cared more for her than he wanted to. One didn't have to be a genius or an expert on men to know he fought his feelings.

Wouldn't he be amazed to discover why she had denied him! If only she were experienced, as everyone believed, taking Neil as a lover wouldn't pose any problem. God knew she wanted to. However, as it was, he would feel obliged to ''do the right thing'' the moment he discovered the truth. She couldn't let him make love to her or he'd know. Thank God she had remembered that at the last moment and stopped him.

Neil would feel duty bound to propose if he took her innocence, and he wouldn't accept no for an answer. She had no doubt they would eventually prove she was not guilty of Terry's murder, but there would still be the stigma of her infamous behavior. No way in the world to disprove that! He would insist on marriage then, and she would be right back where she had started with Terry, running away to keep an honorable earl from wrecking his good name for a hopeless cause. But Neil would find her if she ran, and she wasn't certain she could refuse him forever.

Elizabeth knew she had to protect him. And protect herself as well. Marriage with Neil might be heaven for a while. Until he started to resent her for all the gossip and his certain rejection by society. Parting from him then, with all that hatred in his heart, would be devastating for her.

If only there were a way she could have Neil for a small space of time, just to know once how sweet love might have been. But she couldn't risk his knowing. He must never guess how wrong he was about her.

They should go their separate ways when the investigation was complete and avoid any further contact. She'd head to the hunting box in Scotland, live quietly and try to forget him.

Maybe she'd even keep her new persona; Percival Betts wouldn't have newshounds on his heels or mysterious strangers threatening his life at every turn.

Getting through the next few weeks, perhaps even months, wouldn't prove easy for either of them in any case, but intimacy, as things stood, would be disastrous.

In future, she must see to it there were no opportunities for a recurrence.

# Chapter Seven

Morning arrived with a galloping hangover. Groaning, Neil rose and doused his face with tepid water from the pitcher Bettsy had filled the day before. Filling pitchers, gathering their laundry for Ollie to take out...hell, she even made the beds. Guilt added a pinging to the headache. With all that was happening to her, she still did all those tedious woman things?

*Woman things.* His head swam and he grabbed the edge of the washstand. The previous night's events crowded into his mind with disturbing clarity. Sobriety hurt like hell.

God, had he actually gone to her room and crawled into her bed? And taken advantage of her while she was still in the throes of a nightmare? Not full advantage, thank God! She'd had the good sense to stop him before he mucked things up too royally. Or maybe he had, just by his attempt on her. She was probably cursing him for the cad he was, and he didn't blame her. Somehow, from the moment he'd met her, all his good sense, all his thought processes had become skewed to the point of madness.

Frustrated lust had thrown him into a near tantrum last night. He had thought things about her that were rotten enough to laugh at if he had a warped sense of humor.

No matter what he'd read in the papers and heard at the clubs, Elizabeth Marleigh was no woman of loose morals. Oh, she kissed like the veriest trollop, no doubt about that. But her reactions when their passion heated to the boiling point, the way she waited for him to guide her, screamed inexperience, regardless of how willing she'd seemed at first.

Terry had been her lover, of course, but Neil doubted they had been intimate more than a few times. She was just too unschooled along those lines for him to believe anything else. The more he thought about it, the more he realized that even those eager kisses of hers, deliciously mind-bending as they were, could be the result of simply following his lead. She was a damned quick study, though.

He recalled that reported incident at the Smythes' house party about five months ago, just before he'd left to go abroad. He'd had no indication that Terry was involved with her then, or even that they were acquainted. The story was just another of those appalling misadventures the gossips shook their heads over.

That she had been sexually involved with two men seemed ludicrous now that he knew her better. Why hadn't she explained the situation when it was first mentioned? True, he had not given her much of a chance to deny any of it.

Perhaps all the gossip and ostracizing she'd endured since then had prompted her to thumb her nose at society. That would certainly explain some of her other actions—dancing in the fountain and so forth.

Swimming in her underthings had been necessary, of course, because of the sinking boat. Thank God modesty hadn't overcome her good sense that time.

The incident with the men in her bedroom must have some reasonable explanation. She'd said the fellows were drunk and had been there only a few moments when they were discovered. Had it been a misunderstanding or had someone set her up?

No wonder she had clung to Terry when everyone else turned against her. Neil certainly couldn't blame her for that. Terry had had the right idea—a good, sound marriage to someone above reproach was the only hope left for her. Otherwise, whether she continued on her current path or not, everyone would put the very worst construction on everything she did from now on, and the scandal would never die.

He ran a brush through his hair and straightened his shoulders. The mirror wasn't even kind enough to lie. Red eyed and prickly faced, he looked like hell. Felt like hell, too. It'd take more than a dose of capsicum to set him right this morning. If he walked into her room like this, she'd throw something at him. She might do that anyway, and with very good reason. Best get it over with so he could begin to make things right for her. He sniffed and trudged to her room.

The door stood ajar. He distinctly recalled slamming it shut. Pushing it open, he saw instantly that the room was vacant.

Oh God, she had run away! He'd *made* her run! Fear gripped him, stronger than passion had. She could be out there now, on the streets without any protection! Every peeler in London was after her and someone wanted her dead!

"Bettsy!" he shouted, dashing out into the hall. He tripped on the stairs and nearly fell. "Bettsy?" he called again, sprinting across the foyer and through the dining room. He rounded the corner into the kitchen and stopped, heart thudding.

*Thank God!* She sat on the edge of the table, swinging one booted foot and licking jam off her finger.

*Erotic.* A sharp jolt of desire set the blood pounding in his ears, echoing a lower pulsing. Fully dressed, covered from chin to foot in men's clothes, Elizabeth Marleigh was still the most enticing woman he'd ever seen.

"Good morning," she said, smiling. Innocence itself.

"If you say so." He approached a little unsteadily. Her eyes locked with his, flaring slightly.

Taking her hand, he raised it to his lips, kissed it and took one finger in his mouth. Reveling in the sweetness, he imagined he could feel the separate whorls of her fingerprints against his tongue. He sucked gently, then harder, raking the tip sensuously with his teeth, applying more and more pressure until she made a small, helpless sound.

Why was he doing this? He'd meant to keep his distance,

tell her what an ass he'd been to try to seduce her, ask her forgiveness. This had to stop. Right now.

Slowly, he withdrew her finger and kissed the wet tip of it. Her whole hand trembled in his grasp. "About last night— I'm sorry, Bettsy," he whispered, holding her gaze.

She blinked and glanced away, her face coloring to a charming pink. "Neil, I—"

A staccato rap on the kitchen door interrupted her. She snatched her hand from his with a horrified gasp. "It's Lindy."

"A pox on his timing. Let him in, will you? Give him a cup of tea while I get dressed." Almost as an afterthought, he turned at the dining room door. "We'll talk later."

As he bounded up the stairs, Neil wondered if he should have explained things the moment he found her. Yes, he ought to have made his plans for them clear right away so she wouldn't worry.

"You look worried, Betts," MacLinden said as he stirred three lumps of sugar into the tea she'd just poured him.

She busied herself buttering another croissant, afraid that if she looked directly at Lindy, he'd guess something was wrong.

Her resolve to keep things platonic between Neil and herself had melted away like snow in July the moment he'd touched her hand. Where in the world had she found the will to refuse him last night? Could she ever find it again? Somehow she had to, for his sake and hers. If only he weren't so damned honorable.

In the meantime, Lindy ought not to know how wanton she'd become, how she'd let Neil touch her and make her burn for him. Neil said his friend was very good at guessing things. Lindy's sharp green eyes seemed to miss very little.

Would he realize that she had nearly become what everyone labeled her? Elizabeth thought she had gained a measure of respect from Trent MacLinden, and she hated to lose it. He had begun to like her as a friend. She could tell by how he teased her and the way he shared information, almost as if he considered her an equal partner in the investigation.

Lindy wasn't one to accept rumors as fact, and she sensed he didn't take those circulating about her as hard truth. Yet. His attitude would change if he learned she'd welcomed to her bed a man she had known less than a week. Even if she hadn't completed the deed, the intent had certainly been there. She wanted Neil so badly it must be obvious to anyone with half an eye.

Elizabeth's opinion of herself declined further knowing that she would be upstairs right now compounding her error with wicked enthusiasm if MacLinden hadn't chosen this early hour to arrive.

Best thing to do was put it from her mind for the time being. There were more immediate things to stew about than her foolish infatuation with Neil Bronwyn. As to Lindy's current question, she would simply admit her second greatest worry.

"I attracted too much attention last night at White's," she said. "One of Terry's friends almost choked, and I was the only one who noticed. There was nothing for it but to do what I could. It caused quite a stir."

"Were you recognized?"

"No, but everyone toasted me. I think Neil may have you haul me in for practicing without a license." She laughed ruefully, hoping he wouldn't chastise her as sharply as Neil had.

"Did you learn anything significant while you were there?"

"I learned to keep my head down and my mouth shut, if that's what you mean," she said. More seriously, she added, "No, Terry was barely mentioned. We didn't stay long and I only talked with Lords Biddenton and Turner, two of Terry's mates from school."

"And I spoke privately with Lord Hobbs at his request," Neil said, interrupting the conversation as he returned, still fiddling with his sleeve links. "He was merely fishing for gossip about the investigation, I think. It seems Colin has been speaking out in Bettsy's defense every chance he gets."

"You didn't tell me that!" Elizabeth said, heartened that

her cousin would stand up for her in the face of such over-whelming evidence. "What a pleasant surprise!"

"Oh well, Marleigh did defend you after a fashion when I questioned him. Wise move whether he's guilty or not," Lindy said, nodding and pursing his lips around his unlit pipe. "Makes him look nobler than noble, don't you think?"

"Couldn't Colin be sincere?" she asked hopefully. "Surely you don't believe he killed Terry. Why on earth should he?"

"Didn't your father consider holding the title in abeyance for your future heir, Betts?" MacLinden asked.

Elizabeth's face heated. Only one thing could keep the near-est existing male relative from succeeding to the title, and no one outside the family had ever discussed that secret. If she weren't such a shameless eavesdropper, she would never have heard it herself. Well, Lindy must know the worst already to have asked such a question.

"Yes, Father considered that at one time. I overheard him talking to Mother about it before she died." She hesitated, uncertain how much to reveal. "You see, Father knew by that time that he could never have a son, and Uncle James was already dead then. That would have made Colin the natural heir, but..."

"But Colin was not fathered by James Marleigh, was he?" MacLinden asked. "According to my mother, there were ru-mors at the time," he explained. "Nob watching's a hobby of hers."

"Uncle James acknowledged him," she said defensively. MacLinden waited for the rest, so she gave it up. "You're right, though. Uncle James was away for a year, so Father said. When he returned, Aunt May was well along with Colin. Nobody knew who the father was. She refused to tell, even on her deathbed."

Neil's boot heels clicked on the tiles as he sauntered across the kitchen. He came to stand behind Elizabeth's chair, resting his hands on her shoulders as he spoke. "So, we have a secret bastard who is afraid you'll contest his right to the title?"

"No!" She craned her neck to look up at him. "It's not

like that at all. Father liked Colin very much. Aunt May was a cousin as well, several times removed, so Colin is related by blood regardless of his paternity. Father remarked to Mother that it was best not to saddle me with such a responsibility. He wanted me to feel free to marry where I chose and not worry about producing heirs for the title."

"And will you?" Neil asked, his face carefully blank.

"Will I what?"

"Marry where you choose? Have children?"

"No," she answered curtly, disturbed by the turn of subject and by the way his hands gripped her shoulders. How could she ever marry now?

"Anyway," she said, shrugging him off with a warning look, "Father wanted Colin to inherit, and he put it in writing, though it was hardly necessary. Everyone who knew about his birth is probably dead by now, and I couldn't prove Uncle James wasn't his father even if I wanted to, which I certainly do not."

MacLinden sat quietly through her confrontation with Neil, looking back and forth as though observing a tennis match. Now that they were finished, he continued as if it had never happened. "So, when your father died, his title went to Colin and his fortune to you."

"Colin has money," she said defensively, feeling obliged to return her cousin's loyalty, sincerely offered or not.

"But not a fortune," MacLinden qualified.

"I'm sure I don't know. He never seems to want for anything, and his property's worth a lot. The manor is entailed, you see, and goes with the earldom. I have the town house here and a hunting box near in Edinburgh."

"And all that lovely money, not to mention your father's private investments," MacLinden insisted.

Neil dragged out a chair and sat down. "So, Colin is one suspect. Anyone else?"

The inspector sighed. "Oh yes, assuming that the attempts on Bettsy's life are connected to Terry's death. And I'm certain they are, since someone definitely used her gun to implicate her.'' He looked from Neil to her and began to enumerate the suspects on his fingers, touching them in turn with his pipe stem.

"There's the maid, Maggie Leffing, who sent Betts the tainted chocolate. She acted on someone's behalf, I'm certain. Now the chit's vanished as though she'd never been.

"Then we have Colin's missing father. If the man's someone important, could be that he's afraid of being named if Betts contests Colin's rights to the title. Could spoil his family life if he has one. I'll be checking into this further, though I do think it's probably a blind alley.''

Lindy continued thoughtfully, "I expect the motive is greed or fear. Maybe a combination. Could be the three suspects are working together. Or it could very well be someone else entirely, such as the man Terry argued with in the theater.''

"If it is one of those first three, that would explain the threat to Bettsy, but why would any of them kill my nephew?'' Neil asked, restlessly pushing himself out of his chair to pace the room.

"Terry, if you recall, had studied estate law in depth at the Inns. That was no secret,'' MacLinden explained. "Given his interest in that field and the power behind his title, he could have assisted Betts quite admirably against Colin's claim. And if he had married Betts, Terry would have had excellent reason to do so. The entailed Marleigh property, even without the title, would have doubled Terry's wealth.''

"But what if there is no connection between the attempts on Bettsy and Terry's murder? Someone could have stolen her pistols just to throw suspicion off himself,'' Neil said, bracing his hands against the table.

"Then we must consider young Lord Turner, whom you met last night,'' Lindy said.

"Turner?'' Neil asked, turning away abruptly. "Surely not!''

"I hear he owed three thousand pounds past what he's worth to Terry in gaming debts. Reason enough, don't you think?''

"I don't believe it," Neil declared. "I know Turner, and he's not the sort who would shoot a man, even one who planned to ruin him. Terry would never have insisted on calling in markers on a friend. Surely there would be some sort of written record among Terry's papers if the rumor were true."

"All the same," MacLinden said, downing the dregs of his tea and rising. He picked up his hat and flicked an imaginary piece of dust off the brim. "We can't dismiss the possibility that Turner may have killed Terry and taken the I.O.U.s the same night. Unless you do find those markers, though, I haven't even cause enough to question him. See what you can find out."

He threw his cape over his shoulder and looked directly at Elizabeth. "And do have a care, Betts. Our investigation could go on for months and we wouldn't want anything to…alter your disguise." He looked pointedly at her middle and winked.

Elizabeth knew she blushed to the soles of her feet.

"You told him what happened?" Neil asked as soon as the door closed behind Lindy.

"Are you mad? Of course I didn't tell him! And nothing *did* happen. Not really."

Neil smiled. "So he guessed. Doesn't matter. We are marrying before the week's out anyway, and Lindy will be a witness."

"*Marrying?* You *are* mad! No!" Elizabeth couldn't believe Neil's brain had ceased to function overnight.

"What do you mean, no? Haven't you considered what will result from last night?" His anger increased a hundredfold.

"Were you that drunk? *Nothing* happened last night! There can be no 'result,' as you call it. I stopped you, in case you don't remember!" she shouted, unable to control her own rage.

"You wouldn't have stopped me this morning if Lindy hadn't arrived when he did. You won't stop me next time, either!" His voice continued to rise. "The 'result' will be a full-scale, unbridled affair without anyone's blessing if we don't marry. I can't do that to you, Bettsy."

"You won't do anything at all to me, you self-righteous prig! This stops right here, right now, do you hear me?" She stamped her foot and winced as a pain shot up her leg. "There will be no affair between us! Or marriage! Clear enough?"

The sudden silence lengthened. She watched his anger shift to worry. His emotions read like a large-type news sheet. "You won't try to leave, will you, Bettsy? If I promise to behave, will you promise to stay?"

"Leave? Where in the world would I go?" she asked softly. He would listen to reason now. "Neil, look. I'm at your mercy here. Don't push us into something that could be disastrous for both of us. Can't we put this physical thing aside and try to be friends?" She smiled, trying to cajole him into agreement. "I think we had a good beginning on friendship."

Neil lifted one hand and outlined her face without quite touching her. The tension stretched to breaking. "A good beginning, love? I drugged you, abducted you, held you by force and then dressed you up like a man. What in the name of God would you call a *bad* beginning?"

Elizabeth laughed as she grasped his outstretched hand and shook it. "Come on, Neil, be my friend?"

He nodded seriously. "'Til death us do part. And thereto I pledge thee my troth."

"You're impossible," she said with a defeated sigh.

"I know, but a friend would overlook that." He paused, caressing her hand with his, thoughtfully tracing each finger. "I've been impulsive, reckless, rude and at times downright wicked. I try very hard to control myself, but sometimes I slip when I lose my concentration. You cause havoc with a man's concentration, Bettsy."

He raised his eyes to hers, and she recognized intense yearning of a nonsexual kind. "You really have forgiven me all that, haven't you, Bettsy? You just accept me as I am, don't you? Do you have any idea how amazing that is to me?"

Elizabeth tried to make light of it. She gave him her best

Percival Betts grin. "Well, I'll say this much for you, Doc, you're almost never predictable and certainly not dull." She winked. "That's what I like best about you, I think. I really do hate it when you act like a stuffy old stick. You go all serious on me and get so terribly, awfully *correct*. Could you not do that? Couldn't you just be yourself?"

The strangest mix of emotions crossed his face—confusion, disbelief and finally something like wonder. He laughed aloud and kissed her noisily on the lips—a truly friendly smack that had nothing at all to with lust and everything to do with affection. She considered the bargain sealed. Neil was going to be her friend now. Just a very good friend.

Happy as that made her, she admitted to a twinge of regret for all that might have been.

Boredom set in about three o'clock that afternoon. The place felt empty without Neil. Though he'd been gone for only two hours, it was the first time he had left her alone in Havington House since they had come to London. Elizabeth closed the door to the former conservatory, which would soon serve as their research lab, and started across the hall.

The unexpected clack of the door knocker made her jump. Neil had laid down the law before he left for the medical-supply house. She was not to answer if anyone called. *Anyone.* MacLinden had his own little knocking code and always came to the kitchen door. Oliver, Neil's driver, was somewhere about, but he wouldn't knock on the front door. Who could be calling? she wondered.

Quietly, she tipped through the hall and into the front parlor to peek through the draperies. A shiny maroon coach hitched to a fine pair of grays stood in the front drive, its driver and footman dressed in splendid black-and-silver livery.

Again the knocking, sharp and demanding, broke the silence. She stepped closer to the far edge of the window, anxious to satisfy her curiosity.

"Botheration!" she gasped, and leapt back. Too late. The woman on the steps had seen her, or at least the moving drapery had grabbed the visitor's attention. Well, there was nothing for it now but to see who was beating down the door. It wasn't as though it was someone Elizabeth knew, who might expose her. Probably some relative of one of Neil's soldier-patients. Maybe a society matron come to offer her condolences for Terry's death. No harm in taking the message for Neil and sending the lady on her way.

Elizabeth squared her shoulders, slipped on her spectacles and marched to the front door. The moment she opened it, the woman pushed her way in and stabbed the floor tiles with the tip of her parasol.

"What do you mean, keeping me standing about like some common delivery person? His lordship will dismiss you for this impertinence, see if he doesn't!"

Elizabeth gave the guest the once-over she thought gentlemen might give actresses at the Strand. This one was no actress, though. Pearls dripped from her ears like huge tears. Tasteful pearls. The watered-silk morning gown shimmered like old gold. *Old money.* In her heyday, the beauty must have been what the old ton would have called a diamond of the first water, an original. Probably in her late twenties, she was still lovely beyond belief, if one overlooked the haughtiness. Right now she looked mad as hell.

"Announce me at once, you ingrate!" the dark-haired vision demanded with another vicious tap of her lacy weapon.

The temptation was just too great. Elizabeth nodded once. "Of course, I've been expecting you all morning. You're quite late, you know."

The woman drew in her chin, peered down her nose and glared. "Expecting me? Late? Whatever are you talking about?"

Percival Betts smiled, showing every tooth. "You *are* the new housekeeper, aren't you?"

There was only a split second to enjoy the speechless horror of her victim before a gloved hand cracked across Elizabeth's cheek, causing her eyeglasses to hang suspended from one ear. The sting was worth it, however. She watched in amusement while the woman stalked around the foyer in a royal snit, looking for something to break.

"Forgive me if I've erred, madame," Elizabeth purred, adjusting her eyewear. "If you *aren't* the new hire, do allow me to apologize and introduce myself."

The amber eyes snapped and the lightly rouged mouth sliced a line across the ivory powdered face. "I don't care who you are, you pea brain! Announce me to the earl this instant!"

"Oh dear, you'll be sorry to hear he's not at home," Elizabeth said, trying to suppress her grin.

"Oh yes, he is," a deep voice rumbled from just behind her.

Drat, he'd come in the back way and probably heard it all. Elizabeth wrinkled her nose. Now she was in for it. Neil would rake her over like a leaf-strewn lawn. He was wearing his wait-till-I-get-you-alone look, and she knew better than to expect kisses when he did.

She watched him transfer his attention to the guest and marveled at the sudden lack of emotion on his face. She'd never seen such calculated indifference. This woman meant either nothing at all to Neil or else everything in the world.

"Emma," he said in a clipped tone.

Elizabeth watched, thunderstruck, as the woman swooped at him like a bird of prey. Shapely arms clutched him about the neck in a stranglehold, while the voluptuous body heaved with patently fake sobs. "Oh, Neil, darling, I just heard about your tragedy. Nothing under the sun could have kept me from you!"

"I could if I had a harpoon handy," Elizabeth muttered. Neil's threatening glare silenced her.

"Would you excuse us…Percival?" he growled. It was not a request.

Elizabeth didn't dare take it as one. She sauntered toward the doorway to the conservatory, flicking a glance over one shoulder. "You will call if you need anything, milord? A towel, smelling salts, a stout *stick?*"

Neil didn't answer, but then Elizabeth didn't expect that he would. Ducking through the door, she closed it all but a crack, then listened shamelessly.

The Emma woman's watery assault on Neil's shirtfront dwindled to pretty sighs.

Elizabeth opened the door a little more so that she could see better. Good Lord, the floozy was kissing him! Well, Elizabeth fumed as Neil pulled back sharply, he could have disengaged a little sooner than that!

"Why are you here, Emma?" Neil held the woman at arm's length and asked in a tone that could freeze water.

"Oh, my poor Neil, how you must be suffering. I know how dear your little Terry was to you. Believe me, darling, I know exactly how you feel. Paul died just last year, and though ours was not a love match—"

"Thank you for your sympathy, Emma." Neil's words cut her short. "I must ask you to leave now."

"But, Neil, I know you need someone to talk to, someone who can offer you a shoulder."

*Ha!* Elizabeth thought. Not likely she'd stop with a shoulder! The bloody cow! The urge to dash out and land a bootprint on the backside of that watered silk was overwhelming.

Neil clamped a hand over a dimpled elbow and ushered the woman to the door. "You have to go, Emma. There's no one here to chaperon you. The staff's at the country house and only my assistant and I are in residence. Your reputation's at risk."

He opened the door and had her halfway through when she turned, face earnest as a Calvinist preacher's. "I'd risk anything for you, Neil. You must know that. There's nothing now to keep us apart."

"Goodbye, Emma." His cold indifference never once faltered.

"I'll be back when you're feeling more the thing, Neil. Do take care now!" Emma What's-her-name glided down the steps and into the waiting coach.

The clip-clop of the grays died away before the door closed.

"You can come out now, Betts," Neil said in the same tone he'd used with the woman. Elizabeth shivered at the coldness of it.

She decided on offense rather than defense. What did she have to lose? He was probably as angry as he was going to get.

Her boots rang out on the shiny tile of the hall as she marched forward, right up to Neil, and poked a finger in his tear-dampened shirtfront. "Just who was that wretched watering pot, your former mistress or something?"

"Or something. She's my former fiancée." His eyes looked blank as a frozen pond.

"She slapped my face," Elizabeth said, hoping for some kind of response other than the dead expression he wore. "Cracked my spectacles, too."

"You had it coming," he said without a blink. Turning on his heel, he spoke without looking back. "Don't answer that door again or *I'll* slap your face." The clack of his boot heels grew muffled on the dining room carpet, sounded faint on the kitchen tiles and disappeared altogether with the vicious slam of the back door.

# Chapter Eight

"Well, I'll be damned!" Elizabeth mumbled into the eerie stillness of the foyer. Here was a Neil she didn't know at all.

She'd seen him threatening, loving, twisted by grief, hateful, sarcastic, even fearful a time or two. But now? He showed nothing, absolutely nothing, of the passionate man she knew him to be. This iciness and total absence of emotion was a hundred times worse than heated anger.

Was it only this morning he had promised so reluctantly to stop trying to seduce her and be her friend? Was this the same man whose face she'd been able to read like the Sunday news? Now she'd have to guess just what this Emma person meant to him.

All right. Fact: Emma Thingamabob had been engaged to Neil. He'd either thrown her over or she had reneged. Which? She'd mentioned a Paul Somebody who had not been a love match. A husband. That probably meant Emma had left Neil hanging. Not good, if Emma had been the one to cry off. Neil might still love her.

Surely he was not so dense as to languish over a whiny, overblown termagant who knocked people's spectacles off. No, be fair, Elizabeth grudgingly ordered herself. The woman was drop-dead gorgeous and rich to boot, judging by her trappings. And with a sterling reputation, if Neil's warning about the lack of a chaperon was any indication.

Now Neil had stalked out, obviously angry and upset under that dreadful, forced composure of his. Some friend she was to provoke him so.

Elizabeth's heart picked up speed when she heard the back door open again. He was back! She rushed to the kitchen to meet him and stopped short when Oliver, who served as Neil's groom and driver, appeared instead.

"How do, m'lady. Lord Doc just said I'm t'keep ye company." He doffed his cap and ran a knobby hand over his balding head.

Elizabeth nodded. Oliver was always about somewhere in the house or the stables, but it was the first time he'd dared to approach her and say more than "good day."

"Would you like a cup of tea, Oliver?"

The man chuckled as he ducked his head. "Thankee, ma'am, I'd be obliged. Just wanted ye t'know I'm about, in case ye be needin' me fer anything." He shifted from one foot to the other, picking at the band on his cap before looking up. "'E ain't mad at yerself. Thought ye ought t'know that."

"You overheard my little confrontation with the lady?" She saw by his expression that he had.

"Wouldna been doin' my job if I 'adn't. Lord Doc's right strict about yer well-bein', as 'e should be." Oliver hesitated only a second before adding in a slightly belligerent voice, "An' she *ain't* no lady, if ye take my meaning."

Elizabeth's eyes widened with avid interest. The man was dying to tell her something, and not a jot more eager than she was to hear it.

She had absolutely no qualms whatever about listening to tales out of school. Much of her early education revolved around such, and now, when she had a perfect opportunity to learn more about Neil, she wasn't about to give up the nasty habit.

"Pray, do go on, Oliver, while I put on the kettle." She ushered him toward a chair.

He grinned as he settled in for tea, revealing a wide gap between his front teeth and huge dimples in his weatherworn cheeks. "Aye, well, 'twas she who near done th' Lord Doc in, that's what! Buggered off—beggin' yer pardon—*left* with an old lord twice 'er age. She wuz hanging over th' anvil with that one the very night Doc went with 'is 'at in 'is 'and to 'er old da about wedding 'er.

"Best thing that coulda 'appened, if ye ask me, but Lord Doc was mighty 'eartsore. Stayed drunk fer a week straight once th' word got round. Sobered up then and wished 'em well ter their faces. Doc's got class, 'e 'as. Bought 'is rank and took out to th' war straightaway."

"Ahh," Elizabeth said, nodding thoughtfully. "So the wretch eloped to Gretna Green with that Paul man? Did she ever tell Doc why?" It was pretty obvious without the explanation.

"In a word, money. There wuz th' old lord's title as well, o' course. Doc had just finished schoolin' up in Edinburgh and wuz planning to set up office in Maidstone then. Chucked it all, 'e did.

"Gor, we—Earl Jon, Master Terry and me—all wuz thinkin' 'e was going off to fight and die. Th' earl sent me on after 'im to watch 'is back. Thanks be th' army nobs knowed what wuz what and stuck 'im in Salamanca at th' orspital so Doc wouldn't get hisself kilt."

"Why are you telling me all this, Oliver?" Elizabeth thought it rather strange that the man would open up so freely all of a sudden when he hadn't said more than a passing word to her until now.

"Ye gotta be th' one to save Lord Doc from 'isself, m'lady. Powerful stuck on the woman, 'e wuz. Might still be. 'Er old man's dead now and she's out to git another'n. Lord Doc's a bleedin' earl now, don't ye see, with a bank full o' blunt! Ripe pickin's fer such as 'er."

"Why would you care? If he loves her so much, wouldn't you want him to be happy?"

Oliver grunted in disgust. "''Appy wi' th' loiks of 'er? Give over! She ain't but a cut above a *hoor* if 'e could just see it. I've knowed Lord Doc since 'e wuz a babe peein' 'is nappies.

Ain't a mean bone in 'is body and 'e bleedin' well don't deserve t'be leg-shackled to summat loik *'er!*''

Elizabeth nodded to show she understood. "Quite. Well, Oliver, you've been most enlightening. I'll certainly see what I can do to steer his lordship out of this situation.'' She rose and stuck out her hand.

He shook it with the grip of a wrestler, then jerked his paw back and shoved it in his pocket. "Good tea,'' he muttered, grinning bashfully before ambling out the kitchen door.

Now here was a quandary, Elizabeth thought. She rubbed the side of her face where the woman's hand had struck her. Oliver was right, of course. Neil didn't deserve the likes of this Emma person. Nobody short of a hardened criminal would.

Pity Elizabeth couldn't tell whether he was in any immediate danger of succumbing. His attitude toward the woman certainly wasn't loverlike in the least, but he could be hiding the pain he felt. She promised herself, just as she had promised Oliver, that she'd do whatever was necessary to protect Neil from the clutches of Emma the Witch. She owed him that much.

Neil returned just before dark, his mood immeasurably improved by drink. At least he wasn't scowling.

Elizabeth wrinkled her nose as he swaggered through the kitchen. "What in heaven's name is that smell?''

"Hmm?'' His eyebrows rose over his bleary gaze. "Smell?''

"What have you been drinking?'' She enunciated each word as though speaking to a dull-wit, which he certainly looked to be at this point.

"Oh, gin,'' he stated absently, trying to hang his jacket on a bow-backed chair and failing miserably. He stared at it, frowning comically, as it slid to the floor in a heap. His thought processes seemed to tangle over whether he should risk bending down to pick it up. He sighed over the decision.

"Neil," she said, plucking at his shirtsleeve to get his attention. "Why don't you sit down before you fall down?"

"I must have got…overserved," he said unnecessarily, still staring at the coat on the floor.

"Do tell." Elizabeth fought a grin. Here was yet another Neil she hadn't met. He looked incredibly boyish with his hair tumbling over his brow and his loosened tie dangling to one side.

His expression wavered between shamefaced and defensive. "Driving me t' drink," he said, fighting the slur of his words. "You are. 'S all your fault." He poked her sharply in the chest with a forefinger and then smoothed out the front of her shirt with a clumsy hand. A sudden, happy smile warned her he'd completely lost his train of thought.

"Don't be absurd," Elizabeth countered, grabbing his wandering hands just before they reached her cloth-bound breast. "Emma What's-her-face's visit prompted this, and you know it."

He nodded and swayed to the left, automatically grabbing at the chair. "I wanted to choke her," he whispered confidentially.

"What a coincidence. So did I. Now why don't we get you upstairs and into bed? Come on, lean on me and mind your feet." She slid one arm around his waist and guided him through the door and into the hall.

Neil giggled. He actually giggled, and Elizabeth joined him. She admitted her own glee had little to do with the fact that he was drunk and a lot to do with the fact that he had wanted to strangle their afternoon visitor. He should have started drinking earlier in the day, before the she-cat came to call.

The front door knocker beat out a jaunty little rhythm as they staggered through the hall to the stairs.

"Someone's at the door, Neil!" she said, shifting his weight against the newel post. "Should I answer it?"

He grinned and latched on to the stair rail. "Why not?"

Still she hesitated. It couldn't be Lindy. And if Emma the

Hoor had come back, she'd be pounding instead of tapping a tune.

Whoever it was had no business seeing the Earl of Havington three sails to the wind and in danger of sprawling on the floor. As quickly as she could, Elizabeth grabbed his arm and guided him into the study.

"Sit down and keep quiet," she ordered, parking him in one of the leather wing chairs. Closing the door behind her, she went to see who their evening visitor might be.

"Little Doc!" Biddenton crowed. "Hoped we'd find you home! Told Tun we might if we came by early." He pushed past her and entered the foyer, glancing around with awe at the gilt mirror and the matching rosewood stands with their Imari vases. "Gaw, what digs! Would ya look at this, Tun! No wonder Terry never asked us by. Prob'ly thought we'd nick something!"

Turner followed him in, shoving his cane and hat at Elizabeth. "Offer us a nip, will you, Little Doc? That stinky hansom ride's left me dry as a bull's teat."

"No, I don't think..." Elizabeth hedged. Apparently, Terry had been wise enough to keep company with these two only at the clubs. Too late to follow suit; they'd already breached the fort.

"Aw, c'mon, mate. Old Doc won't care if we dip into his stock. Demmed fine cellar, I'll bet." Biddie slapped her roughly on the back and stacked his hat atop Turner's.

She led them toward the parlor. Just as they passed the study door, Neil's voice rang out. "Bettsy! Where are you? Can't find a glass for the life of me!"

"Oh, Lord!" She rolled her eyes and pushed Biddie toward the front door, hoping Turner would follow. "You two best come back tomorrow. His lordship's in a mood."

"Ha!" Biddie resisted and stood his ground. "Mood, my foot. He sounds foxed to me. This I have got to see!"

"Wait! You don't want to..." She gave it up when Biddie plunged into the study, Turner hot on his heels, as usual.

"Lads!" Neil greeted them merrily from the sideboard,

where he had managed to unstopper a decanter. Apparently, he'd located the glasses. "Wanna whiskey?"

"Does th' devil speak French?" they choroused.

Elizabeth collapsed in Neil's vacated chair with a hand to her head. What *now?* The best she could hope for was that they would drink themselves into a stupor before Neil said anything to ruin her disguise.

Then a greater fear surfaced. What if he mentioned that Turner was one of the suspects in Terry's murder?

God, why in the world had she answered the door? Every time she did, it was like opening a bloody Pandora's box! First Emma and now these two scapegraces.

"To women," Neil was saying as he clinked his glass to Biddie's and then Turner's. "Devil take 'em, eh?"

"Devil take 'em!" the two replied in unison. They knocked back their drinks in a gulp.

"Female troubles, milord?" Turner asked slyly as he held out his tumbler to catch Neil's unsteady offering of a refill.

"Belly cramps," Neil intimated with a suggestive wink, and then hooted, slapping one knee and slopping liquor onto the carpet. After a moment, Biddie got the "female trouble" joke and laughed wildly. Turner was already doubled over, gasping.

Elizabeth rescued the crystal container and most of the whiskey, setting it carefully on the sideboard. "How about a game?" she asked brightly, scrambling for the cards Neil kept in a side drawer of the desk. She fanned the deck. "What shall it be, whist or faro?"

"Can't see th' spots," Neil said, shaking his head. "No, no, I need t'set th' lads straight on thish issue." He sliced the air with one hand for emphasis. "Women!"

"Yes, oh great font of wisdom?" Biddie asked, leaning forward to catch whatever pearls a doctor might drop.

"A scourge, the lot of 'em," Neil said, and directed an apologetic look toward Elizabeth. "Sorry, but you know 's true." He hiccuped. "You…are a case in pint—*point.*"

Biddie looked confused and then concerned. "Little Doc's got woman troubles, too?"

Elizabeth panicked. The only way to shut Neil up was to drown him out. Or drown him, period. "Yes! Oh, yes, I do, Biddie," she said quickly, to forestall whatever else Neil was poised to say about her. "Having a dreadful time with the cheeky little chit. But there you go. It's to be expected, eh? Daresay you've had your share of wrangles with 'em and know exactly what I mean. You, Turner? Been put to the screws lately as well?" Elizabeth snagged a quick breath and plowed on. "Damned shame, all we have to go through just for a bit of pleasure now and again. Not fair, is it? Take heed, though—I mean to prevail in this and won't give up until I have her. No, sir, I mean to keep at her until I coax her right into my—"

"What the *devil* are you bletherin' about?" Neil interrupted, frowning and trying his best to focus. Endearing as he looked, she wanted to crack him over the head with something hard.

"You know very well, Doc," she said with a warning glance. "It was you brought this up. Least you can do is let me tell it. Now *be quiet!*"

She noticed his perplexity waver, then clear a bit. He pressed his lips together and nodded. Maybe the gin was wearing off and the whiskey hadn't hit him yet. She heaved a sigh of relief when she saw him study his glass and then set it aside.

"So tell us, then," Turner urged, leaning forward in his chair. "About your girl."

"Do go on, Betts," Biddie agreed, sipping his drink.

Elizabeth shook her head sadly. "Hate to recount it. Wretched situation." She wondered what in the world she could tell them about a nonexistent woman she'd just manufactured.

"Got you all stirred up, then, and holdin' out on you?" Biddie asked, sighing loudly. "Just like a female, ain't it?"

Elizabeth nodded, trying to look pitiful. "Won't come across. Wants a chap with more blunt, y'see. Can't figure how I'll compete on a doctor's pay, either, so there you are."

"I've got it! We'll help you, Biddie and me," Turner offered, slapping his skinny knee. "We could talk to her, see? And tell her what a canny one you are, bein' a doctor. Say you're up to snuff on what women like and all that. You *are*, aren't you? Up to snuff, that is?" He colored from his collar up, but still managed a sly smile. "Hafta be with all those naughty books from the med library. All th' sweet spots down pat and done to a turn, eh?"

Biddie was virtually dancing in his chair. "Great thought, Tun. Hey, we'll bring Sadie and Janice with us, too. Make it a right old party. Doc—I mean milord—what say you come, too? Find you a bird and tag along with us! We'll make th' rounds."

"No!" Elizabeth shouted, then winced when all three pinned her with unblinking stares. "Well, I don't know," she qualified. "She might not come out with me again. No, I'd best let 'er go."

"Give me her direction and I'll see she agrees," Biddie demanded. "Visit the gel myself and won't leave 'til she caves in to seein' you. Tun here will help me. Got a better idea! Bring 'er to the theater. They all like that. She'll come."

Elizabeth groaned. "Why don't you two toddle off and let me get my wits together? I'll let you know tomorrow." She must get them out of the house before Neil gave everything away. "Come on, I'll see you out." She rose and they followed, talking excitedly about the following night's plans.

"You'll set it up with her, Percy?" Turner asked as they stepped out into the night. "We *have* to meet her and tell her what a huge mistake she's making."

"We'll see. And don't call me Percy, Tun," she said, using the nickname Biddie used for him.

"'Night, Little Doc," Biddie called over his shoulder as he and Turner marched down the walk. "Meet you at the Lyceum at eight! Don't forget now. And make Doc come, too. Had no idea that old rascal was such a rakehell. Got prime whiskey, too."

She stared into the darkness as their footsteps faded away. She couldn't wait until Neil sobered up enough to tell him that because of his big mouth, they now had to scrape up escorts for the theater—two women who didn't exist.

There wouldn't be a real problem, though. All Elizabeth had to do was send round a note to Biddie tomorrow saying that she'd broken with her "bird" and wouldn't be attending, after all.

Sweet of the two to want to fix her problem. She couldn't help but like them. Suspecting Tun of murder was ludicrous.

Elizabeth smiled to herself, proud of her quick resourcefulness in warding off a potential disaster. If Biddie or Tun ever guessed she wasn't a man, word would rush through London like the Great Fire.

A muffled snort evened out to a steady snore as she reached the study door. Neil lay sprawled in the leather chair, his arms hanging over the sides and his booted feet stretched out toward the empty fireplace. She laughed softly at the sight. He looked so human like this, his studied dignity and usual air of competence in total ruin. *Blue Ruin,* she thought, and laughed at her own joke. Dr. Neil Bronwyn, earl of Havington, a gin swiller. Who'd have thought it?

In the stillness, she heard a tapping on the kitchen door. *Lindy.* She backed out of the study and went to let him in.

"Hullo," she said, taking his cape and hanging it on the hook by the door. "This place is a veritable meeting hall today!" She poured him a brandy and proceeded to bring him up-to-date on all their visitors. He listened, nodding now and again until she reached the end of her report.

"Emma Throckmorton actually had the nerve to show her face, eh? Can't say I'm surprised."

Elizabeth rolled her eyes upward and shook her head. "Ooh, that woman!"

"Well, you needn't worry that Doc will let her back in his life. She's had her chance." Lindy polished off his drink and slouched comfortably in his chair, elbows propped on the table. "Can't say I like his going off on a tear like this. Not like Neil at all. Never seen him drunk once, even in the war."

"Oh, he did this before, right after she left him. Oliver said so,'' Elizabeth said, and poured herself a brandy. If anybody deserved a measure of false comfort after a day like today, she did. She coughed as it burned in her throat.

"Go easy on that stuff, Betts," Lindy warned. "One of you flown with drink is enough for one night. Shall I help you put him to bed?"

"No, he's too bloody big to budge. Let him sleep where he is. I'll throw a blanket over him later."

She leaned forward on the table, clasping her hands around her glass. "You don't really think Turner could have killed Terry, do you, Lindy?"

He released his unlit pipe and smoothed his mustache with two fingers. "Not very likely, but you never know. I think you ought to go with them tomorrow night, though. Try to get a handle on what the man is really like."

She laughed. "I *know* what he's like. Turner follows Biddie around like a well-trained pup and rarely has an original thought in his head. He's harmless as a rice pudding."

"I'd still like you to go, and Neil as well, since they invited him along."

"You're forgetting two minor details, Lindy," she said, loosening her foulard with a forefinger. "Our *dolly birds*."

He grinned, pushing away from the table and getting ready to leave. "I'll send two round for you."

"Just like that?" She laughed. "You'll send two round? May I ask who, or will you just surprise us with a couple of unfortunates off the street?"

"I'll send my girl, Helen Trawick, for you, and my sister, Bonnie, for Neil. Not to worry, I'll prepare them for the act."

"You'll tell them the truth?" Elizabeth couldn't believe Lindy would risk it even with women of such close acquaintance.

He patted her shoulder. "Only as much as they need to know. Helen's an actress and Bonnie's game for anything. They'll do."

"I don't like this, Lindy," Elizabeth warned, "not by half."

The inspector stuck his pipe in his pocket and pulled on his gloves. "Well, you and Neil need to get to know Turner a bit better. And there's always the off chance you might come across the man Terry met at the theater that night. Keep a sharp ear, Betts. Everything you learn, even the seemingly insignificant, could be very important to the whole."

Elizabeth reluctantly agreed and said good-night. Lindy was right, of course. So far they had turned up nothing that would help find Terry's murderer. The suspect list hadn't shortened by so much as one.

All they had to show for their ruse at this point was her galloping attraction for Neil Bronwyn and his determination to take up her salvation where Terry had left off.

Somehow she had to put an end to both, get this murder solved and disappear.

Elizabeth climbed the stairs, weary and worried about tomorrow night's fiasco. She doubted sleep would come easily in spite of the brandy she'd consumed. It was almost enough to make her envy the man downstairs, slumbering away in drunken oblivion.

Sick of the whole masquerade, she donned her most feminine nightgown instead of the usual nightshirt. The small, pink, ribbon roses dotting the bodice made her feel girlish again. The silk soothed her flesh where the linen had bound her breasts.

Suddenly impatient with herself for her missish turn of mind, Elizabeth donned a robe, grabbed an extra coverlet out of the chest and went down to settle Neil in for the night. He shifted in the chair as she tried to tuck the blanket around him. He looked so disheveled sprawled there, head to one side, legs outspread, arms dangling. One hand snaked up in a clumsy gesture and gripped her waist. She shivered, feeling his long fingers clasp the top of her hip. No harm enjoying such a meaningless touch, she thought, and leaned into it.

She wanted to kiss him again, just once. It could be a sort of farewell to what might have been if they'd met under other conditions, before she'd become society's favorite bone to worry. In his current state, he'd never know it happened. All she had to do was bend down and press her lips to his. The odor of the liquor on his breath ought to keep her senses intact, if nothing else. One kiss, full out, that was all.

Quickly, she bent and closed her mouth over his. So sweet, despite the gin-and-whiskey flavor. Neil remained motionless. Too motionless, she thought too late. The gentle snoring had stopped. The hand on her hip tightened. The other joined it on the opposite side.

Before she knew what had happened, he'd swung her onto his lap. His mouth plundered hers with such ferocity she couldn't catch her breath. His hands were everywhere at once, grasping, sliding over her skin, under her robe, under her night rail.

Elizabeth's own moan of pleasure took her by surprise. She ought to fight him, she knew. She ought to push away from him and run for dear life.

Then he said it—words that no one had ever spoken to her in the whole of her twenty years. "I love you. God, I do love you." His voice fell on her ears like a benediction.

He didn't mean it, of course. At least he didn't mean that he loved *her*. She knew it at once, but couldn't resist pretending just for that moment.

"And I love you," she answered, realizing for the first time that her own words were as true as his were meaningless. She did love him, with all the feeling that was inside her.

Neil cared about people, cared about her. He was doing everything within his power to save her from a false charge of murder and from her own danger, even though she was nothing to him really. Just his nephew's folly, a sad mistake in judgment.

His hand closed on her breast and squeezed. Need shot through her blood like a flood tide. Fear that he would stop urged her to the next kiss. She found his mouth and opened her own, savoring the taste of cheap gin, good whiskey and Neil.

Her mind searched furiously for some kind of reason to

remove herself from his lap. No, she argued against logic, this was what she wanted with all her soul. Besides, she rationalized, he would never remember it.

And she could remember it always. Through all those lonely nights to come.

At that, a sly thought formed perfectly amidst her fog of passion. If she were not a virgin, she could become his mistress. Her innocence was all that had stopped her from surrendering last night. She knew that a man could tell when a woman had never succumbed. There was the barrier her nurse had told her about and warned her to save for her husband. Well, there would be no husband in her future now. Why not take a lover? Not just any lover, but Neil, the man she really loved.

Neil would insist on marriage, even more strongly than he already had, if he knew all the rumors about her were false. He'd marry her to reestablish her good name, and in turn, he'd lose his own. If he took her innocence and knew that he had, she would be Lady Havington before the week was out. That might be heaven for a while, but he'd hate her for it eventually. He'd be ruined and it would be her fault.

But suppose he thought the rumors true? If he took her tonight and had no memory of it, she could pretend to be as wanton as the world had accused. There would be no need for him to feel obligated to marry her. He would be hers for the duration of the investigation at least, as long as they were together here at Havington House.

If she played her part as mistress well enough after tonight, he would never mention marriage again.

Later, after they had solved Terry's murder, she could hide away in Scotland where he'd never find her and he could get on with his life, marry someone suitable who would give him heirs. No one would know he'd had any dealings at all with the notorious Lady Marleigh. But she would have her memories, stores of them to give her comfort in her isolation.

That decision made, Elizabeth threw herself into another kiss that banished thought altogether.

Neil slid from the chair to the floor with surprising agility, gripping Elizabeth in his arms, rolling on top of her, still kissing her with wild abandon. His mouth trailed wet heat along her neck, nuzzling the ribbon roses and the ties of her night rail until he found an opening. Lips scorched her skin like a brand.

She absorbed his incoherent love words and answered in kind. His touches grew more urgent, spreading from her breasts, down her belly and lower. She arched against his hand and cried out when he found her.

"Now," he groaned against the curve of her neck.

She felt him fumble with his buttons and curse. Brushing his hand aside, she undid his trousers and shifted them down enough to free him.

Oh God, he was huge! Panic almost set in, but she knew it was too late to stop—too late for him and for her. He moved into position—she didn't like to dwell on how automatically he did that—and braced himself unsteadily on his elbows above her.

His lower body probed clumsily, and he groaned in frustration against her ear. More adept, or at least more sober than he, Elizabeth maneuvered her hips to guide him into her.

He lunged. The screech of pain slipped out before she could stop it. Passion, for her, died a swift death in an instant, but she was determined to see this through. Either he hadn't heard her little scream or was too involved to notice.

Holding her breath, she waited while he thrust into her violently, endlessly. She was not at all impressed. It was damned uncomfortable and not much of a memory to make, after all.

The discomfort dwindled after a moment as her body grew used to the invasion. Elizabeth felt a great need to soothe his desperation, but she had no idea what to do. Stroking his face and shoulders, she moved with him as best she could.

Suddenly he tensed, growled with what sounded like agony and collapsed on her like a felled oak. "Mine," he whispered, and the next breath was a snore.

So that was *it?* Well, she admitted, things had been earth-

shakingly pleasant up to a point. And right there at the last...
She knew, from Nanny's teaching, that it was only painful the
one time. Maybe the next, when he wasn't so deep in his cups,
it would be nicer.

One could always hope.

Elizabeth heaved at his deadweight until she managed to
roll him off her and onto his back.

The look on his face should belong to an angel, she
thought—one who had a secure place in paradise. The idea
made her smile. She had done that for him, made him look
that way. Not Emma with her oh-so-perfect nose in the air,
but Little Dr. Bettsy.

Then she chanced to look down at his body, relaxed now
and not quite so fearsome. She saw blood on his member and
her night rail as well. Nanny had said there would be, so it
was all right. Perfectly normal.

And a dead giveaway if he ever saw it.

Leaping to her feet, she rushed to the kitchen for a cloth
and water. She washed him gently, terrified he would wake
up and find her performing such an inelegant chore.

Rearranging his trousers so that she could fasten them was
a major undertaking. That finally done, she covered him with
the blanket and ran upstairs to take care of herself.

Well, the act itself hadn't been all that thrilling, but she
hadn't expected it to be, under the circumstances. Elizabeth
refused to dwell on the specifics of what had just happened.
She had solved the problem of her virginity. That had been
her aim and she had been successful. It felt exhilarating to
take at least this small measure of control over her future.
Now, if she wanted Neil, she could have him without its re-
sulting in any kind of permanent arrangement that might ruin
him.

She rolled up her bloodstained nightgown and stuffed it in
the very bottom corner of her valise, which she stored on the
back shelf of the dressing-room cupboard. She didn't dare include it in the laundry Oliver collected for the washerwoman.

Donning a plain nightshirt like she usually wore, she crawled into bed and hugged her pillow to her breast.

Well, she was his lover now, in a manner of speaking.

If he intended to pursue a course of intimacy—and she was fairly certain it would come to that—she could succumb with a clear conscience and assume all the responsibility.

Once she proved just how experienced she was, he would thank his lucky stars he'd escaped with his bachelorhood intact.

The thought ought to have satisfied her.

# Chapter Nine

Neil rolled to one side and groaned at the agony slicing through his head. He knew it would be hours before he could function with any degree of normalcy. He also knew he deserved it. Pulling himself upright took all the strength he had and then some.

It had been six years since he'd drunk that much. And *gin*, for God's sake. Gin always did this to him, and he should have known better. It was too large a price to pay for a few hours of forgetfulness. Damn Emma.

She wasn't worth a passing thought, much less a bout with a bottle. Her visit wasn't the main thing that had set him off, however. Getting away from Bettsy had been imperative. He'd wanted to shake her senseless for disobeying him and putting herself in danger. It could have been anyone at the door, even the man who had tried to kill her. Before he lost all his wits and took her over his knee, he'd decided to order Oliver to keep watch while he cooled off at the nearest pub. Wouldn't have done to take himself off to one of the gentlemen's clubs in that frame of mind. He'd walked the few blocks that took him out of the prime district and into a modest, working-class neighborhood.

Sergeant Maxwell, new owner of the Dark Horse Inn and a survivor of the famous Light Brigade, offered Neil a free drink when he had renewed their acquaintance. Big mistake. One followed another as they rehashed old times.

Forcing Bettsy and Emma from his mind, Neil eventually began to enjoy the sergeant's company. He couldn't even recall coming home. He just hoped Bettsy hadn't been awake when he did.

Slivers of dreams crept into his mind as he hung over the kitchen lavatory and splashed water on his head. The snick of the pump handle jiggled a memory of the door knocker tapping.

A picture of Biddie and Turner raising glasses confused him. Had they come to the pub? He didn't think so. Then he recalled Bettsy babbling on to them about some trouble with a woman. No, no, he hadn't even seen her last night. Had he?

A wave of sheer lust gusted through him at the thought of her. Tiny silk roses, ribbons. Breasts...Bettsy with her night rail open, inviting, urging. Her hands on him, tugging. Her body beneath him. Moving in her... Suddenly, he was painfully aroused and aching like the devil.

"Dreams!" he whispered to himself as he splashed his face again, fighting to ignore the untimely swelling.

"Well, good morning, Lord Green Gills. Aren't you looking chipper today!" Elizabeth bounced in and perched on the edge of the table. He wanted to drown her in the sink.

"Leave me be," he groaned instead. "I hurt."

"Poor lamb. Tea?"

"No, death," he answered, pulling the wet tea towel over his face. "If you laugh, so help me, I'll beat you."

"Not a chuckle, I promise." She lifted herself off the table's edge and scrounged in the cupboard. Moments later, she mixed a bit of bicarbonate of soda with water and offered it to him. "Drink that and go up for your bath. You reek." When he brushed past her, she continued, "Better have a long nap after that so you'll be refreshed for tonight."

"Tonight?" he asked absently, not really wanting to know. Even if she were proposing to make his dream come true, he wasn't certain he'd be able in spite of his present erection.

There was an obvious lack of communication between his lower parts and his head, which felt ready to burst.

"Theater engagement with Biddie and Turner," she explained.

Something troubling niggled at the back of his brain. "Theater engagement?"

She told him briefly about the plans to take women to the Lyceum for a play. Not much of it registered, only that they really had had visitors last night.

"Biddie and Turner were here? After I returned?" he asked carefully. He watched her nod and apprehension knotted his already sickened stomach. If his recollection of the lads visiting was no dream, perhaps the other... Before he could complete the thought, the question slipped out of his mouth. "Were we intimate last night?"

"Were we what?" she asked with a nervous laugh.

Good Lord, something *had* happened or she would have denied it outright. And she wouldn't be blushing like that.

"Did we...did I make love to you or did I dream it?" He watched her turn an even brighter pink. "Oh God, I did!"

She shook her head and laughed again, louder this time. It sounded horribly forced, he thought.

"I don't remember much about it," she said, and looked apologetic. "We had whiskey when the lads were here and later, when Lindy came by, I had brandy. We did kiss a bit when I came to tuck you in."

"No, I came inside you. I remember," he said softly, hardening anew at the fuzzy memory.

"Perhaps," she said, feigning sudden interest in the teakettle. "Doesn't matter much in the long run. I suppose it would have happened sooner or later, anyway."

He grabbed her arm and hauled her closer. "It damned well does matter, Bettsy. It matters a great deal to me!"

"Oh, leave off the theatrics, Neil. There'll be enough of that tonight, since Lindy's fixed me up with an actress. Go have your bath and get your mind on track, will you? My head's not in best form, either, if you must know. And you stink.''

With a snort of disgust, he shoved her away and stomped out of the kitchen. How was it she could be so blasé about what had happened? Did she really not recall it? Truth told, he could remember only bits and pieces himself. Delicious bits and pieces that were driving him mad.

One thing for certain, the next time he made love to her she would damn well remember *everything*. And then, by God, she'd not be so devil-may-care about it. That there would surely be a next time—and soon—mollified him somewhat.

It wouldn't be today, however. He was too hung over. And too damned angry to trust himself not to do her an injury. Tonight, he decided. Then he remembered the theater plans and cursed. Well, later then. Afterward, for whatever was left of the night. And in the morning as well, damn her eyes.

Elizabeth avoided Neil as best she could. It was no small feat even in a place the size of Havington House. He slept away the morning and then appeared in the laboratory, where she was washing test tubes. She dried her hands immediately and, with as few words as possible, escaped to the kitchen. Once there, she called out to Oliver, who was hanging about the stable door. His presence over a cup of tea prevented Neil from continuing the morning's conversation.

As soon as she could, she retreated upstairs to bathe and get ready for their outing. By the time she dressed and came downstairs, Lindy was there with his sister, Bonnie.

Bonnie was a MacLinden, all right. Her red hair rivaled Lindy's in brilliance and her eyes were the same mossy green. But there the resemblance ended. Where Lindy was stocky and rather short for a man, Bonnie was lithe and tall. Freckles across her upturned nose lent her a piquant, childlike air, though she must be upward of twenty. Elizabeth liked her on sight.

Lindy introduced her to Bonnie as Dr. Percival Betts and showed no indication that he'd told his sister the truth about

Elizabeth's gender. She saw no recourse but to play her role as best she could. Taking Bonnie's hand, Elizabeth dropped a kiss just above the gloved knuckles. "My pleasure, Miss MacLinden."

"Bonnie, please, and may I call you Betts?" The throaty voice sounded like stage quality to Elizabeth. She wondered if this one had acting ambitions like Lindy's friend, Helen.

"Delighted if you would, Bonnie," she responded, and turned to Neil. "You know Lord Havington, I assume?"

"Oh yes," Bonnie said, smiling and stretching out her hand to him. "The doctor and I are old friends."

*How old and how friendly?* Elizabeth wondered, watching the byplay between the two as Neil kissed Bonnie's hand. A sudden attack of unexpected jealousy left her speechless and fuming.

"Helen's performing at the Lyceum. Your mentioning the place is what gave me the idea to include her," Lindy said. "She'll be meeting you after the performance. Duty calls, so I'll leave Bonnie in your capable hands. Good luck tonight."

Elizabeth pasted on a smile and merely watched as Neil set out to charm Bonnie MacLinden on the way to the theater. She got the sneaking feeling it wasn't the first time he'd done so. To Bonnie's credit, she didn't look as smitten as Elizabeth would have felt under his barrage of flattery. There seemed more amusement than anything in her attitude.

"Gorgeous frock, Bonnie," Neil offered, running a long, tanned finger under the edge of the Cluny lace at her belled sleeve. "Dark green becomes you, sets off those devilish eyes of yours. Don't you agree, Betts? Lindy's a madman to let you out of the house looking the way you do. We should have come away armed to the teeth to beat off your admirers." Neil's wide white smile gleamed in the coach's lamplight as he clutched Bonnie's hand.

Bonnie snapped open her painted fan and waggled it under her chin. "If I'm mobbed by the rabble, you must use that rapier wit of yours to protect me, Doc. I've heard it slays 'em like a claymore." Bonnie adjusted the neckline of her low-cut gown and flashed a lopsided grin toward Elizabeth. "Have you a like weapon to defend our friend Helen, Dr. Betts?"

Neil answered before she could open her mouth. "Oh, he's witless and weaponless, I'm afraid. Betts here is a bit backward with the opposite sex." He looked at Elizabeth through narrowed eyes. "Doesn't have an inkling how precious such...discourse can be." Then he turned to Bonnie and lifted her hand, brushing his lips across her wrist. "But you do, don't you, love?"

Bonnie laughed openly and shook her head. "Neil, you are outrageous!" She settled a helpless grin on Elizabeth. "What am I to do with him?"

"His nose needs breaking if you're any good with your fists," Elizabeth replied, unsmiling. Bonnie hooted.

"We've arrived," Neil said pleasantly. "Shall we?"

They descended, Neil taking an inordinate amount of time to lift Bonnie from the coach and settle her on the walkway.

Elizabeth got the distinct feeling he was enacting revenge for her earlier dismissal of what had happened between them the night before. Well, if he expected outraged possessiveness on her part, he could bloody well drop the act. Wait until Helen showed up. Percival Betts would show him *charming!*

Biddenton arrived shortly after with his current amour, Janice. The little shopgirl was plain as pudding, with totally nondescript features. She hung on Biddie's every word. The devotion was difficult to watch with a straight face. The dolt paid her less attention than he did his hat. Conversation became impossible as they ascended to Biddie's rented theater box.

There was no sign of Turner.

The box put them above the rowdy rabble in the orchestral section. Elizabeth wondered if Neil's reference to a weapon was a joke after all when the play, a farce called *Lord Parsimonious,* began. Heckling erupted and grew so raucous throughout the first act, the players could hardly be heard above it.

"Watch, here's Helen," Bonnie said as the curtain rose again.

A tall, dark-haired vision in spangled silver drifted onto the stage, dragging an ostrich-feather fan. The audience grew quieter, finally lapsing into silence. Helen's kohl-rimmed eyes scanned the crowd and the rouged lips opened. Her deep contralto filled the hall, rose above the mediocre musicians like a soaring eagle and captured the audience like a clutch of helpless chicks. Elizabeth smiled in wonder at the stirring quality of the voice. Helen Trawick seemed out of place in this rackety comedy, like a unicorn in a field full of donkeys.

Elizabeth tried to picture Helen with Lindy. He'd said she was his girl. A new kind of respect dawned for the good inspector. His taste in women was excellent if this Helen was half as sweet and sensitive as her stage presence and quality of voice suggested. Yes, Elizabeth could imagine Helen's languid charm tempering Lindy's blustering lack of diplomacy. A good match.

When the song ended and Helen's thespian lover approached her for his part, the heckling resumed. By the end of the third act, Elizabeth's head throbbed from the noise.

They remained seated until most of the patrons milled out. Then Neil led them down the stairs and toward the back of the theater to the dressing rooms.

"We seem to be short some of our expected party. I thought Turner and his lady friend were coming," Neil said to Biddie.

"Said as much," Biddie replied, maneuvering carefully behind Janice's hoopskirt. "Prob'ly meet us later at the Velvet Swing."

Elizabeth and Neil exchanged disappointed glances. The whole night would be a wasted effort if Turner didn't show. They were supposed to get to know him better.

The only dressing-room door being mobbed was Helen's. "She says it's always like this," Bonnie explained as they waited for the admirers to thin. "This is only the second time Lindy's let me come to hear her. He seldom has the evenings off or he'd be here himself. Wasn't she wonderful?"

"Divine," Elizabeth declared with all the fervor of a stricken stage-door Johnny. The woman inside was to be her quarry for the night—at least Biddie and Turner were supposed to think so. Taking the initiative, she pranced forward eagerly and rapped on the door with the head of her cane. "Miss Trawick? It's Doc Betts and friends. May we come in?"

The door opened and a maid stood aside for them to enter. The seediness of the backstage apartment surprised Elizabeth, but she hid her reaction. Biddie surely supposed she'd been in here before. The accommodations might be lacking, but there must have been a dozen flower arrangements stacked haphazardly in a dimly lit corner. The place smelled like a funeral parlor.

The sight of Helen Trawick in dishabille gave the impression of a beautifully plumed bird in a mudlark's nest.

The stage paint was gone now and her walnut-colored hair tumbled about her shoulders and half-exposed breasts in clinging furls. Her rosy lips spread into a welcoming smile that fully encompassed the wide hazel eyes.

"Why, Bettsy Boy, what a surprise!" the woman said with a slightly wicked look.

*Bettsy Boy?* Elizabeth made a mental note to wring Lindy's neck if he was responsible for that sobriquet.

"Smashing performance, my dear. You got my flowers?" Actually, Elizabeth had no inkling where all the blooms had come from, but it was something to say.

One lovely, long-fingered hand gestured toward the corner. "You're too kind," Helen said in a cool, melodious voice.

Elizabeth made belated introductions and managed not to laugh at Biddie's openmouthed awe. She was glad she didn't really have to depend on the fellow to speak in her behalf. Neil and Bonnie offered effusive praise of Helen's performance, and Janice nodded with enthusiasm.

"Would you come out with us for a late supper, my sweet?" Elizabeth asked plaintively as she grasped Helen's hand, kissing the air just above it.

"If you like," Helen conceded with a mere breath of reluctance. "A moment to dress and I'll join you out front." She pulled the silk paisley shawl closer about her shoulders and stood, her obvious sign of dismissal. Elizabeth executed a perfect bow and ushered the entourage out.

"Why don't you and Janice trot on to the Velvet Swing and save us a table? It's bound to be mobbed," Neil suggested to Biddie as they approached the front entrance.

When the couple had gone, Neil turned to Bonnie. "I'm amazed Lindy allows you attend the theater. Tonight, I understand, but you mentioned you'd been before?"

"Oh, yes, we came two weeks ago, when Helen opened. I demanded he bring me along. Helen and I have been friends for years and I'd never watched her sing professionally. He could hardly refuse, now could he?"

Neil scoffed. "He certainly could and probably should have. It isn't considered quite proper these days, even in the Lyceum, which is a cut above the norm."

"Prude," Bonnie exclaimed, tempering her accusation with a smile. "Better not let Lindy hear you say that. He'd take exception to the slur against Helen. She works here, for heaven's sake."

Then she turned to Elizabeth with a droll look. "Don't you find this man a bit tedious, Dr. Betts? How can you stand all that piety, day in and day out? Why, I think I'd have to—"

Neil's shout interrupted her and his shoulder hit Elizabeth directly in the midsection, knocking her completely off her feet. Then he dropped to his knees, covering her upper body with his.

The man had lost his senses, Elizabeth thought, wondering what in the world had set him off. Her lungs seemed to have collapsed beneath his weight. She could see, but couldn't seem to focus properly. The place around them was utter pandemonium. A man's harsh, anguished roar blotted out the other noise.

Neil shouted her name, gripped her shoulder gently, then harder. "Bettsy!"

Elizabeth wanted to answer him but couldn't seem to catch her breath. Maybe she'd just close her eyes for a moment. Then she'd see what he wanted to argue about.

Neil's hands shook so violently he could barely control them. Pressing trembling fingers to the side of her neck, he prayed—disjointed words, promises, threats, pleas.

*Oh God, no pulse!* He tried to call her back. She lay limp, staring at nothing, the brown of her eyes so dark he couldn't distinguish pupil from iris. They slid shut, the dark lashes destroying his only hope. Neil felt his own heart falter.

*Bettsy. Gone. Dead!*

A tidal wave of rage engulfed him as he lowered her to the cobblestones. A killing rage. He staggered to his feet, swinging his head left and right, sniffing like a predator. Gunpowder. His eyes shifted. The alley from which the pistol had spit the death blow loomed to his right. The puff of smoke still hung there, dispersing slowly.

Neil shook off restraining hands and began to run toward the alley at the side of the theater, his prey's escape route. Darkness enveloped him, but his eyes grew keen. When he exited the far end of the long, black void, he stopped and blinked as the street lamps glared.

*Footsteps ahead.* He ran full out toward the sound, scanned right to left. *This way.* Ducking down a dark lane, the only possible source of the sound, he entered another pit of hell. Ahead, he heard the clatter of boots. *Faster!* Just as he broke free of the alleyway, a shot rang out, nicking the stones above his head.

Unarmed and uncaring, Neil rushed into the street, diving directly at the man holding the smoking gun. Death held no fear; Bettsy was waiting. But first, he'd tear this goddamned bastard limb from limb for what he'd done. No quick, merciful death. He would kill him piece by bloody frigging piece.

Fresh blasts of fury welled from deep in his chest and echoed through the foggy night. Another shot exploded near his ear and pinged off the side of the building. He punched and pummeled and tore at the man, yelling like a Viking berserker.

His hands closed around the thick throat and began to squeeze. He watched eyes bug out, heard choking sounds, and squeezed harder. The urge to kill doubled with every ragged breath he took. *Die, you son of a bitch. You killed her! Die slowly and know why. Suffer, you bloody cur!*

Suddenly, strong fingers pried at his own, urging him to release this scum that needed to die. He raged, cursed, tried to bite the interfering hands. He couldn't let go now. He couldn't.

"Lord Havington! Doctor! Leave off, we'll take 'im now. We'll take 'im. Turn him loose," a young bobby urged.

"No!" With one finger Neil dug for the carotid artery, missed his mark and cursed again.

"Please," the officer ordered frantically. "Miss MacLinden says Dr. Betts needs you bad. He's bleedin'. The young man is *bleedin'*, Doctor!"

"Bettsy's *dead!*" Neil shouted furiously, renewing his effort to rip out the throat under his hands.

"No, no, he was groaning when I left. And bleedin', I tell you! You must hurry. He's alive, I promise."

Reason broke through and Neil collapsed backward, sitting heavily on the legs of the man he'd released. Horror over what he'd almost done held him immobile for a few seconds. He stared at the puffy, gasping face of the gunman.

Then the full import of what the young watchman had just said finally registered. *Alive! Bettsy was alive!*

Lurching to his feet, Neil searched wildly for the way he had come, realizing suddenly that his sense of direction had deserted him along with his insanity.

"That way." The officer pointed, and Neil tore back through the alley at a dead run, oblivious to everything in his path until he reached her side.

He dropped to his knees and pushed Bonnie away, taking her place at Bettsy's side. Unconscious. Breathing shallow, but regular. His fingers, steadier now, located a pulse, erratic and faint, but blessedly *there*. He removed the ragged length of linen someone had pressed to her head wound, but the light from the street lamp was too dim to see much. Blood flowed freely still, and Neil quickly replaced the makeshift bandage.

Thank God Oliver had arrived at the appointed time to drive them to the supper club. Still, Neil debated whether to take her back inside the theater, but decided not to. Everything he'd need to treat her was at Havington House. If there was a bullet present, that meant surgery. If not, the ten-minute ride would make little difference.

"Home, make haste!" he shouted to Oliver. Scooping Bettsy up in his arms, Neil climbed into the coach.

Bonnie wedged herself in after him, stepping on his feet and crunching down her crinolines to make room for Helen.

"Get out," Neil muttered to both of them as he slid nearer to the lamp inside, hoping to see the wound better.

"Trent's meeting us. I sent for him," Bonnie said, as though that explained their intrusion. She remained where she was.

Neil promptly forgot their presence as he bent over Bettsy's head. He cursed his trembling hands, hands that had failed to find her pulse. Had just assumed... God, she might have died there in the street because of his dreadful mistake. He bit back the fear as best he could. Control was everything now. Tonight he had totally lost his wits and gone right over the edge. Now was not the time to fail again. Not when Bettsy's life was at stake.

"Steady," he muttered to himself as his eyes probed around the wound just above her temple. He still couldn't tell whether the bullet had entered. He didn't think so, but the light was so low, his eyes so filled, it was difficult to see. "You won't die, Bettsy. You won't."

"Here, let me help," Bonnie demanded, leaning forward and trying to brush his hand aside.

"No!" Neil shouted, and then sucked in a deep breath. He released it with a shudder. "Leave her to me."

The coach rocked violently as it sped along, too violently

to attempt any further examination even if he'd had better light. Neil occupied himself trying to act as a coach spring, cushioning the slight body resting across his lap. He worried at the laxness in her, the total lack of movement. And prayed to God there was no bullet lodged in her head.

He could still see the pistol barrel as the gloved hand appeared out of the shadows at the corner of the theater. Bettsy had stood perfectly positioned between him and the weapon to take the bullet in the back of her head. The aim was as true as a ray of light.

If only he had reacted a split second sooner, it would have missed her altogether. She must have turned sideways when he tried to throw her clear. The report of the gun had come simultaneously with the impact of their bodies. But the bullet had traveled faster than sound, faster than his thoughts.

"Neil!" Bonnie's voice finally penetrated. "Neil, we're here." The coach had stopped.

Without answering, Neil kicked open the door. Hefting Bettsy a bit so that her head rested on his shoulder like that of a sleeping child, he leapt from the coach and dashed up the steps to the town house.

"To the lab! Scrub your hands and set up for me," he shouted to Oliver, who opened the door and rushed in ahead of them.

Tenderly, Neil laid his precious burden down on the long, bare table and rushed to light a lamp. "Help me!" he ordered as he caught sight of Bonnie and Helen standing just inside the door. "All the lights you can find, Bonnie. Hurry! Helen, boil water! Move!" He gestured frantically toward the kitchen.

Oliver shoved a basin under Neil's hands and poured alcohol over the palms. Then he moved the lamp closer to Bettsy's head and began laying out instruments on a towel. The man's brisk efficiency reminded Neil to steel himself. Bettsy's life might depend solely on him, and he'd already failed her once tonight.

He removed his sticky, blood-soaked handkerchief from her wound. Mopping gently with a wad of cotton lint to absorb what was puddled in the groove, he almost collapsed with thanksgiving. No hole. The ball hadn't entered, had only cut a wide gash about two inches long right at the hairline.

The crease quickly filled again, but he didn't panic. Head wounds bled profusely. It only remained to debride it, stanch the flow and stitch it shut. A scar; such a small price compared to her life. His eyes teared again, this time from profound relief.

"Not so bad, eh?" A soft voice interrupted the sound of his harsh breathing. Neil blinked and looked up. Bless Ollie, who had not forgotten his training.

Neil shook his head. "Just grazed her."

"She'll rally," Oliver said, releasing the words with a harsh sigh. "Seen lots worse, ain't we?"

"Yes." Neil breathed out the word, his composure returning fully. He carefully bathed the wound with the salicylic solution Oliver set near his hand and began threading a suture needle as he spoke. "The other women?"

"MacLinden's sis is upstairs fixing th' bed and th'other'n's heatin' up water like ye told 'er."

"Umm," Neil muttered, intent on setting the first small stitch. He tried to make himself think of Bettsy as he would any other patient. But the breaking of that smooth ivory skin, skin he had kissed, tasted, treasured—was it only last night?—made him groan. She hadn't regained consciousness, but still jerked a bit. Oliver braced her head between his hands.

Neil considered chloroform and decided against it. The sooner he had her awake, the better to judge the extent of shock to her system. Besides, last time the stuff had made her sick.

She felt cool to the touch, like smooth marble. And very still now. Neil hoped the devil who'd done this to Bettsy would die from the choking he'd inflicted. It wasn't very likely, but he wished for it with every fiber of his being.

Neil bathed the rest of Bettsy's face and soaked the worst of the blood from her hair. Then he covered the neat sutures with a pad and bound it on. In doing so, he felt a huge **lump** near the back of her head and cursed. She must have hit her head on the cobbles when she fell. The knot was raised, though, and not caved in, so he hoped it didn't spell concussion.

Her pulse was near normal now. She was breathing steadily, and there was no fever yet. There seemed little danger of any permanent impairment. She would be all right. He allowed himself a shudder and a brief moment to recover his equilibrium.

Lifting her in his arms, he headed across the hall to the stairs.

"The water?" Helen asked, meeting him on the way with a steaming kettle in her hand.

"Make coffee. And keep some water hot for an infusion later," he ordered, and continued on his way.

After settling Bettsy on the bed where she usually slept, Neil left her long enough to retrieve one of Terry's flannel nightshirts and lock both doors to the hall.

He hated to undress her this way. She ought to be fully conscious and participating. And well. Her wound wasn't serious, thank God. Nor was the lump on her head. There'd be a little fever and a beastly headache when she woke, but she *would* recover, with no ill effects. He only wished she were in good form right now. Rephrase that, he thought wryly as he slid a hand over her waist; nothing wrong with the *form* at all. Except that it was driving him out of his mind.

Neil felt light-headed, almost euphoric. And randy as a buck in rut. No wonder, since his blood had been pumping full steam half the night. Recognizing the reason for his arousal didn't make Neil like himself any better for it. He fought off hazy recollections of the night before. They seemed all the more tantalizing for their dreamlike quality.

From memory, he recited the *Materia Medica*'s section on astringents to keep his mind off what his hands were doing. He got no further than the first property of *Acidum Tannicum* before he interrupted himself with a whispered curse.

Bettsy's starched shirt lay open to reveal the wide strip of linen that bound her breasts to near flatness. Neil took a deep, fatalistic breath and shook his head. Worse than a damned corset; the thing would have to come off. Gingerly, he reached for the pins fastening it and began expounding on the composition of *Acidum Carbolicum* in a strained voice. Eyes closed, moving on to *Creasotum*, he lifted her and removed the shirt, laying the linen loosely across her chest.

Sweat tricked down his forehead and stung his eyes. *Whew!* At this rate, he knew he'd never apply an astringent again without getting hard.

Moving to the foot of the bed, he tugged off her polished boots and woolen stockings. A smile stole over him. Such pretty feet. Neil palmed one, marveling at how small and smooth it was. How perfect her toes. Ach, he ought to have his head examined! Playing with her feet, for God's sake. How she would laugh at that. He laughed for her and at himself, relieved by his sudden attack of humor.

He unbuckled her belt and slid the twill trousers down her legs and off her ankles. She looked ridiculous in Terry's knee-length drawers. They hung on her pelvis now, the top button pulled loose. Through the soft, thick linen, a distinct tubular bulge rose above her pubis. He smiled. Curiosity overwhelmed ethics. He had to know what she'd put there.

Just as his hand neared the second button, her low-pitched voice jarred his senses. "Touch that and you die!"

He jerked back, startled into a crack of laughter. "You're awake!"

"And you're a louse." She glared at him down the length of her body. "Assaulting a poor fellow in his sleep. Ought to call you out. Pervert."

Holding the linen tightly to cover her breasts, she rolled to one side and tried to sit up. Neil rushed to stop her. "No! Lie back."

She groaned and abandoned her effort immediately. "God, catch my head if it rolls off the bed!" Then her eyes flew open and locked on his shirtfront, which was soaked and stiffened with her blood. "Neil, you're hurt!"

"No, no, it's not *my* blood. How do you feel, other than the headache?" He pried one eyelid wider and examined her pupils for the dozenth time.

"What happened?" she asked, batting his hand away and blinking. "I thought you'd gone bonkers on me, or maybe I was the one. Did I pass out? Had the most bizarre dream..."

Neil debated for a second whether to tell her, but she seemed fully alert and would soon know anyway. "Someone shot you. The bullet grazed your head just here," he said, touching the bandage lightly. Then he quickly added, "It'll leave just a light scar, I promise. My sewing lessons were legend at med school."

She snorted, a rather inelegant sound more suited to Percival Betts than a young lady. "Wish I could believe that. You have to run down an entire volume by heart to get to the part you do next. I heard you just now." Her bravado a little too obvious, she fired the question, "So, who shot me?"

"I don't know his name." Neil rested his forehead on one palm. He thought for a moment he might be sick, just remembering the madness that had overtaken him at the theater. Then he slid his arms around Bettsy's waist and laid his head on her breast, comforted by the steady beating of her heart.

The doorknob rattled and someone knocked impatiently. "A moment," Neil called out, and placed a kiss directly on the spot where his ear had rested. "I couldn't live without you, Bettsy. I really don't believe I could."

Silently, she looked at him with an unreadable expression. He knew she didn't understand yet how vital she was to his existence. But she would. Soon she would.

He covered her to the shoulders with the counterpane and went to answer the door.

# Chapter Ten

Lindy stood waiting as Neil opened the door. "I've sent Helen and Bonnie home," he whispered, "and Sergeant Roarke just brought news of the shooter."

"Then you'd best come in and tell the victim," Bettsy called out, obviously piqued by the attempted secrecy. "You caught him, I trust?"

"Ah, we're awake then?" Lindy stepped inside the room and came over to stand by the bed, shifting uneasily from one foot to the other. He threw Neil a meaningful look, as though to say things were best explained outside the patient's hearing.

From the look on Bettsy's face, Neil knew Lindy had a better chance of making prime minister than he did getting out of the room without a full explanation. "Go ahead, Lindy. She might as well hear it." Placing the back of his hand against her forehead, he added succinctly, "You need something for pain?"

She jerked away from his touch and winced. "Don't coddle me. Just pour us a tot of brandy and let's get on with it."

Neil poured as Lindy began. "Bonnie summoned the watch almost instantly with her whistle. Gave it to her a while back. Good protection for a woman, whistles."

He cleared his throat and took a sip of the drink Neil handed him. "Roarke's man, Mullins, brought the fellow in and questioned him. Could hardly talk, they said." Lindy raised an admonishing brow at Neil. "But he was laughing like a loony."

"Laughing?" Neil repeated, disbelieving.

"Aye, laughing his head off," Lindy said, shaking his own. "Gone round the bend, I think. Admitted to everything. 'Course, the gun was right where he dropped it. Couldn't very well deny it, now could he?"

Neil had marked Lindy's tone as well as his words. "Then why do you sound as though you doubt he did it?"

Lindy's head jerked up, and he pressed his lips together tightly for a second before answering. "Oh, he's guilty all right. Thing is, I'd thought, hoped, that he was in someone's employ and we'd discover our culprit's identity through him."

Bettsy piped up. "You're saying that this has nothing to do with our investigation into Terry's death or the attempts on me? The man simply shot me because I got in front of his pistol?"

"Actually, no. He says he did it because he heard Percival Betts had bragged all through the clubs and hells about despoiling his sister."

"What?" Neil shouted with a bark of laughter.

Bettsy rolled her eyes and covered them with one hand. "You've a dark side I hadn't suspected, Lindy. I'd prefer you kept your little jokes to yourself until my head feels better."

Lindy wasn't laughing. "This is serious, Betts. Someone— likely the man we're after—spread that rumor, knowing what a dreadful temper Thorpe Bensen has and how fiercely protective he is toward his wayward little sis. Vicky Bensen's last lover landed in a gutter down in Whitechapel with his face pulverized and half his ribs broken. Bensen admitted to that as well tonight. Volunteered the fact and was right proud of it."

Neil felt his skin crawl. "You know what this means. Someone's penetrated Bettsy's disguise and knows she's here."

"Then why didn't they simply expose me?" Bettsy asked. "That would seem the more reasonable action—let the law take care of me. If I were arrested and tried, there's little doubt I'd be hanged, as things stand now.''

Her voice sounded steady enough, but Neil didn't miss the tremble of her hand as it tightened into a fist on the coverlet. The other was locked around the stem of her brandy snifter. Her face looked pale as death, her brown eyes almost black.

''I'll have to take her away from here,'' he told Lindy. ''We'll cross to France and lose ourselves in Paris.''

Lindy mulled it over for only a moment. ''And how will you know he's not right behind you all the way, waiting for another chance to do her in? Our man doesn't want Betts found or tried for murder. He wants her dead. That points toward Colin Marleigh. Who else would dread having her hauled into court? Having her under suspicion has left enough of a stain on the family name. He's the one we have to watch, and mark me, we will. Marleigh won't be able to cross his own threshold without having my lads on his tail. When he makes the next move, even if he hires someone else to do his dirty work, we'll have him. We'll follow anyone he contacts who looks remotely suspicious.''

''Colin's not behind this,'' Bettsy said with stout conviction. ''I won't believe it.''

''Be that as it may,'' Neil said to her, ''you're not going anywhere to give him or anyone else a chance at you. You're an invalid until this mess is over and we have him locked away.''

''Then how do we catch him if we don't draw him out?'' Lindy asked.

Neil sighed with exasperation and jerked his head toward the door. ''Bettsy needs rest now. We can talk about this later. It's not as though she's going anywhere until she's recovered.''

Lindy nodded and walked to the door, intimating with a look that the matter was far from finished. ''See you tomorrow, Betts. Try not to worry, eh? You're safe as the queen herself.''

''I'll see you out,'' Neil said, and turned to Bettsy. ''You, don't move a hair. Try not to go to sleep just yet. I'll come back straightaway and sit with you.'' He waited for her nod and accompanied Lindy down the stairs.

"She seems all right. Is she?'' Lindy asked as they reached the foyer.

"Got off with a souvenir scar and a whale of a headache. May have a touch of fever before the night's out,'' Neil grumbled. "I suppose we ought to consider her lucky.''

Lindy turned and rested a hand on his shoulder. "And you, Neil? Are you recovered? Mullins said you nearly did the bloke in right there.''

Neil said nothing. Lindy didn't need to mention the similar incident in Balaclava for him to know he was thinking of it.

"I know it's difficult to see the woman you love injured, but—''

"Difficult? Christ, Lindy, I thought she was dead! A bullet to the head, her pulse so shallow I couldn't find it! Hell yes, I meant to kill him!'' Neil sucked in a harsh breath and released it slowly, struggling against renewed fury. "Bensen was only a tool. Someone out there is still after her. And you want me to use her as bait? I won't have it, Lindy. You might as well know that now.''

"Then she'll spend the rest of her life in your bedroom? Knowing Betts, I doubt that! I give her a week, tops, before she's out and about with or without your permission.''

Neil knew he was right. "Well, at least she needn't pose as a man anymore. I'll allow her up and around, but she doesn't leave this house and that's final.''

Lindy tugged on his mustache and frowned. "Let's not abandon the ruse just yet, shall we? Suppose someone else, maybe someone who has nothing at all to do with the murder or with framing Betts, simply wants Percival Betts out of the way.''

"Who? And why?'' Neil couldn't imagine anyone with a grudge against the innocuous little Percival Betts. "He'' made friends right and left without even trying.

"After what you told me about Betts's little altercation with your former fiancée, even she could be responsible for this. The woman wants back in your good graces, and she knows Betts is against that, even if she hasn't reasoned why yet.''

Lindy shook his head. ''None of this shooting business makes sense. I don't see how anyone could have penetrated Betts's disguise. Who in his right mind would ever imagine you'd give safe harbor to the very woman you think killed your nephew?'' Lindy rested a shoulder against the door frame and cocked his head. ''Though we daren't treat that rumor as such, it could have been merely a joke perpetrated by one of your young friends. One who didn't realize just how dreadful Bensen's temper really is. No, we'd best keep up Betts's disguise until we know for certain who's behind the shooting.''

''Young friends, you say?'' Neil mused. ''Turner? He never arrived at the theater tonight. Perhaps he expected something to happen and decided to stay out of the line of fire.''

Lindy shrugged. ''Or maybe he had better things to occupy his time. My man followed him to rooms let by a Miss Sadie Farnham. He stayed for nearly three hours while your play was in progress, departed alone, and went directly to the Velvet Swing.''

''You don't think he had anything to do with what happened, do you, Lindy?''

''Who can say at this point? Everyone's suspect.''

All Neil knew was that he felt an increasing sense of dread. The pieces of this investigation still lay as scattered as an overturned puzzle. ''Go away now, Lindy. I can't think about this any more tonight. I've just had the fright of my life and I think I'm in worse shape than Bettsy is at the moment.''

''She's a corker though, ain't she?'' Lindy said, grinning as he set his bowler at a jaunty angle.

''That she is,'' Neil agreed softly, ''a corker indeed.'' He closed the door behind MacLinden and went back upstairs to sit with his patient.

Elizabeth was awake when he returned, and she tried to smile. The skin of her face didn't seem to want to stretch in the directions necessary, however. Her limbs felt shaky, almost detached.

"How do you feel?" he asked. "I'm hoping you won't need laudanum if we can get by without it. Be quiet a moment," he said. He took a fat cylinder from his assortment of instruments, placed it against her chest and leaned down to listen to the other end. Gently rolling her to one side, he placed it on her back. "Breathe deeply."

"Why no laudanum?" she asked when he'd finished. She wasn't eager to be drugged to sleep, but her head was throbbing like the very devil. All sensation in her body seemed to be concentrated from her neck up.

Neil sighed and sat down on the edge of the bed. After a moment of silence, he said calmly, "We've had no chance to discuss what happened last night in the study, or what may have gone on before we met. But now we must, Bettsy. You'll need further medication if you become feverish or congested from lying abed. I need to be cautious about what I administer. If there's even the smallest chance of pregnancy, however early on, I mislike giving a woman opiates, or especially astringents. Miscarriage could occur. When did your last menses end?"

Elizabeth blushed. Her old nurse, a sometime midwife, had explained the facts of life in great detail. Included in the instruction was the knowledge of a woman's fertile time in the monthly cycle, so that Elizabeth could plan her family when she married. According to Nanny's expertise, there was very little chance of conception last night, since her monthly had ended three weeks before.

"Don't worry. It's not possible. I could not have conceived last night." Her words sounded clipped, she knew, but the intimacy of the subject embarrassed her. As did that damned brisk efficiency of his.

"Well, we shall see." He busied himself tucking the covers around her and putting his stethoscope away.

Elizabeth hated it when he became so businesslike—Dr. Bronwyn, fixer of all ills. She was piqued that he was so nonchalant about the possibility of her having his child. And worse yet, by his speaking so matter-of-factly about her having someone else's child. She wished he would stand up so she could kick him.

Neil was right, of course. He was always so bloody right. Her thinking was definitely muddled by the injury. For numerous reasons, having his baby would be a disaster for both of them and certainly for the hypothetical child. Still, the precious thought clung in her mind: a tiny Neil to hold and love. But it wouldn't be. Not this time or ever. She'd make certain of that.

"You are to tell me immediately if you even suspect you are increasing."

"It's nothing to you. But I assure you, I'm not."

"You'll bloody well *tell* me if you think you are! Do you hear?" He was angry. And, she noticed with not a little satisfaction, sweating in spite of his cool demeanor.

"No," she said when he clasped her shoulder. "And take your hands off me! Do you think I'm so stupid that I don't know how to avoid a pregnancy?"

He released her with a dangerous look. "You do?" he asked, sounding as though he might choke on the words. Then he closed his eyes and sighed deeply as he turned his face away for a moment. When he looked back, she saw sorrow there, blended with firm resolve. "Bettsy, I only want to keep you safe."

"Is that all you want, Neil?" She wished he wouldn't do this right now—be kind and supportive. It was confusing and made her say things before thinking them through. She had no business asking what he wanted.

"No, sweetheart," he said softly. "That's definitely not all I want. You see, in spite of everything, as ridiculous as it sounds and makes me feel, I'm afraid that I love you."

Elizabeth absorbed the words through a tangle of emotions. They were what she yearned for in the deepest part of her heart and what she dreaded most in her rational moments. Now she would have to alienate him somehow before he realized she loved him as well.

If she became his mistress as she wanted, she could very well conceive. That precious plan would have to die right here and now. Thoughts of proper timing would go right out the window with the first kiss. It must happen to everyone that way or else there would be no unwanted children.

A baby would bind him to her like glue. He'd never let her go. Neil would suffer for that alliance, as much as Terry would have. And the poor, hapless child would bear the disgrace, as a Havington bastard and the offspring of the notorious Marleigh woman who had brought down an earl.

The way was clear. She must disgust him so royally that he would be happy to see the back of her when their mission was finished. Failing that, she would have to give up her part in the murder investigation and disappear forever.

But right now, this moment, she couldn't bear to have him hate her. There were things she could say, things she could do that would set the course against any future for the two of them. But with the pain in her head almost equal to the pain in her heart, she couldn't bring herself to begin the campaign just now. Instead, she willed herself to relax against the pillows and close her eyes in case he should notice they were filling up.

"I'd like to sleep now," she whispered. "Please don't stay." Seconds later, she heard the door open and close softly. Her despair was so deep, tears seemed frivolous.

For the next week, Neil tended her twice daily to change the dressing on her head and check for fever. He kept his questions and comments well within the realm of their doctor-patient relationship and accepted her belligerence without comment.

There was really no reason why she shouldn't be allowed up and about, but he refused her demands and kept her bedridden, except to use the necessary room and to lounge in her pillowed window seat. Her room was the safest place for her, and, he admitted to himself, her seclusion was also a punishment.

He realized his disillusionment wasn't her fault. She had never denied her past. But he'd really begun to think she was innocent of all the rumors until she'd confessed her knowledge of preventing conception. That she had been promiscuous didn't affect his love for her, but it hurt him nonetheless. So, for the past seven days, he had kept his emotional distance, trying to come to grips with the fact that he had lost his heart to the little jade. Undoubtedly he'd lost his mind as well.

"Betts champing at the bit, is she?" Lindy commented as they finished up the dinner his mother had sent over.

"Wishing me to perdition with every breath, I expect," Neil said, pouring them each another glass of wine. "I'll have to let her up tomorrow. She's well and she knows it."

"Then what?" Lindy asked, licking a few errant drops of Madeira off his mustache.

"Keep her confined to the house, I suppose. What else can I do?"

Lindy inched forward in his chair, gesturing with one hand. "Why not entertain here? You could ask your chums to come for drinks and a game or two. I know Turner has brought round his card every afternoon. Perhaps he feels guilty if he had a hand in the rumor that got her shot."

"Or perhaps he simply likes her and is worried. Did you think of that? Biddie has sent regards and would have come had he not been down with a head cold. I thought you'd settled on Colin as the culprit, or barring that, Emma's vindictiveness."

"Nothing's settled at all. Turner may want you both out of the way in the event one of you might yet find his markers among Terry's papers and try to collect," Lindy explained.

"Absurd. He's never even mentioned the debts. Probably assumes he's free and clear now, if the markers do indeed exist. Turner's harmless, Lindy."

The inspector nodded and sighed. "Likely right. I'm grasping at dust motes, I admit. Why don't you invite Colin to come by? Send word you'd like to speak with him. After all, your nephew was supposedly murdered by his lordship's cousin. I expect curiosity will bring him if nothing else, especially if he's our man. Maybe you can divine something in his attitude that I've missed.''

Neil hedged. ''Next week, perhaps.''

''No, it'll have to be tomorrow. He has stopped off at the town house before continuing on to Scotland, so my sources say. Still intent on running his own investigation. That's what puzzles me about all this. Supposing he's the one who had Betts shot, he should know of her disguise. If he is the guilty party and knows she's with you, why is he still trying to find her?''

''A pretense to throw you off, maybe. All right, tomorrow it is then,'' Neil promised. ''I'll have to lock Bettsy in her room if she finds out. Curious little monkey will want to listen in.''

''Well, why not let her? She knows him better than either of us,'' Lindy said reasonably.

Neil wouldn't consider it, afraid Bettsy might overhear something from her cousin that would hurt her feelings. Or trigger an unwanted confrontation if she revealed herself.

While Lindy went up to visit Bettsy, Neil retired to his study and composed a short invitation. He sent Oliver off to deliver it in spite of the lateness of the hour.

Then he leaned back in his favorite leather chair and let his gaze wander around the library. So much had happened here in this room—his last words with Terry, the shooting that destroyed a young life so filled with promise and his own drunken intimacy with the woman who was inadvertently responsible for the tragedy.

He stared sadly at the plush, wine-red carpeting where he and Bettsy had lain together. Try as he might, Neil could recall only flashes of their first sexual encounter. She'd brushed it off as a trivial, tipsy mistake. She was right, of course. It never should have happened at all, especially not here, and certainly not in that way.

How could he possibly love this woman?

How could he not?

The following morning, Colin's answer to Neil's invitation was succinct and to the point. He could be expected at two in the afternoon. Elizabeth was to keep to her room, much as she begged to secrete herself somewhere in the library and listen. Neil was having none of that. In spite of Lindy's suggestion, Neil knew the risk was too great.

There wasn't a shred of proof that Colin had anything at all to do with either Terry's death or the attacks on Elizabeth. He did, however, have a whale of a motive and grand opportunity.

Colin arrived a few minutes early, hat in hand, looking faintly apologetic.

Neil greeted him coolly, as one might be expected to address the cousin of his nephew's murderer. The man's looks disappointed Neil. Someone who would kill or order it done ought to have the grace to look like a criminal. Colin Marleigh certainly did not. His pale blond hair lay neatly combed without thought to concealing its thinning on top. The pinch-featured face and solemn green eyes looked guileless enough. He was a short, stocky man. Foppish, too, in his gaily checked, three-piece suit. Colin was the epitome of a young nobleman of aimless pursuits. But was he what he seemed to be?

Neil led him toward the study. "Good of you to come, Marleigh. I trust you won't mind a few questions, since we were very nearly related by marriage. As I mentioned in my note, I'd like to try and make some sense of what happened if I can. Sit down and I'll pour you a brandy, unless you'd prefer port."

"Uh, port actually, if you wouldn't mind. Bit early for brandy. Be happy to help however I can."

*Happy to help?* Neil noted the way Colin's hands shook as he accepted the wine. He wondered why the man would agree to this interview unless he was guilty and trying to find out how much Neil knew about Terry's murder and the attempt on Bettsy.

"Not much I can say, Havington. Dreadfully sorry about young Terry. Fine fellow. Damned shame." Colin had a real talent for looking sincere, Neil thought darkly.

"You knew my nephew well, then?" Neil asked.

"No, no, not at all *well*. Saw him about here and there. Played a few hands of whist with him at Knuckle's once."

Colin seemed unnerved by Neil's silence. After a few moments, he downed his port in two gulps and sighed. "See here, Havington, I just want you to know the girl is mad. I hadn't the faintest notion she'd go so far round the bend as to do murder. Tried to keep her in hand. Didn't really want to lock her away. I planned to warn young Havington off her but I simply left it too late."

He met Neil's gaze with one that looked like abject sorrow. "I feel somewhat...responsible."

Neil remained quiet for another long moment, staring into his glass, swirling the liquid around. Then he looked up, eyebrows raised in question. "Responsible? Well, I suppose you must have had a rather difficult time with her. Did you really consider locking her up?" He thanked God that Elizabeth was not listening to this tripe.

Colin's nod was effusive. "Oh yes, I did think seriously about committing her! Especially after she whacked off her hair and embarrassed the life out of me. My friends even suggested St. Mary's of Bethlehem."

"*Bedlam?* Good God, man, she's your cousin! And a gently reared lady!" He forgot for the moment that he was supposed to pretend hatred for the woman who'd supposedly killed Terry. He wanted to choke this little bastard, guilty or not.

Marleigh grew defensive at the rebuke. "Here now! She didn't behave as a lady, now did she? Invited those blokes to her room and then screamed the house down when they took her up on it. And that other time, paddling about the pond in her unmentionables! Don't that tell you how far gone she is?

The chit's all about in the head, has been ever since the old man died.''

Marleigh squinted a little and shook his finger in Neil's direction. "If you ask me the old earl was a little off center himself. Never mixed about with people or had a civil word for anyone. Damned old curmudgeon!''

"I'd heard he was rather fond of you,'' Neil said.

Colin looked ashamed. "Maybe. Hard to tell with him.''

"Did you see Lady Marleigh the day she killed my nephew?'' Neil struggled to keep his voice bland.

"No. She kept pretty much to herself after we had words over her...incidents. Didn't like it above half that I gave her a setdown. I left her alone until I could fathom what to do with her. I was in the country when she shot him. Had been for a week.''

Neil cast about for something more direct. "How did you feel about the proposed marriage?''

"Well, neither one asked *my* permission, I can tell you!'' Colin squirmed in his chair and crossed his legs at the knee. He wiggled one booted foot back and forth rapidly, as though he were sitting on a keg of gunpowder.

*Now we're getting somewhere,* Neil thought. "But I'd think you'd approve, Marleigh, since your cousin and her *wealth* of problems would then have been Terry's to sort through.''

The dam broke. Colin leapt from his seat and slammed his glass down on the side table. "Now see here, Havington. I came to do the pretty and say how sorry I was, not to play at what might have been. I'm doing all I possibly can to find the little tramp and put her away, either in a madhouse or in prison. You'll have to be content with that. Now if you don't mind, I'll take my leave.''

He yanked open the study door and strode toward the foyer, snatching up his hat and cane as he passed by the hall tree.

Neil followed at a leisurely pace and barely heard Marleigh's curt "good afternoon'' before the front door slammed.

"That scurvy *worm!*''

Neil spun around at the sound of Bettsy's irate voice. "You were in there?"

"Under your desk," she admitted, brushing off her trouser legs and coughing at the flurry of dust. "You really ought to hire a maid."

"Devil a maid! What did you think you were doing? Can you imagine what would have happened if he had seen you?"

She ran her hands through her hair, wincing slightly as she inadvertently touched the newly formed scar. "Well, do you think he did it?" she asked, ignoring his reprimand.

"Very probably, and he definitely wants your money. The mention of wealth, even out of context, was what set him off." Neil moved forward and pushed her hair back to see if she'd damaged his handiwork. "Keep your hands off that until the redness goes away. Let's put more of that sali salve on just to be safe."

"No, it's fine," she said, jerking away and glancing toward the kitchen. "Lindy's waiting."

"A moment more won't matter. About what Colin said…it must have hurt you terribly. I wish you hadn't heard it."

"Forget it. We have enough to think about with the investigation without you worrying about my feelings."

He took her elbow and pulled her close, wrapping his arms around her. "I can't disregard anything that upsets you, Bettsy. Don't you understand how much I love you?"

She stiffened against him, then pulled away. "Love? What you feel is sympathy, Neil, sympathy for my wretched past and perhaps our shared grief over Terry. And a healthy shot of lust, of course. Don't twist all that into something it's not. For my sake and for yours, at least try to stifle the lust."

She frowned down at the floor. "We were very lucky last week that the timing was not right."

"Right for what?" he asked.

"For conception, of course. Had we lost our senses—or sobriety, as it turned out—merely a few days earlier, you'd have had good reason to worry. Think about that next time you—"

"You've begun your time, then?"

"Not yet, but soon," she answered, coloring a bright red.

Neil nodded slowly, tongue in cheek. "So the rhythm method always works well for you, does it?"

She looked confused, her eyes darting, her bottom lip caught between her teeth. "Rhythm? Oh yes! Yes it does. Always works...very well. Always has."

"You prefer it then, to envelopes or sponges and the like?"

Her brows came together in a most charming way. "Oh definitely. Yes. Much better." She bobbed her head in agreement.

He smiled, hope welling in his chest. "Even better than orange juice? Actually, I recommend the juice to my more fastidious patients."

Curiosity clearly overcame her need for pretense. "Orange juice?"

"Instead," he explained dryly. "Orange juice instead."

"This is a ridiculous conversation. I have no idea what you're talking about." She started to leave, and he grabbed her elbow.

"You don't know a damned thing about contraception, do you, Bettsy?"

"If that means avoiding childbearing, then I most certainly do!" she retorted. "I know everything. My nurse was very well informed."

"Your nurse? Ah, I see," he said, stifling the smile that ran all through him. Why she wanted him to think she was so terribly experienced, he couldn't imagine. But any woman who practiced sex regularly in a nefarious way would either be an expert in the ways to prevent pregnancy or already well caught. It was obvious to him now that Bettsy was never that sort.

He suspected that she had experimented a bit, probably only with Terry, and for some reason wanted him to think she was a woman of the world. Time enough later to ponder all that. It was sufficient for now to know that she was a far cry from what her reputation purported her to be. Relief was so damned sweet he wanted to shout.

"Well, then. Let's go see what Lindy thinks of your cousin's revelations, shall we?" he said, slipping her hand through his arm. "Did I ever tell you what a truly interesting companion you make, Betts?"

She huffed and rolled her eyes. "You've hardly said two words this past week that didn't relate to the stitches in my head or some sort of vile substance you wished to rub on it. I thought I'd go mad!"

"So did I," he said, contemplating what sort of words he'd like to say to her. But apparently, it was too soon for that.

# Chapter Eleven

Lindy wondered why Neil looked so pleased with himself when they entered the kitchen. Betts seemed troubled. Perhaps Colin Marleigh had established his guilt beyond question, then. "So what have you found out?"

Neil seated Betts before he answered, his words coming hesitantly, as though he didn't want to say them in Betts's hearing. "I'd like to see Colin Marleigh hang. I dislike the man intensely. I admit that colors my judgment of everything he said, but I still think he's guilty."

"Not of the murder," Bettsy insisted, shaking her head. "I simply don't believe he killed Terry."

Neil let out a disgusted sigh and threw up his hands. "Why are you defending the toad, Bettsy? You heard what he'd planned to do to you!"

Lindy never underestimated a woman's intuition. She knew Colin Marleigh better than either of them and had obviously turned this over in her mind a number of times. He marked Betts's words carefully.

She rested her elbows on the table and leaned her chin in her hands. "It's not that I think he's too good to shoot anyone," she explained. "He's simply too squeamish. Father worried about the fact that Colin was too lily-livered to hunt. He isn't smart enough to have arranged everything, either."

"He would have confined you to a madhouse. He was certainly canny enough to arrange that!" Neil said, fuming.

"There's no doubt he's after your inheritance," Lindy affirmed. "I've checked with his bankers, and he assuredly has pocket wrinkles. That proves nothing, of course," he continued. "Even should we have some sort of proof that he committed murder, short of a confession, an indictment might not stick. He is, after all, an earl."

"Then what good will come of all this if you can't arrest him?" Neil asked.

Lindy's eyes narrowed as he chewed his pipe stem. "With my men on his coattails, he'll play hell getting up to any further mischief. Can't hire anyone without our knowledge and can't do anything himself. Sooner or later, he'll trip himself up. Maybe brag to someone about how clever he's been.

"That one thing about him still confuses me, though," Lindy continued. "Why is he haring off to Scotland to try and find her? He has to know Betts's identity if he set up the shooting."

Neil pondered that. "He never mentioned the incident or asked about my poor, wounded assistant. That could mean he's either innocent and not at all curious about our Dr. Betts, or that he's guilty and doesn't dare ask questions. I'm convinced of the guilt theory. He may be going to Scotland to assess the property he thinks he'll get with Bettsy's death. Or simply as a diversion in the event anyone begins to suspect him."

"Possibly," Lindy said. "At any rate, after he leaves for Edinburgh, you two should be safe to continue gathering what information you can. Could be Marleigh's already assured someone of his expected fortune. Any little thing he's mentioned to his cronies could be useful when added to the context of our inquiry. If we get enough on him, we might bluff him into a confession. Try to cultivate that set he runs with if you can."

After a round of heated arguments against taking Bettsy with him, Neil finally gave in. Maybe she would be safe with

Marleigh gone north. Lindy had men keeping careful watch, both on Marleigh and on Bettsy. Neil remained apprehensive. Who knew what scheme the devil might have set in motion?

During the next week, they fell into a pattern. In the afternoons they worked, setting up the lab in the conservatory and discussing future research projects. It gave them something productive to do while waiting for the night.

Evenings began at Boodle's, playing at whist or vingt-et-un and listening for anything that might aid Lindy's case. After a round at other, lesser-known clubs, they usually wound up at White's for a drink with Biddie and Turner. All that might have proved great fun if Neil hadn't spent most of the time watching for a would-be assassin.

Bettsy made a point of retiring as soon as they arrived home and keeping both doors to her room firmly locked.

On the last nightly foray, they discovered that Colin had made earnest promises to settle his gaming debts and pay his delinquent bills within a fortnight. Unless he had suddenly unearthed buried treasure somewhere, they were fairly certain where he intended to get the money. Bettsy's death would make the earl of Marleigh a very wealthy man.

Neil brought their club outings to a halt once they learned that much. Lindy might have men watching Marleigh like a bug under a microscope, but Neil worried that Colin might have arranged another attack on Bettsy before he left London. What better alibi?

The sensible thing to do was keep her isolated where Neil could protect her. He, Oliver and Lindy's two men guarded her like the queen's jewels.

Enforced togetherness brought its own problems. Neil made no further advances toward Bettsy, sensing that she felt uneasy and perhaps as embarrassed as he was about their first encounter. Determined not to rush the issue, he treated her as he might have any young, aspiring doctor during their daily work in the lab.

In the evenings, they ate simple fare they could prepare themselves, or meals Oliver brought in from the kitchen down on Peebles Lane. Later Neil would beat her soundly at chess and she would trounce him at gammon.

Their friendship took on a comfortable equality, a new experience for Neil and apparently for Bettsy, as well. Though quelling his constant desire for her proved difficult, that was somewhat made up for by their increasing camaraderie.

Now, Neil realized, he was growing to love her in more ways than he could count—as friend and companion, dedicated assistant and, hopefully again soon, as a lover. Marriage was his ultimate goal, of course. Until he could arrange that, he decided to simply enjoy being with her. It was a satisfying, if somewhat strange sort of courtship, he thought.

As he feared, she chafed regularly at being confined. Feeling restless himself after days indoors, Neil finally agreed to an early morning ride in Hyde Park. Little danger in that, he thought, since no one would be expecting them to leave the house. The guards would have noticed if anyone had been watching the place.

The autumn air felt nippy, but not enough so for cloaks. Oak and maple leaves crunched and scattered under their horses' hooves. The sky had cleared of fog earlier, providing a cheery, blue backdrop for a bashful sun. Few riders were taking advantage of the unusually fine morning, Neil noted. Most of London, at least those of his own class, slept right through it. He couldn't regret that today. The fewer people about, the fewer he would have to be wary of.

Bettsy sat her mare easily and naturally, as though she had ridden astride all her life. Neil stole a sidelong glance and felt a warm glow of pride in her adaptability.

She clicked her tongue and shot ahead even as he watched, reveling in her freedom from hampering skirts and sidesaddle. He nudged the gelding into a gallop and easily caught up.

"Dally's not cut out for racing, you know," he admonished, leaning forward and laughing, as they reined in near the edge of the trees on a sunny, deserted path.

"Neither am I," she said, breathless and beaming. "Shall we walk a bit?" Without waiting for his answer, she slid down from her mare and wrapped the reins around one fist. "I've gotten too used to this. I love it."

"Our masquerade, you mean?" he asked, knowing exactly what she meant. He liked it, too, in spite of the reasons for it. Bettsy dashing about in breeches was a sight to see. Regretfully he glanced at her bosom, severely flattened under her dark green frock coat. What would she would look like in a satin ballgown, breasts half-exposed, ruffled hoops flaring out from that incredibly tiny waist of hers? On second thought, maybe he didn't love the masculine disguise all that much.

"I only wish it were more productive," Bettsy said, interrupting his increasingly carnal thoughts. "Do you suppose we'll go on forever, doctor and assistant, researcher and protégé?" She grew serious as they walked beside the man-made lake. "It's been weeks since we began. All we've gleaned are rumors about Colin's search for me and his plans to pay his debts. What if we never learn whether he really killed Terry? Shall I just disappear after a while, do you think?"

"No," he answered quickly, wanting to erase her frown, charming as it was. "I think we will eventually resolve all this, one way or another. Then we should marry, move to the country and live happily ever after."

"Ha! I almost forget from time to time what a fool you can be. Don't mention marriage anymore, Neil. You know how I feel about it. It's a stupid idea."

He wouldn't give it up. Every time the opportunity arose, Neil casually mentioned marriage. Every time, like clockwork, she refused. He thought he knew why—to protect him—and that salved his pride somewhat. But it did nothing for his burning need to claim her officially, physically and every other way there was. He was totally smitten and resigned to it.

Neil knew his only hope for her acceptance of a proposal was to publicly prove her innocent of Terry's death and then demolish the rumors that, to her mind at least, made her unacceptable as a wife. One feat seemed almost as impossible as the other, but he was determined. It was the only way he could have her.

She obviously liked him very well, and he was sure she would come to love him eventually. He'd see to it. Right now, he had to bide his time and get her used to the idea. Wear her down if he must.

"Oh well, it was just a thought," he said offhandedly, flashing his most ingratiating smile.

"Well, don't think it," she ordered, increasing her pace and looking off in the distance.

"Oh, all right. If you won't marry me, then how about sharing breakfast? I'm suddenly famished. Why don't we—?"

Neil halted midquestion when she stopped with a jerk and grabbed at his sleeve. "Mount up, Neil," she whispered urgently, her voice frightened and her body tense.

"What is it?" He followed the direction of her stare and saw three riders. They were hardly close enough to identify, but Neil didn't think he knew them. The man riding a huge gray reined to a stop facing their direction. Neil felt a sudden flicker of recognition. Something about the posture...

"It's Colin! That's his bay. Hurry!" She swung into the saddle, turned her mount and spurred to a gallop before Neil was fully seated.

He bolted after her, catching up before she reached the path that led out of the park. "Slow down!" he called. "They aren't following."

"Did he see me? Do you think he knew it was us?" she asked, breathless from exertion and probably fear. Her eyes were round and her manner agitated. Neil knew she had taken his and Lindy's deductions to heart, even though she didn't want to believe her cousin guilty of Terry's death. Colin was dangerous and she knew it. He had two men with him. If they had gotten closer and were armed, Neil knew both he and Bettsy might now be lying dead on the ground.

"No, I don't think he noticed us," Neil lied, hoping to calm her. "Even if he did, what could he do in the middle of the park?"

She fingered her scar. Good point, Neil admitted with a

grimace. He knew Bettsy's nerves were near the edge and his weren't in much better shape. None of Lindy's men were anywhere about, that he could see. What had happened to the damned surveillance?

Bettsy had just taken her last morning ride in the park. There could be no more public outings of any kind. They'd be worse than foolish to risk a closer encounter with the man, whether he knew Bettsy's identity or not.

They arrived home shortly before ten. Elizabeth paced the kitchen, pausing fitfully to read over his shoulder as Neil scribbled a hurried message to Lindy. He advised him that Colin had returned to London and demanded to know why they hadn't been warned of his arrival. Once he'd sealed the missive, Oliver took it directly to Scotland Yard.

Regardless of Neil's reassurance to the contrary, Elizabeth was almost certain her cousin had recognized her. His sudden alertness, that stiffening of his posture, had looked like surprise, even at a distance. She was convinced Colin hadn't known before about her disguise or that she was under Neil's protection, but he almost surely did now.

That would mean Colin couldn't have been responsible for her being shot at the theater. He would be planning some course of action to inherit her wealth, though. Like her immediate arrest and certain conviction. Could there be two separate threats?

Had Emma or Turner or some unknown enemy been behind the rumor, after all?

At first Elizabeth had convinced herself that Bensen's shooting her was the result of a joke gone awry. Biddie and Turner were always teasing her, prodding her about her conquests. Secretly, she believed Biddie's overactive mouth had been responsible. She hadn't mentioned it because she didn't want Neil to pound him to a pulp.

Seeing Colin today and knowing he had recognized her suddenly sent her imagination reeling, made her recall the former attempts on her life. It reinforced the fact that someone really wanted her dead. And if Colin had found her, even if he wasn't the one trying to kill her, he could have her arrested for murder now that he knew where she was. Probably had already notified the Yard of her disguise. Thank God Lindy was in charge of the case.

She felt hunted.

By evening, Elizabeth felt like screaming with frustration. Neil had tried his best to keep her busy in the lab, until she dropped a case of his costly test tubes. Luncheon, and later tea, were forgotten. Neither even mentioned supper. Sleep was out of the question, even though it was near midnight.

Neil looked as apprehensive as she felt. Three times he had mentioned taking her to the Continent for her safety. However, all the ports were watched, and they couldn't flee without Lindy's help.

They sat over coffee in the kitchen, waiting, starting at every noise that broke the midnight silence. "Why hasn't he come?" she asked, voicing the question they'd both been asking themselves since midmorning.

"Well, Lindy does have a job, you know. There are other cases besides ours that need his attention."

She crossed one booted ankle over her knee and leaned forward. The masculine pose bolstered her courage a little, made her feel less like a fainthearted damsel in distress, anyway. "If Colin did recognize me, what do you think he will—?"

MacLinden's coded knock interrupted her.

"Where the hell have you been?" Neil barked as he jerked open the door.

Lindy took off his bowler and smoothed down his carroty waves. His usually merry eyes were a dark and somber green. "You'd both better sit down."

Elizabeth pounded a fist in her palm and slumped back down in her chair. "I knew it! Colin's turned me in, hasn't he?"

"Yes, in a manner of speaking," MacLinden replied, shrugging out of his cape. "He came to the Yard about eight o'clock this morning to let us know he'd found you."

"That's impossible! He didn't see us in the park until half past nine," Neil said.

MacLinden's bushy eyebrow rose, and one side of his mouth quirked, throwing his mustache out of kilter. "Ah, I see. Must have cut through there on his way from the Yard. Well, at any rate, he assured me that his dear cousin, Lady Elizabeth Marleigh, was resting peacefully at Kick's Folly in Kent. You know the place, Betts—the fake castle ruin on the Marleigh estate?"

He paused dramatically, looking from one to the other. Then he added in his own inimitable way, "Seems his poor mad cousin has a bullet in her head. From the missing pistol, you see. Dead quite a while—a good fortnight, I'd say. Murder, suicide, with matching guns. Ties things up nicely, eh what?"

Elizabeth couldn't speak. There were simply too many questions to push one out coherently. A quick glance at Neil told her he was having the same problem. MacLinden looked entirely too pleased with the effect, damn the rascal.

"That's where I've been all day," Lindy explained. "Had to go down there and see what was what, of course, and transport the body back to the city. Ugly errand and not quite finished, I'm afraid."

He looked squarely at Elizabeth with something approaching sympathy. "You'll have to see her, Betts. I'm sorry about it, but you must."

"Impossible," Neil said, coming around the table to drape an arm across her shoulders. She welcomed the warmth and the protest on her behalf. "Don't ask this of her, Lindy. Not after all she's been through."

"Necessary, my friend, or you know I wouldn't suggest it. We've got to know for certain if the girl is who I think she is. Best we go on down to the morgue tonight when there are few people about. Hate to insist, but there you are." He raised his palms and shrugged.

Moments later, Elizabeth sank into the corner of the carriage, trying to steel herself for what was to come. If the situation weren't so macabre, the disjointed conversation going on between Lindy and Neil would have been laughable.

"I had Thurston, the old butler, come this evening to view the body," Lindy said. "Insists it's 'her ladyship' without a doubt. The old sod almost broke down. Felt right sorry for him."

Neil rapped the side of his fist on the edge of the window. "I can't believe you'd make Bettsy do this. Damn it, man, she's not up to such a thing."

"Corpse is about the same size as Betts here. Hair's cut the same, color's right but probably not natural." Lindy was trying to prepare her, Elizabeth realized while he spoke. He was subtly reducing the body to an inanimate object. It certainly was that *now*, she thought, shivering. Nothing to fear, just a gruesome sight she'd have to endure. But she did fear it.

Neil didn't appear to hear a word Lindy said. It was as though he had forgotten their presence in the carriage and was carrying on a conversation with himself. "This morning shook her so badly, she was all thumbs in the lab. Completely off her feed all day. Now she has to do this! God." He paused, leaning his head against his hand, elbow propped against the side of the carriage.

"The gun was in her hand, y'see, but I can't think why she'd have had it in her left, when the entry wound was in the right temple." MacLinden nodded toward Elizabeth knowingly. "Exit wound's the messy one, don't you know. That's how you can tell. Entry's fairly neat, as a rule."

Neil spoke again. "I've left my med bag at home and she'll probably be sick all over the place. Faint or something, and me with no smelling salts. Understandable if she does. Cadavers aren't my cup of tea, either. Immediate death is bad enough to witness, but this…? One never gets used to it."

Lindy rambled on, directing his comments to Elizabeth. "I think I have some bay rum in my desk and some extra hankies. The odor, you see, is still—"

Elizabeth clapped her hands over her ears. "Stop this! Just stop it, both of you!"

Two deep breaths later, she opened her eyes and glared at them in the carriage light. "Are you trying to make me sick beforehand? Are you?"

Neil wore the visage of someone just coming out of a sound sleep. Lindy looked chagrined.

"We have to do this, all right?" she said firmly, palm out to ward off any answer before she could finish. "Just be quiet! Don't say another word, either of you."

The basement morgue was worse than her expectation, which was nothing good to begin with. The cold smell of death and acrid chemicals permeated the air inside the building. The low gaslight threw exaggerated shadows over the silent corridor. Elizabeth felt the urge to hold her breath. When they entered the cold room full of sheet-draped tables, she had to.

A gray-faced attendant, who looked as if he might have just risen from under one of those sheets himself, sat writing at a small desk near the door. He paused for a second and, nodding once to MacLinden, returned to his paperwork.

Lindy placed a hand on Elizabeth's shoulder, guiding her quickly to the table nearest the light. Without ceremony, he pulled the sheet back to just above the breasts.

Elizabeth gasped, and the smell of putrefaction filled her nose and throat. Her gorge rose so swiftly it took her by surprise. She ran. Even as she did so, a disengaged part of her mind scorned her reaction.

Outside the door, she stopped, gagged over a dustbin and thanked heaven she'd skipped today's meals. Neil held her shoulders from behind, offering support in the form of muttered curses.

Elizabeth drew in several deep breaths, wondering if she'd ever be able to smell anything pleasant again. Then something inside her clicked into place. She had to do this. Shrugging out of Neil's grip, she reentered the room and strode unsteadily toward the table, where Lindy still stood.

"It's Maggie," she said, staring at the pale, bloated woman

who had sent her a death's brew not six weeks earlier. "It's definitely Margaret Leffing, my maid."

In spite of wobbly knees, Elizabeth managed to walk out under her own steam, batting angrily at Neil's hands when he tried to support her. She had squashed the rolled brim of her top hat and sweated through her shirt and waistcoat, but at least she felt better about herself now. She had done what had to be done and had gotten through it. But courage be damned, she would never forget it as long as she lived.

The men were thankfully silent on the ride home. Mac-Linden leaned out the window after she and Neil had exited the carriage. "That was a brave night's work. Good show, Betts."

"It was a thrice-damned nightmare and you bloody well know it. Both of you can...just go to hell!" she spat, satisfied at his look of shock, the very first one she'd ever seen him wear. Her eyes cut to Neil. "Your mouth's open." Then she turned on her heel and swaggered up the path to the kitchen door.

The whole day held an aura of unreality. She had been profane just now, but life was suddenly profane. Why should she feel this strange, light-headed buoyancy? she wondered. Was this what a mix of terror, relief and fury produced?

She felt the urge to laugh again. *Inappropriate.* That's how she felt—inappropriate, loose and reckless, a bit wild, unraveled. She tamped down the hysteria, bit her lips together and sucked in a deep breath through her nose. What else could possibly happen? Nothing worse tonight, surely to God.

Neil followed her in, lighting the lamp while she tossed her ruined hat toward the coffee grinder. It stuck on the upturned handle. He watched her smile at the small success, more of a grimace really. "Are you all right, Bettsy?"

"Oh, of course! Just wonderful! How about you? Great evening's sport, what? Biddie and Tun would've said as much. We should have taken them with us. Come see our corpse, lads! Was she a friend of yours, Tun? Did you blow out her brains?"

Neil frowned when she clapped a hand over her mouth, uncertain whether she was about to burst into laughter, tears or gag again. He noticed her pupils, dilated even in the bright light from the lamp. A tremor in her legs almost wrecked her balance. *Shock.* Neil's heart contracted at the sight. She must be at her rope's end.

He swept her up in his arms and carried her upstairs. She felt rigid in his arms. Her hands opened and closed frantically as she gripped his cloak. It was a major effort to disentangle them when they arrived in his room.

"I'm all right. I am. I will be," she said like a litany, her voice thick with determination.

Neil lifted her onto the edge of the high four-poster. "Just sit here, love," he ordered softly. "Sit here on the bed for a moment. I'll fetch you a tot."

"No," she shouted, grabbing his collar and drawing him to her. "Don't." Her voice was unnaturally high-pitched, but it dropped to a whisper. "Please, don't go. Don't leave me."

As if he could.

Neil sighed and wrapped his arms around Bettsy, pulling her against him as he moved between her legs. The side of the bed frame braced his knees. He wished something would brace up his resolve. It appeared to be crumbling fast under the force of his untimely desire and the way she was clinging to him. "You're shivering. Are you cold, sweet?"

He brushed a hand over her head and held it to his chest. Bettsy's face burrowed into the opening of his cloak like a kitten seeking warmth. Her hands snaked inside, around his waist, and clutched the back of his waistcoat.

Neil felt the familiar, constant ache for her increase to fever pitch as she pressed against him. The height of the bed where she sat placed her just right to... *No! Not now,* he prayed. *Don't even let me think about that now.*

Her palms gripped his buttocks and forced him closer. Small, slender legs wound around his thighs. He was hard against her warmth, only the soft wool fabric of their breeches between them.

This had to stop.

"Bettsy…"

"Neil," she murmured, then lifted her head and tilted her face back. "Kiss me."

"You're not yourself right now," he said, desperate to do exactly as she asked and knowing she would hate him for it in the morning. He'd hate himself right along with her. "We shouldn't." The words sounded oddly encouraging and he hadn't meant them to. "I ought to—"

She arched against him, an age-old plea. He totally forgot what he ought to do. Good intentions fled like a runaway train. His mouth closed over hers, greeting her iciness with his encompassing heat. His arms gathered her hard against him, hands rushing over her back, around and between them to tug at her buttons.

Clothes flew in a rough and frantic peeling of layers interspersed by greedy kisses and groans of need. When they were both bare, he pushed against her in the same position he had held only moments before. Nothing stood between them now except the part of him seeking entry.

Her fingers found him, squeezing, demanding, guiding. Neil groaned as she shifted her hips and cried out in welcome.

*Home.* The sensation flooded through his mind, just as it had before, the first time. Its shadowy memory overlay reality like a double vision. *Home inside her. Again.* A forever feeling beyond any words. Sustaining it suddenly became his sole ambition in life.

He drove deeper and deeper still, needing all that was there for him, a space in her body, a place in her heart.

*I love you.* He felt the words, wasn't certain if he'd voiced them, didn't know if he could speak even if he wanted to. But she knew. How could she not know?

The delicious, heady sensation billowed, washing through him in tremendous waves, threatening to spill. *Not yet, oh please, a little longer.*

Her body thrust hard against his, and inside her, shudders

gripped him like an insistent fist. Harsh cries rent the night, echoed in his head, throughout the room, the house, the world.

''Mine,'' he gasped, thinking it might be his last breath, not caring if it was.

Neil closed over her as she lay back against the bed. A major effort of strength brought his lips to her lashes to taste whether she wept.

There were no tears, but her words breathed softly against his cheek. *Thank you?* What an absurd thing for her to say. Her lack of eloquence almost matched his own. He would have laughed if he'd had any energy left.

She lay in his arms, totally relaxed and warm. Soothed. Not the way he'd first intended, but he was satisfied with the results and inordinately so with the method of achievement.

When he could make his limbs behave, he moved away from her and lifted her legs onto the mattress, crawling up beside her almost simultaneously. He dragged the coverlet around them and pulled her into his arms, snuggling them both in a cocoon of down-filled satin.

Everything he'd ever yearned for was his tonight, right now, this very minute. If only he could find a way to hold her for the rest of his life.

Hours later, though he was exhausted physically, his mental processes still refused to shut down. Neil knew there would be no rest for him until the matter of Bettsy's future was settled, the murderer caught and hanged. She might be safe from arrest at the moment, with the Yard thinking she was dead, but somewhere out there was a man who knew the body in the morgue was not Bettsy's. The danger to her was acute and, if her fancied ''rhythm'' was just a little out of sync, she might not be the only one in need of saving. Neither thought was conducive to sleep.

Elizabeth woke late. Her rumbling stomach told her it had been a long time since she had eaten her last meal. She stretched languorously, muscles protesting, skin tingling against the satin covers. Getting out of bed held little appeal.

When she did, she'd have to confront the fact that she wore nothing at all but a giddy smile and the scent of Neil Bronwyn.

Yesterday's events tumbled through her mind. Elizabeth Marleigh was safely dead, she reminded herself. For now at least, she needn't worry about being hauled away in chains. Lindy had said Colin had identified Maggie's body as hers. With the search for Lady Marleigh called off, she should be able to leave England without interference.

Colin would inherit most of her money, unfortunately, but not the secret account she had established in Edinburgh under a fictitious name. Thank God she had made preparations to leave before Terry was murdered. If Neil hadn't abducted her that night, she might have been taken into custody before she even reached the border. Even he would have believed her guilty.

Neil had saved her then from certain death, and again at the theater. And last night, when she had endured more horror than she'd have thought possible for one day, he had saved her once more. Had he left her alone in the state she was in, she would surely have qualified for a madhouse.

Neil Bronwyn definitely knew how to fight madness with madness. Had she but known what delicious delights were possible, she would never have waited until she was desperate for comfort. Perhaps that had made it all the sweeter. At any rate, the first time, when she'd been in charge and he stewed in liquor, offered nothing by comparison.

What must he be thinking this morning? The truth, no doubt—that Elizabeth Marleigh was a reckless wanton without a shred of moral fibre. Well, when hadn't he thought so? She had been labeled that for months and wasn't the least bit sorry that it was now true. Hadn't the episode in the study been calculated on her part just to achieve this end?

He would worry about a pregnancy, she knew, but there would be no child. Last night hardly mattered, since her courses were already late and due anytime now. Nanny had been very specific. Elizabeth distinctly remembered her saying many times that two weeks afterward was the proper time to schedule relations if one wanted to conceive. Exactly two weeks.

As much as she would love a child of Neil's, it would be a selfish thing to bear one. She would have to keep scrupulous track of the timing to avoid it if they were intimate again.

She didn't think even fear of pregnancy would have mattered last night. Her courage had failed her at the morgue. She was just glad she had plucked it up until the necessary task of viewing what was left of Maggie was over. And thankful Neil had rescued her from a night of horrible dreams about the whole event.

How marvelous to lose herself in him, if only for a little while. Neil had carried her away in a storm of pleasure to a realm of peace and forgetfulness. Even if he damned her because of it, she would thank him all her life for that.

Elizabeth admitted she loved him, though she dared not let him know it. She would have to make light of last night in spite of her deep feelings. If not, he would insist on following her wherever she went to hide, or making her stay with him, a dangerous proposition for both of them.

At least marriage was out of the question now. They couldn't wed legally without revealing her identity. Even if Lindy and Neil ever discovered the murderer and cleared her of the charge, Elizabeth Marleigh must remain dead. Neil would see the wisdom in that.

# Chapter Twelve

Forcing herself from the warmth of bed, Elizabeth washed and dressed quickly. She dared not let him catch her abed in this soft, reflective mood, mooning over her regrets, wishing for things she couldn't have. Better she should treat last night's lovemaking lightly, as a sort of whim born of her fear. If he thought their intimacy meant little to her, that he was only one of countless lovers, he'd surely give up the idea that they had any sort of future together. His pride might suffer a bit, but better that than total ruin.

Lindy had already arrived and was talking with Neil when she entered the kitchen. The inspector looked disgustingly chipper this morning in his dapper, plaid suit. Neil looked like the wrath of God—hurriedly dressed, unshaven and glowering at both of them through bloodshot eyes.

So much for the sweet aftermath of lovemaking, she thought with a pang of disappointment. He looked like he'd eaten green apples and suffered a bellyache.

"Good morning," she said. Forcing cheerfulness, she plopped down across the table from Neil and took up a scone.

"Afternoon," Lindy corrected, sliding the butter dish toward her. "Mum sent marmalade. Orange. Abominable stuff." He gobbled down a portion of scone slathered with the fruit preserve and licked his lips.

"So I see," she said. "News?"

"We've decided not to hang you," Lindy quipped, grinning at Neil's growled reprimand.

"Lovely, now I can stop practicing my gallows speech. So your chief believes Maggie was the murderess?" she asked, realizing that life as they lived it now would soon change.

"And believes she is you, as I'm certain you've guessed," Lindy said, pausing to sip his tea. "Colin never viewed the woman's body, unless, of course, he was the one who killed her. That's very likely, by the way. He says the gamekeeper found her and notified him. The fact that she wore your clothing and two of your rings rather convinces me he's involved up to his neck. You were right about his being squeamish, though. Refused outright to look at her. Gagged at the thought."

"What about Thurston?" she asked. "When you first told me he had identified her as me yesterday, I figured that Maggie must be unrecognizable. She wasn't quite that. He should have known her."

"Maybe not," Lindy said. "His sight's probably dimmed, and he was expecting it to be you. I'd already shown him the jewelry she had on. The body was a hard thing to look at closely, as you know."

Elizabeth swallowed heavily and lowered her eyes. "Yes, I do know." Neil took her hand and squeezed it comfortingly.

She allowed that, though she knew it wasn't wise to encourage any tender feelings he might have. So far, he'd said nothing to her since she came down.

There were dark circles under his eyes, as though he hadn't slept at all. He wore the spectacles this morning, probably trying to conceal the evidence of his sleeplessness. Or, bleary-eyed as he was, maybe he really needed them to see.

The question foremost in her mind slipped out before she was ready to hear the answer. "So where do we go from here?"

Elizabeth held her breath, options flashing through her mind. She could leave England and disappear, now that pursuit by the authorities was not a problem. She supposed she could simply reappear as the unjustly accused Lady Marleigh, now that Maggie had been found with the other gun. Or she could remain here as Neil's assistant and let Colin have the damned inheritance.

Elizabeth yearned to stay. Aside from the danger, she quite liked the life she had assumed.

Neil started to speak up, but Lindy silenced him with an admonishing finger. The inspector seemed to be feeling his importance this morning. His smile looked sly as a fox stalking chickens. "Now I'll tell you the really good news. I've traced the rumor to Lord John Goodroe. He says he thought to throw suspicion off himself when Bensen started asking pointed questions about who his sister sneaked out to see. Pointed the finger at you, Betts. Shouldn't have beat him so often at the tables. So now we know the shooting is totally unrelated to the murders, and your role is still safe to play. We still don't have our killer. You needn't worry—at least about an arrest. I dare say your reputation might suffer another blow if anyone should ever find out who you really are."

"But that's hardly worth mentioning, is it?" she replied with a humorless laugh. "Shall we continue to march?"

"Aye, lass!" Lindy agreed theatrically. "That we shall." He dropped the Scots accent he affected now and then and became serious, looking pointedly at Neil. "You and Betts must step up your activity. Be seen everywhere. Ask direct questions of anybody you think might possibly know anything about Terry's death. I want all of London to know you aren't accepting this murder-suicide conclusion the Yard has drawn.

"We have our suspects lined up now. There's Colin Marleigh in the lead. Had the best access to everything, including the clothes and jewelry Maggie was wearing. Turner's a close second."

Neil interrupted, shaking his head. "Turner couldn't have killed Maggie Leffing. He didn't even know her."

"Oh, but he could very well have known her. He and Biddenton have cut a wide swath through London's supply of shopgirls, ladies' maids, governesses and companions. Neither fellow is considered top-drawer enough for the debutantes, you see,'' Lindy explained. ''Turner, for all his shy ways, definitely has an inroad with the lassies of modest means. His title, though it's merely a courtesy one, attracts them like ants to a picnic. Simplest thing in the world for him to befriend a maid who might aid him in setting up Betts for Terry's murder.''

Bettsy agreed with Neil, who was still shaking his head. ''That's too far-fetched even for you, Lindy. Turner's not our man.''

Lindy shrugged and clicked his tongue against his pipe. ''That leaves our stranger from the theater running a distant third. I believe it has to be one of the three. Colin and Turner are being watched every hour of the day. If one of them bolts or is bold enough to make a move, then we'll know. I want whoever it is running scared enough to trip over his own feet.''

Neil removed the spectacles and placed them carefully on the table. Elizabeth watched his hands complete the precise movements and realized how tense he was.

His voice sounded even and controlled, too much so to be natural. ''And what if it is our third suspect, Lindy? Or perhaps someone none of us has so much as thought about? I recall your mentioning Colin's natural father as a possibility. We still have no idea who that man could be. Bettsy could be killed by a total stranger while your men are trailing about after the first two on your list. How are we to guard against the unknown?''

''We have two men stationed outside your house who'll follow you everywhere,'' Lindy reassured him. ''They're my best, Neil. There's no chance anyone could get near Betts.''

''Don't be an idiot,'' Neil growled. ''Anyone inside any of the clubs—where your chaps can't follow, by the way—could simply level her with another shot, or a knife.'' His voice rose with each supposition. ''There's no way to protect her fully, Lindy. No way in hell.''

Dead silence settled over the kitchen. Elizabeth rattled her teacup in its dish just to break the tension.

"I'm sorry," Neil said softly, "but I won't risk her life anymore, not even to find whoever killed Terry."

"It's not up to you, Neil," Elizabeth said, placing a hand on his arm. She felt the corded tension through his sleeve. "It is my decision and I think Lindy's right. We have to draw the man out somehow."

Neil shoved away from the table, his chair scraping harshly on the kitchen tiles. Without another word, he strode angrily out of the room. Only when they heard an upstairs door slam did she and Lindy look at each other.

Lindy's smile was slow, but genuine. "Sex makes him surly. You might make a note of that."

Elizabeth burst into laughter. Each time she sobered and looked at Lindy's cocky grin, she relapsed. It was a ridiculous response, a full admission of her intimacy with Neil, but she couldn't seem to help it.

"I love a lass with a sense of humor," Lindy remarked wryly. He stood and donned his hat, giving its crown a satisfied pat. "Send round when he mellows enough to see reason, will you?"

She could only nod and wipe her eyes.

The reprieve made her giddy. She could stay with Neil awhile longer. Might as well admit it, she thought—relief greatly outweighed the fear she felt. And relief equaled laughter. Always had since she was a child.

How many times had that "inappropriate response," as her father had called it, gotten her into trouble? Too many times to count, especially in the past few months.

She had laughed wildly at Neil after he'd abducted her, as soon as he'd convinced her she was safe and offered her a place to hide. Safety for the first time in months had been a heady thing. He must have thought she'd lost her mind.

She had laughed after her escape from drowning. Colin and all his friends saw the whole episode as a lark because of that. All but one, perhaps—the man who had drilled the hole in the boat. Her hysteria must have confused the hell out of him.

There had been no laughter after the knife incident, though.

There had been no relief at all then. After locking the dressing-room door against the attacker, she had remained terrified.

Well, at least she hadn't been the one giggling and dancing about in the fountain afterward. That had been another woman, probably Maggie. The maid had to have been involved; that was almost certainly why she had been killed. Perhaps she had threatened to tell or tried to blackmail whoever gave the orders.

With the tainted chocolate, everything had happened so fast. The little kitchen maid's sudden fit and leap off the balcony; Colin's rushing in that way. Had Elizabeth lost control then? She had. Her own hysteria had prevented her from drinking the glass of something Maggie had fetched for her afterward. Probably saved her life, now that she thought about it. Maggie had disappeared after that. Immediately after.

Well, laughing was better than crying, Elizabeth supposed, even if tears seemed more normal under the circumstances. No one had ever accused her of normalcy, even before all the troubles began. Colin had always said she was a little strange. He was a fine one to cast stones at her, though.

Colin and Maggie. They had to have conspired. And then he'd killed Maggie for fear she would give him away.

Elizabeth hated to believe it of Colin. He'd mostly been kind to her when they were children. Perhaps they hadn't been the closest of friends, but she couldn't recall a really harsh word between them. Except after the awful incidents that he must have arranged himself.

He wanted her wealth, and that was a fact. No one else had a real reason to kill her. He must have promised Maggie the world to get her assistance. And poor Terry had put himself directly in Colin's way by offering her the protection of the Havington name.

Colin had murdered twice and would again if need be. She must make herself accept that and deal with it.

But first, she had to mollify Neil and make him see the importance of solving Terry's murder officially. If they didn't establish Colin's guilt and have him arrested, Elizabeth knew she would be running for the rest of her life. And that life might be woefully short once she was out from under Neil's protection.

Any further relationship with Neil after she abandoned the role of his assistant was out of the question. By the time they had Colin in custody and all this was over, Neil should be sufficiently disgusted with her to let her go gracefully.

With that thought firmly in mind, she tugged down her gabardine waistcoat and braced herself for the necessary confrontation.

A crash and curse from the upper floor halted her at the foot of the stairs. She took the steps two at a time and burst into Neil's bedroom. He paced like a wild animal, pausing only to kick the remains of a broken water pitcher into the fireplace. Elizabeth saw that he'd changed again and now wore his riding clothes.

When he sensed she was there, he rounded on her, throwing one hand in the air and shaking a finger. "Don't you even try to stop me. You stay right here or I'll haul you back and tie you to the bedpost, and that's a promise!"

"Where are you going?"

"To take Colin Marleigh apart, piece by piece, until I get to the bottom of this! Today! I'll rip his mealy little heart out by its roots and make him eat the damn thing!"

Without thinking of the consequences, Elizabeth cracked her palm across his face as hard as she could.

Neil stood there, arm raised, stunned for a good five seconds. She watched the anger drain from his face along with the color, leaving it pale but for her crimson handprint. He seemed to gather his senses as she watched. Slowly, his massive shoulders relaxed, almost drooped. His eyes grew lighter as the pupils contracted. Then he blinked hard and looked away, his jaw clenching several times beneath the dark stubble of beard.

"Sit down!" she ordered in the most imperious tone she could muster. To her amazement, he backed up and sat down on the bed.

"Now then," she said, lowering her voice to a reasonable level and clasping her hands behind her. "Let's be rational about this, shall we?"

"Yes. Rational. By all means," he agreed quietly.

"For heaven's sake, Neil, I'm not going to thrash you. Look at me!"

He kept his eyes on his hands, which lay palms up on his lap. When he spoke, the words were so subdued she had to lean closer to hear. "I want to kill the man, Bettsy. All night long I thought about it. All night after we... I tried for control. Almost had it, too. Until Lindy came."

Neil looked deeply troubled, too much so to be cured by a smack. Elizabeth knew he felt trapped between his primitive urge to do battle and his carefully fostered mask of gentility.

"Neil, anger's a natural reaction under the circumstances, don't you think? Strangling the little bastard appeals to me, too, but you know we can't do that."

He met her eyes then, his looking lost and empty. "I'm supposed to save lives, Bettsy. That's what I've trained all my adult life to do, what I vowed with the physician's oath to do. But, by God, I ache to kill him. Even now. Even if he's not the one who murdered Terry. Removing him would mean one less evil to threaten you. In truth, I want nothing better than to kill them all—Colin, Turner, Bensen. All of them."

She moved toward him, standing between his legs, and put her hands on his shoulders. "Neil, you're making too much of this. It's only frustration."

"No, no." He shook his head, dropping it forward to rest on her chest. "I've killed before, you see. With these." She felt the slight movement of his hands between them. Those sensitive, healing, pleasure-giving hands.

A chill rippled down her spine, a recollection of his training in the oriental martial arts. Every day he practiced in the garden below her window, sometimes alone, sometimes with Oliver. She had seen enough of the moves to realize how lethal they could be. The heel of a hand to the nose, a blow to the windpipe. *No!* She suppressed her shiver of suspicion. Neil was no killer. What he was speaking of must have been some sort of accident, surgery gone wrong or a fluke accident of some kind. Surely. "Tell me."

Instead he sighed, lifted his head and looked straight into her eyes. She saw the dark blue of his clouded by despair. "All my life I've fought against this wildness inside me. Well," he qualified, "at least since I was old enough to know I had to change or be damned for it."

He shifted restlessly against her, but she inched closer and kept her hands on him, afraid to let go lest she run away to avoid hearing this. She knew if she ran, he would abandon himself to whatever devils drove him, and Lord knew what he might do. "Go on," she said as calmly as she could.

"I was five when I realized what I was like. Mother told me often and in no uncertain terms how vicious I was. And then, as soon as Father died, she left me in that place. Reddingote Academy. When I saw her leave, knowing I'd never see her again, I just came undone. I struck out at the nearest person, one of the masters. I bit, I kicked, I wanted to destroy him. Her, really, I suppose, but she was no longer there."

He lapsed into brief silence as though lost in the memory. "He beat me senseless, of course. Most of them did at one time or another. Right away, that first day, they recognized me as a troublemaker. Every time I lost my temper or upset their scheme of things in any way, I was punished. Conformity was a struggle, to say the least.

"By the time I was twelve, I became a model student." He laughed dryly. "Not a very quick study, was I?"

She smiled and smoothed a hand over the cheek she'd slapped. He hardly seemed aware of her touch.

"Everyone liked me after that. I had a handle on life. Followed all the rules, did everything right. Until I met Emma. She brought out the very worst in me. All those lessons in passiveness and self-control went flying right out of my head like birds let loose. Our affair escalated to a near nightly orgy. I reverted to that wild and impetuous beast my mother had named me. That must have frightened Emma, because she ran away to the first man who offered her his name. Left me without so much as a goodbye."

Elizabeth couldn't hold back a snort at that. "Ran from the beast, eh? Straight into a title and money. I think you vastly overrate your scare tactics, Neil. She certainly came galloping back in a hurry when she heard you were an earl. If she was afraid of anything back then, it was that you couldn't afford her expensive tastes."

Neil nodded faintly. "That was part of it, I know. But even if I could excuse the unleashed passions that helped drive her away, there's what happened afterward. I had this urge, almost uncontrollable, to kill her when I found she'd married. And old Lord Curtiss, too, for taking her."

"But you didn't act on that urge. You behaved honorably, don't you see? Wished them well in person."

"I wished them in hell privately, you may be sure," he said. "I convinced myself it was better to beat them down there than to hand them tickets."

"So you went to war?" she asked softly, brushing his hair back from his forehead.

"I sold the house I'd bought for Emma and myself and purchased my commission. Meant to take up a horse and saber for the final tantrum of my life."

"Ah, rid the world of the fearsome Dr. Bronwyn, eh?"

"It was no joke." He brushed a hand over his face and captured her fingers at the side of his neck. "They stuck me in hospital at Balaclava, of course. With cholera rampant, doctors were in short supply. I'll admit the rage had cooled somewhat by the time I arrived there. Literally surrounded by death, I found I wasn't really so eager to die, after all."

He swallowed heavily. "Three weeks later, I killed him."

"Who?" she whispered, feathering her fingers through the hair at his temples, dreading to hear what he was about to say.

"A Russian, a patient. He'd been wounded and captured behind our lines. Apparently, his wounds were not as incapacitating as the attending physician believed.

"I happened on him struggling with a nurse, trying to get

past her through the door to escape." Neil stopped talking, his face so pale the shadows underneath his eyes looked purple. "Poor little bird—one of Nightingale's finest—with no thought in her head but to keep the bastard from breaking his stitches."

"Finish it, Neil," she encouraged gently. "Tell the rest."

"I'd have let him go, I think, but the brute snapped her neck like a twig. I heard the crack. After that I don't remember much...my hands locked around his throat, choking sounds, his eyes." Neil leaned his head back and stared at the ceiling. "They said even after he was dead, someone had to knock me out to make me release him."

"I shouldn't wonder," Elizabeth whispered. The images he painted were all too vivid. She felt him sag against her. This misplaced guilt of his would never do, she thought.

"I love you, but you scare me, Bettsy," he muttered, his hands rubbing her hips just below the waist.

"I do? How so?" she asked, confused by the sudden change in subject, if not the mood.

"I had it all together again until I met you. You make me do things I despair of doing, and without thinking first—kidnapping, abandoning my ethics, ranting like a maniac, wanting to commit murder. Did you know I very nearly killed the man who shot you? Would have done, exactly as I did that Russian, had the watch not arrived in time to save him. I went...mad."

He flexed his hands, staring at them as though they were covered in blood. Then he looked up with a glitter of defiance brightening his eyes. "Even now I can't say that would have been a bad day's work. My lack of regret worries me as much as the violence. I want to regret, but I don't quite feel it. I think I was born a savage. Worst of all—and, honestly, I can't even pretend I'm sorry for it—was forcing myself on you."

She threw back her head with a crack of laughter. "Forcing yourself on me? When?"

"In the study that night. You were foxed."

"Not half as foxed as you were. And I wasn't drinking at all last night," she reminded him.

He straightened a little and clicked his tongue, exasperated by her determined defense of him. "You were terribly upset after our visit to the morgue! I took awful advantage, and you know it."

She grabbed his face in her hands and smiled directly into his eyes. "Umm, awfully wonderful advantage it was, too. Didn't scare me a bit. Maybe I'm just as savage as you are."

Her fingernails dug into his cheeks in a mock attack. Her smile felt as feral as she meant it to look. "We're *all* born that way, Neil. Savagery's elemental, a survival instinct. Danger and passion just thin that veneer of civility." She pulled his mouth to hers and bit his bottom lip. "You rub my veneer away entirely." Again she nipped and whispered, "Do it."

He took her mouth, ravaged it with the ferocity of a determined conqueror, plundered it without mercy. She slid her hands into his hair, grasped two handfuls of the soft, wonderful stuff and gave as good as she got. What a rough, mighty warrior he would have been in olden times, she thought with a primitive thrill. No, not would have been—he *was* a warrior. Her warrior. At least for now.

Suddenly, he pulled away, laughing bitterly, and brushed her aside to get up. "Provoking baggage! See what I mean? Nothing frightens you, does it? You are the most shameless hussy."

She knew he'd begun to recover himself, at least enough to be embarrassed about all he had just told her. No doubt it was the first confession of this sort he had ever made. And a man as strong as Neil couldn't be comfortable baring his soul that way.

"Kiss me half as well next time round, and I may tell you how I got that way." She pinched his cheek. "Now why don't you take a short nap while I go and make you breakfast? You didn't eat a thing this morning."

"Damn it, Bettsy, don't be so bloody kind! I'm trying to warn you I can be dangerous!"

"My God, you *are* blue-deviled this morning! Now shut up

and lie down or I'll kick you in the shins. You haven't seen a vicious rage until you've seen one of mine!''

Incredibly, he smiled. It was slowly formed and a bit lopsided, but at least it reached his eyes. He shook his head. ''I've seen one, thank you.''

''Well then, if we can manage not to have them simultaneously, maybe we can avoid a catastrophe, hmm? Sort of keep each other in check, as it were? So we don't wipe out all our possible villains and put Lindy out of work.''

''You're daft, is what,'' he said with a protracted sigh. Moving wearily, he dragged off his wrinkled tie and shrugged out of his coat. ''And I'm exhausted.''

She closed the door on her way out. He was going to be all right now. Luckily, she'd stumbled on a cure for his megrims this time, but with that attitude of guilt he labored under, the malady would probably reoccur.

Throttling a man who had just broken a woman's neck seemed a perfectly normal reaction to her. His fury at Emma and her rich old lord for their betrayal was reasonable enough. And Elizabeth didn't see how being rejected and deserted by a selfish, unloving mother could cause anything but a blinding rage in a child of five. All in all, she thought Neil had handled himself quite well under all those circumstances.

Neil Bronwyn was a man of action and courage, an aggressive male born in an age of dandies and fops. There must be some way to make him accept himself and quit trying so hard to change.

Elizabeth hoped she could help him do that much, at least, before she had to leave him.

# Chapter Thirteen

Elizabeth glanced around the laboratory with pride. All the sparkling beakers and tubes, Neil's precious bottles of mysterious chemicals and his endless collection of medical books stood in neat, military rows on their respective shelves. Delivered just this morning, several unpacked boxes of equipment and supplies stood stacked near the floor-length windows. The green tile floor gleamed. She smiled at the new American-made Spencer microscope sitting in lonely splendor on the long, polished mahogany table in the center of the room. The scope, Neil's pride and joy, made quite a centerpiece. "Now what shall we do with you?" she asked.

Neil still slept, exhausted by two virtually sleepless nights and his emotional catharsis this morning. It satisfied Elizabeth to keep to this part of the day's routine they had established in the lab.

There seemed little left to do until they settled on a particular field of research. Neil leaned toward the problems of respiratory distress. They had already begun an intensive study of it, and Elizabeth worked just as hard as he. Neil's enthusiasm proved contagious.

The game they played—that she was indeed the young Dr. Betts—satisfied a need in both. Neil explored aloud the projects they might undertake, listing all their possibilities and drawbacks. Elizabeth listened with fascination, both for the subjects he discussed and the respect he accorded her as an equal participant. It was as though he took for granted she'd always be there working by his side, a valuable asset to his mission.

How she wished that were true. Sometimes she even entertained the dream that it really could continue indefinitely.

"Woolgathering, I see."

Startled by the sound of his voice, she turned, laughing. "Ah yes. I thought we'd pen up the sheep in here, over in the corner, perhaps."

"Dreadfully messy buggers, sheep," he said, strolling over to the microscope and wiping away an imaginary swath of dust.

"You look well rested. Could we go for a ride, do you think? It's only half past two." She felt restless and confined, and Neil looked as though he could use a bit of air.

He ignored the suggestion. "I'm sorry about this morning, Bettsy. Can't imagine what I was thinking to ramble on like that. Lack of sleep, I expect. Sometimes makes me maudlin and out of sorts. I feel like an idiot."

She swung her arms behind her and strutted a few steps toward him, tilting her head to one side. "Probably the sex. Lindy says it leaves you surly."

"Oh, good Lord!" Neil said with a bark of laughter. "I ought to sew his ruddy mouth shut. The rascal comes up with the most outrageous things."

She swayed from one foot to the other, feeling a little flirtatious. "Does it? Make you surly, I mean."

He grasped her hands and leaned his head toward hers. "Makes me want to rush you back upstairs and keep you in bed forever."

The loud clearing of a throat interrupted whatever it was Neil was about to do. Disappointed, Elizabeth frowned at Oliver, who stood in the doorway twisting his hands together.

"Pardon, sir, she's here again. Follered me in, y'see."

"Neil, darling," Emma crooned as she pushed past Oliver.

She halted suddenly when she saw Neil standing there, holding both of Bettsy's hands in his. "What's this?"

A skinny, older woman dressed all in black stood directly behind Emma, peering around her. Her pinched mouth formed a perfect O.

Ah, so the lady brought a chaperon this time, Elizabeth thought, tongue in cheek. How very proper.

Neil released Elizabeth's hands and turned to Oliver. "Please show the ladies out."

"I'm not going anywhere until I hear some sort of explanation," Emma said firmly. The sound of her tapping slipper penetrated the sudden silence.

Elizabeth shrugged and headed for the door. "Come on, Mr. Oliver, I think we should dish up some tea or something for Doc's *patients*." Then she winked at Neil. "Suture stuff is in the third drawer there if you feel an urge to perform that last surgical procedure we discussed. And do, please, call me to assist."

Neil nodded, and Elizabeth detected the trace of a smile around his eyes. She hurried out. Emma Nitwit might need sutures somewhere besides her mouth if they stayed in the same room one moment longer. Maybe Elizabeth and Neil had more in common than he realized—the urge to kill.

"What was the meaning of that?" Emma demanded, flouncing toward the lab table, where she deposited her parasol and reticule with a thunk.

Neil decided to be truthful. "The surgical procedure? Dr. Betts would like me to stitch your lips together."

Emma gaped for a moment and then attacked. "You were holding hands, for God's sake! What has that wretched little toad persuaded you to?" She ranted on. "I suspected it before—at least his intentions—from his snippish manner toward me."

"That he wanted me to sew up your mouth?" Neil asked with wide-eyed innocence. Emma's outrage seemed a bit staged to him.

"Of course not, you idiot! That he was...that he had *designs* on you! There, deny it's so if you can!"

"If you imply that either Betts or myself might be sexually interested in members of our own gender, you are much mistaken, Emma. You of all people should know I'm innocent of that."

He turned to the older woman, Emma's maid. "Violet here can attest to it as well, if your memory's faulty. I expect she had the dubious pleasure of tidying up after us all those mornings after our episodes of what one might call wild abandon."

Emma's eyes grew soft. "Oh, Neil, I do remember. I'm so glad you've not forgotten how we loved. I wish it could be that way again. I want it to be." She approached him and placed her palms on his chest. "Tell me you'll send that wretch away and stop all this gadding about town every night. He takes up all your time when we could be—"

"We could be *nothing,* Emma." He removed her hands from his waistcoat and placed them at her sides. "I want you to leave now before I forget myself and throw you bodily into the street." He kept his calm, but the tension inside him coiled like an overwound watch spring.

"It *is* him! I knew it!" she shouted, flouncing angrily around the room, her eyes darting from the boxes to the windows and then toward the shelves. Neil feared she was looking for something to throw. He circled between her and his microscope, successfully backing her toward the door.

She continued to rave. "He's turned you against me and into something vile! He hated me from the first because I'm beautiful and he knows I'll win you back before he can entice you to his nasty ways."

"Damn it, Emma, for the last time, I am not—"

She stopped moving, so that her body collided with his. "Oh, I do know, sweetheart," she said, touching his chest with one hand, whining prettily. "I know you're not like him yet, but can't you see his plan? I've met men like him before.

They're sly, insinuating, persistent sods who'll stop at nothing.''

Understanding dawned. Her husband must have been inclined that way, and so she read the very worst into what she'd seen. Neil would have felt sympathy for her bad luck in choosing the old man if her own greediness hadn't caused it.

The thought of her suffering because of her decision six years ago tempered his anger a little. He still wanted to toss her out. But perhaps she was, in her own obnoxious way, trying to save him from getting caught up in a disastrous relationship like her husband must have done. It was laughable, and yet terribly sad in a way.

"Emma," he said reassuringly, "you need not go on with this. Betts is no threat to either of us." Something chilling stirred in the back of his mind as he spoke the word *threat*. He suppressed the feeling. "I loved you once, but it's over now and can never be again. You made your choice six years ago."

"But he's dead now!" she wailed, wringing her hands together and pleading with a tearful look.

Neil nodded, feeling another chill. "Yes, so he is." He watched her eyes dart from him to Violet and back again. "How did he die, I wonder?"

She appeared at a loss, almost frightened, and then seemed to recover. "His heart. It was weak, you see." Her throat worked to swallow. "He was so very old."

"Oh? How old?" he asked, keeping his voice conversational.

"Fifty-two," she mumbled, dropping her gaze to her hands.

He nodded, stepped back to the table, gathered up the things she had left there and held them out to her. "You'd best leave, Emma. I've work to do and I'm sure you have other calls to make."

Neil ushered her out of the laboratory, toward the front door, with an impersonal hand at her elbow. "I want you to know that I wish you well in spite of everything." With a final, gentle push, he deposited her on the front steps and moved back to allow Violet to join her there. "Please, don't come again."

"But, darling... Neil?"

He closed the door in her face and leaned against it.

Why on earth would the woman think she stood the slightest chance of reconciling with him after what she had done? Emma was many things, but Neil had never thought her stupid. Perhaps he had been the one who was stupid in not recognizing just how thick skulled she really was.

She hadn't left him because of fear at all. Of course, he'd known all along that wasn't the only reason, but some of his wild behavior in bed had jumped to mind immediately when he first heard she'd left him.

He knew he had taken entirely too much license with her enthusiasm during intimacy, but he'd been enthralled by all his newfound knowledge of the opposite sex. A highborn lady was bound to be frightened by the way he'd treated her. Not that he had ever hurt Emma, of course. She had seemed very receptive, but then, at the first chance offered her, had run away.

Betts was right, though. Emma had reappeared at once when he'd put "Lord" in front of his name. A telling fact, that.

"Well, dash it all, she's gone!" Bettsy said, appearing in the hall with a steaming mug. "Now we'll have to cancel surgery. And I had her anesthesia all ready, too. Ah well, I'll just use it on the mad doctor. Here."

She offered Neil the brew with a grin and called back to the kitchen in a loud stage voice, "Oliver, stopper that hemlock for me, would you?"

Neil took the tea and sipped. "Cheeky devil! You *did* lace this."

"Brandy and honey. Covers the bitterness fairly well, don't you think? Drink up now and I'll lay you out prettily in the parlor. You ought to have already died a natural death, though, from all that poison sweetness you just sent packing. I nearly expired myself from the tiny dose I observed. 'Neil, dahling,''' she mimicked. "Jesus, that woman is cloying, isn't she?"

Neil chuckled as he toasted her with his cup. "She thinks you're my jealous little noncy-boy."

"Your what?" Then she guessed what he meant and her eyes grew wide. "Really? Oh Lord, all I need is for *that* to spread around the clubs. First I'm a seducer of young women and now I'm corrupting doctors! My reputation as good old Percival Betts is getting worse than Lady Elizabeth's."

Neil pushed away from the door and laid his free arm about her shoulders in a comradely fashion. "Nah, no one would believe it even if she were inclined to start such a rumor. A gentleman doesn't foul his own nest—it's an unwritten rule. If you were my lover, I wouldn't keep you in residence here and flaunt you about town. Just isn't done."

She halted and looked up at him thoughtfully. "But, Neil, I *am*. And you *do*."

Neil cradled her smooth oval face between his hands, brushing back the darkened curls from her brow. "Ah, but you're not merely a lover of mine, Bettsy Marleigh, you're the woman I mean to marry. Future mother of the ninth Earl Havington and possibly a little Lady Percival. You don't foul my nest, darling, you *are* my nest."

"And you, Dr. Lord Havington, have peas for brains. I swear I can hear them rattle every time you shake your head." She laughed, thumped him on the shoulder and threaded her arm through his. "Marriage, indeed! Fine husband you'd make. You can't even do an honest day's work around here for the females breaking down your door. What you need is an overseer."

They returned to the laboratory, where Neil had begun designing an aspirator to clear the lungs. He found his sketchbook and pencils and took up where he'd left off, calling out parts for Bettsy to list as he began to draw.

Behind exacting efforts to depict the device, though, Neil's mind knitted up the threads of suspicion Emma had strewn about. Could the woman have killed her husband? There was a guilty look about her when he had brought it up, and the man had only been fifty-two—somewhat young to die of an age-weakened heart. Was she capable of killing? Terry's death was extremely convenient for her. It was obvious to Neil Emma planned to rekindle their relationship now that he had succeeded Terry.

Emma's jealousy of his young protégé might well have triggered Bettsy's shooting at the theater. Emma could have put a flea in John Goodroe's ear about starting the rumor.... No, too many things didn't add together. She wouldn't have had any reason for the earlier attacks on Bettsy—even if she had known her then—nor access to the murder weapons from Marleigh House that killed Terry and Maggie Leffing. Emma wouldn't know the workings of a pistol, or have the contacts necessary to hire an assassin. Hell, she didn't have sense enough to plan afternoon tea.

Neil scoffed at himself for grasping at shadows. Was he so eager to have done with the mystery that he'd even suspect that feather wit?

No, Colin Marleigh was their man. Neil discounted Turner altogether, despite Lindy's lingering suspicion of the young man. No real proof existed that Turner had ever owed Terry a farthing. The young man rarely bet more than a few pounds when they had talked him into gaming. Turner was just what he appeared to be—the friendly, quiet son of a minor baron, who spent his time in the frivolous pursuits of his class. And that man from the theater could simply be a tradesman with whom Terry had had a disagreement.

Neil realized the investigation intruded on his every thought and action these days. If only they could be quit of it.

Shoving the troubling thoughts to the back of his mind, he completed his sketch of the reservoir bottle with a two-way stopcock and explained its possible use in lung clearing to

Bettsy. Her excitement about the idea made him forget everything but her obvious pride in him.

A messenger arrived that afternoon with an invitation.

Greetings, friends,
*Macbeth* opens tonight at the Lyceum with Miss Helen Trawick in her first leading role. This is not business, but a respite for us all. Meet you in box #6. Please come.
> Your servant,
> Trent MacLinden

"So formal! Hate that we'll have to send regrets," Neil said promptly, refolding the invitation and laying it aside.

"Oh no!" Elizabeth knew that if she didn't insist on going, Neil would never get over his fear of her going about in public. "Look, we know why Bensen shot me, and Lindy swears it had nothing to do with the murder. I'm as safe now as before the shooting. Maybe more so."

He looked doubtful. "We could run into Marleigh. I don't think we should risk it."

She pleaded, threatened and cajoled. "Colin hates the theater. He won't attend. We can go late," she suggested as her final ploy. "No one has to know we're even there. It's Helen's debut and Lindy really wants us to come. How can we refuse?"

Neil hesitated as he considered it. "All right, but you'll sit well back in the box so you're not visible, and we stay until everyone else is gone," he ordered. "I hope to hell I don't regret this. How you can even consider going to a theater after what happened is beyond me."

At nine, Oliver drove them to the Lyceum in the closed carriage. When they arrived, the play was already under way.

"Sit, sit. That's her cue. Watch," Lindy said, hardly sparing them a glance of greeting as they entered the box.

Entranced, Elizabeth watched Helen become the tragic figure of Lady Macbeth. Neil and Lindy must have been just as mesmerized, for there was no conversation until the end of the second act. The applause was deafening.

"My God, she's wonderful, Lindy," Neil said sincerely. Elizabeth agreed profusely, while Lindy beamed with pride.

"Thank you both for coming. Helen will be so pleased. She's wanted to visit you ever since the shooting, Betts, but I didn't think it wise. She knows everything now, by the way. So does Bonnie, I'm afraid. Neil's reaction to your injuries blew your disguise to hell and gone." He grinned at both of them. "Don't worry, though. We can trust them."

Neil looked doubtful, but Elizabeth hurried to reassure Lindy. "Of course we can."

She looked out over the crowd, a more refined group than had attended the comedy. They were still quite noisy as they mingled during the intermission. Leaning forward out of her shadowy concealment, Elizabeth chanced to look up.

A tall man in a box across from theirs was staring directly at her. To her horror, she saw a flicker of recognition on his face. Then he quickly got to his feet and turned to exit his booth. *That profile!* She grabbed MacLinden's arm. "Lindy, there! That man, it's him! The one who argued with Terry!"

The inspector followed her pointing finger and leapt to his feet. "Did he see you?"

She bit her lip and nodded vigorously.

Lindy squeezed her shoulder hard. "I didn't see his face. Describe him. Anything unusual. Quickly, Betts."

"He's wearing a green plaid waistcoat under a black frock coat. Bright green. And one of those stringlike ties. Oh, and he had on yellow gloves."

"Don't worry, we'll get him. Stay right here," he ordered and dashed out of the booth.

A tense quarter hour passed with Neil stationed outside in the hallway and Elizabeth huddled in an inside corner of the box. She felt ridiculous. And terrified. The man had recognized her; she knew it. The lights dimmed and the third act commenced.

Finally Neil returned to the box with Lindy in tow. "Did you see him?" she whispered to Lindy.

"Only his back as he left his box. Couldn't locate him when I got downstairs. You're certain it was the fellow who spoke to Terry that night? You saw his face?"

"Yes. Without doubt it was him. There was something about his stance as well, you know? An attitude, a way of moving. Lindy, I got the feeling he knew exactly who I am."

"I doubt he did, Betts, but all the same, we won't take any chances. Neil, I found Oliver and told him to bring your carriage around back. Take Betts out the stage exit now and go directly home." Lindy looked pointedly at Neil's coat pocket and raised a brow in question.

Neil nodded slightly. Elizabeth didn't miss the exchange, though she was sure they'd meant her to. Neil was armed. That didn't surprise her. Instead, she felt reassured and hoped he could shoot as well as he did everything else.

Lindy's head bobbed once. "Wait for me there. I'll keep watch on the box in the event our man returns. Have a care."

Neil virtually dragged her down the back stairs and out the door. "Home and keep a sharp eye behind us," he barked up at Oliver.

Elizabeth banged her knee against the carriage door and cursed as Neil shoved her inside. "Damn it, Neil, don't push!"

"Just sit still and shut up!" he thundered as he climbed in behind her. He slammed a fist against the window frame and yanked the curtain shut. "This is all your fault, you know? I told you you should have stayed at home! Where you're safe!"

Elizabeth wanted to smack him. "And then I'd never have seen the man, now would I? How are we ever going to solve this thing if you keep me wrapped in cotton wool, tucked away in a drawer?"

"I don't care if we solve it! You've been almost drowned,

nearly stabbed, framed for murder and shot! And I mention only the high points of your adventures! God only knows what will happen to you next!'' Neil sucked in a deep breath and blew it out through his teeth, shaking his head as if to clear it. ''You ask why I shudder every time you step outside? Lord, it's a frigging wonder I've got any nerves left.''

She threw up her hands, just missing his temple with her gold-knobbed cane. ''Well, if I'm so much bloody trouble, my lord, I can surely find another place to stay—somewhere where *nobody* can find me. Even you!''

''Like hell you will!'' he shouted, and snatched the cane out of her hand. Dashing it to the floor, he grabbed her by the arms and pulled her into his lap. ''You aren't going anywhere, you understand me? So don't even think about it!''

''You brute! Look, you've squashed my hat! My best topper!''

The carriage lurched as they rounded a corner. Neil released her and shoved her aside. ''We'll discuss this further when you calm down.''

''When I...? When *I* calm down?'' She snapped her mouth shut at his warning glare. It was useless to argue. At least not here and now.

The carriage rumbled through the streets, its creaking and bumping unnaturally loud in the sudden absence of conversation. The relative silence dragged on for long minutes.

''Sorry I shouted,'' Neil said when the brewing tension grew unbearable.

Elizabeth crossed her arms and hugged herself, shooting him an offended look. ''And well you should be. I'll bet Lindy would never rail at Helen that way.''

Neil chuckled, then leaned back against the squabs with a sigh. ''I expect you're right. Ours is a unique relationship.''

''To say the least,'' she agreed wryly, and lapsed into a comfortable sulk, hoping he would suffer a little more guilt.

Instead, he changed the subject as though their quarrel had never happened. ''Helen is nice, don't you think?''

Elizabeth nodded thoughtfully, glad enough to dispense with their useless battle. "Yes, she's perfect for Lindy. Do you think they'll marry? He seems rather serious about her."

"Helen's occupation could prevent it," Neil said, tactfully not spelling out that any actress's morals were suspect, at best.

"Nonsense. Lindy loves her. You can see it in his face whenever he speaks her name. And when he looks at her…"

"Would you marry me if I were a peeler like Lindy? An innkeeper's son?" Neil asked. He carefully kept his voice light, but Elizabeth didn't miss the tension behind the question.

"You're asking whether my notoriety's probable effect on your nobility is the reason for my refusing your proposal," she countered, wishing he hadn't brought up the matter.

"I want to know if that's the only reason." She noticed how carefully he watched her in the dim carriage light.

She toyed with the top hat he had squashed earlier and avoided his eyes. "You presume too much after a casual night of lovemaking."

He leaned forward, snatched the ruined hat from her hand and sent it sailing out the window. "Two nights, Bettsy, and there was nothing casual about them, at least not on my part."

Neil's persistence angered her more than his shouting had done. Especially since she wanted nothing more than to give in and tell him how much she loved him, how very badly she longed to be his wife. Were she a bit more selfish, she would have done so right then and there and damn the consequences. It would serve him right.

"Not casual?" she asked with more sarcasm than was warranted. "You were so gin-flown the first time you barely recall the event. I found nothing remarkable about it, either, so I can assure you that you didn't miss much." She paused thoughtfully and then added, "Sober, though, I'd say you're an adequate lover."

"Adequate?" he exclaimed, swinging a fist up and pounding the seat beside him. "Adequate? By God, you're cold! Is that all it was to you? An *adequate* tumble?"

"Satisfactory, then, if you insist," she amended, fiddling nervously with her gloves. The situation began to tickle her sense of the ridiculous. Bruising his sexual pride provided a bit of needed revenge for his tolerance of Emma Throckmorton Curtiss and his gruff attitude tonight. "Shall I write a letter of referral for you to give your next mistress?" she needled.

"You may write your epitaph if you keep this up!" he warned, but she saw the twinkle in his eye and a betraying twitch of his lips. He laced his fingers behind his head and leaned back against the seat, his arrogance restored. "I can see it now, carved all in pink granite. 'Here lies Elizabeth Marleigh Bronwyn, Countess of Havington, *Almost* Beloved Wife of—'"

Elizabeth burst into tears. The sudden weakness appalled her, but she couldn't seem to hold it in. She buried her face in her hands. Loud, hiccuping sobs heaved her body uncontrollably. The harder she tried to stop, the worse it became, so she gave in to a good, hard cry. One moment she was fine, and the next... Damn, but she hated this!

"Oh God, Bettsy," Neil said as he pulled her into his lap again. "Hush, sweeting. It was only a joke, a horrible joke, and I'm so sorry. Please don't cry." He patted her as he kissed the top of her head and nuzzled her hair. "It's all right, I promise. We'll be all right. Trust me."

For the longest time she wept loudly, alternately beating her fists on his chest and clutching his waistcoat, knowing it was a joke, knowing he was sorry about it, knowing that he loved her.

The carriage stopped just as she managed to cease wailing. She looked helplessly up at Neil and sniffed, uncertain what she could say. "Neil, I don't know why I—"

"Shh. It's no wonder you're upset." He brushed her hair from her forehead and kissed it softly. "You're worried and overtired and I've been beastly to you. Let's go in now, it's past time for bed."

Elizabeth felt strangely light-headed and loose limbed as

Neil guided her upstairs with a strong hand at her waist. She made no objection when he entered her room with her and began to remove her clothes.

Maybe he would make love to her again, if only to prove he was better than she'd said he was. At the moment she didn't much care whether he did or not. She had run the gamut of feelings and was past caring what happened next.

Before she realized it, she was covered neck to toe in a flannel nightshirt and Neil was covering her with the quilts. "Will you stay?" she whispered.

"Yes," he said quietly, and began to undress.

# Chapter Fourteen

Neil rose quietly and pulled on his robe as soon as he made certain Bettsy was sleeping peacefully. Guilt ate at him for taking her to task the way he had in the carriage. Poor little thing had just about reached the limit of endurance. He hoped to God Lindy would have something positive to report when he arrived.

After checking with Oliver, who had gone over every inch of the house after their arrival, Neil paced the kitchen and waited. When Lindy's knock sounded, he jerked open the door.

"We finally spotted him," Lindy said immediately, depositing his cloak and hat on a chair.

"You didn't catch him?"

"No, no need just yet," Lindy said. "After all, we haven't a jot of proof he has anything at all to do with any of this. Two of my chaps are following him. I'll find out where he lives and who he is, then go and question him tomorrow. No danger from that one tonight, I assure you."

"He's under surveillance? You're certain?" Neil asked.

"Of course," Lindy said, and plopped down at the table as though invited. He dragged out his pipe. "I could use a cuppa if you got one."

Neil set on the kettle. He felt somewhat calmer now that the stranger was operating under a net. "I suppose I shouldn't say so, but I wish to God we'd not gone tonight. Bettsy's a mental wreck, and I'm not much better." He set out two cups and sat down to wait for the water to heat. Lindy looked a bit offended. "I must admit, we did enjoy Helen's performance, though. She's quite wonderful." Neil smiled when Lindy's chest puffed out. "Your pride's showing. I think you just popped a button off your waistcoat."

Lindy stuffed the unlit pipe back in his pocket and stood up. "We'll marry when this play runs its course. Always been Helen's dream to play Lady Macbeth. Had to give her the chance."

Neil couldn't feature any man in his right mind doing that. No wonder Lindy had never mentioned Helen much during the course of their friendship. "You allowed her to go on the stage, Lindy? Knowing she'd become your wife someday? How could you let her do such a thing?"

Lindy looked pensive. "I'd let her overthrow the queen and crown Helen myself if that's what she wanted. I'd kill for her, die for her. Anything. She takes shameless advantage of it, too, but I don't care. I love her."

Neil said nothing to that. He had never encountered such blind devotion for a woman and thought it patently ridiculous. But then again... His attention fully on his thoughts, he had to ask Lindy to repeat what he'd just said.

"I said, you doubtless know the feeling."

"Hardly," Neil replied, aghast at the thought. Certainly he felt love for Bettsy, but at least he tempered it with reason.

Lindy scoffed. "Of course you do. Betts has had you in a lather since the night you met her, and I'll wager you'll be wed before I am."

"Well, Bettsy's not exactly thrilled by the idea," Neil admitted. "She won't even think about it."

Lindy laughed merrily as he loosened his tie. "Ah, my friend, then you know little about women. They *all* think about it!"

Neil ignored the gibe. "We've got to get this business of Terry's murder behind us, Lindy. Soon, too. I don't know how much longer I can go on like this, knowing Bettsy's in danger, wanting things settled between us. What can we do?''

"Something will break soon, Neil. Don't you feel it? I believe we're very close to catching the bugger responsible.''

Neil sighed. "I hope to God you're right. We can't let anything else happen to her.''

Once Lindy had downed his cup of tea and said good-night, Neil sat alone for a long while, reflecting on what they had discussed. The subject of love disturbed him almost as much as their talk of possible murder suspects.

Lindy hadn't a patch on him regarding obsessiveness. Senseless as it was, Neil knew what he felt for Bettsy bordered on just that. On closer introspection, he could find no reasonableness about it whatsoever. He loved her to absolute distraction and that was a fact.

The thought was humbling and frightening, as well. He'd regressed to where he'd started as a child—totally out of control, reckless and unthinking, capable of driving away the person he held most dear. Somehow he had to get himself in hand and at least maintain a pretense of control over his emotions.

His enraged behavior earlier tonight at the theater and in the carriage would have sent a weaker woman into hysterical fits. Surely Bettsy had limits to what she would endure. He must remember that or he'd lose her as surely as he had his mother.

Lindy had paved a path toward a safe life and respectability for his woman. *Will I be able to do as much for mine?* Neil wondered.

Neil woke just after dawn. Along with the soft pink light streaming through the windows, the night's happenings rushed into his mind. They almost eclipsed the warm sense of well-being he'd experienced waking with Bettsy asleep in his arms. He forced away the worries, determined on a moment of peace.

A smile formed as he examined her close up. A tiny measure of red-gold had grown out from her scalp to blend with the walnut-colored dye she'd applied weeks ago for the disguise.

Her face was fuller and her color rosier, no doubt because she ate better than she had at first. Point of fact, the little rascal packed it away like a stevedore now, especially the sweets Lindy brought from his mother's kitchen.

A bell clanged in his head. *Increased appetite, cravings...*

Carefully, holding his breath, Neil lowered the covers and watched the rise and fall of her breasts. Were they fuller? Gently, he closed his hand over one and squeezed, trying to recall their size when he had undressed her that first night at Bearsden Manor. The nipple contracting under his palm distracted him. He shook his head, both to deny his quickening desire and to clear his mind.

Trying not to wake her, he undid the four buttons at her neck and laid the nightshirt open. Yes, they were larger. That, together with the increase in appetite, no monthly flow yet that he knew of and her sudden, emotional outbursts, explained everything. His heart slammed against the wall of his chest and his eyes clenched shut. A wave of joy like nothing he'd ever known swept over him, leaving in its wake a sheen of quiet happiness. *Increasing.* Bettsy was with child. He just knew it.

A grin stretched wide across his face as he leaned back on the pillow and sighed, feeling tears burn the back of his eyes. No wonder her own tears surfaced so easily! And the poor darling had no inkling why.

It took all of his will not to shake her awake and tell her, laugh with her, make plans for the future. For their baby's future—his heir, perhaps, or a shining little curly top who'd twist him about her finger just as her mother did.

It must have happened that night in the study for the changes in Bettsy to be apparent already. Almost three weeks ago. Then a dark thought intruded. Unless...unless it had happened before then. His teeth ground together painfully.

Unless it had happened with Terry.

Neil quickly rolled from the bed and escaped into the adjoining room before he cursed aloud. Snatching up his robe, he bounded down to the kitchen and busied himself making coffee to keep himself out of the brandy.

The suspicion wouldn't leave him no matter how hard he tried to tell himself it wasn't true. Terry had insisted on the marriage. Bettsy had admitted she didn't love Terry and that he was only marrying her to protect her. She'd been running away from Terry that night. Perhaps...oh God, perhaps it wasn't even Terry's! Neil dropped the empty cup he was holding and slumped down on a kitchen chair, burying his hands in his hair.

The acrid smell and hissing sputter of coffee boiling over dragged him out of his angry trance. Attending to the mundane chore of wiping up restored him to a more normal state of mind.

Neil forced himself to reason. There would be a child; that much was fairly certain. Whose child was anybody's guess. Maybe Bettsy herself wouldn't know. He bit back his fury and settled down in his chair, determined to get the situation straight in his mind before Bettsy woke up.

Worst case, he reckoned, was that the rumors about her spreading her favors were true. In that event, the babe could belong to any number of bucks who had bragged about enjoying her bed.

He squeezed his eyes shut on a roiling fit of jealous rage. No. None of it was true. Hadn't he already decided she was totally lacking in experience? Well, perhaps not totally. There was Terry.

Neil allowed himself a moment of hatred for the boy he'd loved like a son. As he knew it would, the feeling mellowed into exasperation at his nephew's lack of restraint. But how could Neil blame any red-blooded man for wanting Bettsy? And how could he hold against her the need for comfort and protection she must have felt?

Truth was, he loved them both to the depths of his soul. Absolute forgiveness and acceptance might take a while, but

Neil knew it would come eventually. Then he would have not only the woman he loved and needed, but also the only part of Terry that death had not taken away. The child. Terry's child. Probably.

When his hands slid down over his eyes, he was amazed to find them wet.

By midmorning, Neil had worked off most of his distress in the lab. He had accomplished little, but now felt able to confront Bettsy without showing any residual anger. She would be famished when she woke. After putting away his sketches and reference books, he decided to fix her a tray and take it up.

Just as he put on the tea, there was a knock at the kitchen door. Not Lindy's knock, he decided, as he crossed to open it.

"My Lord Havington, a message for you from the earl of Marleigh," croaked a weathered old servant wearing an impeccable black suit and holding a top hat. He offered a folded missive sealed with the Marleigh crest. "I shall await your response, milord."

Neil worried that Oliver hadn't appeared to announce the man's arrival. He looked out and saw no sign of Ollie anywhere. He accepted the paper and stepped back into the entryway. "Come in. And you are...?"

"Thurston, milord. Lord Marleigh's man," the old fellow answered as he shuffled inside.

Strange, Neil thought, to have this ancient retainer deliver a message rather than one of the footmen. Especially since the cadaverous old servant looked ready to fold up and expire on the spot. Then he remembered the name. "*Thurston,* you say? Weren't you in Lady Elizabeth Marleigh's employ at one time?"

"Briefly, milord." The butler's eyes glared at Neil from behind thick, rounded lenses that magnified the bright green irises. Amazing how clear the eyes were, Neil thought. Clear and quick and rather hateful in their expression.

Neil broke the seal on the letter. The message was short.

Lady Elizabeth Marleigh will be interred tomorrow afternoon at three of the clock in Kensington Cemetery at Uxbridge Road, should you be interested in attending.

Your servant,<br>Marleigh

Neil refolded the paper and looked up at Thurston. "Are you aware of the contents of this?" he asked.

"Of course, milord," the man said, lifting his chin defiantly.

"Do you know why her ladyship is not to be buried with her family?" Neil asked. It seemed strange indeed to bury an earl's only daughter in a newly opened cemetery, unless Colin were well aware that the body in question did not belong to his cousin.

Thurston cleared his throat and looked askance. His halting voice crackled like dry parchment. "Lady Elizabeth took her own life and that of another, so I'm told. The consecrated ground at the family church is hardly the place for her remains under such circumstances." He paused. "Have you a reply for Lord Marleigh, milord?"

Neil thought before answering. Why would Colin issue him a special invitation when a mere notification would have been more in keeping? Perhaps to signal to others interested that, by his presence, the earl of Havington accepted the dead woman as Elizabeth Marleigh, his nephew's murderess?

Given this Thurston's defensive attitude, Neil wondered just how much the man knew about the whole situation. Few of the nobility reckoned with their servants' grasp of family doings. The old fellow had worked for both Elizabeth and Colin and had perhaps been with the Marleigh family in one position or another since long before both were born.

"You saw her body, did you not?" Neil asked, watching for and not missing the surprised intake of breath. Obviously, Thurston was unaware of Neil's connection to Inspector MacLinden and the doings at the morgue.

"Yes, milord. Ghastly sight, as you might imagine." The butler shivered, but the reaction looked somehow contrived.

"I don't need to imagine it, Thurston. I saw her myself."

Neil watched the man turn an even pastier white and shift his weight as though trying to remain upright.

The click of footsteps on the hall tiles warned Neil of Bettsy's impending arrival, but there was no time to warn her. Instead he grasped Thurston's arm and ushered him quickly toward the door. "Tell Lord Colin I shall be there." Neil yanked open the door and practically shoved the old man outside.

Thurston turned just as he exited and glanced around Neil's shoulder before the door closed in his face. Neil wondered if he'd imagined the flare of recognition in the old man's avid green gaze.

He leaned back against the closed door and watched Bettsy lift the abandoned letter from the table. She winced as she read.

Neil stood there a moment, shoring up his reserve, fighting back his unwarranted anger—anger he thought he'd subdued.

Her vulnerability excused her from an immediate confrontation, he decided. He wouldn't mention the child now. Time enough for settling that after he had her safe from harm. Neil pushed away from the door and joined her by the table.

"Scones today! Is there ham, too?" she asked, plumbing the basket Oliver had delivered earlier. "Was that Oliver just now?"

"It was Thurston," he replied, and watched her eyes go round with surprise. "Colin sent him with that," Neil said, pointing to the paper she held in her hand.

"He sent *Thurston?*" she asked, settling comfortably on a kitchen chair and tucking into the food.

"Makes you wonder, doesn't it?" Neil poured her tea. "He saw you as you came in."

"Doesn't matter," she said with a negligent toss of her head. "Poor old soul had trouble finding the front door when he worked at Marleigh House." With a flourish, she pushed the letter to the middle of the table and sighed. "He even identified Maggie as me. He thinks I'm dead."

Neil couldn't quite believe that. He recalled the widening of those sharp green eyes and the mouth gone slightly slack. Of course, the reaction could have been due to the rough and speedy ousting Neil had given him.

"How long did Thurston work for you, Bettsy?" he asked, stirring sugar into his tea and hoping his question sounded like idle curiosity.

She thought for a moment, a forefinger tapping her lips. "He came right before Father died. I remember because we'd just returned from Scotland when he appeared, belongings in hand, asking for employment. Colin had taken on a younger man in his place, and there was nowhere else for him to go."

"Colin employed him before he came to your father?" Uneasiness grew in the pit of Neil's stomach. The warning bells in his head increased from jingles to thunderous peals.

"Umm-hmm," Bettsy replied, intent on buttering her scone. "Thurston had worked for Colin's family since before I was born."

Why should Colin turn the old man off and now rehire him? Unless Thurston had been sent to Marleigh House for a very specific reason. The attacks on Bettsy had begun soon after her father's death. And as to that event, Neil wondered just how the elder Marleigh had died.

He watched Bettsy bite into a second buttery scone. She proceeded to wolf down the remainder like a starving street urchin. It should have disgusted him, but instead he found her lapse of manners oddly endearing.

"Father said Thurston even acted as steward while Uncle James went away to India," Bettsy offered, reaching for yet another scone.

"Steward? Must have been quite a comedown, being relegated to butler status once again," Neil said quietly.

Bettsy shook her head. "Oh, I shouldn't think so. Not much difference except that he probably handled the household finances as steward. Mind you, it was only the modest house of an army officer where he served, not some great estate."

Neil noticed a glimmer of unease in her eyes. He'd gone past the point where she believed he was only curious.

"You think Thurston is involved? Is that why you're asking all these questions?" she asked. Her hands splayed over the tabletop and she leaned forward as though she meant to push herself out of her chair.

Neil smiled and wagged his head. "Don't be absurd. The man's so ancient he can barely hobble about. You said yourself he's blind as a mole and bedridden half the time. No danger there. I merely wondered about him."

Her doubtful look persisted, and Neil rushed to change the subject. "Shall we work? I almost finished the aspirator drawings while you slept in this morning. We can complete the order list if you like."

She turned away and drew in a deep breath, letting it out slowly. "Do you mind if we wait till later? I feel a bit queasy all of a sudden."

"Well, I don't wonder, with that bellyful of greasy scones. By rights you ought to weigh twenty stone, the way you eat." He softened the teasing with a laugh. "Why don't you go back upstairs and lie down? Lindy should be coming by or sending word soon about our theater man. I'll wake you the moment he does."

She looked quite pale and kept biting her lips. "Neil, you won't be going out today, will you?"

"Hadn't planned on it. Why, do you need something in particular?"

Her hand hovered around her throat. "I—I may need a doctor. I feel...ill!" She dashed for the back door, flung it open and emptied her stomach, barely missing Lindy's shiny new shoes.

Neil encircled her shoulders from behind and held her head while she retched into the geraniums at the side of the walk.

"Now there's a greeting for you!" Lindy said with a concerned look at the patient. "Wonder what brought that on?"

"Overindulgence in buttered scones," Neil said, warning Lindy with his darkest scowl not to pursue the subject.

"Ah well, it's too late to forgo the indulgence now, eh?" Lindy lowered his head, stealing an impertinent look at Neil from under his ruddy lashes. "At least you might have held off on the butter."

# Chapter Fifteen

Elizabeth groaned as Neil assisted her to a kitchen chair. A lonely scone mocked her from its gold-edged plate in the center of the table. She squeezed her eyes shut against the sight, swallowing heavily. Neil daubed at her face with a wet cloth and had the gall to offer some inanity about her feeling better in a moment.

"Some doctor you are!" she snapped.

"You'll be fine, Bettsy. Trust me, it's an upset that will right itself soon enough."

Lindy snorted as he set a glass of water in front of her. These two were the least sympathetic individuals she'd ever had occasion to meet. Neil disappeared into the pantry and returned with a handful of flat, salted biscuits. "Here, nibble on these."

Elizabeth turned her face away. "Not bloody likely." However, the sickness was already fading a bit. She accepted a biscuit and took a tenuous bite.

"You should go back upstairs and lie down," Neil suggested.

Elizabeth tossed the rest of the biscuit at his head. "You're just trying to get rid of me so you can discuss that man at the theater." She threw him a punishing glare. "What did you find out, Lindy?"

He looked from her to Neil and back again, settling himself

against the sideboard and crossing his arms. "Not much. The rascal ducked into one of the gaming hells in Whitechapel and must have sneaked out a back way. Disappeared."

"You lost him? Damn!" Neil slapped his fist against the tabletop, making the dishes bounce.

"Afraid so. He obviously knew he was being followed. Realized we're on to him. But now I've seen him and my men know what he looks like. Shouldn't be that difficult to find him."

Neil moved behind Betts and laid his hands on her shoulders, a protective and rather possessive gesture that sent a shiver of absolute longing through her. His fingers began working such magic on her muscles, she barely paid attention as he related to Lindy the details of Thurston's visit.

However, she did notice Lindy tense like a hound on a new scent when he read Colin's invitation.

"So, you're going to my funeral?" she asked Neil lazily, her head lolling about as he massaged her neck.

"Lindy and I will both go, so we can see who turns up. And you, my pretty fellow, will remain secluded here tomorrow with Oliver and Lindy's men standing guard below. I'll be away for only two or three hours. You won't be afraid, will you?" Regardless of his forced lightness, Elizabeth sensed his own underlying fear for her.

"No. I expect I'll find enough to keep me busy." Now that she was satisfied the men weren't hiding any information from her, Elizabeth gave in to her growing lethargy. "I believe I will go and rest for a bit. Would you excuse me, Lindy? See you tomorrow after the festivities?"

"Count on it," Lindy said with a curt little nod.

She left them planning details of their trip to the cemetery. Another woman would be laid to rest in Elizabeth Marleigh's place tomorrow afternoon, she thought as she trudged upstairs. Would there be anyone at the gravesite who mourned the passing of Lady Marleigh? Or of Maggie Leffing, for that matter?

"You don't look as thrilled as you might," Lindy said as Elizabeth's footsteps faded and the upstairs door closed.

"She'll have to wed you now, with a babe on the way."

Neil stared at the floor and frowned, cracking his knuckles. "Lord, don't be telling me she *still* refuses?"

"She doesn't know," Neil said. "Or at least she won't admit it. I only realized it myself this morning. How did you guess?"

Lindy couldn't suppress a laugh, though he tried to stifle the worst of it by brushing a hand over his mustache. "I agree with Betts—some doctor *you* are. I suspected a few days ago. She has that look about her. Mum and my sisters had the same way about 'em when they carried, right from the first. Nausea is always the clincher, ain't it?" Lindy sighed, happy for Betts and Neil in spite of the problems they would face. "Just think, Doc, a babe of your own."

Neil's venomous glance was quick, but not quick enough.

"Surely to God you don't think it isn't yours?" But Lindy knew Neil thought exactly that. "You mean that you and Betts haven't, uh... I'm sorry, that was inexcusable. Forget I asked."

Lindy felt his face color up at the misstep. He'd thought surely they *had.* This was no business of his. He should speak up for Betts, though, since she hadn't the chance to do so herself. "You really oughtn't to condemn her out of hand, Neil."

"Christ, Lindy, I don't condemn her! I love the little wretch, but it tears me apart, not knowing. The child *could* be mine, but it's highly unlikely, with Bettsy showing symptoms so soon. The devil of it is I'll never be certain. Don't you see?"

Neil began to pace, his hands shoved deep in his pockets. "The first birth's sometimes a few weeks early or late. Either way, it could be Terry's. Even if the child proves the image of me, it could still be Terry's. Discounting our disparate sizes, you know the resemblance in our features is very strong."

Lindy caught himself packing his empty pipe with nonexistent tobacco, cursed and put it away. "Why don't you simply ask her?"

"Hell, chances are *she* won't even know." Neil's voice

dropped and he shook his head slowly. "I virtually took her from Terry's arms without a pause."

Lindy couldn't say it didn't matter, because he saw very well that it did. A touch of devil's advocacy might do the trick here. "In that case, you should send her away as soon as we have the murder solved. Simply detach yourself from her and from the child before it arrives. It's not as though she needs your support."

"Of course she needs it! And will have it. We'll be married as soon as possible. That was never in question."

"Not wise, Doc. The issue of paternity will eventually drive you apart. Unless you can bring yourself to accept that it is very probably Terry's child and learn to live with it."

"If it is even *Terry's!*" Neil said in a burst of anger.

Lindy grasped his friend's arm, squeezing hard and shaking. "Get hold of yourself, man! Surely you don't believe those rumors about her? Not now, not after knowing Betts as you do."

"No, no, of course not," Neil muttered, running a hand through his hair and across his face. "I thought I had buried that fear so deeply it wouldn't surface again."

Lindy maneuvered him into a chair and sat down on the one facing it. Leaning forward, his face close to Neil's, he spoke from the heart. "Listen to me, my friend. Betts loves you. And you're right, she is going to need you."

This wasn't making any headway at all that Lindy could see. He tried another tack. "Imagine this case if you will," he continued thoughtfully. "You have this affair with a woman you like well enough, but don't precisely love. She bears you a child and then dies. Poof, she's gone just like that!" He snapped his fingers. "There you are, left with this babe of your making. You've awaited the birth for nine long months, perhaps felt its feet kick under your palm, heard its heart beat against your ear. Now its mother, a woman you felt some affection for, is dead."

Lindy leaned even closer. "Quite by chance or design, you meet Betts, who steals your heart like a Shippy Street pickpocket.'' Ah, he had Doc's full attention now. ''But do you think she'll have you with this squalling infant some other lass produced? Noo, not our self-righteous Lady Elizabeth! She wants only her *own* children, you see. If that child came from another woman's body, it's of no account whatever, even if it *is* yours as well, a part of you, the man she claims she loves.''

''You may stop with the supposition,'' Neil said, holding out a hand as though to ward Lindy off. ''Your point's well taken and I'm bleeding from it, if that's any consolation.'' He chuckled. ''Damn you, man, are you sure you're not Irish? That's the biggest load of malarky I've ever heard. Very effective, though.''

''Faith and begorra, me auld mither'd be sa proud!'' Lindy grinned, clutching his heart.

''Your 'auld' mother's not the only one. Will you stand godfather to the—to *our* child next summer, Lindy?'' Neil asked. And did it rather humbly, the inspector thought with a smug smile.

''Gladly.'' They shook hands on it.

Lindy sniffed and brushed a finger over one eye. ''Well, I must be off and running. Got us a Clootie to catch and I'll not do it racketing around here.''

He took his leave quickly and strode off down the back walk toward his carriage. There must be bard's blood in him, he thought. He told a damned good story if he did say so. Perhaps he'd missed his calling.

Even so, he knew he had to tend to the business he had chosen and wind up this case in a hurry now that Betts had inadvertently set a deadline. Perhaps tomorrow's funeral would produce some results.

So far every lead he'd had ran to a dead end. If the chief ever discovered that his new inspector had a clutch of unemployed former soldiers conducting surveillance on the earl of Marleigh—not to mention guarding a suspected murderess— Lindy knew he'd be an unemployed civilian. He needed absolute proof of someone's guilt to officially reopen the case

and justify an arrest. At this point, there was simply none to
be had.

Neil paused at the bottom of the stairs, not delaying what
he meant to do, but savoring the thought of it. Now, today,
before Betts discovered her pregnancy, he needed to confirm
his decision. The child would be as much his as the mother
would be. From this day on, he would proclaim this hour as
the one in which his heir was conceived. If not by the seed of
his loins, then by the determination in his heart and mind.

With a tender smile and a budding sense of urgency, he
counted the treads that led him up to the master suite.

The heavy brocade of the draperies screened out all but the
most feeble light. Curled in sleep, Bettsy looked little more
than a child herself, he thought.

Neil slipped out of his boots and his clothes and climbed
into bed beside her, sliding his arms around her from behind
as he nuzzled her neck. She smelled sweet, a warm, womanly
scent mingled with her lavender soap. He breathed softly in
her ear. She stirred and turned her face to his. Neil buried her
mouth under his, meaning to go slowly, but unable to curb his
mounting hunger to have her. Soft lips opened beneath his
without coaxing, taking him into her as though she'd been
waiting for him. Her wordless murmur of welcome swept
aside his good intentions. He turned her quickly and grasped
her to him, pushing his insistent lower body against hers.

"No, not like this. Not this time," he said, more to himself
than to her. He rolled her to her back and leaned over her to
unfasten her nightshirt. She lifted herself as he swept it up and
over her head and shoved the covers away.

Again he caught her mouth, this time caressing instead of
ravaging, tasting rather than consuming. Tentatively, she made
small forays of her own, touching her tongue to his, raising
her head from the pillow to prevent his moving away. He
fastened his mouth on her chin, raked it with his teeth, then
moved lower. All feeling centered in his lips as the pulse in
her neck quickened under them. He trailed kisses lower, to the

hollow of her throat, over her satiny chest to the swell of her breast.

Soft pleasure sounds from deep within her drove him on. Those and her seeking hands. Her fingers threaded through the dark mat on his chest. Delay became impossible, but he fought for it. This time should be memorable, special, better than before.

He spoke against her breast, briefly touching the beaded center with the tip of his tongue. "You're mine, Bettsy, all of you. Not just this way," he said, suckling her as hard and deeply as he could without causing pain, then releasing her with a soothing kiss, "but every way. I'll have you now, today and always."

Again he took her into his mouth and heard her sound of surrender, felt it vibrate within him, resonant, musical, arousing. His fingers clutched hers, lacing with them, palm-to-palm beside her shoulders as he moved over her. He looked down into her shadowed face. "Let me love you as I will. Don't be afraid."

"No," she whispered with a slight shake of her head, "no fear. Oh, Neil, I want you." Her lips parted and he began again with a soft kiss that quickly deepened to a restless struggle.

Moving back, he drifted lower to tease and claim, first her breasts, one to the other and back again. "So hot…" He abandoned them for the curve of her waist, nipping gently, reveling in her pleas for more. The dip of her navel beckoned and he filled it with a heated caress, breathing softly into the dampness there.

She arched against him, and he could scent her readiness. Too soon. Lower, he nuzzled the curls—red ones, he recalled, and wished he'd pulled back the draperies so he could see. "Open for me," he entreated, and raised himself slightly so she could obey. "Further," he whispered against her, tugging his hands from hers and placing his palms on her inner thighs. "All of you. Mine." Dizzy with need, he took her with his mouth, burying his tongue inside, withdrawing, capturing the swelling point of pleasure now exposed and pulsing rapidly.

Dimly, he heard her cries over the ringing in his ears. Her hands gripped his hair and still he circled and teased with his tongue, pressing his own need rhythmically against the bed. It was no longer enough. She began to thrash wildly, crying out, eager. Like one possessed, he rose over her and thrust in to the hilt. Her inner muscles gripped him so tightly he struggled to withdraw and plunge again. And again.

"Be still," he growled against his will. "Still, Betts, or it's over."

"No!" she cried, and lifted her hips in a swift rotation that ended in almost painful, squeezing contractions around him.

Sweet madness swept him and he moved without thought, pounding ceaselessly. His own shout rang in his ears like thunder as he poured himself into her, giving, giving until he had no more. His very life force exploded into her demanding womb. "Mine!" he cried with a shuddering breath. "By God, you're mine!" He buried his face in the pillow beside her head. "All of you," he added in a fervent whisper, rolling gently to one side, still joined.

Bettsy held on, gripping his back with a much weaker hold. Still gasping, she mumbled against his neck, "You...presume too much."

"For a man who's merely adequate?" he asked with a contented sigh.

"Damned satisfactory," she admitted breathlessly.

"Then don't argue. There's a child in you now. Mine."

"Time's not right."

"Exactly right. Today's the day."

"No chance," she said, planting a lazy kiss on his shoulder. "I'm so certain, you might persuade me to have another go if you're nice about it."

He laughed with delight as he hugged her. "Cheeky devil. Have a little mercy, will you?" But he felt himself stir within her even as she suggested it. This time he knew would last for hours. This time his urgency was spent and he could savor her, prolong her pleasure indefinitely. This time he was in complete control.

Elizabeth had never imagined anything so gloriously sensual. The vestiges of sleep had robbed her of whatever qualms she might have had about letting Neil make love to her. Thank God. Now fully awake, she saw no point in protesting, especially with Neil's body already swelling within her.

The feeling swept away coherent thought, leaving her quaking with rekindled desire. *More* kept echoing in her brain. Her fingers played over his chest as he rose above her. They slid downward to his hips and squeezed the tensing muscles there, urging him to move.

A slow, languid rhythm emerged between them. Tremors of pure feeling darted through her, retreated and returned with each measured thrust. Her eyes met his in the semidarkness and held the heated gaze. He lowered his chest so that the silken black curls teased her breasts with his every movement. Inside, her body clung to his, greedy to keep the fullness of him deep within. "Satisfactory?" he whispered, smiling into her eyes.

"Very...yes!" She clenched her eyes shut at a particularly deep foray and cried out for another.

"Shall I try for *excellent?*" he asked, nuzzling her lips with his tongue as he withdrew almost his full length.

"Oh, please," she moaned, and tried to rise and claim him completely. He held back, poised at her entrance.

"Can you see?" he whispered, looking down between their bodies. "Watch." Her eyes followed his, traveling the length of their shadowed bodies to the place where he barely joined her. "Touch," he offered, waiting.

Her hands moved between them as though he willed their movements, feeling the heat, the pulsing promise. His stones were hard, contracted, his shaft slick as wet satin and hard as steel. A wordless murmur of wonder escaped her lips with a broken breath.

"Now," he breathed, almost soundlessly, and watched as

she drew her fingers around his column. "Move your hand," he ordered softly. "Watch me come in."

Mesmerized, she watched him sink into her, slowly and steadily filling her with his whole length. The sight and sensation combined in an explosion of pure feeling.

Buried within her, he ground himself against her with a groan of pleasure and then began to pull away. She cried out in protest and tried to hold him, but he pinioned her hands with his. She twisted and arched, but still he moved back, leaving her empty.

"Neil!" she pleaded, demanded, threatened.

"Now?" he asked, hovering above her, tormenting.

"Yes, oh, yes, now!"

Suddenly he moved, abandoning her to lie on his back. Puzzled, she rose up on one elbow, ready to plead again if she must. Her body was on fire, longing, bereft without him.

He traced her breast with one finger and looked up at her through heavy-lidded eyes. "Then take what you want. Come over me and claim your pleasure."

Elizabeth mounted him quickly, guiding him inside her. She moved uncertainly, remembering her ineptitude that night in the study when she'd done everything herself.

He touched her where they joined, and she came undone. The world shattered around her into pieces of light and piercing shards of ecstasy. She held on to it for long seconds, suspended in a nothingness that encompassed everything. Neil became her heartbeat, her breath, her life force, her death, her all. His final surge and roar of triumph wrung a last, exquisite shudder from her, and she melted on top of him like a puddle of hot wax.

Elizabeth heard him gather enough air for a single word. "Excellent?" he asked with a shaky laugh.

"Infinitely...superior," she managed to answer.

"To what?" he asked, his hand coming to life against her neck and idly stroking the fringe of curls at her nape.

"To everything in the world," she whispered. "In the universe."

"I love you, Elizabeth." He kissed her. "My sweet Bettsy."

His words held a conviction not to be argued with. Hers slipped out before she could catch them. "I love you, too."

"I know. We'll marry on Saturday in Charing Cross."

"No!" she said, pushing herself up to glare at him. "It won't do, Neil."

"We'll have a grander wedding later if you like. This one's only to legitimize the child in the event I drop dead of exhaustion. Judging by my heart rate, that's a real possibility."

She sat up quickly, dragging a sheet over her breasts and huffing with exasperation. "There is no child, I tell you!"

His lips turned up crookedly as he laced his fingers behind his head, regarding her steadily. "Of course there is. We just made one. Mine and yours, a feisty little girl, I think. With red hair and a nasty disposition."

Elizabeth blinked and looked away, hysteria threatening. She felt the urge to laugh wildly at his determined complacency. "You are mad."

He was the one who laughed. "An adequately, excellently, infinitely superior madness it is, too. Saturday, Bettsy, at Charing Cross. Are you hungry?"

She fell sideways on the bed and turned away from him, mirth erupting inside her like a live thing. She laughed until the tears came. This reaction didn't signal hysterical relief, though, she realized. Only a sort of dark humor at the whole situation.

For the first time, after the episode at breakfast, she had finally admitted to herself that Nanny might have inadvertently misinformed her. Her courses were very late and she had been sick. She might very well have taken more than Neil's inebriated body on the floor of the study that night almost three weeks ago. A baby. Wouldn't that be icing on the cake? Wouldn't it just?

The laughter degenerated into weak little sobs as she felt Neil's arms surround her. One of his hands settled on her breast and the other on her abdomen.

Why couldn't she have him? she asked herself in a fit of righteous anger. Why not? She'd done nothing wrong to cause this tangle of events. Nothing! Could she help it if someone plotted against her? This wasn't fair!

"I won't let you go, Bettsy," Neil rasped against her ear. "You're mine, and I promise I will never let you go."

Elizabeth sighed and covered his hands with hers. Poor Neil. He did love her, probably as much as she loved him, if such were possible. It would be his ruin, and ultimately hers, if she agreed to the marriage. She would have to leave him. But not just yet. Oh God, not yet.

She turned in his arms and searched urgently for his mouth, hungry for another hour of joy, another cherished memory to store away for later.

# Chapter Sixteen

Elizabeth realized Neil would never let her go willingly, certainly not with a baby on the way. God knew she didn't want to leave, but somehow she had to make herself do so. Neil was determined to wed on Saturday next.

Why couldn't he understand? No decent home in England would ever receive them. Neil would be either shunned or ridiculed if he wed her. Probably both.

Her emotions lay too close to the surface. She felt vulnerable, especially to Neil's particular method of persuasion. What if, in a weak moment, she agreed to his madness? She had to go now, while she still had strength to resist what he offered.

As much as Elizabeth hated the deceit, she practiced it assiduously until that next afternoon, when he was to leave for the funeral. She indulged in Neil's lovemaking, weeping at the sweetness of it. She smiled at his plans for their future, saying nothing, secretly deciding how she would escape to Scotland.

The funeral provided the perfect opportunity. Neil assured her that one of Lindy's best men remained on duty, watching the front of the town house. Oliver covered the back from his upstairs window in the carriage house. Both of her guardians were well armed and vigilant; they would be watching for anyone trying to enter the house. However, neither suspected her scheme to leave.

"I'll be fine," she promised Neil as he drummed up excuses to delay his departure for the cemetery. She memorized his every feature, tracing them with trembling fingers, imprinting them in her heart. How she wanted to throw herself into his arms, beg him to forgive what she had to do. Instead, she laughed a little unsteadily. "You'd best be off or Lindy will come looking for you! One more kiss?" She kept it light, a sweet, quick buss, such as a wife might give her husband to see him off for the day.

Neil made a petulant face when she pulled away. "That's supposed to do for three whole hours?"

She shoved him toward the door. "Go!"

He chuckled, a contented sound that wrenched her insides. As he exited, he turned, winked and blew her a kiss.

With a playful grab, she caught it and placed her palm over her mouth, stifling a sob as the door closed behind him. For a long moment she stood perfectly still, feeling hot tears track down her cheeks. Then she sniffed and shook herself into action. Three hours seemed a very short time to escape London.

A scant quarter hour later, Elizabeth stashed a quickly packed valise and Terry's three-caped coat behind the kitchen door. Then she stepped outside and beckoned to Oliver. She needed him away from his watch post in the carriage house just long enough for her to collect her mare from the stables and sneak out the back gate.

"Milady?" He shuffled inside. One callused hand rested on the butt of a pistol tucked through his belt. "Aught amiss?"

"No, everything's fine, Oliver," she said, smiling. "The thing is, I need your help in moving some books from the attic down to the lab. They're all ready, stacked right by the door. Should take only two or three trips."

"I'll tote for ye later, milady, but Lord Doc says t' keep a sharp eye peeled out yonder." He gestured toward the small garden and gate that led to the back alley.

Elizabeth shrugged. "Tell you what. I'll keep watch from my bedroom window and scream like a banshee if I see anyone. Shouldn't take you more than a few minutes."

He started shaking his head, but she ignored it. "Just bring the books down and stack them on the table. You can go right back out. Soon as I see you return to your post, I'll come down and put them on the shelves."

Oliver tilted his head to one side as though he were considering and then gave a short nod. "Mind you watch close, then. Anybody approaches that gate, you holler."

"Don't worry," she said, "I've more at stake than you do!"

She followed him to the stairs and up as far as her room. As soon as he disappeared up the next flight, she retraced her steps at a run and flew out the back door. She kept behind the overgrown hedges in the event he looked down from one of the attic windows, then made a dash from her cover to the stable.

Just before she entered, she caught a whiff of sulfur.

Darting into the dark interior, she tossed the coat and valise aside and peeked back out. A trail of sparking smoke snaked its way to the floor-length conservatory windows. One pane near the bottom was missing. Frozen with horror, she watched the hissing serpent eat its way across the terrace stones, through the broken windowpane and into the laboratory. A split second of silence ensued, then an explosion jarred the stable door shut. Its force slammed her backward to the straw-strewn floor.

Stunned, Elizabeth lay breathless for a moment before the reality of the disaster sent her scrambling for one of the empty stalls. Curled into a ball, she snuggled deep in the sweet, fresh straw and shuddered uncontrollably.

Just as Oliver's predicament dawned on her, she heard his shouts. Thank God! He was outside, not blown to pieces as she had feared. Within moments, it sounded as though half of London had descended on the back garden to view the disaster. Shortly after that, bells clanged, signaling that fire wagons approached. Voices rang out, Oliver's louder than the rest.

Elizabeth huddled deeply in the corner, drawing the hay up to cover her completely. She didn't dare show herself now, even though she realized Oliver must be frantic. Who knew how many people were out there? And any one of them could have blown up the place where she always spent her afternoons. Sudden nausea attacked and she swallowed with difficulty.

Neil would come soon, she told herself. He would be here in a few hours, maybe sooner if Oliver could get word to him. Until then, she couldn't risk discovery. Her thoughts evened out with the prospect of rescue, and the violent shivering finally abated. Relaxing her arms, which she'd clasped tightly around her middle, she forced herself to breathe normally. Neil would come.

Who had done this thing and why? Had the man or men who'd planned this meant to kill them both? Who knew that she habitually worked with Neil every day in the lab? Everyone they knew. But who had had access to the laboratory to lay explosives?

The powder had to have been set the night before or in the early morning hours before Oliver was awake. Even then, Lindy had a man stationed at the back gate. Whoever it was must have climbed the wall under cover of darkness, broken out the glass where it would not be noticed, shoved in a quantity of black powder and trailed a fuse to where it could be ignited from outside the gate. It was certainly an unexpected form of attack.

Elizabeth sighed, mourning the probable loss of their precious microscope. Thank goodness the conservatory-turned-lab had been built onto the back of the four-story house. That made extensive damage to the rest of the structure improbable. The whole laboratory was likely in cinders, though, and they'd have to start all over. *They?* No, she remembered, she wouldn't be there to assist Neil any longer. She meant to disappear.

But she couldn't leave right now. He would be frantic, thinking first that she had expired in the explosion, and then, when he found no body, that someone had taken her away. No, she would have to wait and reassure him that she was all right. A wry smile tugged her lips. A reason or a rationalization? The disaster provided her an excuse to stay a while longer. Just a few more days. Then she would go.

Secure in the knowledge that Neil would come home soon, and that the immediate danger was past, Elizabeth deliberately dismissed the troubling mystery. She focused on Neil and the virtually sleepless night they had shared. Closing her eyes and making herself relax in the bed of prickly straw, she blocked out the horror of the explosion and escaped into her memories. Eventually she fell asleep.

Neil rode through the streets like a demon possessed. His mount galloped full out, dodged pedestrians, carriages, and even leapt over one street vendor's cart. Somewhere in his wake rode Lindy and the messenger, the man who had been detailed to keep watch with Oliver. Self-recrimination and fear for Bettsy blacked out Neil's anger at their failure to keep her safe. He should have been there, shouldn't have left her side for a moment.

The air smelled like a bloody war zone, he thought darkly as he leapt from his mount's back before it had fully halted. Dropping the reins, he dashed up the steps, threw open the door and stopped short. The entrance hall stood undamaged except for bits of debris. The door at the far end by the stairs hung on one hinge, its inner side blackened and pitted.

"Jesus, no!" he breathed, half in exclamation, half in prayer. Then his feet began to move of their own accord, taking him swiftly toward the lab. Terror knotted his insides and made his movements uncoordinated as he reached the portal of what now looked like hell burned out. In the midst of the smoking rubble stood a sooty Oliver.

"Bettsy?" Neil whispered, his heart in his throat. She *could not* have been in here! He met Oliver's woebegone gaze and watched the man shake his head slowly.

"Where, Ollie? Where is she?" Neil demanded, scanning the knee-deep, smoldering wreckage—tons of glass from the skylights, plaster and shards of the wooden shelves and furniture, beams, shattered equipment, a tortured half of his microscope. He fully expected to find her hand or foot protruding from the mess. His stomach clenched and he thought he might be sick. He thought he might die.

"She ain't nowhere else, sir. We searched," Oliver said as he stooped and began raking up a pile of broken boards.

Something inside Neil snapped. Grunting with fury and exertion, he began shoving things, lifting anything large enough to conceal a human form and hefting it aside. He ignored pain as scattered shards of glass bit into his hands through the gloves and sliced his trousered legs above the boots. He fought off Lindy—apparently just arrived—when he tried to stop the search.

"Neil! Wait! Man, listen to me!" Lindy grappled with his arms, intent on restraining him.

Neil cursed foully and fell to his knees, tugging at a slab of the collapsed table. A sharp blow to his head stunned him. He teetered to one side, dizzied but conscious, and felt hands lifting and dragging him away.

Reason returned when he found himself prone on the floor of the hallway, just outside the laboratory door. He looked up to see Lindy gesturing and barking orders to several men. They disappeared into the room, and Neil could hear them sifting through the wreckage. He sat up and ran a bloodied hand through his hair, biting back fright and struggling to breathe normally.

Lindy knelt and tugged off Neil's glove to examine his right hand. "We'll find her for you," he said, wrapping a handkerchief around Neil's palm. "Sorry I had to clout you, but you're like a goddamned mule. Had to get your attention." The inspector reached for Neil's other hand, and they locked gazes. "Don't you go berserk on me again. Betts might need these paws of yours if she's hurt."

Neil's throat convulsed as he glanced toward the lab. "Hurt? No one could have lived through—" He broke off and lowered his head. *"God!"*

Lindy shook him by the shoulders. "Don't you go mourning her yet. We don't know that she was in there."

A voice from the front entry interrupted Lindy. "Inspector? I stabled his lordship's mount. Thought you might want to know I stumbled over these." The man held up a small valise and a coat.

Neil scrambled to his feet, grabbed the case and tore the thing open, spilling out the contents. Bettsy's clothes! Her woolen stockings! Terry's, rather—the ones she had appropriated. He flung them aside and picked up a pair of breeches. He shook them at the man and demanded, "The horses? How many horses?"

"Three in the stalls, milord. A mare, the coach pair and the one you just rode. I gave him some oats and—"

Neil dashed through the dining room and kitchen, still clutching the garment in his fist. She was in the stables! *Had* to be there. He slammed through the kitchen door and ran past the carriage house to the building at the back of the garden.

"Bettsy?" he shouted as he shoved the door open and all but fell inside. Scrambling to his feet, he overturned oat sacks and anything else large enough for her to hide behind. *Nothing!* He began throwing open the half doors of empty stalls, and with a cursory glance inside, progressed to the ones occupied. Yanking the horses out, slapping rumps to hurry them, he found their enclosures empty except for a few droppings and trampled straw.

He drew in a deep breath, willing his harried brain to function. Lindy was examining a spot on the floor. "What do you make of it?" Neil asked, forcing a steadiness he didn't begin to feel. "She was here, wasn't she? Tell me she was here!" He noticed Lindy gazing past him, a burgeoning grin on his face.

Slowly Neil turned and saw her. His heart nearly stopped with relief. She rested on all fours just inside one of the empty stalls, looking up at him through sleep-glazed eyes. Straw littered her tousled curls and clung to her rumpled suit. Her lips widened with a happy smile and parted to form his name.

Suddenly he was there, with no recollection of crossing the stable. His arms ached with the force of his grip on her. His mouth raked her face, hungry to taste every inch of it. He wiped his tears on her hair, half laughing, half weeping. *She lived!*

She yelped, giggling, as his hands ran over her, roughly pinching and sliding in rough caresses. "Neil, stop!"

Collapsing back against the stall door, Neil pulled her into his lap and encased her in his arms. His lips sought her ear. "Christ, I thought you were dead!"

Her hands found his face and she kissed him. Neil knew he'd never tasted anything so wonderful in his entire life.

Lindy's rough-edged reprimand dragged them back to sanity. "Do this later, if you don't mind. We've a crime here, remember?"

Bettsy pulled away, but only far enough to rest her palms on Neil's chest. Her words were for Lindy. "How bad is the damage?"

"Total to the laboratory. Very little to the rest of the place. They're sorting through the mess now."

"I saw how it happened, how they set it up," she offered. "There was a trail of powder, or perhaps a long fuse, that led into the lab through a broken pane near the ground. I think it was too far away for me to stamp it out." She ducked her head as though ashamed of her failure. "The truth is I didn't even try. I simply froze when I saw it burning."

"Oh, love," Neil muttered, dragging her head to his chest and holding it there. "You silly henwit, if you'd tried, it might have killed you! It doesn't matter about the lab. Nothing matters but that you're safe." He kissed the top of her head, ignoring the stalks of straw scratching his lips.

"I wouldn't exactly say she's safe," Lindy argued, pacing back and forth in front of them. "Whoever did this had to have gotten into the laboratory somehow and planted the powder. How did they sneak in with a cache large enough to do the job?"

Elizabeth snapped her fingers and then pointed at Lindy. "Suppose we watched them bring it in?"

"What do you mean?" Neil asked.

"The deliveries! The man from the supply house stacked some of the boxes right by the windows. Just this morning, he brought more. He put a few across the room near the shelves. We hadn't time to examine any of the contents." She frowned. "But suppose we had? How could he know we wouldn't open them today and find it before he set it off?"

Lindy brushed his mustache with two fingers, darting a glance toward them. "Question is, how did he break a windowpane, string the fuse across the garden and out the gate?"

Neil shook his head. "Very carefully, I expect. Most likely came over the wall at night."

"All academic now. It's been done and that's that," Lindy said, halting his pacing. "For the moment, I think we should let our madman think he has succeeded. I'll go and speak with the lad who found the valise and coat. He shouldn't mention finding anything out here. Betts, you'll lie low until dark. Doc can bring you inside after I've dismissed the men who are sifting through the wreckage."

Elizabeth watched Lindy pull the door shut, encapsulating her and Neil in relative darkness. Her fingers were growing numb in Neil's tight grasp. The silence grew ominous, broken only by the sounds of the horses snuffling and shifting idly in their stalls.

Neil's sudden accusation startled her. "You were leaving."

She tried to tug her hands free, but he strengthened his grip. "You're hurting me."

He released her immediately and got to his feet, turning his back. "Why were you leaving?"

She gritted her teeth and expelled a long sigh. If he knew the reason for her going, he would guard against it happening in the future, especially when the danger to her life no longer existed. Lying to him disturbed her, but she saw no alternative. "I thought I'd be safer out of the country. Seems I was right."

He turned back to her then, but she saw only the shadows

of his features. "You would have gone without even a good-bye? What of all the plans we made?"

She forced a laugh. "You made. *You*, Neil. I had no choice but to agree, now did I?" Elizabeth busied herself brushing the straw from her suit. "What if I don't want a future here with you? What if you, as my self-appointed protector, assume too much after a little bed sport?"

His growl of anger frightened her a little, but she held her ground. His large hand gripped her arm just below her shoulder. "Bed sport? Is that all I mean to you? Tell me the truth, Bettsy."

Elizabeth cringed at his hurt and anger. She steeled herself, knowing that he would get over this, over her, if she could only maintain the fiction for a while. Disgust would take hold soon and he would no longer want her. "You made an admirable diversion for me, my lord, but I'm afraid you took our dalliance too seriously. It's time for me to go."

"On to bigger and better things, then?" he asked, his jaw clenched with fury, his fingers biting into her arm.

She forced out a bitter laugh. "Oh, your *things* are certainly big enough to suit any woman. In fact, your ego is overlarge. Tell me, have I bruised it?"

He shook her. Hard. "The hell with my ego, it's my heart you're breaking!" Then he released his grip on her and brushed his hands over her sleeves, as though to wipe away any hurt he'd caused. "Bettsy, damn it, you know I love you. Why are you doing this? Even if you mean what you say, what about the child? Don't you care about creating some kind of stable life for it with a father who will—"

"There is no *child!*" She pushed away from him and staggered backward over the rough floor, rubbing her suddenly chilly arms. Neil knew she was pregnant. It only made her look stupid to keep denying it. Elizabeth realized the time had come to admit her condition, to herself and to him. She sank down against the wall of the stable, holding up one hand to warn Neil not to approach her.

Somehow, she had to make him release her and relinquish

his claim on the babe they had created. Maybe that was why he wanted her to stay, for this possible heir. That thought, along with all that had happened to her in the last traumatic hours, melted Elizabeth's resolve. She rested her head on her drawn-up knees and began to weep softly, hating herself for the weakness.

She was so damned tired of fighting.

Neil crouched in front of her, not touching her in spite of the concern he felt. She looked so fragile, he thought, but he knew better. Bettsy had more courage in her than most men possessed. Neither horrible slander, nor bullets, nor a keg of gunpowder had weakened her spirit. He suspected these tears were a result of the pregnancy, not defeat. She would cry this out and then raise that defiant little chin of hers, spitting out more anger or well-meant lies to drive him away. He knew her reason, too.

How could he make her understand that life without her, whether he was socially accepted or not, meant absolutely nothing to him? His work held no meaning, either, unless she continued to share it. Simply saying so wouldn't do the trick, but he couldn't very well hold her against her will forever.

He blew out a deep breath and settled down beside her, a few inches away, leaning against the wall. Her sobbing had stopped, but her forehead still rested against her knees, hiding her face.

"I want you to know that I don't believe anything that's been said about you, Bettsy. All those rumors were just that. We've established why you were swimming nearly nude—you almost drowned and had to shed your heavy clothes. Anyone with any sense would have done the same. Obviously someone, probably Maggie, danced that night in the fountain. I'd wager she looked enough like you from a distance. Those men found in your room that night were no doubt lured there by whoever wanted you to look guilty. Or mad. Probably Colin. The rest of your escapades originated in the mouths of cup-shot knaves building their own reputations as rakes around the clubs. None of that was your fault. Why should you punish yourself for it?''

She said nothing. Didn't move.

He tried another tack. ''If it's guilt about your pregnancy, you mustn't let that worry you. I'll love any child of yours as though it were mine. I've made it mine.''

Her head shot up with such a look of surprised hope, he drew back from her. ''That's it!'' she said quickly. A bit too quickly, he thought. ''You wouldn't want a baby someone else fathered! I can manage by myself quite well, and that's why I need to leave immediately. So that—''

''Ha! It *is* mine!'' Neil felt his face crack with delight. He knew without a doubt under the sun that she lied through those even little teeth of hers. She'd been resigned to the fact that he knew she was pregnant and would insist on keeping what was his. Only his clumsy offer to claim it gave her a way out of staying. ''It is my child and, by God, you know it is!''

''No, no, you're wrong, Neil.'' She rushed on, gathering speed as she went. ''I swear you couldn't count the lovers I've had since Father died. So many I forget names and places and dates. Anyone could be the father, anyone in London or—''

''Maybe even Terry?'' he suggested helpfully.

''Yes, that's right! It probably was him.'' She nodded eagerly, rubbing her legs with excitement.

Neil grinned. ''No. You were never intimate with Terry.''

He watched doubt shadow her face. Ah, she was wondering just how much Terry had told him about their relationship before he died. ''Well, maybe not,'' she qualified, ''but it could have been anybody else.''

''Lame, Bettsy. Very lame,'' Neil chided. ''I was the first and only. You were a virgin. Admit it.''

''But you were drunk!'' She snapped her lips together and frowned, realizing her mistake when he laughed out loud.

''Drunk as a lord, and sorry as hell to have missed it. Must have been dreadfully awkward for you when I might have made it less so.'' He snaked his arms around her and held her tight as she struggled. ''You minx, I ought to thrash you with a buggy whip.'' He laughed with pure relief and wonder. ''Ah, Bettsy, I do love you and your warped little mind.''

She shoved away from him, red faced and furious. ''You're dead wrong, Neil. Wishing won't make it true.''

He settled back against the wall, smug and happy. ''Give it up, love. You're going to marry me as soon as I get you out of this stable and into a dress. I flatly refuse to stand up with a bride in breeches, however well they suit you.''

''I won't do it,'' she declared, arms folded across her chest and her chin in the air.

''What? Wear a dress?'' he joked, his mood light as air.

''Marry you! You're a fool, Neil Bronwyn, if you think I'll let you wreck your career and your good name over this horrible mis-mistake.'' A sob broke the last word. ''This is all my fault,'' she wailed. ''I don't want to cry! I won't!'' She held her breath.

Neil gathered her in his arms and rocked her. ''It's all right, sweetheart. Little mothers do a lot of that when they're increasing. Perfectly natural. Go ahead and soak my shirt.''

''Beast!'' she groaned into his chest, striking his shoulder with a weak fist.

''I know. Curse of the male gender. You'll straighten me out, I'm sure, but it could take years.'' He sighed, a rush of well-being such as he'd never known filling him completely. ''A whole lifetime.''

A short time later, Neil wondered if he would ever again know such comfort. Bettsy lay against him, totally spent and lost in slumber. Her tears warmed his chest, seemed to seep right through it into his heart. He rested a hand lightly on her still-flat abdomen, eagerly anticipating a swell there in a few weeks. The combined smells of fresh hay, horse dung and oiled leather permeated the air around him, but he imagined the scents of love and Bettsy.

Soon. Very soon now, he would hold her in the marriage bed and love away her fears and doubts. No matter what the future held, Neil promised himself he'd never let her face anything alone again. When the birth pangs came, urgent and frightening, he'd be there sharing, encouraging her every step of the way.

Somehow, he and Lindy would have to corner the monster who had killed Terry and who threatened Bettsy. The investigation had dragged on long enough. Perhaps the relief when it was over would soften Bettsy's stance on the marriage. If not, Neil would simply remain firm on the matter.

He had exaggerated about the wedding, of course. They couldn't afford to risk her life by revealing that she had survived the blast. But the delay wouldn't be a long one.

Neil had little doubt that the murderer knew exactly who Bettsy was. There remained an outside chance, however, that the explosion today could have been meant for Neil himself. After all, Terry had been a victim, and now Neil held the title. Everyone knew he and Bettsy spent their afternoons in the lab. It was quite possible that someone wanted to destroy them both.

In any event, he meant to keep Bettsy hidden completely until the matter was resolved.

Everything pointed to Colin as the culprit. Marleigh admitted he had planned to declare Bettsy insane. Perhaps he'd decided that wasn't permanent enough to suit his needs. Very likely he had tried to frame her for Terry's murder, had killed Maggie Leffing to keep her quiet about it and had arranged the explosion today. Neil couldn't imagine a better motive than the Marleigh fortune. Yes, he thought, idly caressing Bettsy's arm. Colin must be the one. But if Lindy accused the earl of Marleigh of murder, he'd better be able to prove it.

Neil couldn't quite dismiss the man who had argued with Terry at the theater. Damned suspicious, that one, especially after the altercation with Terry that Bettsy had overheard. But how could the stranger have gotten the weapons from the Marleigh town house? A partnership with Maggie to implicate Bettsy? But why try to kill Bettsy afterward, when he must know she would hang? Well, Neil admitted, the man might have feared she would remember him and what she had overheard.

Neil couldn't seriously consider Turner. But then, the boy had said nothing about the gambling debts. He knew about Terry and Bettsy's friendship and could have stolen the guns to try to throw suspicion off himself. And if Turner had guessed Bettsy was really Elizabeth, he might even have suggested the rumor Goodroe started that caused Bensen to shoot her. Turner had been conspicuously absent when she was shot. Hadn't he mentioned once that he dabbled in fireworks displays? That would give him some expertise with black powder, certainly.

Hell, though he favored Colin Marleigh, it could be any one of them, Neil realized. He ran a hand through his hair, wincing when he disturbed the glass cuts on his palm. All he knew for certain was that he and Lindy had to redouble their efforts and find the guilty party before he struck again.

Bettsy was even more vulnerable now that she carried a child. Even the threat of further attacks might worry her enough to cause a miscarriage. His heart nearly stopped at the new thought.

"I'll keep you safe, Bettsy. I promise. You and our little one," he murmured softly so as not to wake her. "God help me, if it's the last thing I do, I'll catch this bastard and give you the peace you deserve."

# Chapter Seventeen

Lindy rapped on the front door for a change, purposely altering his routine on arriving at Havington House. One didn't take a visitor to the back door, after all. Especially not an important visitor one was showing off. Five in the afternoon wasn't precisely proper for a formal call on an earl, but that small breach of etiquette would surely be overlooked.

The door opened, revealing a disheveled Neil dressed in a dirty, rumpled shirt and trousers. His boots wore traces of soot. Lindy knew he'd been clearing out the mess in the laboratory.

"MacLinden?" Neil greeted Lindy perfunctorily, his gaze locked on the guest he'd brought.

Lindy grinned with triumph. "Lord Havington, I'd like you to meet Alfred Ward, our fellow theater aficionado."

Neil's eyes widened with surprise. "Well. Do come in."

MacLinden allowed the man to precede him through the wide oak door and into the foyer. His discovery of Mr. Ward meant only partial success, but even that proved a great step forward in solving the crime. A narrowing of the field, so to speak. Lindy was immensely pleased and was certain Neil would be. They trailed after the doctor into the formal, sunswept parlor. MacLinden laid his dapper bowler on a piecrust side table and watched Ward follow suit with his beaver stovepipe.

The man showed no awe in an earl's presence, as many

commoners did; Lindy noticed and admired him for it. His distinguished appearance certainly belied his ancestry. Few nobles carried themselves as well as did Alfred Ward. He stood as tall as Neil, though more sparely framed. The aquiline nose, expressive face and silver hair lent him a rather dramatic presence. Almost theatrical, like the voice.

"May I assume this call for drinks, Inspector?" Neil asked, wearing a look of anticipation.

"Without question," Lindy replied, rocking back on his heels, hands clasped on his lapels.

"Oh, I think there'll be questions, all right," Neil said with a smirk. He doled two fingers of whiskey into each of three glasses and handed them out. "Mr. Ward, let's hear about your...disagreement with my nephew. You are the man who spoke with him at the theater, are you not?"

"Yes," Ward agreed, nodding once. "We did have words."

"Harsh words, by all accounts," Neil continued, thumping his glass down on the table beside the hats. His hands clenched with what Lindy recognized as growing impatience. Amazing how Doc had all but abandoned that cultivated calm of his since Betts had come into his life. Much like a domesticated animal reverting to the wild.

Ward reached into his coat with one hand. A harsh scream of warning sounded from the doorway. Betts launched herself across the room and, with an admirably high kick, landed a booted right foot in Ward's midsection. His tall frame bent double and he collapsed in a gasping heap at their feet.

Lindy found himself speechless with awe and embarrassment at the unwarranted act. Poor Betts had finally cracked under the strain. He squatted down to assist Ward in rising.

"He's the one!" Betts cried, grabbing Neil's arm as she righted herself. Her face looked the color of rice paper.

"Easy, love," Neil warned, putting his arms around her.

Lindy wondered whether Betts needed comfort or restraint. He'd never seen a woman do what she had. Amazing move.

Ward's groan drew his attention away from the girl. "Are you all right, Mr. Ward?"

The man's somber features cracked in a slow, self-deprecating smile. "Well, my dignity hurts worse than anything else." He rubbed his stomach with a long, slender hand. "May I ask why you attacked me, young man?"

Betts's wide-eyed look settled on Lindy. "He went for a gun!"

Ward laughed then, a low, rumbling sound. "No, no, lad, merely documents I meant to share with his lordship. If you'll permit?" He reached slowly into his coat pocket with two fingers and withdrew a flat sheaf of papers, which he held out to Neil. "My findings, requested by the former earl, on incidents involving a Lady Elizabeth Marleigh."

"Findings?" Neil asked, shooting Lindy a questioning look.

"Yes," Ward confirmed. "And my billing, of course, all itemized. Your nephew and I argued over advance payment, I'm sad to say. Now that the job is complete, I assume you will honor his debt, my lord? Investigative work is frightfully expensive these days and, if you will note as you read, not a few bribes were required in the process."

"You're an *investigator?*" Neil parroted in disbelief.

Lindy decided to relieve Ward of some of the explanation. The poor man still looked a bit short of breath and small wonder. "Mr. Ward is a former Bow Street man. Best in the business, so they say. Works independently now. Apparently, Terry hired him to disprove the allegations about Elizabeth in the news sheets and around the clubs. Made a thorough job of it, too." Lindy smiled at Betts's expression of chagrin. "Good news, eh?"

Betts nodded slightly, still unconvinced, he could see.

Neil tore open the seal and unfolded the papers. Backing up, he sat on the divan, drawing Betts down beside him with a tug on her elbow. Lindy took a chair facing them and motioned for Ward to do the same. For some ten minutes, Neil read and passed the papers, one a time, to Betts, who in turn gave them to Lindy.

The inspector knew the contents already, but still relished the black-and-white proof of Betts's innocence. When the last page had been handed over, Lindy smiled all around. "Barring your atrocious handwriting, Mr. Ward, you've done a most excellent piece of work. Wouldn't you say so, milord?" He cocked an eyebrow at Neil, who looked ready to embrace Ward on the instant.

Neil did better than that; he rose and offered his hand. "Alfred—may I call you that, since I consider you one of the best friends I shall ever meet?—please accept my heartfelt thanks and a doubling of your fee. If ever there's anything, anything at all you need that's within my power to provide, you've only to ask. I don't believe I can ever thank you enough."

"Perhaps one thing, my lord," Ward said.

"Neil. You must call me Neil," he insisted, pumping the man's hand. "Now what may I do for you, Alfred?"

"I'd like an introduction to her ladyship. You see, I feel I quite know her after all my efforts on her behalf, though I've only seen her twice at a distance." Ward smiled suggestively at Betts, looking for the world like the aging Lothario he must be. Lindy noted a flicker of jealousy darken Neil's expression.

"This high-kicking lad is Lady Marleigh, Mr. Ward," Lindy said, stepping in quickly before Neil made a fool of himself. "But then, her disguise didn't fool you at all, did it, sir?"

Ward reached for Betts's hand and let his lips hover just above it. "Her beauty shines right through, now that I know. That night at the theater with your party, I suspected, but I only knew for certain when his lordship expressed his affection so openly this afternoon. Congratulations, my lord, on your exquisite taste in women. Now may I also ask a harmless boon of the lady?"

Neil mumbled something sounding like acquiescence under the gun. The loss of his usual dignity tickled Lindy.

Ward released Betts's hand. "May I inquire who your *sensai* is, my lady? You pack a wicked blow behind such a tiny boot."

Betts looked confused. "*Sensai?* What's that?"

Neil stepped between them. "I am her *sensai*. Taught her

everything she knows." His pride bordered on belligerence. Then he turned, asking her sotto voce, "How *did* you learn to kick like that?"

Betts colored a bright pink. "I watch you every morning in the garden. Especially when you practice with Oliver." She wrinkled her nose, looking a little ashamed at her admission. "I asked you to teach me once. When you didn't, I simply watched and tried to copy your moves."

Lindy shook his head in wonder. "You learned that merely by watching? Good God, Neil, can you imagine what she could do with a bit of real training?"

"It boggles the mind," Neil replied, laughing. "So you watched me, eh? Every day?" He shot a self-satisfied look at Ward.

Lindy eyed Neil's swelling shirtfront, expecting the buttons to pop at any moment. Arrogant rascal. "Much as I hate to break up this little admiration-society meeting," he interrupted, "oughten we to discuss Mr. Ward's findings and see how they might relate to our investigation?"

"Of course," Betts agreed, obviously eager to change the subject. "So we know Colin is behind the slander."

"A fact with proof to back it up," Lindy said, resuming his seat when Betts took hers. "Since he instigated the events that destroyed your reputation, he also might have tried to frame you for Terry's murder."

"Because of the money I inherited," she said dully.

"Quite so," Ward agreed. "Lord Marleigh even went so far as to initiate confinement papers for you at St. Mary's of Bethlehem, signed by a Dr. Brunbaum, one of the administrators."

"When?" Neil asked, one fist clutched tightly in the other.

"The day your nephew was killed," Ward said. "One of the Marleigh footmen admitted that he accompanied his employer to her ladyship's town house late that very evening to take her up, but she had already left. They had no idea where she had gone, you see."

Ward paused and looked at Lindy. "In my opinion, it would

have been a simple matter for Lord Marleigh to have seized the dueling pistols at that time, seen to young Havington's demise and rushed it to his country estate to establish his alibi. None of his people would betray the time of his arrival for fear they'd be turned out. What do you think, Inspector?''

Lindy stroked his mustache for a moment before speaking. "I think I'd best have a witness with an ironclad reputation for honesty and no secrets in his past before I haul the earl of Marleigh before a magistrate. Else I'll be scratching out a living in Whitechapel with the rest of the beggars. At this point, all we have is circumstantial.''

Neil cursed foully and with real feeling. He paced the room a couple of times like a caged tiger. "I say we beat the truth out of the son of a bitch. Now. Today.''

"Think a moment, Doc,'' Lindy suggested, dispensing with his official formality. "Why would Marleigh kill Terry when he already had commitment papers signed to put Betts away? He'd have had control of her money. God knows that Betts—pardon this, my dear—wouldn't have lasted a week in that hellhole.''

"Bugger that theory, Lindy. You know as well as I that this woman would probably have been running the whole hospital in that length of time. Colin shot my nephew because he knew Terry would never have left her in such a place. Not for any longer than it took him to hear of it. Also, if you'll recall, Terry might have been a threat legally if he had questioned Colin's right to the title. We discussed that at the very beginning. Colin had every reason to kill Terry, foremost of which his desire to implicate Bettsy. She'd have been hanged. That's much more final than incarceration in a mental ward.''

"And he'd have had the documentation of her supposed madness as well,'' Ward added for good measure.

"Stop it! Stop it, all of you!'' Betts cried. "I know it's true, but I can't hear any more.''

She dashed from the room, and Lindy heard the rapid click of her boots on the stairs. "Better go see to her, Doc. We'll let ourselves out.''

Ward winced at Lindy as Neil brushed past them on the run. "Lordship's got his hands rather full, doesn't he?"

Lindy nodded and picked up his hat. "Aye, he does that. He's good for your fee, though, doubled like he said. I'll wager you have it by messenger before the end of the day." He glanced up the stairs as they passed. "If he gets our Betts calmed down in time to regain his senses. He's usually much more dignified than he was today, but what with the murders, falling in love and such, he's been under a bit of stress these past weeks."

"Not to worry," Ward said, giving his top hat a pat to settle it on his handsome silvery locks. "He can pay me when I've done with the case."

"Ah, so you're going to help us, Mr. Ward?" Lindy asked with an ingratiating smile.

"Oh, absolutely, Inspector. You couldn't pry me off this investigation with a bloody crowbar."

Lindy pulled the front door shut and nodded at the guard he had positioned just across the street. Taking longer strides than usual, he managed to keep pace with Alfred Ward as they made their way down the block to his waiting carriage.

All in all, the day had gone rather nicely, Lindy thought. The suspects were narrowed to two, he had gained the services of a famously successful Bow Street man and Helen would be waiting for him after her performance. Life didn't get much better than that. The arrest of a murderer and the proof of guilt in hand would have been preferable, of course, but one shouldn't be greedy. Perhaps that would be tomorrow's treat.

Elizabeth slammed her fists against the bedcovers. Damn Colin! How could her own cousin plot against her so foully? Terry was dead because of her. Colin had killed him, just to ruin her life. And he had ruined it beyond repair, no matter what those papers proved. There would always be a question in everyone's mind.

"Ah, Bettsy," Neil crooned as he came in and lay down

beside her. He stroked her hair with his hand and tried to pull her close.

"Leave me alone!" She turned her back to him, sniffing loudly.

"Of course I won't leave and you know it. Sweetheart, you ought not to let this upset you so. Don't you see what this means? We can clear your name as soon as Colin's arrested. Everyone will know he arranged all those ugly situations for his own benefit. We'll expose him for the murdering scum he is and have an end to this."

"Terry's dead because of me," she cried.

"He's dead because of Colin, Bettsy. You mustn't blame yourself. No one, least of all me, thinks you're to blame for anything. Colin won't have the final victory in this, you know."

Elizabeth laughed bitterly. "And I thought I was naive."

Neil slid his arms around her, wishing he could ease the rigidity of her body and the hopelessness in her heart. "You've done nothing wrong, Bettsy. Nothing. Everyone will know that once they learn the truth."

"Ah," she said, her soft voice rife with sarcasm, "so the whole of London's crème de la crème will welcome me with open arms. We'll have the wedding of the century and live happily ever after, the good doctor earl and his poor, wronged countess. Oh, and her little bastard. Let's not forget the fruit of our experiments. 'Just whose could it be?' they'll ask, 'Lord Terry's, Lord Neil's or the lords legion who marched through her bedroom?'"

Neil rose above her, grasped her shoulder and shook her gently. "Stop this, Bettsy! Stop it right now. I know the child is mine. No one will ever doubt that when I've had my say. I promise you."

She turned her red-rimmed eyes to meet his determined glare. "Take out an advertisement, will you? Even you have some small doubt hidden down there in the recesses of that overlarge heart. Don't deny it. That doubt will grow, fed with everyone's snide innuendos. You'll have nothing left but the pity of your peers. Their pity, ridicule and rejection. Your life's work will become a standing joke. Even if you still believe in me after that, what you feel now will change to bitterness and regret.'' She hid her face in the pillow. Through the thickness of her jacket, he could feel her choke back a sob. "That will truly destroy me, Neil. You have to let me go.''

"Never. Not in a million years. And there's not a doubt in my mind whose child you carry. You and Terry were merely friends.'' Neil wished his voice hadn't sounded so desperate when he said it. He did believe her. He did.

She shook her head and squeezed her eyes shut. Her fists curled against her stomach. "I loved him.''

Once again Neil brushed his hand over her hair, watching the short curls spring against his fingers. He lowered his lips to her temple and kissed her softly. "Of course you loved him. We both did.''

Suddenly she turned in his arms, her face, earnest and pleading, only inches from his. "I could stay at your country house! You could come to me—to us—whenever you want. I'll be your mistress, and no one need ever know we're together.''

He caught her chin, cupping it with one hand. "Don't you know I have no life without you beside me every day? I refuse to hide you and the child, to sneak quick couplings with you and give a chuck under the chin to my heir before I ride away. You think I'd do that just to avoid a little gossip? You must be mad as old King George. You'll be my wife, my countess, and the world be damned.''

"'Tis you who'll be damned, Neil,'' she said with a sad sigh.

"Then so be it. Better damned with you than blessed with anyone else. I love you, Bettsy.'' He lowered his mouth to hers and blocked any further protests.

Words got them nowhere at this point. He knew he'd never change her mind with that sort of argument. Somehow he had to persuade her to stay, convince her that marriage offered the only solution. Were it not for the baby they'd made, he would take the time to court her when Terry's murder and the rumors about her were put to rest. As things stood, no time remained for wooing. He'd make her agree to marry him, coerce her with passion if all else failed. Neil deepened the kiss.

Desperation lent a wild urgency to his efforts. He slid a hand under her jacket, unfastened her waistcoat and tugged at the tight binding over her breasts. Damn all this cloth! Lowering his mouth to her neck, he felt her pulse pound under his lips—whether with excitement or resistance, he didn't know. Nor did he care much at this point. "Bettsy, I need you," he growled against her throat. "Please." Again he raised his lips to hers, and felt her response as much as heard it.

"I will have this," she murmured with fierce determination. "I will!" She kissed him back, meeting that need of his with more eagerness than he thought possible for a body as small as hers to hold.

"Damn right you will," he answered into her mouth, yanking off his own coat so fiercely their teeth grated together. "Help me."

Clothes flew, tangling around wrists and ankles. Buttons popped, falling heedlessly to the bed and floor. He grabbed the edges of the linen wrapping her chest, ripped it with one vicious jerk and fell on her breasts like a starveling.

Somewhere in the back of his mind, a voice urged caution, and he lightened his attack. "Sorry," he whispered against her, touching her gently with his tongue. Her fingers slid through his hair and gripped his head like a vise, holding him to her, demanding, insisting. He took her in his mouth and suckled fiercely, first one hard peak and then the other. She writhed, incoherent and pleading, her half-covered hips grinding against his.

Cursing vilely, he reared over her and slid off one of her boots, tossed it over his shoulder and pushed her trousers and linen drawers down as far as he could. She pulled her leg free, and he lowered himself to her the same instant.

He felt her hand between them, seeking, finding, guiding. With a groan, he felt her close around him, liquid fire and light. "Oh God, let this...be forever. Last forever." He lay still, reveling in the frantic movements under him that sent ripples of pure and undiluted pleasure streaking through his veins, his muscles, his brain.

"Neil," she whispered, more an exhalation of what seemed to be her last breath. Then a wisp of reason sneaked through his fog of ecstasy. Maybe it *was* her last breath. He must be crushing her.

He braced himself on his elbows, freeing her upper body. Her swift intake of air told him he'd been right. For the space of a minute, he studied her face, a means to distract himself from the demands of his lower body. Her eyes were glazed, dark and slumberous. Her lips tightened, then opened, a sound emerging that slowly registered as words. "Move, damn it. Move!"

A sharp denial formed in his mind. *Not now!* He couldn't stop now! Then, when her nails carved into his buttocks, he understood. Oh, *move!* He moved, more swiftly than he meant to. The frantic thrusts erased whatever reason remained— thrusts she met passionately, raising him to a pinnacle that begged a leap he couldn't deny. "Now?" His question was a plea.

She took him over the edge without pausing to answer, joining him with a quaking that shook him to his very soul. Shudders rippled through them—sharp, sweet aftershocks, drawing sounds from his throat that seemed foreign, a language born of deep need assuaged.

They lay pressed together for what seemed like hours before either moved. Then he heard her soft, short laugh. He opened one eye and followed her glance down the length of their bodies. Her breeches were bunched around one small foot, which waggled back and forth. She slid her other leg, bare except for a sagging stocking, up to catch the waistband of the trousers that hung about his knees. Good Lord, he was still wearing his sooty boots. His shirt, minus most of its buttons, was draped over one shoulder like a wrinkled rag.

"Aren't we a pair?" she asked, clicking her tongue in mock disgust.

"Forever a pair," he answered with a satisfied grin.

Neil ignored her long-suffering sigh. So he hadn't exactly convinced her he was right. Small wonder, considering his roughness and haste. He'd remedy that shortly, however, when he made long, slow love to her and with ecstatic duress extracted her promise to marry him.

How could she possibly give this up, this wondrous, steel-to-lodestone magic between them? For him it was much more than that, and to her, it soon would be. He'd make her love him, want him, crave his nearness above everything. The sexual pull drew both ways, he knew, and that would hold them together. It had to until she, too, possessed the deeper, more elemental need for him that he felt for her.

Bettsy accepted him for what he was, even seemed attracted to the reckless, heedless, impulsive part of his nature that had always turned others—important others—away. That alone provided reason enough to love her, but it made up only the small, selfish part of what drew him to her.

He loved her courage. And her wit. Lord, she probably had more innate intelligence than he, given the way she took to the research without any formal training at all. That ought to foster envy in a man, but it only made him proud of her.

He spared a moment to thank whatever powers directed fate that Emma Throckmorton had thrown him over for rich old Lord Curtiss. To think Neil might now be saddled with a petty, grasping bitch of a wife and doomed forever to long for the beautiful, brave and selfless Elizabeth Marleigh. Bettsy, now his for the taking. Thank God.

That moment of thanks had lasted too long, Neil realized when he looked down at her, nestled against his shoulder. Her long, thick lashes lay in repose. Her breathing was even and soft. She was asleep, and still unpersuaded to share his life the way he wanted. But she would.

Easing back on the pillow, he stared at the intricate pleats of the canopy overhead. The scent of their loving and the feel of her bare skin against his own stirred him anew. He ignored the fact out of deference to her need for rest.

Later, he promised himself and her. "Later we'll finish this, Elizabeth Marleigh, and you'll find no mindless, sex-starved idiot dragging down your pants then. There'll be only an experienced, dedicated physician, using every trick known to man and the medical world to seduce you into marriage. We'll see then who has the last word, no matter how smart and protective you think you are."

Elizabeth woke alone, naked and wonderfully exhausted. Dusk peeked in the window, pink and soft and promising rain. She stretched and sighed, treating her skin to the pleasurable rasp of feather-stuffed linen. Her problems forgotten for the moment, she simply enjoyed snuggling, drawing comfort from the warm Neil scent in the pillows. With a palm on her abdomen, she felt as well as heard the rumble of hunger and smiled. The rest of the day had flown while she played slugabed. Neil must have finished undressing her after she fell asleep. Ever the doctor, seeking her comfort, she thought.

With a major effort, she slid out of bed and padded to the water closet. By the time she had bathed and dressed, the afternoon's dilemma had resurfaced full force.

Neil presented a strong case for marriage, especially in regard to the child. If she thought for a moment her reputation wouldn't dash his life on the rocks, she would marry him tonight. But no one knew better than she how rumors possessed a life of their own. How they grew and spread. How the smallest conjecture mushroomed into blatant accusations and felled the subject like a blow from a cricket bat. As a victim, she knew.

And Neil thought the truth would right all that? Foolish tom noddy! Not a soul within the medical community would credit him with enough sense to apply a leech if he proved stupid enough to marry a woman like her.

Taking no for an answer seemed beyond him. If she couldn't convince him to settle for an affair, she would simply have to disappear as she'd originally planned. Not yet, though, she decided. She had been wrong to try and hie off unprepared. Danger lurked around every corner until they had Colin, or whoever might be the murderer, safely in custody.

## Chapter Eighteen

Neil poured himself a snifter of brandy, settled by the lamp in the study and opened the book he'd just found. The thin blue volume had slid out of the middle of the tome on modern obstetrics he'd just pulled down to study. That rascal Ned Mazer had given him this as a graduation gift when they'd finished medical school together. A hundred years ago, he thought, smiling.

"Don't try page 34," Ned had warned him then, "unless you relish a month in traction." Silent laughter shook him as he turned to the page Ned had mentioned and held the volume closer to the light. Now this really went beyond strange. Twisted torsos and tangled limbs... Even the author didn't recommend it very highly, and stated he had included it only as an odd variation. It certainly merited *that* description! The poor old sod must have tried it and probably ended up with more sprained muscles than added pleasure. Even the unabridged *Kama Sutra* had left out this one, no doubt with sound reason.

"*Variations on Sexual Congress?*" Elizabeth's crack of laughter sent Neil scrambling, too late. Oh Lord, she'd seen it.

"A friend...gave it to me as a jest," he murmured.

"What a lie! Not even a good one, either," she replied, and

laughed again. "Ah, Neil, you never cease to amaze me. Why in the world would you think you needed to read *that?*"

He slammed the book down on the table and grabbed for the snifter. "I refuse to discuss this, Bettsy. If you had any decorum at all, you'd pretend such books don't even exist."

She flopped down at his feet, propping her elbows on his knees. Fighting a grin, she widened those chocolate eyes in a feigned look of adoration. "Ooh, enlighten me, oh great *sensai*. Instruct me, Master! I would know the dark secrets of the East."

"Tempted, are you?" he asked with a warning glance.

Her lovely brow creased with pretended worry. "Certainly not with page 34! Dreadfully contrived and probably quite difficult, I should think." She took his glass and sipped.

"Good God, you've seen the book before?"

"Umm," she said, nodding. "Read it, too. Found it in Papa's library stuck behind *Figg's Listing of Roman Ruins* when I was fifteen. Never laughed so hard in my life."

Speechless, Neil knocked his head against the padded back of the wing chair with a gusty sigh of disbelief.

He felt her hand on his knee, squeezing it with what seemed like reassurance. "Ah, don't be such a prude, Neil. Girls have to learn by hook or crook. Nobody tells them anything. My mother died before we had any talks of that nature, not that I expect we would have done until I'd signed a betrothal contract. Probably not even then. Nanny gave me some idea, bless her heart, but little more than the essentials of what goes into where and why. I expect that's all most females get beforehand, if they're fortunate enough to learn that much."

"Reading this sort of thing, it's a flaming wonder you weren't put off…sexual things for good and all."

"Certainly made me curious, I can tell you that!" She held up the glass and studied the remaining swallow through the light. "I know what you're up to, Neil," she said, shifting her gaze to his. "It won't work."

"I'm sure I don't know what you mean."

"You're laying a trap for me, of course. You want to tie me to the marriage bed with a neat little bow."

"Page 20, I believe," he said, grabbing the book and riffling the pages, trying to distract her with humor.

She leveled him with a serious look. "Increased efficiency under the covers—assuming that's possible in your case— won't make me marry you, Neil. I won't do it."

"You will." He reached for her.

She scuttled away and rose in a lithe movement to stand before him. "Agree to a secret arrangement and I'll stay with you."

"You'll stay as my wife!" His voice rose, filling the study, as he stood and loomed over her.

Oliver cleared his throat. "'Scuse me. Ye've a visitor, sir. Says 'e's got t' see ye. Urgent like."

Neil took Bettsy by the shoulders and pushed her into the chair he had just vacated. "You sit there and don't move until I get back. You're supposed to be dead, remember?"

She reached for the book, and he snatched it away, stowing it on a top shelf. Bettsy made a face. "May I breathe while you're gone?"

He didn't dignify that with a response. Motioning for Oliver to precede him, Neil closed the door behind them and headed for the parlor.

The identity of the visitor surprised him. Then he recalled what he had just said to Bettsy. Everyone thought she had perished in the explosion. Still, it was awfully late for a condolence call, and where the deuce was Biddie? The two almost always ran as a pair. "Turner," he acknowledged. He held out his hand, which the young man ignored.

"My lord." His voice sounded gritty, almost angry. "I have something for you. Something that wouldn't wait."

Neil stood only an arm's length away. He watched Turner's hand disappear inside his coat. Bettsy's attack on Ward flashed through his mind, and three thoughts coalesced in the blink of an eye: that Turner looked hostile, was one of their last two murder suspects and was reaching for a solid, oblong lump

Neil spotted inside his vest. Automatically, he grabbed his visitor's wrist and twisted it sharply. A bone cracked and Turner screamed.

Neil reached for what he thought was Turner's pistol and came away with a packet wrapped in brown paper. "What's this?"

"Three monkeys," Turner gasped, dropping sideways into a chair and cradling his arm. Tears streamed down his cheeks and his teeth gritted audibly.

"Fifteen hundred pounds?" Neil asked in disbelief, tearing a corner of the package. "Oh God, Tun, I'm sorry. Here, let me see to it." He dropped the money on the floor and knelt before the lad, reaching for his injured wrist.

Turner jerked away as far as he could, groaning an inarticulate plea.

"Come now, I won't hurt you," Neil said.

"You just...broke my arm!" Turner accused, his slender face contorted with pain.

"Well, Christ, I thought you had a gun! It was a reflex act, and I said I was sorry." Neil pried Turner's good hand loose and began to examine the injured limb. "Umm, it's merely cracked, I suspect. Don't move it. A shot of whiskey will fix you right up."

Turner staggered out of the chair and made for the door. Neil caught him by the coattail and forced him to sit. "I said don't move! Now mind what I say!"

Turner cringed, obviously terrified, while Neil shouted, "Oliver! Bring the whiskey, man, and be quick. Get my satchel while you're at it." Then he turned and took the chair next to Turner. "Look, you needn't be afraid. I'll explain everything. I've had a bit of trouble and I thought for a while you might be responsible. I see now why you came tonight and I do apologize. Why don't you keep the money?"

Turner swallowed hard and sniffed. His trembling lessened a bit. "I owed Terry twice that. Thought you'd wait for the rest when I owned up to it. Had to wait for my allowance, but that's all I can get this quarter."

Neil nodded. "I knew of the markers, but you never mentioned them. That's why I thought you might be involved in my recent problems."

"The explosion?" Turner asked, dumbfounded. "The one that killed Betts?" He paled, resting his head against the back of the chair. "God, no! You don't think I...?" His mouth tightened as he swallowed heavily. "Of course you do. I'd have had reason, wouldn't I? To destroy the place and you. But I swear—"

"No need for that," Neil said, taking the whiskey from Oliver and holding it to Turner's lips. "Drink this and try to relax. That arm must hurt like the very devil. I can't tell you what an idiot I feel. Consider your debt canceled as of this moment. I insist."

"Can't do that," Turner said, holding up the glass for a refill. "Honor my debts. Always. Thing to do."

"Oliver, get a deck," Neil ordered, watching Turner's eyes glaze over as he polished off the second whiskey. Neil poured yet another while Oliver produced a deck of cards. With a deft motion, Neil shuffled and offered the cards to Turner. "Cut?"

Turner tapped the top. "What's the bet?"

"You draw high card, the debt's null and you stay away from the tables. I draw high and I get to return your money and charge you two quid for setting the arm. Deal?"

Turner nodded and slid the top card off the deck. A four. "Devil take it! Just my luck," he moaned, closing his eyes.

Neil quickly thumbed a two off the bottom. "Deuce. You win."

Blue eyes snapped open and a wide grin split the skinny face. "I won?" He stared at the two of diamonds.

"Drink to your luck," Neil ordered, and lifted the decant-

An hour alone in the study exhausted Elizabeth's patience. She climbed on a footstool and replaced the little book on the top shelf, where Neil had put it. The noisy patient in the parlor had quieted, and Oliver hadn't returned. Odd, a patient calling here. Must be a neighborhood emergency. Curiosity drove her to crack open the door and peek into the hall.

She recognized Turner, even though she couldn't see his face. He staggered a bit as Oliver helped him outside. Neil held the front door, speaking softly, but she couldn't hear his words.

Once the door had closed, she rushed out to confront him. "What happened to Tun? He was hurt?"

Neil sighed and pressed a thumb and forefinger to the bridge of his nose. "I broke his arm."

"What? Why?"

He shot her a rueful look. "Same reason you kicked the stuffing out of Alfred Ward. *Turner's* weapon turned out to be half the money he owed Terry. I feel like I just kicked a puppy."

Elizabeth nodded knowingly, falling into step as they returned to the study. "Embarrassing, isn't it?"

"Very. Well, at least we know now that Turner's innocent."

She poured Neil another brandy and handed him the glass. Kneeling beside his feet, she rested her head on his knee. "We should send word to Lindy."

"Oliver's going to find him after he sees Turner settled at his rooms. Boy's going to have the devil of a head in the morning from all that whiskey. Maybe it'll take his mind off his arm." Neil shook his head. Sighed deeply. "God, what a day!"

"So Colin's guilty by process of elimination," Elizabeth said. Colin had to be the one. He was the only suspect left. Unless... "Neil, could Colin's real father, some man we don't know, be behind all this? We talked about that once, remember?"

He reached for her hand and rubbed her palm with his thumb. His eyes looked black in the lamplight. And very tired. "No, it has to be Marleigh, Bettsy. I really am sorry. I know you don't want to believe it, but it has to be true."

She sighed and rested her forehead against his knee. "It's

just hard for me to think of him as other than a teasing older cousin. He was something of a comfort when Father died.''

Neil caressed her back and dropped a kiss on her head. ''He would have comforted you right into Bedlam if he had found you the night he killed Terry.''

Her head shot up. ''I know that. I simply can't believe he would shoot anyone in cold blood.''

He set her away from him and gave her a gentle shake. ''Bettsy, we've run out of suspects. Ward certainly didn't do it. Neither did Turner. Who else could have taken your father's pistols? Who else had reason? You must face the fact that Colin murdered Terry, and later, Maggie Leffing. He's tried to murder you. We have proof that he set up those incidents that ruined your reputation. A man who would do that...'' Neil's angry voice drifted away when he saw her tears fall.

He traced their path with his finger. ''Don't weep over this, darling. I promise you everything will come right. In a few days, all this will be behind us.... We'll move out to the country,'' he suggested, his voice soothing. ''Would you like that? We'll set up a lab there and replace all the equipment that was destroyed. Begin again, together, as partners both in the research and as man and wife. When the baby comes, we will—''

''Hush!'' Elizabeth pushed herself away and scrambled to her feet, looking down at him. She dashed from the room, across the hall and took the stairs two at a time. When she reached her room, she threw herself across the bed and buried her face in the pillow. Neil's persistence was driving her crazy.

She rolled to her back and kicked off her boots. This would never do, she thought. She could hardly believe she had let herself get into such a fluster. Even her father's death and the slander in the news sheets hadn't caused this deep a sadness. Her emotional state was exaggerated by the pregnancy, of course. She decided enough was enough and she was done with tears. They never solved a damned thing.

The time had come to face what must be faced. Colin had killed Terry, as surely as he had tried to get rid of her and take her inheritance. At least now she knew for certain where the danger lay and how to avoid it. Now was the perfect time to leave.

She would disappear while Neil and Lindy were tied up with apprehending Colin. They'd be so busy, she would be well away before they knew she was gone. As soon as Lindy called off his men and she could catch Oliver off guard, she would slip away.

Neil would thank God for it after he got over the initial hurt. He had recovered from Emma Throckmorton's desertion, hadn't he? Elizabeth knew Neil loved her as much or more than he had loved Emma. But she also knew that she would bring more disaster to the man she loved than Emma ever could have done.

He would have survived a greedy, simpering wife like Emma. At least he would have retained the goodwill of his peers. Now that Elizabeth thought of it, she realized Neil wouldn't have lost the nephew he loved like a son if Terry hadn't become involved with the notorious Marleigh woman. Someday soon, when his passion cooled, Neil would realize that and hate her for it.

Resolute and dry-eyed, she pushed herself off the bed and washed her face. In the dressing room, her valise sat waiting, still half-packed from her last attempt to leave. And leave she would, just as soon as opportunity presented itself.

The best she could hope for was one more night in Neil's arms. *Please God, just one more night.* Perhaps only what was left of this one, she bargained.

But it was not to be. She realized it the moment she returned downstairs and saw Lindy in the kitchen. Neil, the men Lindy had hired as guards, as well as Mr. Ward, stood around checking their weapons and talking among themselves. This was it, then. They would converge on her cousin without delay.

"Ah, Betts!" Lindy greeted her with enthusiasm. "Guess Neil told you it's all over but the shouting."

"You have the proof now to arrest Colin?" Elizabeth clasped her hands behind her to keep from reaching for Neil.

His look of concern made her want to throw herself into his arms. Not possible.

"Well, not exactly," Lindy admitted with a rueful quirk of his mustache. "Neil has a plan. We'll confront Colin with Ward's findings and run a bluff that we have proof of the rest. Should shake him enough to get a confession. At least we hope so."

Elizabeth nodded, her gaze resting on the floor. "Well, I suppose I should wish you luck. Are you going now?"

"Yes," Neil answered, moving to her side and gripping her shoulder. She relished his nearness, for she knew it would be the last contact they would have. He spoke in a deep, low voice, one she thought he must reserve for the terminally ill. "Bettsy, I want you to go back upstairs and rest. Try not to think about what's happening. Oliver and Tom Weaver will be here to protect you, but you'll have nothing to fear, since we'll be with Colin."

She brought her head up, but couldn't look at him. Another fit of tears would spoil everything, might even make him stay with her himself. "Where is he?" She hoped Colin had left the city so she would have more time to get away.

"At Marleigh House. Lindy's men are already watching him and will be outside in the event he gets away after we confront him."

"Sounds reasonable," she said, shifting slightly away so that Neil's hand fell from her shoulder. The loss of his touch hit her like a sharp pain. "Why don't you take Oliver and Tom with you? The more protection you have, the better, and I won't need it now. Colin may have men—"

"No," Neil interrupted. "We certainly won't leave you here alone. Oliver will watch the back door and Tom the front. All the windows are locked tight, so you needn't worry."

"I'm not worried in the least for myself," she said with not a little frustration. "Everyone thinks I'm dead, anyway, both as Elizabeth Marleigh and as Percival Betts! I don't need protection, you do! You said yourself that Colin's a murderer."

Neil stepped forward, reaching for her as she backed away. "Bettsy, are you all right?"

She nodded and braced herself, lifting her chin and staring over his left shoulder. "I'm fine, just fine. Go, do whatever it is you have to do. I'll...keep myself busy."

Neil brushed a hand over her jaw, catching it in a firm grip and forcing her gaze to his. He mouthed the words *I love you.* She forced her lips to turn up at the corners.

"Well, shall we?" Lindy suggested, restless as a hunter waiting for the horn.

Elizabeth watched the men file out. Her eyes filled when Neil hung back as though he would have another private word.

"Go!" she whispered. "And take care of yourself." She wanted to say so much more. *Remember only the good times. Don't hate me for leaving. I'll care for our child and love you forever. Be happy.* Instead, she shoved him lightly toward the door, her fingers lingering on his sleeve.

She watched as Oliver stationed himself just outside the back door. As soon as he and Tom had settled down for their watch, she would let herself out one of the French doors in the study and be gone. Half an hour—she'd wait that long for Oliver and Tom to relax, and then she would quietly slip away.

The fifty quid Neil kept in his desk drawer for incidentals, plus what she had in her own purse, would see her through to Edinburgh by train. Once there, she could withdraw funds from the secret account she had set up by mail before Neil abducted her.

The sheer logistics of executing the trip would keep her distracted from heartbreak for a while. She wondered what she would do when there was no further crisis to consider.

# Chapter Nineteen

"You will keep a cool head, won't you, Doc?" Lindy asked as he, Neil and Alfred Ward approached Marleigh House. Neil looked ready to attack the moment Colin Marleigh appeared.

"Of course." The words popped out too quickly for Neil to have given any thought to them. A muscle ticked on the left side of his jaw, and Lindy could see the tension in the set of those wide shoulders.

The inspector stopped walking and halted Neil with a hand on his arm. "You realize that if you throttle the bastard, we'll never prove a damned thing? He can bring charges against you for assault and order me to arrest you. Let's do this correctly, Neil."

Their eyes met. Neil nodded and took a deep breath. He rolled his shoulders once in a circular motion, and a haughty mask of indifference dropped over his features. Lindy watched, fascinated, and nudged Neil's elbow with his own. "I love it when you go all aristocratic like that. Gives me a sudden urge to curtsy!"

Neil's soft bark of laughter cracked his facade for a second before he repaired it. "Is nothing sacred to you, Lindy?"

"Certainly not a title, if that's what you're asking."

"Thank God for small favors. You may be hauling someone

with one off to the magistrate today if we have any luck." Neil grasped the heavy knocker and clacked it three times.

A young, burly butler answered in place of old Thurston and admitted them when Lindy gave their names. "This way," the man said, ushering them into a well-appointed library. "I shall inform his lordship."

Lindy had noted Neil's step halt a fraction as they passed the stairs on the way in. A soft expression had sneaked past the haughty mask. Must have been right there that Doc first met Betts.

Neil nodded assessingly as he glanced around the book-lined shelves. His gaze fell on an intricately carved pistol box and he raised a brow in question.

"Aye, right in plain view. Anyone could have pinched 'em."

Neil's lips barely moved with his low-voiced inquiry, "Are you certain Colin's guilty, Lindy?"

Now this was surprising. "Doubting, are you?"

"No. Bettsy still does, though, in spite of everything we know. And something nags at the back of my mind about it, though I can't see how we could be wrong."

Alfred Ward cleared his throat and they all turned toward the door. Neil, as the highest-ranking visitor, stepped forward when Colin entered. Neil neglected to offer his hand, which Lindy thought was wise. Cracked knuckles might be considered assault.

"Marleigh? You've met Inspector MacLinden of Scotland Yard. This gentleman is Mr. Alfred Ward, an associate of mine."

Ward bowed as gracefully as a well-schooled actor, and Lindy made a halfhearted attempt to copy him, just to see if he could.

Colin Marleigh regarded each of them with nervous curiosity. "To what do I owe this visit, Havington? Am I to assume this has to do with my cousin's foul deed and subsequent death?" He remained standing near the door and showed no inclination to offer them a seat. Instead, he shifted from one foot to the other, hands locked behind him. "I've told you all I know."

Neil sidled past Marleigh, causing him to turn and effectively cutting off any chance the man had to bolt. With a studied nonchalance, Neil quietly closed the library door and stood with his back against it. He crossed his arms over his chest and tilted his head to one side. The clipped nature of his words made Lindy frown. "Oh, but we have further information, Marleigh. Mr. Ward here is a private investigator, former Bow Street man hired by my nephew before he died."

"Whatever for?" Sweat popped out in small beads on Marleigh's forehead. A lank strand of thinning hair drooped over his brow, and he raked it back with trembling fingers.

Neil's mouth stretched into a parody of a smile. "To ferret out the truth behind your cousin's outrageous behavior, of course. Terrence did plan to marry her, you know."

Marleigh's hand shook as he brought it up to cover the bottom half of his face. Then he dropped it and turned away from them to look out the window to the terrace. "She was mad," he whispered, sounding a little desperate. "She was!"

Lindy shook his head slightly at Neil, who had moved nearly within reach of Marleigh. That stalking maneuver didn't bode well at all. Looked as though he might go for the kill. *Keep your head, Doc!* Lindy silently cautioned him.

Telepathy didn't seem to work between the classes. Time to step in. Lindy cleared his throat. "My lord, shedding one's clothing to avoid drowning is hardly the act of a madwoman. Elizabeth Marleigh found the hole in her boat before it sank. A deliberately made hole, I might add."

Colin whirled around, stepping back smartly when he realized how close Neil stood. "How can you know that?"

"Oh, we know considerably more than that, Marleigh," Neil said, his voice smooth and cold as a sheet of ice. "We know all about the swinging blade that severed her braid and the woman you hired to provide the midnight dance for your friends."

He drove on without mercy while Marleigh quailed. "Maggie Leffing, wasn't it? And of course, the notes you passed inviting those randy lordlings who invaded your cousin's room at the Smythe house. Clever of you to rouse your hostess in time to find them together. Then there were the rumors, exaggerated out of proportion by your false outrage and dealings with reporters. We know all of it, Marleigh—those incidents just mentioned and the tainted-chocolate episode that went awry. Everything."

"But—but I didn't personally have anything to—"

Neil stepped closer, visibly struggling with himself not to touch the man. "She was incredibly hard to kill, wasn't she, Marleigh? But then her reputation lay in tatters, her sanity in question. So you arranged to forcibly incarcerate your innocent cousin in a madhouse. We have proof, solid evidence, that you intended Elizabeth's death. When your efforts in that direction failed, you deliberately set out to lock her away so that you could gain control of her fortune. A fortune you considered rightfully yours."

"No, no, I..." A loud sob burst through Colin Marleigh's trembling hands as he once more clapped them to his mouth. "Oh, God!"

Lindy quickly stepped in then for fear Neil might send the man crashing through the floor-length window. "Lord Marleigh, I shall have to place you under arrest for the murders of Terrence Bronwyn, earl of Havington, and Miss Margaret Leffing. Will you come quietly?"

Marleigh's hands dropped from his face and he stared at Lindy in disbelief. Words tumbled out of his mouth. "Maggie's not dead! She can't be dead!"

Lindy shared a glance of confusion with Neil.

Alfred Ward spoke for the first time. "You buried her in place of your cousin."

"No," Colin cried. "It *was* Elizabeth! He saw her dead! He swore she was dead, even after I thought I saw her in the park."

"Who swore?" Lindy asked, moving closer. "Who did you hire to kill Elizabeth, Marleigh?"

Colin threw up his hands and backed against the window, "No one! She shot herself! She killed Havington and shot herself!"

Lindy watched the quivering mass of nobility crumple like a deflated balloon. Both he and Ward moved forward to catch the earl as his knees buckled. Depositing him in the nearest chair, they stood over him and waited for his sobbing to subside. The man blubbered noisily, his eyes wet, his nose beginning to run.

"Here, drink this and stop sniveling," Neil instructed, grasping one of Marleigh's hands and placing a glass of brandy in it. "You realize you'll hang alone if you don't name your accomplice."

They watched Marleigh gulp the fiery liquid and cough. He wiped his nose on his sleeve. Ward knelt beside the chair and placed a comforting hand on the earl's shoulder. "My lord, you'd best tell us everything now." His hypnotic voice was smooth as butter. "Lies won't serve, you know. We've proof."

Colin took another gulp and rocked back and forth for a moment, his teeth raking his bottom lip. Then, as if in a trance, he began to speak, an occasional tremor punctuating his narrative. "It was his idea. He badgered me every day after uncle died. 'The money should be yours,' he said. 'It's rightfully yours. We can do it this way,' he said. 'Make everyone think she's gone round the bend. They'll take care of her,' he said. He promised she'd get good care and want for nothing."

Marleigh shot a pleading look at Ward and rushed on, "We knew she could swim. There was never any danger she would drown! She got out, didn't she? And the hair thing. He said he cut it off while she slept. Then Maggie did her bit, dancing about, laughing. It was more like a jest than anything. No one hurt Elizabeth. I wouldn't let anyone hurt her." Marleigh fastened his pleading gaze on Ward.

Ward patted the thin shoulder, giving it an encouraging squeeze. "You sent the notes inviting the men to her chamber, didn't you?"

"Yes!" Marleigh admitted eagerly. "Yes, but I knew they'd not have time to—to do anything before we got there. No harm done, you see? They didn't touch her at all."

"Your friends bandied her name about the clubs and you allowed it, didn't you? Sort of let gossip take its course?" Ward nodded, smiling at Marleigh with feigned sympathy.

"Exactly! That's exactly how it was! And the newsmen I spoke with only asked what I saw take place. I couldn't deny what I saw, could I? I begged them not to print it, but I knew they would. He said they would beforehand and he was right."

Lindy watched Ward and marveled. The man really ought to join Helen on stage. What a talent! A glance at Neil showed him to be in awe, as well—too much so to unleash his violence just yet, thank God.

Ward spoke again, his monotone soothing. "Did you order the chocolate drink that resulted in the kitchen maid's death?"

Colin looked blank. "Chocolate? What do you mean?"

"Never mind that for now," Ward murmured. The mesmerizing note in his voice seemed to do the trick. "On the night young Havington died, you couldn't find your cousin when you went to take her to hospital, could you?"

Marleigh shook his head, his gaze focused on the floor between his feet. His voice sounded broken and sad. "No, she had already gone to Havington House, I suppose. I wish I could have stopped her. She was mad, you know." Then he produced a long, dejected, very sincere sounding sigh. "I might have saved Havington had I been in time."

Ward twisted his distinguished head to meet Lindy's equally confused expression. It was Neil who spoke next, and it was not a question. "You didn't shoot Terrence."

"Of course I didn't shoot him. The poor wretch did nothing but fall in love with my cousin." Marleigh hung his head. "I wish I hadn't exposed her, you know, even though she wasn't quite herself. I wept when I found out she was dead. Poor Lizzie."

He raised a sorrowful gaze to Lindy, pleading for understanding. "I couldn't bear to look on her in the morgue."

Neil whirled around and began to pace restlessly. "What about Maggie Leffing, Marleigh? Who killed her?"

"Maggie's not dead," Marleigh insisted. "She left the morning after that kitchen maid jumped to her death. He said we should let Maggie go. That she'd served her purpose. He—"

Neil pounded a fist in his palm. "Who the devil is *he*, Marleigh? Who?"

Elizabeth's cousin hesitated a second and then his words were almost inaudible. "My...advisor."

Neil shoved his face down until he was nose-to-nose with Marleigh and stared into the wide, frightened eyes. "His name, man, his name!"

The seconds ticked by in thick silence until Marleigh gave a defeated sigh. His face contorted. "Calvin Thurston."

Lindy almost choked. "That old man? Your *butler?*"

Marleigh released a harsh breath and collapsed against the back of the chair. "No, no, he was never that."

Lindy saw Neil close his eyes and nod slowly. His face relaxed as though he had just solved the puzzle of the universe. Surprisingly, his voice sounded calm and steady, devoid of anger for a change. "Thurston is your father, isn't he, Colin?"

"Yes," Marleigh breathed.

A silence fell over the room. Neil looked at Lindy and then at Ward before he focused once more on Marleigh. "And Maggie Leffing was your lover?"

"Since we were youngsters," Marleigh admitted. "I doubt she'll be back, though. Father admitted he told her of my plans to marry. She would have found out soon enough, anyway."

"You planned to marry?" Lindy asked, wondering what other lady would be devastated by this mess.

"Yes. I guess that's out of the question now, isn't it? Lady Emma has already endured my family scandal involving Elizabeth. Wouldn't announce our betrothal yet because of it. I doubt I'll ever recover her affections if she learns about all of this."

"Emma Throckmorton Curtiss?" Neil's voice was flat as a flagstone.

Marleigh's agitation suddenly reared like a horse spying a whip. "You mustn't reveal publicly that Thurston sired me, must you?" He dragged at Neil's sleeve, darting looks at Ward and Lindy as well. "Please say you won't! There's no proof of it. Uncle meant for me to succeed him and he knew all there was to know. Just before he died, he hinted as much right in front of Thurston and me. Please don't expose me. I'll do anything you say! *Anything!*"

Neil's eyes met Lindy's and they nodded in unison. The inspector allowed Neil to set the terms, and he did so with a firm command. "You will visit every gentlemen's club in the London area and broadcast what you did to sully Lady Elizabeth's reputation. Everything you did, in detail, and give your reasons for it—do you understand?" He waited for Marleigh's hesitant nod. "Then you will contact those selfsame reporters and any others who will listen and give them a story that will absolve her completely of any wrongdoing. I want it made overwhelmingly obvious to everyone that she was a victim of your greed and malice. And I want it in tomorrow's news sheets. If I do not approve fully of everything I hear and read, I shall personally see that your title is rescinded and that your properties revert to the crown. Then I will find you, wherever you may choose to hide, and tear you limb from limb. I won't just hurt you, Marleigh. I will kill you, regardless of the consequences to myself. Do I make myself clear?"

Marleigh's head bobbed furiously. His wide green eyes blinked in terror. Lindy looked at Marleigh's lap for a wet spot, surprised when it didn't appear. Maybe he was too scared to piss.

It was past time to complete the most important part of their mission. Lindy was eager to be done with it. "My lord, I think you'd best have someone fetch your *advisor* so that we can get on with this."

The earl gulped, one hand clutching at his throat. "He, uh,

he's not here at present. He offered to escort Emma home. I was just saying goodbye to her when Jimson announced you.''

''Elizabeth!'' Neil dashed for the door.

Lindy followed at a run, calling out a hasty order for Ward and the men they'd brought to stand fast and detain the old man should he reappear there. Betts would be safe, of course, Lindy thought. But he felt a knot of apprehension gather in his stomach, nonetheless. Neil's fears must be contagious.

Nothing suggested that Thurston's sudden departure had anything to do with their arrival at Marleigh House. The man couldn't know Betts was alive. Still, Lindy didn't object when Neil shoved the driver aside and grasped the reins. Nor did he protest when they took the street corners on two wheels, the sturdy bays galloping madly and straining at their traces. He just shut his eyes and prayed for any unfortunate who happened to get in their way.


Elizabeth patted her pocket, assuring herself the money pouch was secure. She slid the antique dagger she'd found in the study into the top of her right boot and wiggled her foot to make certain her stocking was thick enough to cushion it. Satisfied, she donned her cloak, took up the traveling case and tiptoed toward the head of the stairs.

Only one lamp burned below in the entrance hall. She could easily slip down and out through a side window without anyone being the wiser. Then she heard the front door close. *Damn!* Tom must have come inside for something. It was too soon for Neil and Lindy to have returned. Nothing for it but to wait until the way was clear. She set down the valise and shrugged off her cloak.

A feminine voice murmured in anger, the words indistinct. Tom must have thought it safe if he'd let someone into the house. Perhaps it was Helen or Bonnie, come looking for Lindy. Bettsy decided to sneak down and see who the woman was.

She made it halfway down before a creaking tread gave her

away. Two forms quickly materialized at the foot of the stairs. Light from the hall lamp flickered off metal in the man's hand.

"Do come down, *Dr. Betts!*" Emma Throckmorton Curtiss advised, mockingly seductive with the invitation. When Elizabeth stood fast, she spoke again. "I must insist."

With measured steps, Elizabeth complied, keeping her eyes fastened on the revolver aimed at her chest. The two backed away as she reached the bottom.

With a start, she recognized the man. Only now he wasn't bowed with age. His wrinkled face no longer drooped with its usual slackness, and his bright, green eyes sparkled with menace. "Thurston!"

The realization dawned: Thurston had been here the day before the explosion! He must have set the fuse, perhaps trailed it in as he approached the back door. A few steps off the path and he could have kicked out the glass and inserted it. But why? "It was you who tried to kill me!"

"Many times," he growled. "But you do have a remarkable aptitude for survival. I saw you making for the stables after I lit the fuse. You'll not escape today, any more than your old man did in the end." He waggled the pistol to indicate she should step away from the stairs.

Her old man? Thurston had murdered her father! Elizabeth thrust the thought aside. At the moment her own death appeared too imminent for her to dwell on past killings. Clearly, this was no dueling pistol he waved around. The repeater held six shots, if she judged correctly. Enough to slay them all— Oliver, Tom and herself—with bullets left over to kill Neil and Lindy if they returned too soon. "How did you get in?"

Emma laughed, a low-pitched, frightening sound. "That's neither here nor there, Elizabeth. The point is, we shan't be here long." She flicked her wrist in Thurston's direction. "Go ahead, Calvin. Have done with it."

Thurston's face crinkled with what looked like exasperation. "Not here. That's why we brought your carriage, remember?"

"What do you intend to do, Thurston? Shoot me?" Elizabeth forced herself to challenge him, hoping his usual servile manner would reappear. The man had always been a subservient sort. "You forget yourself," she added for good measure.

It wasn't good enough. Thurston straightened even more, his body looking younger and sturdier than she would ever have guessed it could. Regardless of all those sun-baked lines on his face, this man fell far short of the years he'd pretended. His defiant eyes bored into hers again.

Before tonight, she could never recall his looking directly at her. The distinctive color of those irises suddenly hit her like a fist. Colin's eyes! Green as bottle glass. "*You* are his father!" she gasped.

Emma laughed. "And you thought *your* disguise was good! I suppose it's true that people see exactly what they expect to see. You even fooled me the first time we met. Thurston knew you immediately when I described Neil's obnoxious little assistant, but then he already suspected Neil had you secluded somewhere after you ran off together that night. Your little tweenie admitted that the good doctor had called rather late in the evening. You meant to throw everyone off your scent with that argument and leaving in separate carriages. Not quite good enough, though."

Thurston shot Emma an impatient glance. "We should go now."

"Oh, we needn't hurry," Emma said, brushing his sleeve with a dainty gloved hand. "Neil and that wretched bobby friend of his are quite busy chasing shadows."

"They're questioning Colin," Thurston said with a scowl.

"So what? They can't possibly have any proof against *him*, and they wouldn't dare arrest an earl without it." Emma smiled sweetly at Elizabeth. "It's fortunate they *are* with him right now. My darling Colin will have the perfect alibi when they return and find you missing and your guards dead at their posts."

"Your *darling*? Colin?" Elizabeth sputtered.

Emma chuckled at her disbelief. "Of course. I had my sights set on Neil, but he's grown dreadfully difficult of late.

He'll come around once you're out of the picture, I expect, and I'll still marry him. Once he's served his purpose and I'm his widow, Colin should make a delightful husband.''

"You two have been in on this from the start, haven't you?'' Elizabeth asked, truly stunned to find herself standing in the hall with her former butler about to take her life and Neil's former fiancée abetting the deed. An odd pair, to say the least.

"Well, Thurston wants his only son to have what he's entitled to, of course,'' Emma explained with a gloating smile. "And I wanted Neil to make me a countess. He couldn't very well do that with little Terry in the way.''

Elizabeth sucked in a breath and expelled it with a rush. "It was you! You killed Terry so Neil would—''

"Become an earl! And you a convicted murderess. And Colin a wealthy man. You see, Thurston's sister is in my employ. You've met her briefly, if you recall? My dear companion and chaperon? She realized my needs and Thurston's coincided, and brought us together.''

Elizabeth knew she had to play for time. Once she left the house, she would have very little chance of survival. "So with Thurston's help, you framed me for Terry's murder.''

"Precisely,'' Emma agreed. "That would have been sufficient to realize both our goals if you hadn't dashed off with Neil that night. No matter, though. We'll muddle through, won't we, Calvin?''

"There's no point to all this talk. Let's go,'' he ordered, motioning with the pistol.

Elizabeth stood fast, hoping he wouldn't shoot just yet. "You plan to kill Neil? Why? He'll marry you, won't he? You'll have the title, the Havington fortune.''

"Don't play the imbecile, darling. Of course he'll marry me once you're gone. We didn't plan on his death at first, but I've realized these past few weeks that he's hardly my type.'' She wrinkled her perfect nose in disgust. "He's so...intense. Not very tractable,'' she added. "I'm afraid he'll have to go.''

"And then you'll marry Colin.'' Elizabeth frowned at

Thurston. "What's to keep her from killing your son after she's gained his fortune as well? And what of you and your sister? Emma won't need you any longer, will she?"

Thurston's frown grew darker, his wizened face contorting with impatience. He glanced at the hall clock as it chimed the half hour.

*Ten thirty.* Neil had been gone nearly an hour. His return might be her only chance of survival. Elizabeth knew she had to keep Thurston and Emma here until Neil and Lindy arrived. Oliver and Tom must be dead as Emma had said or else these two would never have gained entrance.

Divide and conquer, Elizabeth decided.

Before Emma could agree to leave, Elizabeth goaded her further. "So you think Colin will make you countess of Marleigh? You really believe he will take Neil's leavings? Ha! If I know our Colin, he'll find himself a younger, more-qualified woman to bear his heirs. Listen, Thurston, do you really want this conniving witch for your son? Mother of your grandchildren?"

Thurston hefted the gun and inclined his balding head toward the entrance. "We must go. Immediately!"

It was now or never. As Emma turned, Elizabeth leapt forward, ducking behind her as she drew the knife out of her boot. Holding the point to the woman's neck, she threatened, "Put the gun down, Thurston! I know Emma set you up to all of this. If you do as I say, you won't hang."

Thurston held the gun steady, a menacing gleam in his eyes.

"Put it down!" Elizabeth shouted, "or so help me—"

He fired. The impact of the bullet threw the two women against the wall. Before Elizabeth could recover from the shock, Thurston stood with one booted foot on her wrist, effectively trapping her while he removed Neil's dagger from her powerless grasp.

"Get up," he ordered. Stunned, she wondered what had happened to the wrinkled old retainer she'd felt so sorry for less than a month ago.

Elizabeth struggled out from under Emma's weight. *Dead-*

*weight*, she realized as her gaze caught the woman's unblinking stare. A ragged round hole decorated the middle of Emma's chest.

Thoughts scrambled through Elizabeth's head like a cage full of terrified mice. *Delay.* Her only chance was to delay. Thurston had nothing to lose by shooting her right this minute, just as he had Emma. Unless she could make him think he had a chance for escape. "You can't just leave her here, you know. They'll see her the moment they come back, and you won't get far."

Obviously, that had occurred to him already, since he agreed without further ado. "The cellar?" he asked calmly, as though requesting a drink of water.

"Around that way." Elizabeth pointed to a door toward the back of the hall, beneath the stairs.

"Drag her with you," Thurston ordered, pointing his revolver at her head. "And no more antics, if you please."

As Thurston reached for one of the lamps on the hall table, Elizabeth quickly rolled Emma over, hoping her blood would leave a clear trail on the tiles. Once they reached the cellar, her chances would be almost nil. But, by God, she didn't plan to rot in that dark hole amid Neil's wine racks. She wanted someone to find her. Perhaps, by some quirk of fate, the bullet would not be lethal.

*Keep your wits, stay calm, think,* she chanted under her breath as she slowly dragged Emma toward the door. Thurston grumbled for her to hurry. She pulled the narrow door open and deliberately wedged the body sideways, still playing for time—time to plan, time to live. The pistol hammer clicked in warning. Elizabeth managed to wriggle through the door and slide her arms beneath Emma's, lifting her up like a shield while staggering down the steps.

The strain on her back was excruciating. She experienced sudden worry for the child in her womb, a small entity she hadn't dared stop to consider in all this. *Wits,* she reminded herself, and snatched her thoughts back from the edge of panic to the problem at hand.

When she reached the bottom, her feet landed on solid stone and Elizabeth staggered anew under Emma's weight. A small, square space gave way to ceiling-high racks holding the Havington wine stores. The dank, earthy odor of the cellar chilled her as much as its trapped, cold air. *A tomb.*

Elizabeth shuddered and clutched Emma's form against her chest. Thurston stood halfway down the stairs, wearing an eerie grin as he brought the gun up and aimed it. Time slowed to a crawl. Elizabeth imagined a bullet spinning toward her, reaching her forehead before the sound echoed around her.

"No!" she screamed, dropping to her knees. The swish of a bullet brushed the top of her curls and smashed a bottle behind her. *Bottles!* She reached back, snatched the nearest at hand and threw it, followed by another, and another. Two more shots thundered. He'd come closer, prepared to fire not six feet away. He couldn't possibly miss! Elizabeth rolled to one side even as she hurled the last bottle within reach. The lamp he held shattered from the impact, plummeting everything into absolute darkness.

Elizabeth realized she lay in a slight depression worn down by hundreds of years of foot traffic in front of the wine racks. She scrambled to pull Emma on top of her. If the witch had stopped the first bullet, she could damn well stop another! Another shot pinged off the stone wall. Thurston grunted as if in pain and cursed foully.

How many bullets left? One? Two? Maybe the gun was empty. Elizabeth's breath stuck in her throat. Emma's weight bore down on her like a winepress.

Miracle of miracles! Thurston was leaving! Elizabeth heard him stumble up the stairs and heaved a gusty sigh of relief. Then the horrible truth dawned: he wouldn't quit the house until he made certain she was dead. He'd only gone for another lamp. And to reload.

No place to run. No place to hide. There were no exits to the wine cellar except the one Thurston had just taken. Cut from underlying rock, the room held nothing but a score of open, partially stocked shelves—no protection at all. Her only refuge was to lie beneath the bloody body of Emma Throck-morton.

"Oh, Neil," she whispered, terror rifling through her. "Why don't you come? I've done all I can. I can't do any more!"

Slipping her hands under Emma's corseted back, Elizabeth placed them protectively over her abdomen. The gesture would mean nothing in the end. But at least Neil would know her final thoughts had been of the life they'd created together.

# *Chapter Twenty*

Neil yanked on the reins and leapt down before the carriage wheels stopped rolling. "Wait, you fool!" Lindy shouted, but he ignored him. Tom, the front-door guard, was missing from his post. An unattended brougham sat half a block down the street with its lead horse tied to the wrought-iron fence. Neil sailed up the steps and found the door bolted. He smashed one of the floor-length windows that framed it and squeezed through.

The sight of Thurston in the middle of the hall, aiming a pistol, brought him up short. Neil dived to one side. Instead of firing, however, the man just stood there, his left hand clutching his neck and his right holding the weapon. Slowly, the pistol barrel dipped downward and the gun slipped to the floor. Thurston folded like a limp piece of linen, blood flowing from his neck, forming a widening pool on the black and white tiles.

Neil scuttled toward him, not bothering to get to his feet. Quickly, he shoved the old man to his back and clapped two fingers over the wound. "Where is she?"

Thurston's wide, ugly grimace showed several rotting teeth and an inordinate amount of satisfaction. "Dead," he mouthed.

Neil removed his fingers. The glass-green eyes stared up at him, unblinking, mocking even in death.

Lindy wheezed noisily as he crouched beside Neil. "Betts?"

Neil sprang to his feet and shouted, "Bettsy? Bettsy, answer me, damn it! Where are you?" He hurried to the study and threw open the door, then ran to the stairs.

Glancing down as he reached the bottom riser, he noticed the splatters of red on the floor not three feet away. Blood. *Not Thurston's,* his fevered mind taunted. A puddle and a wide, uneven swath of it, already darkening, drying, trailed toward the back of the foyer.

Neil stumbled in his haste to follow, in growing dread of what he would find. The crimson path led to the cellar door.

"A light," he shouted, even as he saw Lindy running toward him with the oil lamp from the study. The flame flickered wildly with the jarring movements. Neil snatched the lamp away and clattered down the wooden steps. When he reached the bottom, his heart stopped cold.

Broken bottles littered the floor, and pungent pools of wine reflected the light. A body lay in the flickering shadows, its cloak and silken skirts tangled in wild array. A scream stopped at the back of Neil's throat as the sight registered. *Skirts!* His pulse thundered in his ears. Relief surged through his veins like a tidal wave. *Not Bettsy!*

He rushed forward, almost dousing the lamp in his haste. It was Emma, a ragged red hole through her heart. He didn't bother kneeling. Instead, he began checking the deep shadows behind each rack of wine, looking for Bettsy.

"Here," Lindy said in a hushed whisper. "Here, Doc."

Neil turned and followed Lindy's gaze. One small masculine boot protruded from beneath Emma's skirt, well to one side of Emma's own French-heeled feet. "No," he whispered. Then louder, "No!"

He froze. Denial ripped through him, as it had two times before. It had worked then. Denial had worked, hadn't it? She had lived both times when he feared her dead. For some reason, his body wouldn't obey his brain's command to confirm the fact. He stood there in silent agony, holding the lamp, staring, while Lindy rolled Emma's corpse away. Hope and despair struggled desperately.

Bettsy lay underneath as if she had fallen asleep there. Her hands lightly clutched her abdomen. Her eyes were closed, their inky lashes like small fans against her cheeks. Her chest remained perfectly still.

Neil dropped to his knees beside her simply because his legs wouldn't hold him any longer. Just as he set down the lamp, a burst of anger knifed through his gut like a sawtoothed dagger. He grasped her shoulders and shook her hard. "Don't do this to me, you little wretch! Don't you—"

Her eyes flew open. "Neil?"

Words failed, so he simply stared at her, wide-eyed and disbelieving, unable to draw a breath. She threw herself at him and they landed on the floor in a sprawl. A glass shard bit into his backside and the pain roused him from the numbing shock.

His hands left her shoulders and flew over her frantically. Lord, she felt so wonderful, all rough, checkered wool and soft, soft skin. Warm. *Alive!* Her cheek brushed against his as she sought his mouth. He ran a hand through her curls, clenching them in his fist until she groaned against his lips and pulled away.

Residual fury made him gruff. "I ought to beat you! You scared the life out of me! For the third time, Bettsy, the third *time!* I won't have this again. I will not!" He heaved her off him and sat up, reaching for her again.

She scooted sideways like a crab. "Hey, I was playing dead! Thurston went up to get another lamp. I knew he'd be back and there's nowhere to hide in this god-awful place. Do you know that? No way out! I thought you were him coming back. *Ouch!*"

She raised one knee and brushed it with her hand. "Oh."

"What?" he asked, suddenly coming to his senses. "Are you cut? Don't move!" He jumped up, ignoring the sharp stab in his buttocks. Lifting her in his arms, he started up the cellar stairs, mumbling half-formed reprimands along with rough assurances. "Are you hurt anywhere else?" he finally remembered to ask.

"Cut knee is all."

He pressed her head to his shoulder as they passed through the hall, but she managed a peek. "Is that Thurston? Is he dead?"

"I'm trying to spare you that, you little fool. Haven't you seen enough blood for one night?"

"Put me down!" She wriggled furiously until he set her on her feet. Neil's arms shook as he released her. Sweat cooled under his clothes, the aftermath of the bloodcurdling excitement. When would Bettsy's reaction hit? he wondered. Right now she moved fitfully, as though she couldn't hold still.

He followed as she limped over to the body, prodded it with one toe and then scooped up the pistol to examine the chamber. Good Lord, she was likely to shoot someone, with her hands trembling like that. He snatched the weapon out of her grasp and laid it on the hall table. "Come upstairs, Bettsy. You ought to rest."

"No!" She pushed him away. Her fingers dug into her sides just below the waist, clenching, unclenching. She shifted from one small boot to the other. The rise and fall of her chest looked shallow and uneven, but there was absolutely nothing wrong with her voice. "If you think you're going to tuck me up like some naughty child, *my lord,* you're much mistaken. Why do you order me to bed all the time, anyway? For heaven's sake, I've just had a pistol emptied at me, have dragged a body from here to the cellar, wrecked several years' worth of good wine and sliced the bloody hell out of my knee. You think I could *sleep?*"

"Fine then," Neil agreed, hoping she would settle down if he didn't argue. "Let's go into the study and I'll light a fire. We'll see about that knee of yours and let Lindy and his chaps take care of all this."

At least she allowed him to put his arm around her. Tension vibrated in her body like a tuning fork.

Lindy appeared in the doorway just as Neil settled Bettsy in a wing chair.

"Doc, we've found Tom and Oliver. Oliver got off with a bloody lump on his head. He'll do, I think, but he's only just come round. Tom's dead." Lindy spared a look at Bettsy, then continued. "Appears as though Thurston caught a ricochet off the cellar wall and then staggered up the stairs. The men are removing the bodies."

The inspector crossed the room and set Neil's medical bag down beside him. "You left this in the carriage. Thought you might need it. Are you all right now, Betts?"

She nodded. Neil wondered if she'd meant to or if it was due to the shudders now coursing through her. She looked so small and defenseless, sitting there with her hands clasped between her knees. She shook like a frightened fawn. He was surprised when she said in a fairly normal voice, "Thurston is—was Colin's father. He killed Terry. And Emma..."

"We know," Neil assured her. "We know everything. It's all over now, Bettsy. Everything's going to be fine. You're safe. We'll hash through all the details tomorrow."

He had her boot off and was already rolling up the leg of her trousers to check the cut knee. "Look here, it's stopped bleeding. Won't even need stitches." He retrieved cotton lint and a bottle from his bag and daubed the liquid on the wound.

"Brute!" She winced and brushed his hands away.

Neil knew she must be nearing collapse. He tried to think of a way to get her upstairs to bed without a further row. It was nearly midnight and his own body felt about ready to shut down.

"Bettsy, I'd like you to do something for me now if you feel up to it," he whispered. He shot a look at Lindy that sent the inspector backing out of the study with a knowing grin on his face.

Certainly not *that*, Neil thought. Sex with Bettsy was never far from his mind, but now was definitely not the time to get amorous. He turned back to her and explained, "I could use a bit of medical help myself, Dr. Betts."

She leapt forward and grabbed his face. "Were you shot? Where? Oh God, I forgot to ask if you were—"

Neil covered her hands with his, shaking his head and laughing. "No, no, not shot. I'm afraid I sort of sat on the broken remains of a particularly bad vintage down in the cellar."

"Come with me," she ordered, grabbing the open satchel and nearly spilling the contents. She slammed it shut and stuffed it under one arm. He followed her rapid, unsteady progress out of the study and up the stairs to his bedroom. This had been one hell of a night, he thought as he hurried behind her, ready to catch her if she faltered.

He could hardly believe everything was settled so suddenly. Terry's murderer was dead. Damn! Why hadn't he listened to Bettsy when she'd said she doubted Colin's capacity for murder? Neither Neil nor Lindy had ever considered Thurston. Maybe they would have done if only Neil had trusted Bettsy's intuition.

Emma had been involved in the murders. He wasn't certain just how or why, exactly, but now that she was dead, it hardly mattered. Figuring that out was Lindy's job.

Colin Marleigh was his. Marleigh would pay for his perfidy one way or another. Unless he blew his brains out tonight— and coward that he was, that seemed highly unlikely—the bastard had better repair the damage he'd wrought to Bettsy's reputation. Marleigh's life depended on how well he did it. Neil hoped the man realized how precarious his existence really was at this moment, that his very survival depended on tomorrow's newspapers.

All Neil needed to do after that was settled was see to Bettsy's health and the well-being of their child. And as to that, he had to make her rest. Her steps were flagging. She would probably give in to exhaustion as soon as she reached the bed.

He was wrong.

"Off with your breeches," she ordered the minute they entered the room. With a flurry of sudden energy, she set down the medical bag, rushed to the occasional table where he kept the brandy and unstoppered the decanter.

Neil sighed with resignation. Well, he could certainly use a drink. He peeled off his coat, waistcoat and shirt, using the crumpled linen to wipe off the accumulation of sweat. Turning his back to her and facing the bed, he kicked off his boots and peeled off his trousers.

She reached around him to hand him his snifter. "Drink it down quickly. This may hurt if the glass shard's still in there. And this stuff you put on my knee stings like the very devil."

Neil complied. He felt the brandy burn a trail down his gullet, making him cough. Then the smoky, bitter aftertaste hit him. "Aaag! Laudanum?" He spat, but it was too late. "How much?"

"Couple of drops," she said, sounding for all the world like the physician in charge. "Lean over the bed."

He leaned, trying to look back over his shoulder. She shook her head, her gaze trained on his right buttock. "Hmm."

"What?" he asked, worried that she might have to take after him with tweezers. Or worse yet, needle and suture.

After a few more noncommittal grunts and mumbles, Bettsy administered the same treatment he'd given her knee. Neil winced. She was right—the antiseptic was wicked stuff—but a sweet wave of lassitude stole over him that counteracted the sting. The feel of her hands touching him overrode the discomfort completely, and his body stirred against the mattress.

Her palm brushed over his uninjured left cheek and gave it a gentle slap. "Climb up. Time to go night-night."

Neil forced his weighted muscles to comply. He settled on his left side near the middle of the bed. She reached to pull up the coverlet, but he closed his hand over hers. "Stay with me." He hadn't wanted to sound quite so desperate, but, damn it, he was. Desperately longing to hold her through the night and know they would never be apart again. Just hold her.

Bettsy hesitated, her dark eyes heavy lidded and slumberous. Maybe the laudanum in his system only made them seem so. He realized he couldn't hold a thought much longer than it took to breathe in and out again. Laudanum. Few drops, indeed.

She withdrew her hand from his and traced a warming path down his chest. The haze of heat wiped out everything but the feel of her palm against his skin. Neil moved into the touch, craving more. His eyes closed and his breath shuddered out when she stopped at his waist. Again he took her hand, this time with insistence, and pushed it lower until he felt her fingers close around him. He squeezed. "Please," he heard himself whisper.

His chest rumbled with vague disappointment when she pulled away, but his eyes refused to open. Vaguely he heard sounds of rustling cloth. The bed dipped and he felt her against him. *Satin.* Skin like satin, smoother than the coverlet. Hot.

Soft hands—her hands—slid over his body, leaving exquisite pleasure. He stirred—writhed, more like—under the veils of love and laudanum. The idea made him want to laugh, but he hadn't the energy. Instead he curled his lips into a smile.

He rolled to his back, willing her, with what was left of his mind, to follow. The slide of her bare leg across his made his breath catch. He released it slowly, wondering whether he'd be able to draw another. "Please," somebody said. Him, he hoped.

Tight, wet heat gripped him, held him, played over him in flowing swirls and eddies. Suddenly he surged upward, his drifting awareness converging on his lower torso. A high, keening sound echoed in his ears.

With Herculean effort, he forced his eyes half-open. Bettsy rose above him, an Amazon in miniature—head thrown back, full high breasts tightly drawn with passion, slender hips melded to his where their bodies joined. In the throes of ecstasy. Again he surged upward. Once more, then he felt himself melt into her like steel gone liquid. "Mine," somebody whispered. Her, he hoped.

Elizabeth gently extricated herself from Neil's arms and crawled out of bed to dress. Dawn peeped through the crack in the draperies and threw a weak streak of light across the plush Ottoman carpet. Morning already. If she'd kept her scrambled wits last night, she could have been halfway to Scotland by now. She couldn't say she regretted staying, though.

Falling asleep after their lovemaking hadn't been her intention at all. Making love hadn't even been her intention, but she could hardly let him suffer, given the condition he was in. He had needed her. Faugh! She had needed him. Would need him as long as she lived, she suspected. But now was not the time to dwell on her feelings for Neil Bronwyn. Or his expertise between the sheets.

Did laudanum affect all men that way? she wondered. If so, the stuff ought to be priceless. And sell by the gallon.

Regret sliced through her more painfully than ever when she looked at him sleeping, ebony hair tumbled over one eye, his jaw shadowed with morning whiskers. Unable to help herself, she leaned over the side of the bed and brushed her lips over his. He stirred restlessly and smiled, but slept on.

Moving away quickly, Elizabeth dragged on her trousers and boots. If she hurried, she could make a clean getaway before Oliver was up and about. She felt guilty that Neil hadn't seen to the poor man's head last night, but Lindy had said he was probably all right.

Her cloak and valise lay by the upstairs railing right where she'd left them when she'd first heard Emma and Thurston in the hall. She grabbed up the case, shouldered the cloak and moved quietly down the stairs.

The house appeared deserted. There had been no point stationing guards about after last night's events, she thought. Elizabeth entered the study only long enough to scratch a quick note so Neil would know she'd left of her own accord. Then, she headed to the stables, quickly saddled her mare and led her out the back gate. Once mounted, she rode as fast as she could without attracting attention.

Northeast through the narrow streets and lanes she rode, keeping an eye on the sun to maintain her direction. Two hours later she reached the railroad hard by Tottenham. This seemed as good a place as any to board the train for Edinburgh.

Neil would guess her final destination immediately, of course. He would look for her at the hunting box. With his persistence, she doubted he would have much trouble locating it. Losing herself in Edinburgh, the only city she knew well besides London, seemed her only recourse for now. Later, once she had borne the child, she could retire to the country. By then Neil would have given up or forgotten her.

Perhaps, after the note she'd left for him, he wouldn't pursue her at all. She wiped her eyes with the heels of her hands and sniffed. That would be best all around.

He would be safe now. Safe from the ravages of powerful tongues that could reduce his status to that of a pitiful, misguided earl who'd let a trollop wreck his life. Now he could get on with his research without having his peers question his rationality because of a foolish choice of wife.

The matter of the child worried her, but that was as must be, she thought. If she bore a girl, he could still claim and sponsor her when she came of age. A bastard son might inherit if Neil chose to adopt him. God willing, he would. Years could pass before that became a cause for contact. Years in which Neil could form a suitable alliance. Elizabeth refused to envision the type of woman who would be worthy of him.

Only after Elizabeth had seen to delivering the mare back to Neil and had settled herself in one of the Norwich Line's passenger cars did she allow the burgeoning sadness to overtake her. She pulled her stylish slouch hat down over her eyes and leaned her head against the rattling window. In the guise of a sleeping young gentleman, she let her heart finish breaking in two.

Bettsy had been gone two weeks. Neil reread her farewell letter for the hundredth time, trying to ascertain some hidden meaning. It still seemed straightforward. She wanted out. She would rear the babe alone. She wished him happy.

Dear Neil,

This is to assure you I leave of my own will. Do not worry for the child. You shall have the chance to secure its future when the time is right. Remember me fondly when you win a rubber at whist or lift a tot with Biddie and Tun. My gracious thanks to Lindy. And to you. I owe you my life, but my future is mine alone to decide. As of this moment, Elizabeth Marleigh and Percival Betts cease to be. Their one last and dearest wish is for your future happiness and success.

She must take him for a fool if she thought he would simply let her go, when she was as necessary as his next breath. His whole life had been a charade before he met her, an even greater piece of tomfoolery than her dressing up as a man. He had spent all those years trying to be someone he was not—doing what was expected, putting up a false front to please and earn affection. Then she'd come along, dragging out all the worst of his hidden traits from the very first minute they met, and loving him in spite of them. Maybe even because of them.

Bettsy accepted his faults right along with his virtues, loved him in his entirety, just as he did her. She was willful, irreverent, courageous to the point of carelessness, and stupidly overprotective of him. But she wouldn't be Bettsy otherwise.

She seemed to relish the wildness he couldn't hide from her. Well, he would show her *wild,* by God, when he found her. If she didn't come home with him immediately and let him love her, let him banish those demons that drove her, she'd find out exactly what *wild* meant.

Neil couldn't imagine what he would do the rest of his life without her, if the last two weeks were any example.

He refolded the letter and stuffed it into his pocket. The slow clacking of the train ground to a billowing, screeching halt at the Edinburgh station. The nearly four hundred uncomfortable miles he'd traveled hadn't dimmed his determination one whit. By God, he would find her, and she would marry him if he had to drag her screaming to the church. Fractious little baggage.

Neil retrieved his bag and brushed through the throngs of departing passengers. His anger had at times cooled to a simmer in the intervening days. But it had a way of returning to a rapid boil whenever he thought of how she'd left him lying in a drug-induced stupor. Just lying there, sated as a satyr after an orgy, sprawled naked on his bed, never dreaming that when he woke, it would be to nothing but her cheerful little goodbye note. What hurt the worst was that she hadn't trusted him to make things right. Well, devil take it, he would, once he found her.

He'd checked the hunting box first, but hadn't really expected to find her there. The canny little fox would wait until she thought he'd given up on her to go there. Neil spent a good two hours purchasing a closed carriage and hiring a competent driver. The deal completed, he went straight to the new part of town, to the North Loch Hotel.

Thank God for the telegraph, or he'd have spent months searching instead of weeks. He hoped she was still here, since the last cable confirming her presence. If not, he had a way to go yet. But go he would, to the ends of the earth if need be, until he had the foolish chit back where she belonged.

The very idea, her haring off like some fugitive—carrying his child, no less—just when he believed they had everything ironed out to perfection! The more he thought about it, the more he wanted to shake her till her teeth clicked. Or spank her round little bottom until she couldn't sit.

He glanced up briefly at the famous, angular gray castle dominating the whole of the city, old and new. The spectacular sight did nothing to lighten his mood. His anger brewed like tea steeped overlong—dark, strong, unpalatable.

The carriage stopped and he ordered the driver to wait for him. Neil strode into the lobby, demanded the register and flipped back to the date she had arrived. Ignoring the blustering threats of the clerk, he noted the room number of Miss Bettsy Neilson. He had tried every possible combination of her name and his in the telegrams and had finally hit on it. A bloody fortune in telegrams to every inn in Edinburgh! He slammed the book shut with grim satisfaction and stormed up the wide, curving stairs.

Moments later, he returned through the crowded lobby, a screeching, pummeling bundle of fury and petticoats all but obscuring his frontal vision. The clerk and two baggage boys approached him, obviously overcome with chivalry.

"Runaway wife," he explained in his most imperious voice, daring them with a menacing look to interfere in his conjugal problems. They backed away. Neil shouted at them as he exited, "Room 215. Pack her bags and bring 'em to the coach."

He didn't stay to see whether they complied, but kicked open the double doors, stomped down the steps and dumped Bettsy into the waiting carriage.

"Neil, will you lis—"

He clamped one hand over her mouth and shook his other forefinger in her face. "Don't you say anything! I don't want to hear it!"

She nodded. He released her mouth and turned away, unwilling to face her again until he could regulate his breathing.

The least timid of her would-be rescuers approached with her bulging, old valise, plus a newer bag, and started to speak. Neil silenced him with a look and grabbed her baggage. She was already packed? Lord, he had almost missed finding her here! He slung everything inside, climbed in the vehicle and slammed the door. The coach lurched once and barreled off down the street.

Neil's heart resumed a somewhat steadier rhythm as they reached the edge of the city. He'd found her and she was all right. He hadn't admitted until now how afraid he'd been for her—alone, pregnant, at the mercy of anyone who cared to accost her. For sanity's sake, he'd cloaked most of his fear with anger at her leaving. But everything was fine now. Fine. As it should be.

"Thank God," he said aloud, and leaned his head back against the leather squabs.

*  *  *

Elizabeth peered out the coach window, wondering how long he expected her to keep silent. She could hardly believe he had come all this way, gone to so much trouble, gotten so upset. Flattering, but how foolish he would feel once she told him she had already been on her way back to him. If only he had given her a moment to tell him instead of hauling her out like a pig for market!

She glanced at his profile. He was calmer now, eyes closed in what she supposed he regarded as a satisfactory end to his bullying tactics. Should she smack him or kiss him?

Leaving him hadn't been a mistake. These past two weeks of soul-searching had taught her much about feelings she could never have understood had she stayed. Nothing in the world mattered so much as Neil, and she knew now that he must feel exactly the same about her. He had made no secret of that.

If she had stayed away as she'd planned, she would at least have his child to love. Neil would have nothing of her but hurt and angry memories at her desertion.

If his desolation at being apart was even half of what she'd felt these past two weeks, it would be cruel to remain separated forever because of false rumors he didn't even believe.

Most important, though, Elizabeth realized now that if the situation were reversed, and Neil suffered the enmity of all England, it wouldn't lessen her love for him in the least. She would probably love him even more.

She had wronged him by that lack of trust, and he had every right to be angry. His coming for her like a bull in a mating frenzy did upset her plans, but she couldn't say it surprised her much. Impetuous rascal.

Neil finally turned toward her, unsmiling. "Colin's left town. What he did to you is, unfortunately, no crime other than malicious slander. Lindy said we hadn't enough evidence to warrant charging him with attempted murder, but he never really meant to kill you, anyway. There's no proof other than hearsay that he is not your uncle's true son, so I'm afraid he'll keep the title.''

Neil's voice sounded weary. ''Before he left London, he did do a creditable job when it came to confessing his deeds. The news sheets were alive with his retractions for over a week. You're completely exonerated now, you know. Everyone's abuzz with how his dear little cousin Elizabeth almost wound up in Bedlam because of his greed. You're the talk of the town, only this time in a sympathetic light. There's absolutely no reason for us not to marry. None whatsoever.''

She opened her mouth, and he placed a warning finger over it. ''I'll hear no objections.''

She inclined her head and glared at him silently. He didn't act very ecstatic about being in her company, but he had come the length of England and more to find her. She had missed him dreadfully these two weeks without him—so much so that she'd rationalized away all her fears about ruining his future. The two London scandal sheets that made their way north had helped reinforce her decision. But even before she figured they stood a chance of overcoming the old gossip, she had bought her train ticket home.

''I'm abducting you. Again. And you might as well not protest. Won't do you any good.'' His scowl was thunderous.

Her eyes rolled heavenward and she flounced back against the seat, folding her arms over her breasts. He was going to be sorry for this, the high-handed wretch!

''We're heading for Dalkeith Kirk.'' He slid closer and snaked one arm around her waist. The other hand touched her lips again. ''It's all arranged. I have a special license. Be warned—if you deny me again, Bettsy, I won't be responsible for my actions.''

She shook her head, dislodging his hand. ''If you'll only listen, Neil. I had already planned to—''

Again he shushed her. ''You will be my wife. Today! And I'll not hear another word! Not one. Do not open your mouth!''

He resumed his moody contemplation of the countryside,

obviously lost in his somber thoughts. Elizabeth carefully kept her tongue behind her teeth and her lips in repose, but the smile inside her began to bloom, full and sweet. Let him wallow in his anger. He deserved to. She'd bet her last farthing it wouldn't survive past the ceremony, though. If he planned on any kind of wedding night to speak of, he'd damned well better turn up sweet.

When they reached the kirk, she noticed the vicar there seemed to be expecting them. They entered the neat stone chapel, where a small, rotund woman approached her with a bouquet of dwarf mums. The stems were soaked, as though they'd been waiting in a vase. Another witness—a gardener, judging by his attire and grubby hands—stood silently by while the vicar intoned the few words that made Elizabeth countess of Havington.

She only nodded in response to her vows, gaining a glare from Neil. When the vicar pronounced them man and wife, Neil kissed her perfunctorily and quickly turned away to see to the signing of the marriage lines. Elizabeth obediently scratched her name where he indicated with a stab of one finger.

They were married. She hardly dared believe it. Her stunned look must have masked her joy.

"Sulking will do you little good, Bettsy. You might as well come down off that high horse and act like an adult for a change." He heaved out an angry breath. "For God's sake, will you please *say* something! Anything!"

"I do," she said immediately, and then bit her lips together to keep from laughing.

"Do what?" he asked gruffly, ushering her into the carriage.

"Promise all the stuff the vicar asked if I would. And if you'd not acted such a horse's ass and shut me up every time my mouth opened, I'd have said so at the proper time."

His eyebrows rose as he settled himself into the seat beside her. "And if you'd not pouted all through the ceremony, and had made those promises as you should, I'd have kissed you properly.''

Elizabeth couldn't keep her face straight any longer. Her smile grew with every word. ''Well, my lord, I've made amends in private, haven't I?''

He wrapped his arms around her, his mouth hovering just over hers. ''So you have, my lady wife. And so shall I.''

The kiss lasted until Elizabeth felt a little dizzy from lack of oxygen. Or maybe from desire. Probably desire. When he released her mouth, she laughed and brushed an errant hand over his lap. ''All ready for the honeymoon, I see!''

He nibbled at her chin. ''More than ready. It could last forever.''

She tweaked his ear with her teeth, biting a bit harder than she might have, just to punish him a little. ''Umm, forever. It might get repetitious after a while, though, and you could find me either bored or boring. Perhaps you should have brought along your little book for reference?''

''Is page 34 daring enough to keep you interested?'' he growled suggestively, sliding one hand under her petticoats.

''Well, we are heavily into research.'' She tugged off his tie.

''Shortly to take up orthopedics, if we go that route.''

She giggled. ''Behave yourself! We can't really make love in a coach!''

''Oh, did you skip that page?''

Laughing helplessly, she slapped at his prowling hands. ''Arrogant beast!''

''Arrogant, *hungry* beast,'' he growled against her ear.

He knelt on the floor of the coach between her knees and began tugging off her garters. His lips found her knee. ''Umm, lace at last. How well it suits you!'' Fingers trailed gently up her inner thigh to the seam of her silk pantalets, then prodded frantically. ''Good God, it's gone! You've lost your mighty manhood, whatever the hell it was.''

''Neil?'' she said, halting his play, suddenly feeling quite serious. She took his face in her hands and looked deeply into his eyes. "I was leaving the hotel. I was coming home to you."

He smiled in surprise—the first sweet, sincere smile he'd worn since he had found her. "You were? That's why you were already packed?"

"I couldn't live without you a moment longer."

His growling chuckle sent shivers up her spine. "Ah, now there's the wicked truth at last, you little henwit. That's precisely what I've been trying to tell you all along."

\* \* \* \* \*

*Bestselling Medieval author of*
***KNIGHT'S RANSOM***

Continues her exciting
Sommerville Brothers series with

Watch for the spectacular tale of a valiant knight accused
of murder and a beautiful woman who takes him captive!

Don't miss this searing story, available in March,
wherever Harlequin Historicals are sold.

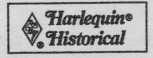

From the bestselling author of *Scandalous*

# CANDACE CAMP

Cam Monroe vowed revenge when
Angela Stanhope's family accused him
of a crime he didn't commit.

Fifteen years later he returns from exile, wealthy
and powerful, to demand Angela's hand in marriage.
It is then that the strange "accidents" begin. Are the
Stanhopes trying to remove him from their lives
one last time, or is there a more insidious,
mysterious explanation?

*Impulse*

Available this March at your favorite retail outlet.

LOVE *or* MONEY?
Why not Love *and* Money!
After all, millionaires
need love, too!

**Suzanne Forster,
Muriel Jensen
and
Judith Arnold**

bring you three original stories
about finding that one-in-a million man!

Harlequin also brings you
a million-dollar sweepstakes—enter
for your chance to win a fortune!

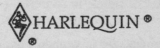

HTMM

# Heartbreak RANCH

Four generations of independent women...
Four heartwarming, romantic stories of the West...
Four incredible authors...

## Fern Michaels
## Jill Marie Landis
### Dorsey Kelley
### Chelley Kitzmiller

Saddle up with Heartbreak Ranch, an outstanding
Western collection that will take you on a whirlwind
trip through four generations and the exciting,
romantic adventures of four strong women who
have inherited the ranch from Bella Duprey,
famed Barbary Coast madam.

Available in March,
wherever Harlequin books are sold.

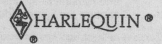

HARLEQUIN ®

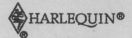

# HARLEQUIN®

## *Not The Same Old Story!*

HARLEQUIN PRESENTS® — Exciting, emotionally intense romance stories that take readers around the world.

*Harlequin Romance®* — Vibrant stories of captivating women and irresistible men experiencing the magic of falling in love!

HARLEQUIN® *Temptation.* — Bold and adventurous— Temptation is strong women, bad boys, great sex!

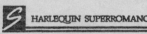

HARLEQUIN SUPERROMANCE® — Provocative, passionate, contemporary stories that celebrate life and love.

AMERICAN ROMANCE® — Romantic adventure where anything is possible and where dreams come true.

HARLEQUIN® INTRIGUE® — Heart-stopping, suspenseful adventures that combine the best of romance and mystery.

LOVE & LAUGHTER™ — Entertaining and fun, humorous and romantic—stories that capture the lighter side of love.